**Also available from Melanie Hansen
and Carina Press**

Point of Contact
Loving a Warrior
Keeping a Warrior

Also available from Melanie Hansen

Pieces of Me
See My Words

D0733253

Trusting a Warrior deals with topics some readers may find difficult, including descriptions of grief therapy and a suicide survivors' support group.

TRUSTING A WARRIOR

—

MELANIE HANSEN

carina
press

carina
press®

Recycling programs
for this product may
not exist in your area.

ISBN-13: 978-1-335-47471-1

Trusting a Warrior

First published in 2020. This edition published in 2021.

Copyright © 2020 by Melanie Hansen

This edition published by arrangement with Harlequin Books S.A.

For questions and comments about the quality of this book, please contact us at CustomerService@Harlequin.com.

Carina Press
22 Adelaide St. West, 40th Floor
Toronto, Ontario M5H 4E3, Canada
www.CarinaPress.com

Printed in U.S.A.

In *Trusting a Warrior*, I've chosen to focus on veteran suicide, which is rapidly becoming an epidemic. Men and women who've survived multiple combat tours are coming home only to take their own lives in record numbers. Post-traumatic stress, traumatic brain injuries and the stigma that prevents veterans from seeking help are all contributing factors. Thankfully, it's starting to be recognized that the mental injuries of war can be just as debilitating—and just as fatal—as the physical ones.

If you're the suicide survivor of a military member, I urge you to reach out to TAPS (Tragedy Assistance Program for Survivors), taps.org/suicideloss. There you will find a wealth of resources geared toward survivors of military suicide, including peer-to-peer support. Those in need of immediate postsuicide support should call 800-959-8277.

If you are a veteran dealing with thoughts of suicide, the Veterans Crisis Line is there twenty-four hours a day. Their number is 800-273-8255, and press 1.

For others who are struggling with the suicide of a loved one, samaritanshope.org/our-services/grief-support-services is an amazing resource. They offer free, nonjudgmental peer support and fellowship to those bereaved by suicide.

You are not alone.

TRUSTING A WARRIOR

Prologue

George Monteverdi leapt into the void, his sixty-five-pound Belgian Malinois dangling from his body harness.

A three-second slide down the rope, and then the helicopter dipped its nose and clattered away, its cargo delivered safely. For the space of several heartbeats, the strike team stayed frozen, weapons to their shoulders, scanning for threats.

At last the team leader twirled his finger in a "let's go" motion. Geo unclipped his dog, quickly stepped out of the harness, and stowed it in his ruck. Then he bent down and cracked the chem-lites hanging from the dog's vest, activating them. That way he'd be visible to the SEALs at all times through their night-vision goggles.

"How 'bout it, Bosch?" he murmured, giving the dog a quick scratch behind the ears. "Ready to go to work?"

A low whine was his reply, the dog's intelligent eyes gleaming up at him, tongue lolling. "I was born ready," he seemed to say, and with one last pat, Geo stood.

"K9's off-leash," he informed his teammates over the troop net. "Heading south."

Grunted acknowledgments echoed in his earpiece, and he exhaled long and slow, adrenaline humming through him, the weight of responsibility settling heavily on his shoulders.

"Walk point with me," he said to the new guy, a tall white dude named Kelly whose whole body vibrated with the nervous, first-op jitters Geo could remember all too well.

Kelly gave a short, jerky nod.

"I'll be watching for Bosch's tells," Geo went on, gesturing toward the dog. "You watch for everything else, okay? We got this."

Geo's calmness was contagious, and Kelly visibly settled down as his training kicked in. "Roger that."

With a reassuring nod, Geo gave the dog his search command, then set out after him, Kelly slightly behind and to the right, the rest of the team fanning out in their wake.

Geo briefly scanned their surroundings to get his bearings before gluing his attention to Bosch, who trotted on ahead, his powerful nose alternating between sniffing the ground and the air. Ignoring the birds he startled into flight, Bosch's sole focus was on detecting the scent of explosives—or humans.

About a mile out, the team paused in the shelter of a palm grove to do one last coordination.

"According to the tactical operations center, nothing's changed since the op brief," the team leader, a Black guy named Jaxon, said. "HVT's stationary, like he has been for the last eight hours."

They all looked at each other. High-value targets

never stayed in one place for long. Eight hours? Unheard of.

"Smells like a trap," Geo said, his tone blunt.

Mutters of agreement went around the circle of guys, and Jaxon waited patiently for everyone to get the requisite bitching and moaning out of their systems before saying, "Oh, I have no doubt this is a trap, gentlemen." He paused. "We just have to outsmart it."

Wolfish grins replaced the sour expressions, because if there was anything SEALs loved more than a challenge, it was a challenge with seemingly impossible odds.

Geo glanced at Kelly. He had a feeling this was going to be a baptism by fire.

Hope you're ready, kid.

Jaxon gave the signal to move out again, and as they walked, Geo pictured the compound. Walls, eight to ten feet high, with a metal gate for entry. Farmland all around, scattered trees. The drone feeds had shown no animals, no women and children. In fact, there was no movement at all. If this was a high-ranking insurgent commander, where were his bodyguards on the roof, or snipers in the trees?

The whole thing stunk to high heaven.

Yet, despite the dangers, everyone from the top down had decided the juice was worth the squeeze. Geo couldn't help but shudder. He'd seen video of the commander's handiwork—the kidnapping of local police, the torture, the murder, the stolen uniforms used to infiltrate coalition ranks. One attack had missed a U.S. general by mere minutes, although several other people had been killed.

Yeah, they couldn't pass up this chance to take the guy down, no way. Maybe he hadn't moved all day because he'd gotten complacent, careless. Maybe he was sick, or injured, and unable to be moved. Maybe he was dead.

No matter what, the intel said he was here, so the SEALs were going on. After all, they had stealth on their side, they had training. Geo's lips curved. They had a hair missile.

A hundred yards out from the target, he called Bosch to him as the team took a knee to observe the compound through their binos.

"Ten to one that shit's wired to blow," Jaxon muttered, his binoculars pointed at the gate, which appeared to be ajar. "Might as well have a goddamn welcome mat out front, too."

"'Come on in, boys. Get blown up!'" someone cracked, and mirthless chuckles went around the group.

Jaxon lowered his binos. "Send in the K9."

Geo uttered a few terse commands, Bosch's lithe form a dark blur as he streaked toward the compound. To the SEALs, he was easily trackable by the chem-lites hanging from his vest, but to the naked eye, he'd be all but invisible.

Unable to keep from tensing, Geo waited for shots to ring out, the bloodcurdling yelp of an animal in pain…

All was silent.

Bosch sniffed along the bottom of the rock-and-mud wall as he'd been trained, looking for buried explosives, then moved on to inspect the gate. Nothing.

"Okay. Let's move in."

At Jaxon's order, the team fanned out and headed

for the compound. At the base of the wall, their sniper unhooked the collapsible ladder from his ruck, set it up and scaled it to the top. He scanned the interior courtyard.

"No movement," he reported.

"Over the ladder or through the gate, boss?"

At Kelly's question, Jaxon glanced at the dog, who'd returned to Geo's side and stood in an alert stance, ears up, body forward. "Gate," he said. "K9 cleared it."

A rush of warmth and pride settled in Geo's chest at the vote of confidence. On a SEAL team, trust was never just given—it had to be earned, and at this moment seven men were putting their lives in his hands, in his training of his dog.

And their work wasn't done yet.

Geo moved to the gate and inched it open far enough for everyone to squeeze through one by one. Once inside, the men spread out across the courtyard as their sniper covered them from his prone position atop the wall.

With Bosch at his heels, Geo headed toward the main structure, a small one-story house. That door, too, was ajar. When Bosch didn't alert on the threshold, Geo moved in behind him, using the barrel of his M-4 to push the door open wider. The smell that assaulted his nose made bile rush into his throat, and he gagged.

"Got something," he croaked into the troop net. "Something dead."

Instantly their platoon medic, Cade, and Jaxon were by his side. Geo let his rifle hang from his shoulder as he slid the powerful flashlight from its sheath on his belt and switched it on, illuminating the single room.

"Jesus *Christ*."

The interior of the small structure was splattered in blood, huge rusty pools of it soaked into the earthen floor. A machete lay on a table underneath some frayed ropes that dangled from the ceiling.

At his feet, the dog let out a distressed whine, something Geo had never heard him do. He reached down to give him a reassuring pat. "I feel it, too, bud."

The evil permeating the room seemed to brush along Geo's skin, echoes of screams lingering in his ears.

"Let's get the fuck out of here," Jaxon said grimly. Cade's face was bone white, eyes stark as he backed from the doorway.

"Boss?" Kelly called out. "Something wrong?"

Jaxon put his hand up to stop him from striding over. "Spare yourself. We've seen what they wanted us to see."

Which was what? A warning? A diversion? Why was the cell phone planted to lure them here in the first place?

Geo could see the wheels turning in Jaxon's head as his sharp gaze darted around the compound. This dude was a leader Geo would follow into the fiery depths of hell itself—calm, decisive, his emotions locked down and firmly in check. In contrast, Cade was shaking, his upper lip gleaming with sweat in the moonlight.

A frisson of alarm moved through Geo. This was *not* the time to be losing it. They had to get their asses out of this mess first.

As if hearing his thoughts, Cade made a visible effort to pull himself together, and when he spoke, his voice was calm. "What's the plan?"

Jaxon turned to Geo. "Is there any other way out of here?"

Instantly he knew what he was thinking. "Yeah. There's another gate by the animal pen."

The small pen and nearby shed had just been searched—no bad guys or explosives—so if the cell phone wasn't planted to lure them here and blow them up, then the ambush must be waiting for them outside.

As they grouped up to move toward the secondary gate, Bosch suddenly tilted his head back, sniffed the air, and bristled. Although he hadn't made a sound, Geo paused. He knew all his tells, and this one was saying, "I smell something."

Had the wind shifted? It *had* been coming from the north, and the dog hadn't hit on anything before now. Geo held up his wind gauge. Sure enough, it was now coming from the east.

He gestured to get Jaxon's attention. "I think we're looking at contact from the east," he said quietly. "They've crept up on us while we've been busy in here."

"What's over that way?"

Pulling up his mental maps, Geo replied, "Palm groves. A shit-ton of irrigation ditches. If they're coming from that direction, the sniper couldn't have seen them from here."

The men shuffled their feet in anticipation, and one of them growled, "If they're lookin' for a fight, I say let's give 'em a goddamn fight."

They had a choice. Jaxon could call in air support, get an A-10 to swoop down from the sky and strafe the area with its powerful cannons. The bad guys would never know what hit them, and the last thing they'd

hear would be the roar of a plane. They'd look up, and
boom, lights out.

Geo glanced around the circle of grim faces. No.
The men in the grove were ones who didn't hesitate
to burn young pilots alive in cages, or behead journal-
ists on camera, or hang people up by their wrists and
butcher them like pieces of meat. They deserved to see
their death coming straight at them.

"Let's go."

In an overabundance of caution considering the rest
of the compound was clear, Geo sent Bosch to inspect
the secondary gate before anyone touched it, the hair
on his arms prickling when the dog took a few whiffs,
then sat.

"Nobody come any closer," he said urgently. "He's
on odor."

The SEALs froze.

Pulling out his flashlight again, Geo crouched and
aimed the powerful beam at the base of the gate. Sure
enough, a few thin wires gleamed.

"Fuckin' toe-popper," he pronounced. "Not enough
to kill, but it would've taken off a leg or two."

Heartfelt curses all around as the realization hit.

If someone had triggered the gate, in those first
few minutes of confusion and chaos, the insurgents
would've had the advantage. They would have swarmed
in from the palm grove to pin the SEALs down in the
compound like sitting ducks, turning them from aggres-
sors into victims forced to fight for their lives. Booby-
trapping the back gate instead of the front showed that
the insurgents had a better understanding of SEAL tactics than they'd given them credit for.

But the bad guys had made a fatal miscalculation. They hadn't expected the dog.

Jaxon didn't have to give any orders. No one made any covert hand signals. They slipped out through the main gate and moved swiftly, silently, toward the palm grove. Next to Geo, Bosch trotted, head held high. His whole demeanor was different now—muscles coiled, body straining, as if he knew his next command wouldn't be to search, but to attack…

"Reveiren!"

At Geo's hiss, the dog streaked off, low to the ground. He veered straight toward a thicket of heavy brush, and with no hesitation, plunged through it. A beat of silence before unearthly screams pierced the air.

Not bothering with stealth anymore, the team ran into the thicket, ignoring the thorns that tore at their uniforms. Busting through to the other side, they were greeted by the sight of Bosch crushing a man's right arm in his powerful jaws. Blood sprayed everywhere as the dog shook him violently, the dude's AK-47 falling uselessly to the ground.

Arrayed on either side of him, his fellow insurgents knelt frozen in shock and horror. One of them caught sight of the SEALs looming out of the darkness, and with a shout, he raised his weapon.

Too little, too late. A ferocious burst of gunfire later, six enemy fighters lay dead.

Growls and screams suddenly came from yet another thicket, and Geo darted over to see Bosch clamped onto the forearm of a man who didn't look to even be out of his teens. He eased his finger from the trigger when he saw no sign of a weapon, and called the dog off.

The boy was sobbing, his arm a mess of blood.

Bellowing "Medic!" Geo jerked the barrel of his gun to motion the kid out of the brush, only then seeing a narrow black tube with some familiar-looking shells lying next to it.

An RPG launcher.

Disillusionment burned in Geo's gut. This was no innocent kid, but the guy tasked with shooting down any American helos rushing to help the SEALs.

Shaking his head, Geo pulled some flex-cuffs from his cargo pocket and bound the boy's wrists together in front of him, then pulled him to his feet and shoved him over to Cade, who already had his med bag out.

"He's got a chunk taken out of his arm," he said briefly, leaving Cade to it while he headed back to collect the weaponry—no way would they leave it behind for someone else to use. In the same vein, the other guys were busy gathering up the dead men's AK-47s, and they piled everything up on a tattered old blanket one of them had been using as a bedroll.

When Cade saw the RPG launcher, he froze in the act of irrigating the kid's wound. "Whose was that?" he asked tightly. "His?"

"Yeah. Probably the helo spotter—"

Before the words had even left Geo's mouth, Cade was yanking his combat knife from the sheath on his thigh and putting it to the kid's throat.

"What the hell?" Geo took a step toward them, only to stop in his tracks when Cade tangled his fingers in the guy's hair and pulled his head back into a painful arch. A thick bead of blood formed under the razor-sharp blade and slid down his smooth skin to stain the neckline of his shalwar kameez.

Cade's eyes looked unfocused, wild. "Can't let him live. Can't let him shoot down any more helos."

Horror turning his blood to ice, Geo fought to keep his voice calm. "Barlow, don't do this. He's unarmed. He's injured."

Several feet away, Bosch shifted uneasily. His training had been exhaustive in identifying threats, and he'd been taught not to go after American uniforms. This scenario confused him, and Geo could see his hackles go up.

"*Foei*," he whispered urgently. *No.*

The dog didn't move any closer to Cade, but he didn't back down either. He stayed in an aggressive stance, legs splayed, chest up. A low growl rumbled in his throat.

Hearing it, Cade let go of the kid's hair and pulled his pistol, which he aimed directly at Bosch's head. "Keep him away from me, George. Keep that bastard away or I swear I'll put a bullet in his brain."

That bastard. The dog that'd just saved eight lives. Angry muttering came from the SEALs now arrayed in a circle behind Geo.

For the space of three heartbeats—the longest of Geo's life—Cade didn't waver. Bosch growled again, and Geo braced himself.

He's gonna shoot my partner right in front of me. Holy shit.

The silence stretched, broken only by Cade's harsh breathing and the prisoner's whimpers, and then Geo's knees went weak with relief when Cade suddenly clicked on the safety and put the gun away. Calling Bosch to him, Geo tethered him to his belt, trying to hide how his hands were shaking.

After that, the fight visibly leached out of Cade. His shoulders slumping, he dropped his knife to the ground. Immediately a couple of SEALs grabbed the teenage insurgent's arms and hustled him away.

Jaxon strode up to Cade and got in his face. "What the fuck was that?"

Blinking rapidly, his jaw clenched, Cade forced out, "Just lost it for a second, boss, when I saw that RPG launcher. It's exactly a punk like that who brought down our guys on Three-Five."

Jaxon's expression softened, and he reached out to grip Cade's shoulder. "I know, but fuck, we're not into vigilante justice here. This asshole will not pass 'Go' on the way to jail, man. You need to let the spooks handle it, aiight?"

Cade gave a jerky nod, and with one last clap to his shoulder, Jaxon strode off, his mind already on the next task.

After a moment, Cade looked over at Geo, his eyes dark with shame and remorse. "I'm sorry, Georgie," he said quietly.

"You pulled a goddamn *gun* on your goddamn *teammate*," Geo ground out, striving for every ounce of control he possessed. "Sorry isn't enough."

"I know." Cade dropped his gaze. "There's no excuse. Not much else I can say."

With that, he bent and picked up his knife. Then he moved around Geo and approached the insurgent, who gave a loud, frightened cry at the sight of him.

"Shut the fuck up," Cade grated, shoving the knife back into its sheath. "Need to treat your arm."

Standing frozen, Geo could only watch everyone get back to business as usual, as if someone they all cared about hadn't just had a serious emotional breakdown right in front of them.

After Jaxon got off his radio call, Geo beckoned him a little bit away from the group. "I think Barlow needs help. What just happened isn't normal, boss."

"For someone who's been through what he has, I'd say yeah, it's pretty normal. He just needs time."

Before Geo could push the issue, Jaxon was already turning away, shouting, "A-10 inbound in twenty, people. Let's hump all this shit over to that courtyard."

There wasn't anything for Geo to do but let it go.

Gritting his teeth, he grabbed a corner of the blanket filled with weapons, and with three other guys, ran it over to the compound, a tethered Bosch easily keeping pace with him. The SEALs unceremoniously dumped the blanket into the rocky dirt, then sprinted back through the gate and across the field for about a hundred yards, where they threw themselves into a ditch next to the rest of the guys.

Cade had jammed a hood over the prisoner's head, and the kid lay curled up on his side in the dirt, blood already seeping through the bandages on his arm. He was quiet, as if resigned to his fate.

And why wouldn't he be? Geo saw guys like this as more hopeless than cowardly, more sad than evil, all of which made them that much more dangerous. It was one thing to fight an enemy; something else completely to fight a hopeless one.

What must it be like, to be so devoid of hope that shooting down helicopters or blowing themselves up seemed to be the only way young men like this could find honor? What sort of leadership asked that of them?

Geo looked away. One who preyed on the hopeless.

Suddenly, with a scream of powerful jet engines, a huge A-10 roared overhead.

"They're cleared hot," Jaxon called over the troop net. "Keep your heads down!"

Before Geo buried his face in the dirt, he saw a blinking object falling from the sky. A split second later, the huge fireball that erupted sent rocks, dirt and pieces of white-hot metal raining down all around them.

Geo was practically lying on top of his dog, and he dug his fingers into the warm fur along his sides, feeling his ribs rising and falling with his reassuring breaths. Secondary explosions cracked through the air as the horrors of the compound were obliterated.

Cleansed by the fire.

Chapter One

One year later

"Smile, honey. It can't be that bad."

Behind the bar, Lani Abuel grit her teeth. This dude was on her last nerve, and tip or no, she was about to go off on him. "Hey, you really don't know what someone else might be going through, so—"

"You're too beautiful to frown like that," he persisted without missing a beat. "C'mon, baby, gimme a smile."

She'd had enough. She planted her palms on the bar top and stared the guy right in the eye. "I don't owe you a smile," she said evenly. "In fact, I don't owe you anything, unless you want to order another drink. What'll it be?"

Spinning around on his stool, the guy stalked off, muttering "Bitch" under his breath. Lani grabbed his empty glass and threw it in the dishwashing basket, where it made a most satisfying clatter.

With a few vicious swipes of her towel, she got rid of the condensation rings he'd left behind. Then she tossed the damp towel away and dusted her hands together, the guy effectively erased from existence. Her existence, anyway.

"Is it safe to sit down?"

She glanced to the side, where a different man now stood with his hands stuffed in his pockets, eyebrows raised in inquiry. Shrugging, she waved at the empty barstool. "Be my guest. Smiles not included in the service tonight, gotta warn you."

"Good thing all I want is a Jack and Coke, then. Actually, make it two."

She mixed both drinks with brisk, efficient motions and placed the glasses in front of him. "Sorry. Not up for small talk right now."

"Works for me. Just came to drink and people watch."

"Great. You wanna run a tab?"

With a nod, the dude fished his wallet out of his back pocket and passed her his credit card. "Please. Just keep 'em coming."

"You got it." Lani turned to her register and set up the tab, swiping his card and taking a peek at the name before handing it back to him. "Thanks, George."

"I go by Geo." The man put his wallet away. "But I guess it doesn't matter since we won't be talking, though, right?"

"Right."

True to his word, the man—Geo—didn't try to speak to her, and luckily, the rest of the upstairs bar was relatively quiet on this Wednesday night. Lani kept busy filling the cocktail servers' drink orders and making sure Geo's Jack and Coke was periodically refreshed.

She noticed he only drank from one glass, though,

leaving the second one untouched. Curiosity pricked her. What could *that* be about? Was he waiting for someone who didn't show?

Grateful for the distraction, she indulged in spinning a few different scenarios. A Tinder meetup? An illicit affair? An undercover cop leaving a signal for his contact that it's safe to approach?

Think you've watched one too many episodes of Law & Order, *my girl.*

At last she leaned her hip against the counter to take a breather, the pesky nausea rearing its ugly head once again. Fishing a sleeve of saltines from a shelf underneath the register, she took a few discreet nibbles before washing the cracker down with a gulp of ginger ale.

She saw Geo watching her and sighed. "Morning sickness—it's not just for mornings anymore."

"Ah." He nodded. "Congratulations."

"Oh, Mama ain't happy." She had no idea why she'd said that, and her cheeks heated with embarrassment. "Sorry. Forgot we're not talking."

He shrugged. "I never said I *wouldn't* talk. It's up to you. If you *want* to talk, I'm all ears. If you don't, I'll just drink."

They spent a moment appraising each other. He was olive-skinned, with dark hair and eyes. Italian, she suspected, with that last name—Monteverdi—but his husky voice held a faint hint of the South.

He wore his hair close-cropped, and his ears stuck out just a tad to frame a pleasant but unremarkable face. His eyes, though, were anything but ordinary. A deep brown surrounded by thick black lashes, they held a wealth of self-confidence tinged with an arrogance that sent an unwilling quiver down Lani's spine. Pair that with muscular shoulders, bulging biceps, a torso without a hint of fat on it, and she just knew…

"You're a team guy, aren't you?"

To her enormous satisfaction, she could tell she'd surprised him.

"Good guess," he said slowly. "You married to one?"

"Almost. My ex-fiancé is a PJ attached to Team Three."

"Ex?" When his gaze dropped to her stomach, Lani could feel herself flush.

"Baby's not his, and yeah, it's quite the mess," she said, then caught herself and snapped, "Why am I even talking to you? I thought we weren't gonna do that."

She spun away to draw the man at the other end of the bar a beer. Stomping back over to her register, she fully intended to ignore Geo, but he said, "You know, sometimes it's easier to talk to a stranger than it is to friends. Just saying."

Biting her lip, Lani finished ringing up Beer Guy, then busied herself wiping down the bar. Geo didn't say anything more, but she was aware of his steady gaze. At last she grabbed a couple of lemons and a knife, plopped her cutting board down in front of him, and began slicing them into wedges.

"Most of my friends were other team wives, so my ex—Rhys—took them with him. I haven't heard from any of those women in months." Chop, chop, chop.

"What about the baby's father?" Geo asked softly. "Is he in the picture?"

She barked out a bitter laugh. "I don't even know his real name."

Before she knew it, she was telling him about that *stupid* weekend hookup at a house in Malibu, a house she'd driven back up to one weekend to see if she could track the guy down, only to find out it was an Airbnb and the owner wouldn't disclose her renters' names or contact info.

"I asked her to pass along a message to call me, but so far nothing."

She appreciated the lack of judgment, and pity, in Geo's eyes. "That's rough," he said. "What're you going to do?"

Thoughts of all she'd lost welled up again. Without answering, she walked over to greet the small, rowdy group of people who'd just arrived. As she worked filling their drink orders, she couldn't help but glance at Geo.

He didn't have his nose buried in his phone, like virtually everyone else did. Instead he sat loose and relaxed, glass in hand, watching the room. And her.

Those confident eyes. The quiet and sincere interest on his face. He raised an eyebrow as she approached him again.

Sometimes it's easier to talk to a stranger...

"I want to keep the baby," she said abruptly. "Maybe I'm crazy, but I want it."

He'd just opened his mouth to reply when Lani's morning sickness suddenly roared back with a vengeance, the intensity of it warning her that this time crackers and ginger ale wouldn't be enough. Gagging, she bolted toward the employee lounge next to the bar and the restroom there.

She barely made it to the toilet, where her stomach emptied itself in heave after wrenching heave, her whole body shaking with the spasms. A warmth knelt behind her, then gentle hands gathered up her hair and held it high.

"Oh, God," she choked out. "No!"

"Hey, it's okay." Geo's voice was low and soothing. "I'm just a stranger you're never going to see again, right? We can pretend this never happened."

Lani wanted to argue, but the nausea refused to abate, even after everything was purged. Geo continued to hold her hair out of the way as she hunched over the toilet, trembling.

Unable to bear the awkwardness, she gasped, "So are you married? Kids?"

"Neither."

"Married to the teams?"

"Nah." He waved one hand behind her neck, and the cool air fanning against her sweaty skin made her want to sob, it felt so good. "Just never been the type to settle down, I guess."

When the queasiness *finally* eased its grip, she collapsed on her butt to lean against the wall. Geo let her hair go and wet a paper towel at the sink, which he handed to her before crouching back down to her level.

She pressed the cold towel against her hot cheeks. "Sorry. This is getting dangerously close to small talk territory, isn't it?"

His sudden laughter was rich, and the grin that spread across his face punched the last remaining breath from her lungs.

Ordinary? No way.

Because his cheeks crinkled and his eyes danced

with genuine amusement, and Lord, in that moment he was absolutely beautiful.

"Thanks, Geo," she mumbled.

"You're welcome…?" His voice trailed off inquiringly.

"Lani."

"You're welcome, Lani." Knees cracking, Geo stood, then extended his hand down to her. After he'd pulled her to her feet, she shakily made her way into the employee's lounge, where she drew herself a small paper cup of water from a nearby dispenser.

After a moment Geo said, "I guess I'll go back to the bar. My drink is melting," and the door closed gently behind him as he left her blessedly alone.

Sinking to the edge of the battered leather couch, she buried her face in her hands. Jesus, a strange man had just held her hair back while she puked. How mortifying. How ridiculous. And it could only happen to Lani, the Human Disaster.

Grimly, she tamped down another wave of self-pity. "Get over yourself, bish. This is *your* shit to deal with. It's not anyone else's fault."

Struggling to her feet, she brushed her hair and refreshed her makeup, then changed out of her sweaty logo tank to replace it with a clean one. Making a mental note to stash some mouthwash in her locker for next time, she fished a mint from her purse.

Not much, but it'd have to do. It wasn't like she'd be kissing anyone anytime soon.

Back out at the bar, she patted her co-worker's shoulder. "Thanks for covering, Josh. I'm okay."

"Good." Josh was busy wiping down the counter.

"Oh, the club manager just called," he said. "They're closing us down, so if you wanted to go serve…"

Lani shuddered. "God, no. I can't handle that tonight."

"I didn't think so, and she said don't worry about it, just go on home." Josh paused. "Why don't you close out your tabs, hon, and I'll reconcile the tip jar."

After dealing with her other open tabs, she approached Geo, who was idly twirling his coaster with one finger. He lifted his chin toward Josh. "That dude said you're shutting down up here?"

"Yeah, they do that on slow nights." She moved to her register. "I'll have to close your tab, but the main bar will be happy to open another one for you."

"Nah, I was going to take off anyway. Let's settle up."

She rang him out, and he signed the credit slip before stuffing a twenty in the tip jar. Lani gave him a rueful smile. "Probably should be tipping *you* for the hair-holding service, right?"

"Why don't we just consider it my good deed for the day?" Geo pushed back from the bar with a quiet, "Take care."

"I will."

As she watched, he picked up his glass and lightly touched it to the other one in a silent toast, then turned and disappeared down the stairs toward the dance floor.

Sudden tears pricked her eyes. *Ah. He's mourning someone. I'm sorry, Geo.*

"You okay to walk to your car?" Josh asked. "I'm happy to—"

"I'm fine," she reassured him as she pulled on an

oversized hoodie and grabbed her purse. "Gonna walk on the beach for a little while, let the fresh air clear my head. Then home to a hot bath and some tea."

"See you Friday, then, doll."

After saying goodbye to the other bartenders and servers, Lani headed out the employee entrance, which opened up mere steps from the Mission Beach board-walk. It was busy, even on a weeknight, with runners and skateboarders, and people hanging out on their decks, along with the sound of laughter, music and screams coming from nearby Belmont Park and its rollercoaster.

She sucked in a deep breath of the salty sea air and, hanging her purse across her body, shoved her hands in the kangaroo pocket of her hoodie and scuffed along the boardwalk, head down. Well, she couldn't avoid thinking about it any longer. Tonight's bout of morning sickness and its aftermath meant reality—that old bitch—was trying her damndest to get Lani's attention.

How was she gonna do this, work and raise a baby on her own in one of the most expensive cities in the U.S.?

She was barely hanging on as it was. Her job paid well, and on a good night the tips were amazing. Still, the cost of living ate into most of what she made, leaving little left over for things like diapers and everything else a baby required. Childcare? Forget it.

She'd need to move home.

That thought sent a giant shudder through her, along with nausea of a different kind. No. Home wasn't home anymore. Home was a place where awful memories lurked. Her parents still lived in that house…

Pressing her palm against her abdomen, Lani choked

back a sob. She wanted to raise her child in *this* place, a place she associated with love, laughter and friendship. No matter that everything was changing, San Diego would always be the city where she'd been the happiest.

It was home now, and she didn't want to leave.

Suddenly, a delicious smell cut into her anguished thoughts. The pretzel stand. Unexpected hunger made her empty tummy give a giant rumble, and before she knew it, she was headed that way. Maybe a big, soft unsalted pretzel and a cup of Sprite would lift her spirits.

They did. The pretzel was hot, and buttery, the soda crisp and cold.

"Let me keep it down, baby, please," she whispered, patting her stomach.

"Feeling better?"

With a start, Lani glanced to the side where a low wall ran along the edge of the boardwalk. Geo perched there, lips quirked, cup of coffee in hand. After a moment's hesitation, she ambled in his direction.

"For now." She tossed the greasy parchment paper into a nearby trash can. "It smelled so good, I couldn't resist."

"I'm glad." Standing, he threw his coffee cup away, too, and by unspoken agreement, they started meandering down the path side by side, hands crammed in their pockets.

"Hey, thanks for listening earlier," she said at last. "It did feel good to talk about it."

"You're very welcome." Geo leapt to the side to avoid a skateboarder barreling at them, and when they came back together, he said, "We can talk some more if you want. I don't have anywhere to be."

"What? A SEAL with time on his hands? How'd you manage that?"

He chuckled. "I do have to check on my dog at some point, but other than that—"

"You have a dog?"

"Well, sort of. I'm a K9 handler, so he's not my pet, he's technically my teammate."

"Really?" Lani knew next to nothing about the military working dog community, just that they existed, even on SEAL teams.

"Yep, his name is Bosch."

"Bosch? As in Hieronymus Bosch, the artist?"

Geo's glance held a tinge of surprise. "Yeah. You know Bosch?"

Unable to keep from bristling, Lani snapped, "Why is that so astonishing? Despite outward appearances, I'm not some uneducated hick—"

"Whoa, now, did I say anything like that?" Geo stopped walking and turned to her. "I can count on one hand the people who've gotten that reference immediately, okay? It's *always* surprising to me when someone does, no matter who it is."

Pinching the bridge of her nose, she blew out a calming breath before mumbling, "I'm sorry. I don't know why I'm so defensive. It's just—"

After a moment, he gestured toward the ocean. "C'mon, let's walk on the beach."

The water was dark, and frothy with waves. She kicked off her shoes, and the cool sand squelched between her toes, easing some of her tension. "You must think I'm an absolute mess, don't you?"

"'An uneducated hick.' 'An absolute mess.' Hmm."

Geo shook his head. "Is that how I see you, or how you see yourself?"

Her throat tightening, Lani stopped walking. He swung around to face her. "Because what I see is a woman who stood up for herself against some dude harassing her. A woman who works hard, who's smart, funny, easy to talk to. Definitely not a 'hick,'" he said, complete with air quotes, "or a 'mess.'"

Blinking rapidly, determined not to cry, she whispered, "You don't even know me. Don't blow sunshine up my ass—"

"I'm not. I would never do that, ever. Ask anyone." His grin lit up the night. "I don't like bullshit, have never had time for it, especially as a K9 handler."

Curiosity pricked her, made her ask, "What does that have to do with anything?"

"Because reading Bosch's body language, his cues, is how I keep him, myself and my crew alive. Is there a buried explosive under that pile of trash? A bad guy in the ditch over there? I have to make split-second decisions, instant judgments, about situations and people, almost on a daily basis."

His solemn gaze met hers.

"So no, I'm not blowing sunshine up your ass, not for one second, when I say that I see strength, not weakness, when I look at you." He paused. "You just have to see it in yourself, too."

The hot tears spilled over at last, and Lani wiped them away on her sleeve. Before the roaring in her ears could get too loud, Geo said, "Let's walk."

They were quiet as they made their way closer to the water, and the hard-packed sand there. The ocean roared around them, the waves surging to within inches of their feet.

"Fear isn't your enemy," he said at last. "If there's anything being a SEAL has taught me, it's that success in life has very little to do with the situation you're in and everything to do with how you react to it. It's what you do in *spite* of that fear."

When he touched her shoulder, Lani glanced up at him. "Fear isn't the polar opposite of courage. Just because you're scared doesn't mean you're not also strong, okay?"

All she could do was nod.

"Assess, prioritize, eliminate what you can't control and fix what you can. That's your SEAL life lesson for today," he said, smiling. "You're practically one of us now."

"But I don't want to be a SEAL. I hate exercise."

A pause, and then Geo threw his head back and laughed, the low, husky sound stroking along her nipples like a rough, warm tongue, hardening them painfully.

"God, you didn't miss a single beat. I haven't laughed like that in forever." His incredible eyes were admiring as he gazed down at her. "You don't have to be a SEAL if you don't want to. We do exercise a lot."

They continued on down the beach, and as they strolled, she thought about her friends—well, her former friends, the wives of the guys on Rhys's team. From the beginning she'd felt out of step with them, with their Barry's Bootcamps and CrossFit classes. Of course men who lived and breathed physical fitness would gravitate toward women who did the same, but for Lani, a night in with a cheese plate and a good book was infinitely more appealing than hours of lifting weights, yoga or Pilates.

Luckily, she'd found a kindred spirit in Sarah, the wife of one of her and Rhys's oldest friends. While the guys were gone, the two of them delighted in spending their days searching out local eateries, gourmet grocery stores and funky little tea shops. They'd cook together, glasses of wine in hand, while they tried out different recipes and experimented with foods from all over the world.

I've lost her. Just like I've lost Rhys, and Tyler...

Tears sprang to her eyes again, and as unobtrusively as possible, she wiped them away. Still, Geo noticed.

"What's wrong?" he asked softly. "Not feeling well?"

"Feeling alone." The admission came easily, too easily, but Lani didn't care. After tonight she doubted he'd spare her another thought. Right now she had his full attention, and damn if it wasn't exactly what she needed. "My friends were all team wives, remember? So now that I'm not with a team guy anymore..."

"Ah." He nodded. "Guess that means time to expand your horizons. Find friends outside the community. We're all pretty much assholes anyway."

She snorted. "Pretty much."

"You're better off without us. You really are."

They snickered together, and she said, "I wish moving on was that simple, though. I was with Rhys for ten years."

He glanced at her. "Wow. High school sweethearts?"

"Sort of." She bit her lip. How could she explain to a stranger everything Rhys was—and wasn't—to her?

Finally she settled on, "My brother died suddenly when I was fourteen. Rhys and I were friends, and afterward, we clung to each other. As time went on, it was easy to convince ourselves it was love."

"But it wasn't?"

"Well, let me put it this way. I've had a more meaningful conversation with you this past hour than I've had with Rhys in years." She shrugged. "Looking back, we were going through the motions, that's all."

Needing something to do with her hands, she fished a hair tie out of her pocket and pulled her hair into a ponytail, aware of Geo's sympathetic gaze.

"The end of a ten-year relationship is no joke. I'm sorry."

His quiet sincerity was a balm to her ragged emotions. "Thanks."

They strolled on in a companionable silence, their shoulders so close together, they almost touched. Lani glanced at his moonlit profile. "So. Who were you drinking with tonight?"

His lips tightened into a thin line, and for a moment, she didn't think he'd answer. Then he grunted, "A teammate. Died one year ago today."

She winced at the pain threading through the terse words. "Aww, shit, Geo. I'm—"

"Yeah," he interrupted. "Me, too."

He didn't want the pity. Well, she could relate. Painful memories surged, of morbid curiosity, intrusive questions, or worse, judgmental silences followed by disgust. After a while, she'd stopped mentioning Tyler's death to anyone, leaving Rhys to carry that particular burden alone…

"One-year anniversaries are hard," was all she said. "I know."

After a long pause, Geo exhaled slowly. "Yeah, I imagine you do."

"How long did you and your teammate serve together?"

"Oh, God, off and on for ten years. I actually met Cade before I went to BUD/S, before I was even a SEAL."

"Yeah?" Instinctively, she kept her tone light, encouraging, remembering her own clawing need to talk to someone, *anyone*, about who Tyler *was*, and her desperation not to define him by his death. "How'd that happen?"

Geo shrugged, although a tiny smile played about his lips. "You really wanna know? It's kind of a cool story."

In answer, she dropped to sitting in the sand and looked up at him expectantly.

Grinning now, Geo sank down next to her and lifted one knee to drape his wrist over it. The pose drew his jeans tight across his lap and powerful thighs, the sight of both drying Lani's mouth up. She gulped, then thought, *Fuck it*. There was no law against appreciating a beautiful man, and it'd sure give her a nice memory to hang on to during the long, lonely nights ahead.

When he didn't immediately say anything, she prompted, "So ten years ago, you were—"

"Twenty years old, and convinced I knew everything."

"You weren't a SEAL yet?"

"No, but I was in the Navy, had been for going on two years. In those days, you enlisted the regular way and then applied for Naval Special Warfare. Now you're sent to a bootcamp that feeds directly into BUD/S, but when I first went in, you had to apply and then wait to hear."

"That must've been hard, the waiting."

"Shit, you have no idea," Geo said fervently. "After two years with no word, I'd pretty much convinced myself it was never gonna happen. Then one day I was called into my department head's office. He had some news for me."

"You'd made it!"

"Yeah." He shook his head. "I couldn't believe it. A couple other dudes were in the office, too. They were part of a SEAL platoon we'd seen around the ship, and when they heard the news, they decided to come check me out."

"And bust your balls, of course."

He fell back on his elbows in the sand, his T-shirt riding up a bit with the motion. Tearing her gaze away from the hint of hair-roughened skin below his navel, Lani shivered as Geo's husky chuckle washed over her again.

"Of course," he said. "They laughed at me, told me there was no way I'd make it, that I should just decline the SEAL contract right now instead of embarrassing myself at BUD/S. This one guy, I think he could see I was getting pissed, so he told me to speak freely."

When he didn't go on, she prompted, "Did you?"

The wicked curl to his lips sent another quiver through her. "Oh, yeah. I got up in his face and said, 'Fuck you *and* the horse you rode in on. I'll see you in the teams.'"

"Oh, God." She clapped her hand over her mouth to suppress her giggle. "Did they give you a beat-down?"

"Nah. I think they were more amused by my arrogant punk-ass routine than anything else. My Chief dismissed me, and as I was heading back to my duties, I heard my name being called. It was one of the SEALs, and yeah, I figured it was time to get my ass kicked. Before I could say anything, he goes, 'Me and my buddy made a bet. Wanna hear it?'"

Lani groaned. "Let me guess. Something about how long it'd take you to wash out."

"That's what I thought, too, but nope. The bet was whether I'd make it or not." Geo shook his head wonderingly. "Believe it or not, this guy bet I'd *make* it. You could've knocked me down with a fuckin' feather when he said that. Then he punched me on the shoulder, said his name was Cade Barlow and that I should look him up when I got to the teams. Not *if,* but *when*."

Knowing what she did about the eat-your-own culture of special operations, she couldn't help her fervent, "Wow. That's truly amazing."

"Yeah." A few beats of silence, and then Geo said softly, "Some of the worst people I've ever met are in the SEAL teams, but Cade, he was one of the best."

His ragged sigh made her heart ache. "Someone worth toasting, then. I'm honored to have been a part of that."

His jaw rippled, and a haunted look flitted across his face. "You have no idea how much you saying that means to me." His voice was barely audible. "Thank you."

"You're welcome." Drawing her knees up, Lani

wrapped her arms around them, unable to keep from wondering what'd happened to Cade. A firefight in a distant country, the full details of which might never be known? An IED? A training accident?

Something about Geo's body language kept her from asking. Besides, in this moment it didn't matter. They were celebrating Cade's *life*, not his death, and the impact his simple gesture of encouragement had made on a young man on the verge of an enormous mental and physical challenge.

She sifted the cool, damp sand through her fingers. Next to her, Geo had his eyes squeezed tightly shut as he wrestled with his memories, until at last he exhaled slowly and sat up again. They both stared out over the dark, roiling ocean, the silence not uncomfortable.

Suddenly he grimaced, and he fished his buzzing phone from his pocket. He glanced at it briefly, then silenced it.

"You need to go?"

When he nodded, the regret that shot through Lani startled her. Surprisingly, his eyes mirrored that regret back at her as he stood and dusted off the seat of his pants before reaching down to help her to her feet.

Squeezing her fingers, he said, "Thanks again for listening. I, uh, had been wondering how I was going to get through tonight."

She gazed up at him. "Well, thanks for holding my hair, and listening to my tale of woe. I'd been wondering how I was going to get through tonight, too."

They smiled at each other.

"Guess it was fate, then, huh?" he said lightly. "Does that mean we should keep in touch?"

A tiny bolt of happiness sizzled through her. "I wouldn't mind."

Of course it'd never go anywhere. He'd soon disappear back into the depths of the spec ops world, while she'd be busy trying to work out her own very uncertain future. Still, it'd be nice while it lasted, and she couldn't deny it felt *really* good to know she'd been what he needed tonight, puking, hair-holding and all.

They'd reached the boardwalk by then, and Geo waved his hand at a sleek motorcycle parked at the curb. "That's mine." Pulling his wallet from his back pocket, he extracted a card and handed it to her.

She glanced at the simple black lettering, which read GeoFrog Tactical K9, followed by a phone number. "You have your own K9 business?"

He shrugged. "I own a bite suit, and sometimes I'll go work with law enforcement, things like that. It keeps Bosch and me sharp." Tapping the edge of the card, he said, "Call me anytime, okay? You'll probably talk to my voice mail a lot, but I promise to call back when I can."

With that, Geo straddled the bike and unlocked his helmet. "Take care of yourself, Lani. You got this."

Lifting his hand in a final wave, he roared off, and she stood there long after his taillights had disappeared into the distance.

"I got this? Glad *you* think so."

But there's no one else, is there? It really is up to me.

Okay, so…

Assess the situation.

She wanted to keep the baby.

Prioritize the tasks.

Talk to the manager and find out her work options. Evaluate her insurance coverage. Start saving money.

Eliminate the things you can't control.

How she'd feel when she first held her child in her arms.

Impatiently, she dashed yet more tears from her eyes. "God, stop with the waterworks and grow the fuck up already. All you can do is your best."

With a sigh, and one last glance after Geo, Lani took the first halting step into her new normal.

Time to go home and find herself a good OB.

Chapter Two

"Dude, you gotta tell Drew something before you leave town. We're at the club. Get over here."

Geo punched the Bluetooth button on his handlebar to disconnect the voice mail. Guilt burned its way through him, almost immediately followed by a secondary wave of annoyance. Shit. He'd been hoping to avoid this.

Gunning the engine, he leaned into the next curve, the chill San Diego wind whipping at his T-shirt and jeans. Brake lights glowed on the interstate up ahead, but instead of slowing, he threaded his motorcycle in between the lines of stopped cars. They flashed past on either side of him, row after row of colorful, glinting metal.

As he drove, he rehearsed what he'd say to Drew.

"I don't want you to wait for me. Go find someone else."

Yeah, that'd go over like a fart in church.

"If I was going to be with anyone, it'd be you."

Geo grit his teeth. No way would Drew fall for that "It's not you, it's me" bullshit.

"It's over, kid. Bye."

Groaning under his breath, he took the next interchange to head inland, where the traffic thickened even more, demanding every bit of his attention. When he roared into the parking lot of his destination at last, he killed the engine and sat for a minute staring up at the brightly lit building, fists clenched on his thighs.

How things had changed. For so many years he'd had to sneak here, heart in his throat, afraid someone would see. Now he could walk in whenever he pleased, openly and without fear, but Geo *still* found himself glancing around, searching the shadows, wondering who might be watching him.

Old habits died hard.

Inside the bar, he paid his cover and received his wristband, then ran lightly down the stairs to the main part of the club where the music thumped and strobe lights flashed. Even on a weeknight, the dance floor was packed with writhing bodies, most of them shirtless. He felt the admiring glances slide over him and even held a few hot gazes himself before making his way toward the bar and the man who sat at the end sipping a club soda with lime.

He smiled when he saw Geo. "Buy you a drink, sailor?"

Geo leaned down to kiss him lightly. "I'll get something in a second, Ash. Where's Drew?"

"Around." Ash hooked his foot over the barstool next to him and pulled it closer. "C'mon, sit down for a minute. He'll find you."

With an annoyed huff, Geo sank down onto the stool and pinched the bridge of his nose. Fuck, the pounding music was already giving him a headache, and he really didn't feel like shouting his way through a breakup, especially not tonight.

He glanced over to meet Ash's shrewd gaze.

"How're you holding up?"

Shrugging, he said, "I'm dealing. I knew tonight would be rough, but I got through it."

He smiled. With a little help from a new friend.

"What're you thinking about?" Ash asked curiously.

Stretching, Geo linked his fingers behind his head. "Just this bartender I met earlier tonight. Lady had some serious knife skills." He smirked at the memory of Lani and her angry lemon chopping.

"Yeah?" Ash lifted an interested brow. "What'd you do, piss her off?"

"Strangely enough, no. I think I made a friend."

"Mm-hmm. It won't last."

"Hey, now." Geo kicked him lightly on the shin. "I *am* capable of friendships, asshole. It's the other I have trouble with."

"Time to tell Drew that, I guess." Ash lifted his chin toward a blond man who'd just walked into their line of sight. He nudged Geo's ankle with his foot. "Go on, now. Be sure to thoroughly break his heart."

A wave of sadness and regret swept over Geo as he looked at Drew. He was a good guy and they'd had a lot of fun together, and goddammit, there'd been way too many of these scenes over the years. Aware of Ash's sympathetic gaze, Geo stood, crammed his hands in his pockets and ambled over to where Drew was talking and laughing with some friends.

Geo studied him as he approached. Tall and slender, with soulful blue eyes and a smattering of freckles on his nose, Drew was a third-year engineering student at UCSD. He also had a wicked sense of humor and an enthusiasm for sex that many a night had left Geo gasping for mercy.

The dude was a catch, for sure, and now Geo was about to toss him back into the sea.

Drew caught sight of him just then, and with a pleased exclamation, flung himself into Geo's arms. Geo hugged him briefly before pushing him gently away. "Can we go outside and talk for a minute?"

The smile faded from Drew's lips. "Yeah, sure," he said, his voice flat. "Be back in a sec, guys."

The gazes of his friends turned hostile, and fighting the urge to squirm, Geo followed as Drew silently led the way outside.

Right outside the door, he whirled around. "Are you breaking up with me, Geo?"

"Yes."

At the sound of the one quiet word, Drew's animated face crumpled, his lower lip starting a heartbreaking quiver. He blinked rapidly before turning to brace his palms on the wall, his head drooping.

"You knew this was temporary going into it," Geo said softly, and he rested his hand on Drew's shoulder and squeezed. "I never meant to hurt you."

He could've kicked himself when Drew lifted his head, renewed hope flaring in his expressive eyes. "Is it just because you're leaving?" He attempted to move into Geo's arms again. "Because I don't mind waiting. I *want* to wait." Sucking in a deep, shaky breath, he blurted, "I love you."

Oh, damn. Dammit, kid. He didn't want to do it like this.

Geo firmed his lips. Better to rip the Band-Aid off all at once. "But I don't love you," he said roughly, his gut churning. "This was never about falling in love, or being boyfriends, or you *waiting* for me. You're cute, and I like you, but believe me, once I ride away from here, I seriously doubt you'll ever cross my mind again."

An awful beat of silence, and then with a cry, Drew tore himself away and turned to run back into the club. Geo watched until he was safely inside before collapsing back against the wall to wait. Sure enough, it was only a few minutes until Ash pushed through the door, caught sight of him, and came to prop his shoulder nearby.

"So. Really good job at breaking his heart," he said almost conversationally. "Dude is bawling. What'd you say to him?"

"He thinks sex is love. What do you think I said?"

Ash winced. "Ouch."

Despite his outward calm, Geo's throat felt tight. "I had to be brutal, you know? Otherwise he was gonna *wait*."

"Ah, babe." Ash heaved a sigh. "You need to stay away from these young guys with stars in their eyes. They're a lot different than we were at twenty-two or twenty-three."

Wasn't that the truth. At that age, Geo had already been through BUD/S, and SQT, and had earned his Trident. After two years of training, war was on his mind, and a relationship with a man wasn't even a possibility unless he wanted his career to go down in flames.

Tilting his head back, Geo stared up at the night sky. "I never promised him anything, you know that."

"Yeah, I know. You never do." Ash studied him for a moment. "You gonna be okay?"

Other than the fact I'm a colossal asshole who manages to let everybody down?

"Yeah," he croaked, shoving away the toxic mixture of guilt and regret that seemed to have taken up permanent root in his chest. "I just needed to get through tonight." Attempting a smile, Geo pulled Ash to him for a hug. "Give Nick a kiss for me, okay?"

"Now that I can do." Ash waggled his eyebrows. "Or you can come kiss him yourself. Up to you."

For a moment Geo was seriously tempted. Ash and his husband Nick were open, and Geo had spent many a hot night in their bed. After debating with himself for a minute, he reluctantly let him go. "Can't. Gotta go check on Bosch."

Ash huffed. "Geez, cockblocked by a dog. So great for the ego." Walking backward away from Geo, he called out, "I think I'll see if that luscious Drew wants some, er, comforting. You mind?"

"Comfort away." Geo pulled his phone from his pocket and, with a few swipes of his finger, deleted Drew from both his contacts and his life.

It was over. Time to move on.

As he rode toward the base, he couldn't help but wonder how Lani was feeling, if she'd managed to keep her snack down. Geo winced at the memory of the violent heaves shaking her body, her breathless mortification as he'd held her hair out of the way.

Yet, despite her obvious physical misery and emotional turmoil, her determination and sense of humor shone through it all. She'd made him laugh, and listened to his story about Cade, and she'd lost someone, too...

The sudden, fervent hope that she'd call took him by surprise.

Why would she? She had *way* too much on her plate to think about calling some dude who'd never be around. They'd shared a moment in time, that's all, two strangers whose lives briefly intersected and then diverged once again.

It won't happen.

Even so, the kernel of hope stubbornly remained. Geo racked his brain, trying to remember how long it'd been since he'd looked forward to *anyone's* call like this.

Sadly, it'd been a really long time.

Chapter Three

The knock on the door startled Lani into a yelp.

Pushing her laptop away and dragging herself up from the table, she trudged over and peered through the peephole. The large green eye staring back at her first made her jump back in alarm, then huff in annoyance. She unlocked the door and yanked it open. "God, I hate when you do that."

Rhys Halloran grinned back at her. "I know. Why do you think I keep doing it?"

"Because you're a mean, gross boy, that's why."

Stepping aside, she let Rhys inside her apartment before leaning back against the door with her arms crossed over her chest, heart pounding. Why on earth was he here?

When his gaze dropped to her midsection, she knew.

"Sarah told you?"

"Aaron did. Honey…" Rhys took a step toward her. "Why didn't *you* tell me?"

She shrugged, unable to meet his eyes. After another beat of silence, he drew in a deep, shaky breath. "Jesus, Lee-Lee." The paleness of his cheeks made his freckles stand out in sharp relief. "What're you going to do?"

The sight of his distress brought a lump rising into her own throat. "I honestly don't know yet. Still trying to figure some things out." She spun around to walk into her tiny kitchen, where she grabbed up her teakettle and started to fill it.

After a moment came the sound of his footsteps behind her. "Tell me about the airfield yesterday. The truth this time, not that bullshit you spouted about wanting to fuck with me."

"The airfield?" Shame and embarrassment made her tone sharp. God, what had she been thinking? Well, she *hadn't* been thinking, not about anyone except herself. Even knowing that Rhys had fallen in love with someone else, Lani had *still* met his plane after his deployment, a homemade sign in hand, one that begged him to try again.

Behind her, Rhys said something, but the loud *ping* of the water into the kettle drowned him out, even as the memory flushed her hot with remembered humiliation. Along with the other team wives, girlfriends and families, Lani'd waited for him, the chill spring wind tugging at her skirt, her palms clammy with desperation, heart in her throat…

"Lani?" The gentle touch of Rhys's hand on her shoulder made her jump, the now-overflowing teakettle giving a mighty slosh.

She pulled away and wiped her eyes on her sleeve, saying thickly, "It's pretty simple, really. I'd just found out I was pregnant, and I was scared shitless, okay? Instead of trying to figure things out on my own, I ran to you." Letting out a mirthless laugh, she went on, "Pathetic, right? I knew about Devon, knew you were in love with her, but I'd already convinced myself she didn't matter. I thought, '*I* need him. He's *mine.*'"

Slamming the kettle onto the burner, she viciously twisted the on switch. "God, Sarah was horrified when I told her what I was going to do. You should've heard her try to talk me out of it."

After a moment's hesitation, Rhys leaned his hip against the counter near her. "I about had a heart attack when I got off the plane and saw you holding that sign," he admitted.

"Yeah, I could see it in your face when you walked toward me, like a man to his execution."

"Shit, really?" His voice was full of genuine remorse. "I'm sorry."

Unbelievably a chuckle welled into her throat. "Probably the way I looked during your flash-mob proposal, huh?"

Which she'd accepted, not wanting to hurt him, but then immediately regretted.

His own embarrassment flickered across his face. "Fuck, don't remind me. Why I thought that was a good idea—"

They'd actually pretended for a while, had the engagement party, made a few plans, until their always-shaky foundation had fallen apart for good.

Lani sighed. "I guess if we need to put each other on the spot to get our way, then the universe is really trying to tell us something, isn't it?"

A brief silence shimmered between them, the gossamer threads of the past that bound them together slowly parting and falling away, leaving the faint echoes of their childhood friendship behind.

Moving closer to him, she said, "Rhys, I'm so sorry I did that to you, and Devon. I just didn't know where else to turn."

He settled his hands gently on her shoulders and squeezed. "I can't imagine how scared you are right now," he said quietly. "If there's anything I can do—"

Besides sacrifice all of your newfound happiness for me? When will I stop asking you to do that?

She firmed her lips. Right fucking now.

"There's really nothing you can do," she said, proud of how steady her voice sounded. "This is *my* mess to deal with, so what I want is for you to walk out of here and go back to Devon."

The relief in his eyes made her heart ache.

"What are you—"

"Me? I have a plan," she said flippantly. "I'll be fine. More than fine." She shut up before he could detect the lie in her voice; after all, he knew her better than anyone.

Sure enough, skepticism twisted his lips. "What's your plan, Lee-Lee?"

"None of your business." She put her palms on his chest and pushed. "Now shoo."

"Uh-uh." Planting his feet, he pinned her with his gaze. "I'm not leaving till you tell me your plan."

He wouldn't either. Lani didn't think she'd ever met a more stubborn person in her entire life. Racking her brain for something to tell him, it hit her, the one thing that would convince him beyond a shadow of a doubt that she was serious about handling this herself.

She lifted her chin. "I'm going to use Tyler's money."

He flat-out gasped. "What?"

She couldn't blame him for that. How many times had she sworn never to touch a penny of the life insurance money her parents had insisted on giving her? Even when she and Rhys had been living paycheck to paycheck and subsisting on ramen noodles and cold cereal, she'd refused to even *think* about using it.

Her father had put it in a savings account for her, and for ten years it'd sat completely untouched. It wasn't a fortune, but it was decent. She shivered. Blood money.

"Yep, I'm going to use it. Maybe go back to school. Do something to better my life. Take care of my baby."

Concern written all over him, Rhys reached out and took her cold hands in his. "Tyler would've liked that," he said gently. "He would've loved having a niece or nephew."

All Lani could do was nod. It was true. His girlfriend had had a big family, and whenever she saw pictures, it seemed Tyler always had a child or two hanging from him.

"What a waste."

At those anguished words, Rhys gave an almost imperceptible flinch, his fingers tightening involuntarily on hers. He straightened, as if bracing himself, his eyes full of a weary resignation that hit her like a fist to the gut.

He was waiting for her to fall apart. Again. Like she had each and every time she was confronted with a major life event, and God, if an accidental pregnancy wasn't one doozy of a stressor.

As always, he had come to pick up the pieces, no matter his personal cost. Tyler had been the one who died, but Rhys was the one made to pay for it, to *relive* it, over and over and over.

No.

"I see strength in you."

Geo's words from the night before suddenly cut through the roaring in Lani's ears, and she clung to them. She pulled them close and used them to make herself let go of Rhys's hands.

"That's my plan," she said firmly. "Use Tyler's money for something good—my baby."

He stared at her, dumbfounded. "I'm so proud of you," he said at last. "I know that decision didn't come easily."

"It does help to think I'd be using it for him or her—" she touched her abdomen "—and not for myself. I think Tyler would've wanted that."

Rhys searched her face a moment longer, and then he nodded. "Okay. It's a good plan."

"You approve?"

"I do." He paused. "You know I'll always be here for you, Lee-Lee. No matter what."

Lani sighed to herself, knowing it'd take more than a mere declaration of intent to convince him otherwise—now she had to *live* it. This was her show now.

Still, an enormous surge of tenderness made her reach up to cup his stubbly cheek. "Hey, you wanna know something?" When his eyes met hers, she whispered, "You're the best friend I've ever had, Peanut Butter."

At the sound of that old childhood nickname, his lashes grew spiky with unshed tears. "Back atcha, Lani-Bo-Bani."

"I'm gonna be fine," she said, standing shakily on the foundation of Geo's words. "So go on now. Be happy with Devon. Do awesome shit."

He turned his head and kissed her palm, his warm lips lingering on the sensitive skin, and then he stepped away. Holding her gaze, he backed toward the door, opened it, and when it closed behind him, the quiet *snick* carried with it such a sense of finality that Lani clapped a hand to her mouth to hold back her sob.

Thank you, Rhys, for going down into that basement so I didn't have to. For staying with me that day, and every day after that for the next ten years.

No matter what the future held for her, she'd made the right decision in giving him his life back.

One more thing had to be said, though.

"Devon, girl, if you ever hurt him, you'd better watch the fuck out."

A few hours later, the teakettle was empty and Lani was a knot of anxiety.

Dropping her head onto her folded arms, she let out a loud groan. Budget, done. Medical coverage, verified. She'd talked to her boss, who told her the club didn't offer *paid* maternity leave, but that as far as she was concerned, Lani's job was safe.

"You're one of the best bartenders we've ever had," she'd said. "The customers love you."

Prioritize. Assess.

Okay, she'd done that, but unfortunately, no matter which way she ran the numbers, she wouldn't be able to do it without the insurance money.

"It's for the baby," she said out loud to the empty kitchen. "Not for you. Remember that."

Steeling herself, she got up from the table and went to the tiny hall closet, where she pulled out her lockbox of important papers. A few spins of the combination, a lift of the lid, and then the savings account book her father had given her after Tyler's death was in her hand.

The feel of the cheap vinyl immediately catapulted her back in time, to when she'd thrown the book at her dad's feet and run from the room, crying that she didn't want money, she wanted her brother back. A well-meaning family friend had followed her, had taken her aside to remind her that she needed to be strong for her parents because Tyler had been their only son.

As if they didn't still have a daughter, one whose grief was a physical pain carving her up from the inside out. One whose guilt was eating her alive because *she'd* been the last one to see Tyler. *She'd* had the chance to save him.

Her parents' suffering hammered it home each and every day—it was her fault. She should have been able to prevent it. She should have *said something*!

Lani fought to hold them at bay, but all the "should haves" she waged constant, fierce battles against reared their ugly heads once again. They started screaming out everything she'd done wrong that day, their strident voices crumbling her earlier resolve into dust and sending the doubts flooding through her in a painful rush.

So much for all that strength Geo saw in her. She wasn't strong, she was one second away from texting Rhys and begging him to come back...

Her jaw clenching, she jumped up and started to

pace. "You got this," she whispered fiercely. "Take it one day at a time. You don't need the money yet, but it's there if you do, okay? What you're *not* going to do is call Rhys. There. Is. No. Rhys."

Still, she cast a longing glance toward the phone before turning her back on it. Ugh. No, goddammit. Too bad Geo wasn't here to give her another SEAL pep talk, because she could really use one right now.

So why don't you call him?

She froze. No, she couldn't.

He invited you to. It was his *idea.*

But what if he doesn't call back?

Would that really be the end of the world? It'd be a little embarrassing, sure, but no real harm done.

As she grabbed up her phone, Lani's throat tightened, her skin growing prickly and hot. A giant fist squeezed her lungs and made her gasp for air. Oh, God, she needed to talk to someone. Needed to pour her heart out. Needed to fully articulate her anger, her heartache, her grief, her *guilt*.

I couldn't keep my brother alive, so how will I ever be able to raise this baby?

Suddenly, a deep crack formed in the protective wall surrounding her heart and sent a wave of terror surging through her body. She doubled over, sob after sob exploding from her chest.

I'm so scared. I need help. Please, somebody help me.

With a shaking finger, Lani swiped open her phone and dialed.

Chapter Four

"Oh, hey, Geo. It's Lani, the puking bartender from Mission Beach."

Geo tightened his grip on his phone, which he'd mashed hard against his ear.

"Shut the fuck up!" he yelled to the guys brawling in the back of the van. "I'm trying to listen to something!"

In response a tennis shoe whizzed by his head and smashed into the windshield, narrowly missing the driver. Geo gritted his teeth and hunched over in the passenger seat, his finger jammed in his other ear to try to block out some of the noise.

SEALs on a road trip—grown men or out-of-control middle schoolers? It was really hard to tell sometimes.

"...calling to thank you," Lani's message was saying. "Not just for the hair-holding, as appreciated as that was, or the awesome life advice—which I've already taken some of, by the way—but for showing me how good it feels to, you know, just *talk* to someone."

He could hear her take in a gulp of air, then blow it out slowly.

"So...here's the thing. Ten years ago, my older brother died by suicide."

Geo's own breath whooshed from his lungs. *What?*

"I thought I was coping. I mean, it's been ten years, right? But the truth is, I haven't really gotten better, and now something's made it so I can't ignore it anymore. That 'something' is my baby, and believe it or not, talking to you the other night has given me the courage to take my first step toward getting help. I'm talking *real* help, not just the dump-on-the-people-who-love-you-the-most kind that I'm used to asking for."

Another pause, and behind Geo, the yelling escalated even more. He gripped the phone tighter and strained to hear, his heart threatening to pound its way out of his chest.

Lani's voice wobbled the tiniest bit. "I had a complete emotional breakdown a few days ago, and after I stopped crying, I called my OB's office. They were able to recommend a therapist. Did you know there are some who specialize in suicide survivors? I didn't either. But yep, there are, and I made an appointment for Thursday next week. I know myself, though, and I know when that day comes, I will *not* want to go through with it."

Geo could only sit frozen, his whole body numb with shock.

"So what I'm going to do is I'm gonna remember our walk on the beach. I'm going to remember that I shared with you a tiny bit of my fear, and how darn *good* that felt afterward."

A long pause.

"Anyway, I just wanted you to know how grateful I am for everything you did that night. I, uh, well, I guess that's it. Bye."

The message ended.

Holy. Christ.

Memories that Geo was desperate to keep buried fought to rise to the surface and, his stomach roiling with nausea, he jammed his finger on the window button and powered it down. Although it wasn't refreshing, the blast of hot desert air hitting his face helped clear his head. It also distracted the other guys from their brawl.

"Hey, Rocco, how 'bout a goddamn piss break?" a few strident voices yelled from the rear of the van.

The driver shook his head. "I said no breaks, didn't I? Use some of that shit rolling around on the floor."

"Aww, c'mon! Bastard."

A few more mutters of disgust, and then a blessed quiet fell as bruised and bloodied SEALs attempted to pee into the various cans and bottles they found littering the floor of the government van.

"Hey," the driver hissed at Geo. "Watch this."

Geo glanced over at Rocco, a tall Latino guy whose baby-faced good looks belied years of combat experience and a razor-sharp tactical mind. His brown eyes were full of mischief, the light in them telling Geo exactly what he was about to do. Gripping the door handle, Geo braced his feet, and sure enough, Rocco jerked the wheel to the side. The van rocked violently as it swerved onto the shoulder.

Outraged yells from the back. "Son of a bitch! You made me piss myself!"

Rocco roared with laughter as an acrid, unmistakable smell filled the air.

"Fuck, I'm covered with it! You're gonna pay, asshole!"

Geo glanced over his shoulder, unable to keep from snickering at the sight of his teammates frantically blotting at the urine splashed on the seats and themselves.

He fished some more napkins from the console and helpfully tossed them back.

Next to him, Rocco pounded the steering wheel with the heel of his hand and shouted, "Gotcha, muhfuckahs!"

The furious muttering behind him made Geo wince. It might not be today, it might not be tomorrow, but in the near future Rocco was gonna find himself duct-taped to a tree somewhere, and if he was really, *really* lucky, they'd let him keep his clothes.

Rocco met his eyes and shrugged. "Worth it," he mouthed before directing his attention back to the road.

Shaking his head in both disgust and amusement, Geo turned to stare out the window at the relentlessly brown landscape flashing past. Every SEAL, at one point or another in his career, found himself duct-taped to a fixed object. For him, it'd been—

Geo struggled to keep it closed, but his mental box of Cade memories burst open.

"Get 'em!"

A vicious tackle, and Geo crashed to the floor of the hotel room. All around him came the crunch of fists on flesh, the sound of bodies slamming into furniture, into walls. Geo kicked, punched and fought, but soon found himself trussed hand and foot and tossed next to Cade, both of them stripped to the waist.

Shouting, laughing team guys poured liquor down their throats, and drew on their chests with Sharpies. When the women finally burst in with outraged screams, they discovered Geo and Cade thoroughly shit-faced and covered with crude Sharpie penises.

Cade's fiancée, Renae, put her hands on her hips and glared around the room. "You fucking assholes," she grated. "Cut them loose. Now."

Like chastened little boys, the SEALs obeyed, and Geo rubbed the blood flow back into his wrists as Renae yanked Cade to his feet.

"Really, guys?" Her voice was furious, but controlled. "He's getting married in less than twelve hours!"

Shaking her head, Renae led Cade away to get him sobered and cleaned up.

Geo's date, Vanessa, crouched next to him, red-faced and teary-eyed as she scrubbed with a wet napkin at the pendulous "balls" drawn right between his pecs. "What were you thinking? You're the best man! Cade and Renae's wedding is ruined!"

Geo didn't reply, his energy consumed with trying not to hurl. How could he explain to her that this is what team guys did, how they showed affection for each other?

Despite their antics, the wedding went off without a hitch. Geo had to enjoy the festivities dateless, since Vanessa had packed up and left.

"Sorry, dude," someone said, and Geo shrugged. It took an extremely strong-willed person to be with a SEAL and the close-knit, unique culture he brought with him. Renae both understood and accepted that. Vanessa didn't.

"Best wedding I've ever been to. God, I miss you, bud." Geo squeezed his burning eyes shut.

When the van finally pulled up at the transient quarters of the base, the SEALs dispersed, leaving the two FNGs—fucking new guys—to clean up the pee-soaked seats and flooring.

Geo unloaded Bosch's crate and gear himself, and after getting it all settled in his room, bent to ruffle the dog's ears. "How 'bout a run?"

He wrapped a reflective Velcro belt around his waist and clipped one end of Bosch's three-foot lead to a ring attached to it. Geo tucked his phone into the pocket of his shorts, and they left their quarters at a slow jog to run along the nearby flight line.

Fighter jets roared down the runway and rocketed up into the night sky, their afterburners glowing. Next to him, Bosch trotted along at a steady pace, his tongue lolling out of his mouth.

"What a long-ass day, buddy," Geo grunted, the endorphins warring with exhaustion. "I work with a bunch of pricks—"

Understatement of the fucking year.

"—and I got a phone call from this beautiful woman that I don't know how to handle."

He paused, as if waiting for Bosch's reply.

"Yeah, you're right, she does come with a lot of baggage. Not really sure if I'm interested in tangling myself up in that, you know?"

A recent breakup. An unplanned pregnancy. A painful past, one that threatened to poke at Geo's own wounds.

He slowed to a walk and laced his fingers behind his head.

"But am I overthinking this?" he asked Bosch, who

ignored him to sniff along the base of a fire hydrant. "It'd just be talking, right? She's an interesting person, and she knows what life in special operations is like."

A friend worth their weight in gold. Most people—like Vanessa and Drew—didn't understand the demands of Geo's life, or else they had unrealistic expectations of it. If he was being perfectly honest with himself, he knew a big part of his attraction for people was so they could tell their friends they were fucking a Navy SEAL.

Maybe with Lani he could just be himself, not the video-game version.

Before he could overthink it any more, he fished his phone from his pocket and dialed.

Chapter Five

"Hey, Lani. It's Geo."

Closing her eyes, Lani let the sound of his voice wash over her again for the fifth time that day, and probably the twentieth time that week.

"It's 9:00 p.m., a balmy ninety-six degrees on the outskirts of Phoenix tonight, and Bosch and I have been out running in it, which is why I'm out of breath and wheezing like a freight train. Sorry."

He was sorry? The slightest bit of Southern drawl and breathlessness, along with Geo's natural husky quality, all combined to make this voice mail one of the sexiest things she'd ever heard.

"Anyway," he went on, "just wanted to call you back, say hi. We're going off the grid a bit tomorrow, so I won't be around, but keep your therapy appointment, okay? I'll be your accountability partner if you want. Next time we talk, I'll expect to hear all about it."

"Lani?"

A soft voice broke in to her concentration, and she glanced up to see a smiling, middle-aged Black woman wearing a dark-blue pantsuit, a silky patterned scarf elegantly draped around her neck, large gold hoops in her ears. "I'm Maura Grant."

"Hello." Fumbling to put away her phone, she stood and extended her hand to her new therapist, surprised when, instead of shaking it, Maura took it between both her own.

"So delighted to meet you. Please come in."

With a motherly pat to her fingers, Maura released her and led her into the office. Lani glanced around in awe, taking in the butter-yellow walls, polished wood laminate and colorful throw rugs. Instead of the stiff Naugahyde couch she'd been expecting, there was a well-worn leather loveseat across from an elegant wing-back chair.

The polished coffee table in between held a sterling silver tea service on it.

"This is beautiful," she mumbled. "Cozy."

"Thanks." Maura chuckled. "It's definitely my home away from home." As she moved to her desk to pick up a legal pad, she asked, "Would you mind pouring us some tea while I get situated? Even if you don't care for any, dear, I'll still take some."

"Uh, sure." Lani set her purse down next to the loveseat and sank down onto it before reaching for one of the delicate flowered teacups. "What kind of tea is it?"

"Roiboos with organic hibiscus and lemongrass. One of my favorites."

The act of pouring the fragrant tea was soothing, and by the time Maura took her seat and murmured her thanks for the cup and saucer Lani placed in front of her, Lani's anxiety had almost totally eased.

Give me a small task to perform so that I feel like a

guest making myself at home rather than a bug under a microscope. Oh, you're good.

As she sipped, she glanced around the room. In addition to the seating area, there was a large wooden desk and matching bookshelf, the latter holding an eye-pleasing mixture of books and a few framed photos. One in particular caught Lani's attention, that of a young man dressed in crisp green/brown camouflage, his sleeves rolled neatly to his elbows.

A Marine.

"That's my son, Vincent," Maura said softly, following her gaze. "It's the last picture I have of him. He completed suicide two weeks later."

Lani gripped her mug in suddenly cold fingers, unable to stop staring at Vincent's bright, seemingly happy smile. "*Why?*"

She hadn't realized she'd whispered the word aloud until Maura said, "I wish I knew. That's one of the things I've had to learn to accept, the fact I'll never know why."

"He didn't leave a note?" Lani's voice was hushed. "There weren't any warning signs?"

"Oh, in hindsight there were things, but they were things that never struck us as out of the ordinary or were easily explained away by puberty or teenage angst. When he died, he didn't leave a note, no explanation at all."

"How long ago?"

"Eleven years."

With a bitter snort, Lani put her mug down with a muffled clink. "You seem so much farther along than I am, Maura, and he was your *child*, not just—"

"Not just a brother?" Maura said gently when she didn't go on. "Like you're not allowed to grieve because he's not someone you gave birth to?"

Lani shrugged and twisted her fingers together. God, she wished she was anywhere but here.

"After Tyler died, my parents seemed to forget I existed," she said. "All the focus was on them. Everyone kept telling me to be strong for *them*, to be there for *them*, since I was the only kid they had left."

"The forgotten mourners." Nodding, Maura sipped her tea. "I've heard that a lot from sibling survivors. I was guilty of it myself with my own surviving children." A spasm of pain crossed her face. "It's taken years to repair that damage."

Maura's openness chased away a little more of Lani's tension. She picked up her tea again. "So how do we do this therapy thing?"

With a smile, Maura said, "Well, we just keep on doing what we've been doing. We can talk about stuff that's bothering you, stuff you'd like to get off your chest. I'm here for *you*, Lani."

A short silence fell, broken only by the clink of cup hitting saucer. Maura sat relaxed, one leg crossed over the other, her legal pad casually open on her lap.

Lani's eyes went to Vincent in his uniform again, and she bit her lip.

"Lani?" Maura's voice was soft, encouraging. "What are you thinking about?"

"My ex."

"What about him?"

"He's military, too. Air Force special ops."

"A pararescueman?" When Lani nodded, Maura went on. "He must've been gone a lot."

"He was. All the time."

"Is that why you broke up?"

"No." To her horror, Lani felt tears sting her eyes. "We broke up because all I did was let him down."

"What do you mean? How did you let him down?" There was no judgment in Maura's tone, only gentle inquiry.

"Because I couldn't cope."

"With what?"

"With everything," Lani said harshly. "With his absences, the things he tried to share with me—"

She broke off, unable to go on. After a beat of silence, Maura said, "About what he saw on deployment?"

"That, and—and about my brother. Rhys is the one who found him."

"Oh." There was a wealth of understanding in that one breathed word. "Tell me."

Lani did, about hearing the gunshot, about Rhys rushing downstairs and then back up, how he'd refused to let her go see, too.

"He called the cops, and when they got there, they handcuffed us and treated us like criminals."

Maura winced. "That's actually standard procedure. They need to ascertain it's not a murder made to look like a suicide."

"My parents fell apart. They blamed me—"

"Why do you think they blamed you?"

Lani grit her teeth as the memories clawed to the surface. "Because I'm the one who missed all the warning signs. Everything."

"Like what?"

Plopping her cup down on the table again, she clasped her trembling hands between her knees. "He'd quit his job out of the blue. He said 'Fuck Dad' when I knew he idolized our father. His eyes were distant and sad."

"And did the thought ever cross your mind, even for one minute, that he was going to kill himself?"

"No!" Lani gasped. "Oh, my God, no! If it had, I would have—"

"You would've done everything in your power to stop him," Maura said softly. "But you didn't know."

"I should have—"

"You. Didn't. Know. You can*not* accept responsibility for that."

The last of Lani's tenuous control slipped away. "Yes, I can," she shouted. "I was the last one to see him alive. I could have *stopped* him! Don't tell me I couldn't have."

Leaping to her feet and grabbing up her purse, she strode toward the door, her whole body shaking with a combination of rage and confusion. Therapy was supposed to be *helping*, not ripping her skin off layer by layer.

"How do you know you didn't?"

The quiet words stopped her in her tracks. "What?" She dashed the back of her hand over her cheeks. "What the hell are you talking about?"

"How do you know there weren't other times you *did* stop him? Something you said, something you did?"

Lani could only stand frozen, her sobbing breaths loud in the room. She remembered coming into the living room once to find Tyler sitting in the dark, staring into space, and she'd cajoled him up and into the dining room where Rhys and Aaron were raiding the fridge. They'd all ended up playing cards for hours, and while Tyler was quieter than usual, he'd seemed to enjoy himself.

Had she stopped him that night? Had she bought him a little more time? Tears stung her eyes as the realization slammed into her: Even if she had, it didn't change the ultimate outcome, because a week later he was gone. That meant...

"That's right. There wasn't anything you could have done." Lani's gaze snapped to Maura, who was looking at her steadily. "You, my friend, have taken the weight of the world on your shoulders, haven't you?" She got up from her chair and walked toward her. "You're supposed to be all-seeing, all-knowing, a mind reader at fourteen years old."

The hot tears overflowed and streamed down Lani's cheeks.

"You're supposed to be the perfect girlfriend to a man who has a dangerous, stressful job that takes him away from home for months at a time. You're never, ever supposed to be human, not ever, because that's letting him down."

Slipping her arm around her shoulders, Maura led her back to the couch. "Because you failed to keep Tyler alive, you must be a failure at everything, right? Especially impending motherhood."

Lani lost it then, and for long minutes she could only sob, tissues magically appearing in her hand.

"I can help you," Maura said, her soft tone cutting through the roaring in Lani's ears. "I can help you because I've been right where you are. I know everything you're feeling, everything you tell yourself. It gets better. I promise you, it'll get better."

Mopping her eyes, Lani sucked deep breaths, in and out, as she fought for control. "I want to get better," she croaked. "I want to let go of the anger. I want to stop blaming myself. I w-want to be a good mom."

"You will be." With one last pat to her shoulder, Maura moved over to sit in her chair again. "The only thing we're going to focus on in here is you. Tyler is gone, and we're not going to analyze his death anymore. We want to grieve his *absence* and celebrate who he *was*—a beloved brother to you for fourteen years."

Lani picked up her teacup again, not to drink, but to hug the comforting warmth close. "He was so smart," she croaked. "Funny, kind. He had goals, and dreams. He l-loved me…"

Maura leaned forward and waited for her to meet her eyes.

"Yes. A life worth remembering," she said softly. "A life not defined by that moment in time, that choice he made in the midst of a pain you couldn't have known about or understood. Assuming responsibility for his death invalidates that pain, and his desperate need for relief from it."

Another sob welled up in Lani's throat.

"No amount of self-blame can change that outcome. No amount of analyzing it is going to help you understand it. You know the how, but you're never going to know the why. *You're never going to know the why, Lani.*"

Lani started to shake.

"Accepting that is the first step toward healing, and we're going to take a thousand steps together, you and me. As many as it takes, okay?"

All Lani could do was nod, the tears dripping from her chin.

"You're not alone, my dear. You're not alone."

God, she needed to pee.

Lani hurried up the walk toward her apartment building, the bags of Chinese food she juggled emitting the most mouthwatering smell.

And all the tea she'd drunk at Maura's sloshing painfully around in her bladder.

Even the brush of the light sea breeze over her skin hurt, everything still raw from the emotional therapy session, and the only thing she wanted to do was curl up in her pj's to watch reruns of *Friends* while she chowed down on some good, old-fashioned comfort food.

Ah, the sweet, sweet relief.

After washing her hands, she trudged toward her bedroom, her old friend—self-pity—doing its best to rear its ugly head. *Forever alone. Maybe I need to get a damn dog.*

The thought made her roll her eyes at herself. "Yeah, right," she said aloud. "A dog *and* a baby to take care of. Good plan."

Still…having a furry little body to snuggle up to at night and give her unconditional doggie love sounded infinitely appealing. Human love, after all, was vastly overrated.

She'd just settled down on the couch, the different cartons of food arrayed before her on the coffee table, remote in hand, when her phone buzzed. With a sigh, she muted the TV and grabbed it. Hopefully it was just a robocall that she could decline and move on, because that Kung Pao was really calling her name…

The screen said Geo.

Her breath caught.

"Hey, Geo," she answered, praying that she sounded natural and breezy and not like her heart was threatening to pound its way out of her chest. Which it totally was.

"Hey, you."

Oh, hello, sexy voice. Lani shivered.

"Did you go today?"

Surprised that he'd actually remembered the date of her appointment, she croaked, "Yep, I did."

"Good for you. How, uh, was it?"

"Well, honestly, it sucked like you wouldn't believe."

He gave an audible wince. "Yikes. I'm sorry."

"Don't be. My therapist warned me I'd feel worse before I feel better." Lani put her legs up on the coffee table and crossed them at the ankle. "There's ten years' worth of shit to unpack, you know."

He didn't reply, his sudden discomfort radiating through the phone, along with the awkwardness of two strangers separated by hundreds of miles being confronted with a difficult topic. Taking pity on him, she changed the subject. "What're you doing in Arizona?"

"Desert training." He grunted. "It's about a bazillion degrees here, which is good practice for us since we'll eventually be going, um—"

"To a galaxy far, far away?"

"Yeah." His relief at not being pressed on exactly *where* rang in his voice. "You understand that I can't say, right?"

"Of course I do. OPSEC, the subject of every predeployment family meeting ever."

Geo's chuckle this time sounded much more genuine, and the husky sound brushed along her skin, tightening her nipples and making her breasts ache. She cupped her hand over one and squeezed.

Ugh. Stupid hormones.

Clearing her throat, she asked, "How's Bosch?"

"He's good. Chilling in his crate."

"Is he there right now?"

"Yep. Right next to my bed."

She could hear rustling, as if Geo was moving around on crisp sheets. She shoved away the visual. "He doesn't sleep with you?"

"Nah, he's not my pet. When we're home, he lives in the base kennels, not with me. On the road, he has a crate."

"How long have you worked with him?"

"About three years."

"Did you pick him or did he pick you? Or didn't you have a choice?"

"I had a choice, and shit, that first day was insane." He paused, and Lani heard what sounded like him punching up his pillows. "Sorry. Just getting comfortable."

A frisson of warmth went through her at the thought

of him settling down in bed to talk to her. Stretching up to turn the table lamp off, she curled up on her side on the couch, phone wedged between her shoulder and ear. The TV flickered silently in front of her, the *Friends* gang drinking their coffee and laughing.

"So I walked into this kennel," Geo said, "and was immediately overwhelmed by what seemed like hundreds of barking, whirling, high-energy dogs. I, uh, was actually afraid of a few."

"Yeah?"

"Oh, yeah. Some of them are real snappish and aggressive. I remember this one, he had a crazy look in his eye like he wanted to kill me. At that point I was seriously wondering what the fuck I'd gotten myself into, and then I looked over and saw this other dog gazing around at all the chaos with what I swear was a sneer on his face, like, 'You peasants.' That was Bosch."

She stifled a giggle, picturing Geo on that barstool, his own expression exactly what he was describing.

"So you picked him?"

"Yep. I asked to work with him, and after two days, I knew he was the dog for me. One of our final exercises was to clear this house. He found the explosive odor right away, and then we were supposed to run out a side door into the yard where a dude in a bite suit was waiting to fight with him. Instead of going out the door, though, Bosch went out a window that nobody realized was open and fuckin' *pile-drove* this guy to the ground. *Boom!*"

The little-boy enthusiasm in his voice reminded her so much of Rhys that tears sprang to her eyes. It'd been so long since she'd lain in bed and talked to a man like this, and she'd forgotten how nice it was.

She wiped the tears on the neckline of her pajama top. "Wow," she said hoarsely. "That sounds intense."

"It was." He fell silent, and after a moment asked, "You okay?"

"What? Yeah. Yeah, I'm fine."

"You don't sound fine," he said, then went on, his tone rueful, "I'm such a tool. You said you'd had a rough day, and here I am, just babbling on about myself."

"Well, I like hearing you babble." Her face burned. "I mean, I'm really interested in, you know, dogs. And stuff."

Lani, you idiot.

"Have you ever had one? A dog, I mean."

"No." She sighed. "Rhys and I moved around so much, and we both worked, so it seemed unfair to have a pet."

"That's too bad," Geo said softly. "Dogs are great."

"Did you have dogs growing up?"

For a moment he didn't answer, and then he said, "I had a fish once. But no, no dogs. My dad was too sick for us to have pets like that."

"Oh. Did he—"

"He had MS. Died when I was eleven."

Lani winced. "I'm so sorry, Geo. That's rough."

Her heart aching, she waited, knowing there was nothing she could say, no platitudes he'd want to hear.

He blew out a breath. "Anyway…"

She could tell he'd revealed way more than he'd meant to, and intending to distract him and hopefully put him at ease, she asked, "Do you think I could have a picture of Bosch sometime?"

He cleared his throat, then rasped, "Sure. He's quite the ham when he wants to be."

"Awesome. Text it to me?"

"I will." His voice sounded stronger. "I'll do it as soon as we hang up. And on that note…"

"Right. Guess we should probably get going."

"Guess we should."

Neither one of them said anything, or made any move to hang up, until Lani whispered, "Bye, Geo."

"Bye."

For a long time, she lay on the couch, staring unseeingly at the TV, her Chinese food ignored.

Geo'd lost someone, too. Not as suddenly as she had, but it'd certainly been traumatic. And he'd been a child, just like her.

A wave of pure empathy flooded her, which made the inevitable tears come. She sobbed until she had nothing left, until she was curled in a tight ball, her gasping breaths slowing to occasional sniffles. Finally she pushed to sitting, only to groan at the nausea now surging into her throat.

Trudging into the kitchen to make some ginger tea, she thought, "I don't need this. I've got too much of my own shit going on to spend my energy crying over someone else's past."

Besides, Geo was a SEAL, one of the most mentally tough people on the face of the earth. He wouldn't need her sympathy. He'd only followed up because he said he would, and if her baggage hadn't scared him off before, it probably had now.

After her tea was brewed, she picked up her phone again. Yeah. No text, no pic of Bosch. In fact, it was highly unlikely she'd ever hear from him again.

Well, maybe it was for the best. For both their sakes.

Chapter Six

"Oh, God, I fucked that up."

Groaning, Geo tossed his phone aside and slammed a pillow over his face.

Real smooth there, dumbass, bringing up your dad.

He hadn't meant to. All of that was *long* into the past, when he'd been a different person with a different life. What in the hell possessed him to bring it up now? And why was it *hurting* so much all of a sudden?

Next to the bed, Bosch twitched his ears, his face impassive, although he cocked his head as if to say, "What *was* that?"

Geo groaned again. "Yeah. Here I am, talking to this great girl, and not only do I choke when she's trying to tell me about something important, I dump *my* shit on top of all *her* shit."

Dragging himself up from the bed, he buckled Bosch into his harness and clipped the leash on. They made their way out into the stifling hot night and headed toward the small greenbelt a few blocks away.

Once there, he let Bosch loose to wander, and explore, just be a dog for a little while. An occasional fighter jet screamed overhead as the pilots practiced night landings and touch-and-gos. With the combination of that sound and the heat, if Geo closed his eyes, he could almost imagine himself back in Iraq. The only thing missing was the scent of honeysuckle. Each war zone had its own distinct scent. Afghanistan's had been pine, from the forests high in the Hindu Kush. Iraq's was honeysuckle.

Pulling a tennis ball from his pocket, Geo held it up. Immediately Bosch went into prey mode, muscles quivering, tail held high. Geo made him wait for a beat, then flung the ball into the darkness.

Bosch took off like a shot after it. This wasn't a game of fetch. Once Bosch had his ball, he wouldn't give it up unless commanded to. It was his to gnaw, to crush in his powerful jaws, to carry around, until Geo told him to drop it. Ambling after him, he let the dog have his reward for one full minute.

Upon the command to release, Bosch dropped the wet, slobbery ball at his feet. Geo scooped it up and threw it again with a sharp instruction for Bosch to hold, which he did, his whole body straining toward the direction it disappeared in.

"*Zoek!*" At the command to seek, Bosch tore after the ball. A moment of silence, then, instead of the happy snuffling sounds of a dog with a toy, out of the gloom came a long, low growl.

"Oh, fuck me." Heart pounding, Geo hustled in that direction. "Whoever you are, stand still!"

Bosch was trained not to attack without the proper Dutch command, but Geo wasn't taking any chances.

"Uh, don't worry. Not moving." The reply was the tiniest bit shaky, and no wonder. When Geo ran up,

Bosch had his front legs spread, hindquarters lifted, every hackle he owned standing on end. The rumbling growl emanating from his throat meant he was ready and willing to fight the man standing in the crosshairs, frozen in place. Holding the tennis ball.

"Dude, toss the ball to me. Slowly."

The man did, and once Geo had possession of it again, Bosch visibly relaxed. At the "come" hand signal, he trotted to Geo's side and sat, his unwavering stare fixed on the interloper.

"I'm so sorry." The man kept a wary gaze on Bosch, too. "I was out for a run and this ball came bouncing right at me. It was instinct just to grab it."

When he took a hesitant step into the pool of light cast by the streetlamp, Geo blinked in sudden recognition. "Hey, you're one of our new straphangers, aren't you?" He stuck his fist out. "Don't think we've formally met. George Monteverdi."

"Matt Knytych." The man returned the knuckle bump with a quirk of his lips. "And yeah, I'm part of your temporary backfill. My regular troop's on block leave, so…"

Geo nodded. Guys hungry for all the experience they could get, especially new SEALs, would ask to join other platoons' training trips. If Matt's platoon was on block leave, that meant they'd just returned from deployment, but instead of taking time off, Matt had decided to get right back to it.

Matt was still eyeing Bosch suspiciously, so with a chuckle, Geo introduced them.

"Really sorry I hijacked your ball, Bosch," Matt said,

sincere apology in his tone. He glanced at Geo. "I didn't even think a tennis ball might be a training evolution."

"It wasn't, actually. It's playtime. The thing is, this ball is also his reward for working, so he takes it *very* seriously."

Now that his toy was safe, Bosch was the canine version of all smiles, his head cocked as he stared at the new person in his orbit. Matt continued to look uneasy, so Geo said, "Since he's not working, Bosch wouldn't mind an ear scratch, if you wanted to give him one."

The dog didn't rip off the tentative hand Matt extended, and visibly relieved, Matt relaxed and fondled his ears. "What's his job? Explosives detection?"

"He's considered a multi-purpose K9, so he does a lot of scent work, and every now and then he gets to do his favorite thing of all—bite people."

Matt froze, and Geo laughed. "Sorry, couldn't resist. He only bites on command, and believe me, he wouldn't bother with your hand. He goes for the whole arm."

With a gulp, Matt croaked, "Jesus. Glad he's on our side." A few more ear scratches, and then he said, "Can I—"

"Sure. Go ahead and make friends."

Crouching down to Bosch's level, Matt studied him as he petted his neck and sides. "Handsome fella. Is he a German shepherd?"

"Belgian Malinois. They're smaller and lighter than shepherds, and that makes all the difference considering how many times per day I lift him out in the field. This guy fast-ropes with me, jumps out of planes with me. He's considered part of my combat load."

"Shit, that's amazing. I can't wait to see him in action."

"Your troop doesn't have a K9 handler?" Geo asked.

"No, we don't." Matt grinned. "But we had someone special attached to us. A CST."

It took Geo a moment to connect the dots. "Cultural Support Team? I've never gotten to work with one of those women. What was it like?"

"Awesome as fuck." Matt launched into a couple of stories about Devon—the CST—which left Geo shaking his head in almost disbelief.

"Wow. I'd love to meet her someday."

"Everyone should meet her. She's great, calm under fire, an all-around fantastic person."

"Which platoon are you with?"

When Matt told him, Geo winced. "Shit. I heard through the grapevine that a couple of your guys ran afoul of an RPG over in Afghanistan."

Matt pointed to himself. "One of the guys. The other was my—" his throat worked "—my best friend."

"Oh, man."

"I was driving," Matt went on raggedly, "and the RPG exploded over the gun turret. Shane was bleeding out, but I didn't stop…"

The first rule of combat medicine: win the fight. Injuries didn't matter if everyone was dead. Once fire superiority was established, *then* aid could be rendered.

"Your buddy's okay?"

"He'll be in Germany for another week or so, but yeah, he's gonna be okay."

And in the meantime, you needed to keep busy. Understandable.

"How about you?" Geo asked.

"Me?"

"Making the decision to keep driving can't have been easy. You coping with that?"

Matt's eyes looked straight into his. "It was my duty to keep driving. I couldn't sacrifice the entire convoy to save Shane, and he wouldn't have wanted me to. If I'd stopped, and more people were hurt or killed, he would've hated me for that in the end. It wasn't a choice, it was the only thing to do. And I'd do it all over again."

Despite his seeming calm, the pain evident in the set of Matt's jaw and compressed lips told Geo how much that decision had cost him emotionally.

"A bitch of a no-win situation, isn't it?"

"Ain't that the truth." Matt pinched the bridge of his nose tightly, voice growing even more hoarse. "Stop and save him, and have him hate me for it, or keep going and have to live with his death."

"He's going to be okay, though, yeah?"

"But for a few hours, I didn't know that. All I knew was that he was hurt so fuckin' bad." Matt drew in a shaky breath. "And I didn't stop…"

Geo stood by silently as Matt wrestled for control. At last he glanced up at him, his intense dark eyes glistening with unshed tears. "I'm sorry."

"Oh, dude. Nothing to be sorry for." His heart aching, Geo reached out to grip his shoulder. "The longer you're in this business, the better you'll learn how to compartmentalize this shit."

Matt shook his head. "That's what I'm afraid of. Compartmentalizing so much that I stop caring." He smiled ruefully. "I'd rather *feel* the pain than have that happen. You know?"

Unbelievably Geo felt his own eyes start to burn, but with sheer force of will, he forced it back. "Well, there's only so much pain you can allow yourself to feel before it eats you alive. Take it from me."

They stared at each other for the space of a few heartbeats, and Geo could almost *see* the questions trembling on Matt's lips. Before he could say anything, Bosch's loud snort broke the spell, and in an instant, Geo retreated back into the safety of his macho armor.

"You'll just have to figure it out for yourself, kid," he said, giving an inward wince at the patronizing tone to his voice. "It sucks about your buddy, but don't let yourself dwell on it too long."

In the sudden awkwardness, Matt's expression smoothed out, his own emotion now tightly locked down. "Yeah. Thanks for the advice, George," he said evenly. "It was nice meeting you. Later, Bosch."

With a lift of his hand, Matt turned and jogged away. Bosch gazed up at Geo almost reproachfully.

"Hey, what was I supposed to do?" Geo grunted. "Spew all over a guy I don't even know, let alone trust?"

Besides, Matt's pain was different than his own. What happened to Shane could be laid directly at the feet of a senseless, never-ending war. What'd happened to Cade...

Shame, guilt and helplessness flared back to life in the pit of Geo's stomach. Matt wouldn't understand anyway. How could he? A wet-behind-the-ears new guy with next to no combat experience didn't get to judge Cade's actions, or Geo's. He had to goddamn *earn* that right.

Back in his room, Geo gave Bosch a bowl of water before dropping to sit cross-legged next to his crate. Bosch finished his drink and ambled over, then flopped on the rug and curled up to rest his head on Geo's thigh.

Geo sifted his fingers through his fur, some of his tension easing. The soothing weight of the dog's head on his leg, the warmth of his body, the comfort and companionship of this creature he loved and knew loved him back…

Right now it was just what he needed.

And all Lani wanted was a picture of him.

At the thought, Geo closed his eyes on a fresh wave of guilt. She'd been dealing with so much, and feeling so alone, and after they talked he'd ignored her simple request because he'd gotten *sad* over his dad's death, something he hardly ever thought about anymore.

On impulse he pulled his phone from his pocket and rifled through his photo album. After finding the one he wanted, he scrolled to Lani's name in his contacts and opened a text. I'm sorry about tonight, he typed, before attaching the pic and hitting Send.

No immediate answer. With a sigh, Geo pushed to his feet and headed for the shower, his silent phone tossed to the bed. When he emerged from the steamy bathroom, towel around his hips, his screen lit up, then faded to black as he eagerly reached for it.

Anticipation burning through him, he pulled up her reply.

Don't be sorry. It was a weird night for both of us, I

think. But thanks for the pic! I'd love to hear the story behind it sometime.

I'd love to tell you. His heart beating a bit faster, Geo typed, Can I take you to dinner the next time we're in town? We should be home in a week or two.

It seemed forever until her answer came, although it was only a couple of seconds.

Sure. I'd like that.

An idiotic grin spreading over his face, Geo replied, It's a date.

"Holy shit."

Lani stared at the picture on her phone screen. In it, a shirtless Geo crouched next to a sleek black-and-tan dog, who sat looking stoically into the camera. Geo's lips held a rueful twist, one hand braced on his thigh, the other held up to display his muscular forearm—a forearm crisscrossed with lurid stitches in the shape of a bite mark.

What was he saying, that Bosch had bitten him? What would make a dog turn on his handler? Holding the phone high, she peered into Bosch's intelligent brown eyes.

"Why would you do that?"

Bosch gazed back at her, his ears upright, chest up and out, for all the world looking most pleased with himself. Damn, it sounded crazy, but the expression on his face reminded her of someone...

But who?

When it hit her a split-second later, she clapped her hand over her mouth to muffle her giggle. He reminded her of Geo himself—completely self-assured, with a bone-deep confidence that bordered on arrogant.

"Oh, my God, Bosch. You're a SEAL in canine form, aren't you?"

Of course he was. Spec ops dogs would *have* to have much the same traits as their human counterparts, who were all Type A mixes of stubbornness and competitiveness. But what'd happened between Geo and Bosch to cause this?

She couldn't wait to find out.

Heading into the kitchen to make sure all the Chinese food was put away, the new journal sitting on the table caught her eye. Lani glared at it.

"Get those thoughts down," Maura had said at the end of their session when she'd handed the journal to her. "Let them flow. Even if some days all you manage to write is what you had for dinner, I want you to get used to putting your thoughts and emotions into words. You've been holding them inside for far too long."

Daily homework. Great.

With a grunt, she snatched up her favorite pen with the purple ink and flipped the journal open to the first pristine white page. The first few sentences came out stilted, flippant, as she attempted to describe her day. When her hand started to cramp, she tossed the pen down and slammed the journal closed. "Ugh, this is dumb."

How was writing stuff down supposed to help her accomplish jack-shit anyway? All the assignment had done so far was contribute to her ongoing sense of failure, and that was something she *definitely* didn't need.

She could manage that part all on her own, thank you very much.

Giving up for the moment, Lani grabbed her tea mug and headed to the living room and her couch. She got comfortable, then took a sip of the fragrant brew while she regarded the phone resting on her thigh.

Unable to help herself, she opened the picture again, this time ignoring the dog to focus on Geo. He looked sweaty, dirty, as if he'd just completed an exercise. She traced her eyes over his camo pants and boots, his ridged abs and well-defined chest. That wound on his arm had to hurt, yet he was crouching next to Bosch as if they were still best friends. What in the world…?

She dropped her head to the back of the couch and blew out a long, slow breath. "I can't believe I'm talking to another spec ops guy," she said to her ceiling. "And I really *like* him. Why can't he be a lawyer or something? Ugh."

The ceiling didn't have an opinion to offer her, so she reached for her mug again. As she did, the journal caught her eye. Pulling it to her, she traced her finger over the drawing on the cover, that of a little boy and girl holding hands, the thought bubble over the girl's head reading, "You're the peanut butter to my jelly."

Peanut butter. Rhys's Peanut Butter Cup.

"Write it all down." Maura's voice echoed in her head. "No matter what it's about. Put your feelings into words as best you can. Scream, cry, get angry, mourn. No one will ever read it but you."

Grabbing up the pen, Lani started to write:

Hey, Rhys, I miss you. I miss your smile, your stupid jokes, and that goofy laugh that always made me laugh, too. I miss your friendship. It scares me to think I might not have that anymore. After all, I've had it for most of my life, and all my best—and worst—memories have you in them. It's so fucking hard to think of making memories without you.

I have to try, though. For your sake, and mine, I'm gonna try, and maybe someday we can build a friendship that isn't based on me needing you anymore. I've gotten so used to needing you, Rhys, that I have no sense of my own strength, or who I want to be. Well, except a good mom. Now that I know. It's a start, isn't it?

And oh, by the way, I have a date with someone. A nice guy, funny and sweet, and damn if his voice doesn't make me shiver. Mmm.

It's really too bad he's a SEAL.

Chapter Seven

Geo shifted uncomfortably on Lani's doorstep, his feet hot and sweaty in the unfamiliar loafers.

The khaki pants he wore were rumpled, and his dark blue polo shirt had a musty smell from being crammed at the bottom of his dresser drawer.

Sighing against the butterflies in his stomach, he rapped twice on the door and stood back under the porch light so she could get a good look at him out of the peephole. After a moment came the scratchy sound of the bolt turning, and then the door swung open.

Geo gulped. "Hi."

"Hey, frogman." Lani stood framed in the brightly lit entryway, the smile on her face warm and welcoming. "Come on in."

His heart tripping a mile a minute, Geo stepped inside, an uncharacteristic shyness stealing his tongue.

"Are those for me?" She reached for the bouquet of carnations he clutched, and with a sheepish grin, he passed them over.

"For you, from me and Bosch. He sends his regards, by the way. Said he'd totally be here, but he'd rather have a spa day."

She giggled. "Bath and toenails?"

"Exactly. They might even throw a massage in there, who knows?"

"Sounds amazing."

They grinned at each other, and then her gaze drifted over him, all the way down to his shoes. Geo tugged at his shirt collar. "Is this okay? I wasn't sure what you wanted to do tonight." He grimaced. "Guess when I texted, I should've asked."

"Well—"

He crossed his arms over his chest. "Did you have something in mind? Tell me."

"Let me get these in some water and we'll talk about it."

Lani's apartment was small, but homey and comfortably messy. His nervousness evaporated as he took in the mismatched furniture, the hoodie thrown carelessly over the back of a chair. For someone who lived in a barracks room and carried most of his life in a duffel bag, the casual vibe of her home put him completely at ease.

As did Lani herself. Her hair twisted up in a loose bun, she wore a pair of drawstring linen pants and a white tank top, no makeup that he could see. As unobtrusively as possible, he checked out her tummy. Maybe there was the tiniest bit of roundness there, but if he didn't know she was pregnant, he didn't think he'd be able to tell just by looking.

In the kitchen, she dug a vase out of a cabinet and started to fill it with water. "I'm not really a wine-and-dine kind of girl, so I thought maybe we could eat here?

I love to cook." She smiled. "But since you're dressed to go out, I'm totally fine with that, too."

A great wave of relief washed through him. "Staying in sounds amazing, and it just so happens I have a change of clothes in my gym bag. Be right back."

He jogged down to his truck and grabbed the duffel stashed behind the seat, which contained a faded Metallica T-shirt and a pair of cargo shorts, along with some beat-up leather slides.

"Ah, much better," he exclaimed when he emerged from her tiny bathroom. "Not that I didn't enjoy trying to look nice for you…" His voice trailed off, and he winced.

Real smooth there, pal.

"Go ahead and wash your hands." Her eyes sparkling with laughter, Lani pointed toward the sink, then carried the vase of carnations to the table. "These are beautiful. Thank you."

"You're welcome," he mumbled as he scrubbed up. He couldn't remember the last time he'd bought anyone flowers, and the pleased smile on her face made him glad he'd given in to the impulse.

"So you ready to pitch in?" She picked up a bowl covered with plastic wrap and waved him toward a wooden cutting board. As he watched, she pulled off the wrap and tipped a large, smooth dough ball out onto the board. "Punch that down for me, and then knead it, okay?"

"Punch it down…?" Geo glanced over at her dubiously. "Like, *punch* it?"

"Yep." She balled up her fist and slammed it firmly into her other palm. "Punch it."

Still skeptical, he poked at the dough tentatively with his knuckles. "What does that do?" When he continued to hesitate, she stepped up next to him and gave the dough a quick, sharp jab right in the middle. It instantly deflated.

"See? Punch it." She grinned at him, and for the first time, Geo noticed she had a smear of flour on her nose and down one cheek. Those pesky butterflies winged to life all over again.

He gulped. "So how do I knead it?" He pushed the dough around with his fingertips. "Like this?"

"No, like this." She reached out and put her hands over his. "Squeeze it. Work it around." She demonstrated the motion with him, her grip strong. "Put your back and forearms into it."

Her body brushed against his, their fingers practically entwined. Her touch, and the bird's-eye view of her full breasts squeezing together and releasing with her movements soon had him rock hard and aching. He pressed closer to the counter to hide it, teeth gritted, mentally ordering his cock to behave.

"That's good." She released him and wiped her sticky hands off on a towel. "You'll do that for about ten minutes while I work on the salad dressing."

Geo kneaded as if his life depended on it while Lani moved briskly around the small kitchen, measuring, whisking. When she bent over at one point to peer in the fridge, the sight of her rounded bottom in the air tightened his pants all over again. He snapped his gaze back to the dough.

Jesus, stop it. She's having a baby, and you'll eventually be leaving. Those two things do not *go together.*

He cleared his throat. "So what're we making?"

"Mmm." She leaned her hip against the counter next to him. "Pretzel monkey bread. Did you ever have that as a kid?"

"What? No, I don't think so."

She smiled. "It's what we always made with my Lola—my grandma—when we visited her house. I'd do what you're doing, knead the dough and roll it out, while my brother got to cut the pieces and put them in a baking soda bath."

"What's that?"

"It's what makes them pretzel-y." Now she grinned at him, her nose wrinkling. "God, when they'd first come out of the oven, they were so golden brown, so yummy. Tyler and I just couldn't wait for them to cool off, so we'd burn our fingers and mouths eating them right away." She sighed. "Those are some of my favorite childhood memories, cooking with my family."

Geo stared down at the countertop, not quite sure what to say. *His* childhood dinners usually consisted of cold cereal he ate alone in front of the TV, and he couldn't remember ever baking with anyone.

Then he shook himself impatiently. Who cared? This wasn't about him.

"Geo?" Lani's voice at his shoulder made him jump. "Everything okay?"

He blinked, suddenly realizing he was *pummeling* the dough. With a forced chuckle, he stepped away from it. "Yeah. I'm, uh, just making sure it's done."

"It is now." She sounded amused, but her eyes searched his face briefly before she handed him a towel to wipe his hands. "Why don't you get yourself a beer while I finish this?"

The beer was cold and smooth, and by the time he'd taken a long swig, the weird knots in his stomach had loosened. He propped his butt against the counter not far from her, determined to get this date back on track. "So what kinds of things do you like to do, you know, besides *not* exercise?"

"Ha, I can't believe you remember that." She shot him a surprised look, and he grinned at her, one eyebrow raised.

"Well?"

"Hmm, let's see. Obviously I love to cook. And eat what I cook, of course. And for *other* people to eat what I cook. Oh!" Setting down the rolling pin, she moved to the fridge and grabbed a magnetic notepad with an attached pen hanging there. "That reminds me. I need to figure out what I'm gonna bring to my first support group meeting. It's a potluck."

Geo gulped, all his tension immediately roaring back. "Support group…?"

"For suicide survivors." She wrote busily for a moment while he wallowed in an agony of discomfort, the beer suddenly losing all its flavor. The sharp *clink* of the bottle as he put it down made her look up.

She frowned at what she read on his face. "Anything wrong?"

"No, no. Nothing's wrong," he said hastily. "It's just—"

She waited while he sucked in a deep breath. "It's just… I'm not sure what to say."

"About what?" Her eyes widened as the light

dawned. "Oh, about my brother? It's okay. You don't have to say anything."

Her voice was even, but the slight tinge of weariness to it stabbed deep. Suddenly, he could picture it—the avoidance, the discomfort, the ignorance. Hadn't he experienced that same thing with...

Before he could think it through, he blurted, "But I *want* you to be able to talk about it with me."

Jesus, what the fuck are you doing? No, you don't *want to talk about this! What if she asks...*

Cramming his shaking hands in his pockets, he fought the urge to mutter an excuse, *any* excuse, and flee the apartment. "I guess I'm just afraid of saying the wrong thing."

"Ah." When her gaze met his, there was a warmth to it that made him quiver. "I appreciate that, and your honesty, Geo."

He let himself relax a bit. "Um, were you guys especially close?"

"Oh, man." Lani picked up a round cookie cutter and started to cut out pieces of dough. "Depends on the day, for sure. We were typical siblings, one minute best friends, the next at each other's throats. But we loved each other. We—" She broke off. "I miss him every day."

She sounded sad, but in control, and sudden admiration banished the last of his hesitancy. Stepping over to her, he reached for the cookie cutter. "Can I go ahead and finish this?" he asked gently.

When she passed him the cutter, her cool fingers came to rest briefly on his. "Just so you know, asking about him, about the person he *was*, is always the right thing to say." She let him go with a squeeze.

For the next several minutes, they didn't speak, except for Lani's quiet directions. The pieces of dough first went into the baking soda bath, and then Geo arranged them tightly together in a parchment-lined pan and stuck it in the oven.

"C'mon." She grabbed him another beer and a bottle of water for herself, and then led him into the living room. "I wanna hear the Bosch story." Plopping down on one end of the worn leather couch, she patted the cushion next to her eagerly, and after he'd seated himself, pointed at his right arm. "Can I see the scar?"

He canted his body and extended his arm, enjoying her awed, "Oooh," at the sight of it.

"Can I touch it?"

When he nodded, she traced her fingertips lightly over and around the puckered skin. "That must've hurt."

The memory of that particular agony crashed over him, chasing away the tingles left by her touch. "Hands down the worst pain I've ever felt," he said, "kind of what I imagine being run over by an eighteen-wheeler is like."

Lani winced. "Wow. So does Bosch jump out of planes with you?"

"He does, and he loves it."

She tilted her head to the side. "Are you sure about that?"

"Totally sure. He told me so himself."

They snickered together, and Geo said, "Actually, special operations dogs start their training as puppies.

He's been acclimated to water, air, gunfire, explosions, you name it, since he was a baby. Nothing fazes him."

Her fingers slid away from his arm, and she picked up her water. "If that's the case, why don't you let him sleep with you? Why can't he live with you if he's that well-trained?"

"Well, let me put it this way. This—" Geo pointed to his scar "—is me and Bosch in a nutshell."

"What, him biting you?"

"Yep," he said, infusing that one word with as much pride as he could muster.

She studied him, her brow wrinkling. "I don't get it. Explain why that's a good thing."

Her adorable confusion made him grin, even as he said, "Because that night, I was stupid, and Bosch let me know it. He reminded me that this isn't a game."

Pulling one knee up on the couch, Lani turned to face him. "This I gotta hear."

"Okay. So it was early in our partnership, and we'd been training in the mountains east of San Diego, balls to the wall, lots of detection and bite work. Bosch had performed well, and I was feeling bulletproof, as if our success was all because of me instead of the fantastic decoys we'd been working with."

She held up a hand to stop him. "Decoys are the ones who wear the bite suits?"

"Yeah, or just a bite sleeve." He pantomimed sliding something over his forearm. "A good decoy is the difference between making or breaking a military working dog, and that night we'd had some of the best. They got Bosch in the *zone*."

She nodded, and Geo sucked in a deep breath. "So

after the evolution, Bosch and I were still really hyped. I decided to take him on an off-leash run along the fence line in the team compound before bedding him down for the night. Great idea, right?"

"Sure."

"That's what I thought, too. Until he caught a scent— the guy who'd been our decoy."

She gasped. "Oh, shit!"

"Right. Dude'd had the same idea as me, a short run to bleed off some adrenaline. Of course, Bosch didn't know we weren't still training, that the guy wasn't wearing a bite suit and wasn't ready for him. All he knew was that he smelled the same 'enemy' he'd been ordered all night to attack, and *boom*, time to get it on."

"Fuck, what happened?"

"I managed to yell out a warning, and you should've seen that guy scale the fence. He was like a goddamned lizard running up a wall."

"So Bosch didn't get him?"

"Nope, just missed him." Geo shuddered at the memory of Bosch's lunge, how he'd missed the guy's bare legs by mere inches. "And then, because he was *pissed* on top of being totally amped, he whirled around, leapt, and tore my T-shirt off."

She clapped her hand over her mouth to stifle a gasp, although her eyes were huge.

"I kicked him away, and just like he'd been trained, he went for my arm. Clamped down on that sucker." He held up his forearm again. "The doc who stitched me up said it was the worst dog bite he'd ever seen."

As her eyes fell to his scar, she gulped, her cheeks a tad bit pale.

"Got my ass handed to me by the decoy when he came down off that fence, too," Geo said ruefully. "I was so damn green back then. I should've kept him leashed at all times until we both had more training, until I could read his moods better. Running with him loose so early on in our partnership was totally irresponsible, and I paid for it, but at least it was me and not anyone else."

Letting go of her death grip on her water bottle, Lani set it down on her coffee table before collapsing back against the cushions with a breathless, "Wow."

"My point is this. He wasn't raised to be a pet. It's not the heartwarming story of an abandoned shelter dog who became a Navy SEAL. He's a highly trained weapon in my arsenal, and while I love him, I'm not going to forget that fact again. Blurring those boundaries—confusing him—by letting him sleep on my bed or hang out with us in the team room while we watch a movie is not gonna happen. Shit, he'd probably go after one of the guys for his beef jerky."

As if on cue, her tummy gave a giant rumble. "God, I probably would, too. I'm so hungry right now."

She sounded so serious, so deadpan, that Geo choked on a laugh. "Yeah?"

"Oh, I'd totally pile-drive a Navy SEAL to get his snack," she assured him. "Got any beef jerky? You'd better run."

That set him off completely, and when he'd wheezed to a stop, he gasped, "The visual on that is priceless, Lani. Priceless."

"Glad I could amuse you," she said drily, eyes twinkling. "And on that note, let's go finish making our dinner."

Getting to her feet, she held her hand out to pull him to his and lead him to the kitchen. Once there, she put him to work mincing garlic for the butter sauce while she set the table. The smell of baking bread absolutely made his mouth water, and when she finally pulled the perfect, golden brown rolls from the oven, the sense of ridiculous pride Geo felt over them tugged his lips into a smile.

As if reading his mind, she glanced at him. "You did most of the work. You want to do the honors?"

He nodded, and stepped to the counter to dip a spoon into the garlic butter mixture on the stove and drizzle it all over the top of the steaming hot bread. He touched her arm when she reached for the pan again.

"Go sit at the table," he urged as he leapt to pull a chair out for her. "I'll bring it."

When she was seated, Geo slowly, carefully, lifted the parchment paper from the pan and arranged the rolls on a large platter. He set it proudly down in front of her, next to the bowl of spinach salad and the carafe of bacon dressing she'd made.

Lastly, he grabbed his beer and slid into the second chair. Holding her eyes with his, he tilted the tip of the bottle toward her. "To new friends."

Smiling, she clinked her glass with his. "And badass dogs."

Geo couldn't remember the last time a meal tasted so delicious. He stuffed himself to the gills, finally leaning back in his chair to hide a satisfied belch behind his hand.

Forking up the last bite of her spinach salad, Lani groaned. "I'm so full. I need to get out and move."

He couldn't resist. "I thought you didn't like to exercise. Ow!"

She glared at him as she kicked his shin again. "You're not supposed to make fun of me." She surged to her feet in mock outrage and started clearing the table. As she bent over him to pick up his plate, he found himself reaching up to brush the backs of his fingers down her smooth cheek.

"You had some flour there," he said huskily. "Got it."

Their eyes met, the spark of desire in hers kicking his heartbeat into a sudden gallop.

"Mmm, well…" As he sat breathless, she picked up his napkin and dabbed it gently along the corners of his mouth. "Had some butter there. Got it."

They stared at each other, and she leaned in closer. Helplessly, he lifted his face, lips parting…

Crash!

The fork sliding from his plate to the table broke the spell, and with a self-conscious chuckle, she straightened and turned to carry the dishes to the sink.

Geo raked a hand through his hair, once again willing his body to calm down.

She's having a baby and you're leaving, asshole.

Shit. If he repeated that enough times to himself, maybe he'd eventually be able to remember it.

I almost kissed him.

Dropping the plates in the sink with a clatter, Lani twisted the faucet on viciously.

I wanted *to kiss him.*

Oh, Lord, had she wanted to kiss him. Her lips still tingled from coming within a whisper of his, and pretty much everything throbbed. Jesus, these pregnancy hormones were fucking insane.

Behind her, the chair scraped as Geo got to his feet, and she tensed, wondering if he'd come over and attempt to continue what she'd so foolishly started.

Instead, he quietly excused himself to use the bathroom. Slumping against the sink, she tamped down the stupid disappointment. Why *would* he want to continue it? The man was thirty years old, and by his own admission had never been married, had no kids. He was obviously a master at avoiding entanglements of any kind, and she'd be one hell of an entanglement, wouldn't she?

When his footsteps sounded behind her, she couldn't help but tense again, praying she could say goodbye coolly when he told her he had to leave.

"Is this your brother?"

The question was so unexpected that Lani froze, her brain scrambling to catch up. She turned slowly to see him holding one of the small framed pictures she kept on a table in the hallway.

She nodded. "That's us at the Grand Canyon." In the photo, Tyler leaned backward and flailed his arms, Lani's tight grip on the front of his T-shirt and the angle making it appear he was about to fall in. "My parents kept yelling at us to be careful, but I love it because that picture is *so* us. Silly, goofy." She paused. "Have you ever been?"

"To the Grand Canyon? Nah. It's just a big ditch."

She threw him a reproving look. "Well, that was such a fun summer. We went to the Canyon and Disneyland,

one of the last family trips we took before Tyler died."
She sighed. "Anyway, I'm so grateful for the memory."

After he'd put the picture back where he found it and
they'd settled on the couch, he said, "I've never been to
Disneyland, World, whatever."

Lani was about to let out a dramatic gasp and make
some flippant remark about "What kind of childhood
did you *have*?" when, just in time, she remembered *exactly* what kind of childhood he'd had.

She nodded, careful not to let any pity show on her
face. "It must've been too hard for your dad to travel."

"It was." He shrugged, his lips tightening a bit. "I
asked every summer, but we never got to go. As an
adult looking back now, I can't even imagine how difficult and expensive it would've been for my mom to
find a caregiver for him so we could go, but as a kid…"

As a kid, disappointments became disasters.

Her heart aching, she said, "Well, you should go.
Rhys and I went a while back. It's only a couple of
hours from here, you know."

To her relief, a smile banished the remoteness from
his eyes. "What, did you borrow somebody's kid to
take with you?"

"Nah. We just went."

"Two adults going to Disneyland?" He sounded so
astonished that she giggled.

"Yeah, silly. It's not just for kids. It's fun for everyone."

"If you say so." With that, he got up and wandered
aimlessly around the living room, looking at the pictures on the walls—mostly of Tyler—and examining
her meager Blu-Ray collection.

Suddenly he grabbed a case and held it up. "*Call of Duty*? Really?"

He sounded so disgusted that she laughed. "Oh, shit. We got that at a command holiday party as a white elephant gift. I made Rhys play it with me a few times, and when he helped me move out, he must've stuck it in with my stuff while *he* kept the Xbox. Asshole."

"Did he win?"

"Ha, nope. I'd kick his ass by spraying bullets everywhere, and then he'd sulk and wouldn't play with me, said he refused to reward bad tactics." Lani couldn't help but grin at the memory.

"You still love him." It wasn't a question.

With a sigh, she tilted her head back to stare at the ceiling. "As a friend, always and forever. I think he feels the same about me. As lovers, we never quite... worked. It's hard to explain."

"You don't have to." Wincing, Geo sank down next to her. "It's none of my business."

"Well, either way, it's over," she said firmly. "Ancient history. Been there, done that, got the T-shirt."

She could feel the weight of his gaze, but he didn't say anything. At last she rolled her head along the back of the couch to look at him. "What?"

"Nothing." He grimaced. "It's just..."

"What?" She reached over and touched his knee. "It's okay. Ask me."

He shook his head, lips pressed tightly together, and then suddenly burst out, "What *happened* between you two? Together for ten years, and now you're..."

He broke off, the horrified look that spread over his face causing an inexplicable giggle to rise to her throat.

"Now we're broken up, and I'm pregnant by some *other* random dude I'll probably never see again?"

"Oh, God." He sounded downright agonized. "I'm so sorry, it really is none of my business."

Lani gave his knee a reassuring squeeze, the feel of hard muscle and warm skin sending a renewed tingle through her. She pulled her hand away reluctantly before saying, "That's why you're here, though, isn't it? For us to get to know each other?"

He shrugged, though she was gratified to see his jaw unclench a bit. "Yeah."

"So I'll answer, and then I get to ask *you* something. How about that?"

A wary look flitted over his face before he smoothed out his expression, and nodding, he said, "Okay."

Hmm. What kind of secrets are you hiding, my friend?

After getting comfortable, she picked up her water bottle and took a long, slow drink. "So Rhys and I, we met when we were five. Instant friends, you know? By our freshman year of high school, we were almost inseparable, but it wasn't romantic. Not then."

Geo drew his knee up and mirrored her pose, his elbow propped on the back of the couch, head resting on his fist.

"This one day after school, he was supposed to come over and help me with my math homework, but he was late." Remembered frustration tightened her lips. "Seemed like he was *always* running late, and it pissed me off. Besides, I didn't like some of the people he'd started hanging around with, and he was doing stupid shit like ditching class, that sort of thing."

"Sounds like a typical freshman boy," he commented, grinning.

She shot him a sour look. "Well, it pissed me off," she said again. "While I was waiting for him to show, my brother came home early from work. When I asked why, Tyler said he'd just quit. It floored me, because he'd been working at that restaurant for years, and it was part of the condition of my parents paying for community college, that he have a job to pay for his car insurance and spending money."

"And he'd just quit?" His voice was hushed, as if not to break her train of thought.

"Yeah. I asked him what he was gonna do, and he goes, 'Who cares? Let's go have a snowball fight!'"

"A snowball fight?"

"Indiana in January, there's gonna be snow, Geo."

"Ah. Right."

"I didn't want to, but something—I'll never know what—made me say yes." Memories washed over her, of crisp air, a backyard full of powdery snow, and Tyler's cold-reddened cheeks and happy grin.

"We horsed around throwing snow at each other," she said huskily, "and made snow angels, and then we went inside and Tyler fixed me some Mexican hot chocolate."

Bowing her head, Lani squeezed her eyes shut, those last images of her brother alive swirling behind them. "It's surreal, looking back now. He'd seemed down for months, not himself, and that afternoon it was the old Tyler again. What happened next didn't—doesn't, will *never*—make sense."

Geo's warm hand came to rest on her shoulder, but

he didn't say anything, which she appreciated. "Tyler didn't touch his hot chocolate, just watched me drink mine. Suddenly he got up, kissed me on the top of my head and whispered, 'See ya, lil sis.' Then he went down into the basement where his room was, and shot himself."

"Oh, Jesus." Geo's whisper was heartfelt. "Lani..."

"I was standing there in shock, wondering what I'd just heard, when Rhys burst in shouting. He pushed past me and ran into the basement, then almost immediately came flying back up. His face was— I'll never forget—"

Geo squeezed her shoulder as she fought for control. "I'm sorry, Lani. No wonder you two are close."

"We clung to each other, you know? For months I couldn't even let him out of my sight. He'd sneak into my room every night because the nights were the worst, for both of us."

"And eventually—"

"Yes. He was my first, I was his first, and because we didn't know any better, we took all of that trauma, all of that clinginess, added sex to the mix and called it love."

"I'm sure he really does love you," Geo said gently. "Of course he does."

"Well, he deserves to find out who he is without my codependent mess of a life dragging him down," she said. "And I deserve more than pity masquerading as love."

Too bad it's taken us ten years to realize both those things, huh, Rhys?

Geo's hand slid down her arm, squeezed once, then

fell away to rest in his lap. She appreciated the steadiness of his gaze despite the tinge of discomfort she could see in his eyes.

"Thanks for listening," she said at last. "I know it's not an easy story to hear."

"I know it's not an easy story to tell. I'd, uh, love to give you a hug, but I wouldn't want you to think it's pity."

With a cross between a laugh and a sob, she scooted closer. "Hey, if you're offering pity-free hugs, I gladly accept."

Geo opened his arms, and she went into them to nestle against his broad chest. He held her close, his heart a steady thump beneath her ear, the familiar male scent of spicy deodorant and fabric softener tickling her nose. She let out a quiet sigh.

"Do you have any siblings?"

"No." His voice was a low rumble. "My dad got sick when I was still pretty young. They chose not to have any more."

"How old were you when he died?"

"Eleven."

She splayed her palm over his chest. "I'm sorry. Such a rough age to lose a parent."

"Everyone kept telling me to be strong for my mom, that I was now the 'man of the house.'" He winced, as if ashamed of the bitterness in his tone.

"So many times people forget that children need to grieve, too," she whispered, her thumb moving in a slow circle. "They give all their support to the parent, or the spouse, while the children are told to be 'strong.'"

The painful memories stabbed into her like a million

tiny needles, of childish bewilderment and a desperate need for attention smashing up against an impenetrable wall of grief time and time again. She'd had Rhys to cling to, but who did Geo have?

"At eleven I didn't have a clue how to be strong," he went on roughly, "so I got angry instead, and rebellious. I was a fucking nightmare, to be honest, so it was a relief for both of us when she finally kicked me out at seventeen."

"Do you ever talk to her?"

"Obligatory birthday and Christmas calls, mostly. We never had the chance to really get to know each other, so the only thing we have in common is my dad being sick, then my dad dying. It's so much less painful not to talk at all."

"Well, I was a different kind of nightmare after Tyler's death," she said. "Needy, bordering on self-destructive. My parents and I definitely have our own healing to do, so yeah, I know exactly where you're coming from with your mom."

Geo went quiet for a long moment. "It's a shitty club to be in, isn't it?" he said at last.

"The worst. But it's nice to know another member."

He rested his cheek on her hair in silent acknowledgment, his arms tight but not restrictive. Lani soaked in the comfort he offered and wallowed in it for as long as she could, before reluctantly pulling away. The last thing she needed was to start clinging to someone else.

To fill the void, she clicked on the TV and scrolled aimlessly through the channels, settling on an old rerun of *Law & Order.* The warmth of his body next to her, along with the emotional mood swings of the evening, soon had her curled up in one corner of the couch, her eyelids doing touch-and-gos.

At one point she woke with a start to find him gone. A massive wave of disappointment swamped her. "Just great," she groused, struggling to her feet to find her phone. "Real smooth. Fall asleep on the guy after he's been so sweet."

Rubbing her eyes, she trudged to the kitchen, gradually becoming aware of the sound of running water, along with some tuneless whistling. When she rounded the corner, she gasped. Geo stood at the sink, up to his elbows in soap suds.

"You're cleaning?"

He glanced at her, then shrugged and turned back to the sink. "You cook, I clean. Only fair."

Holy fucking Christ on a cracker. Was there anything sexier than a man cleaning a kitchen? At that moment, Lani didn't think so. She couldn't take her eyes off his muscular forearms while he wrung out the rag, or the way the water that'd splashed on his shirt made it cling to him.

He hung the rag over the spigot, then faced her with a smile, and to her everlasting horror, she burst into tears. In the next instant, she was in his arms, her own wrapped tightly around his waist.

"I'm sorry," she sobbed. "I d-don't know what's wrong with me."

He held her close as he rocked her. "I think you're tired," he said softly. "And therapy is hard and sad, and you've been lonely because you just broke up with your boyfriend."

"And I'm *pregnant*," she wailed.

His chest rumbled under her cheek as he chuckled. "Oh, yeah, how could I forget that part?"

"I have to pee all the time, and it makes me sleepy, and crabby, and sometimes horny as fuck..."

She really hadn't meant to say that, and to his credit, Geo only froze for half a second before continuing to rub her back soothingly. His hands didn't wander, and he didn't try to take advantage, and why, oh *fucking* why did he have to be a SEAL?

At last the storm abated, and Lani pulled away to wipe her eyes on the neckline of her tank top. "Wow, that was embarrassing. Are you sorry you came?"

"Never." His eyes crinkled. "But I do think I should go now, give you some privacy."

She didn't want him to. She wanted him to stay, and snuggle her on the couch while they watched TV, and maybe kiss her goodnight. But she didn't say any of that, only nodded. "I guess. I've kinda got a long day tomorrow anyway."

She watched as he gathered up his wallet and keys, and then she walked him to the door. "How long are you in town for?"

"A week or so."

"Well, maybe we could get together before you go. I won't fall asleep on you again, I promise."

He smiled. "Sure, I'd like that. Did you have anything in mind?"

"Oh, man." She hesitated, unsure whether or not to ask, but Geo reached out to touch her arm encouragingly.

"What is it?"

"Could you, uh, maybe take me to meet Bosch?"

Wincing, she waited for him to refuse, because hadn't he said Bosch wasn't a pet, but a weapon? It's not like she'd ever ask to visit his gun.

"That would be my very great pleasure." The sincerity in his voice sounded genuine, and she couldn't help a tiny squeal of delight.

"Yay! Text me when you're free?"

"You got it." Stepping closer, Geo reached out to tuck a lock of her hair behind her ear. "Gonna be okay?"

"Gonna be fine," she whispered. "You?"

"Yeah." He drifted his thumb lightly along her jaw, leaving delicious tingles in its wake. Then he bent his head, and it felt like the most natural thing in the world to lift her face, even as she thought, *"Oh, please, God, don't let me have a booger hanging from my nose right now."*

Well, even if she did, it didn't stop him from kissing her gently on the cheek and leaving her with a most reluctant goodbye.

Chapter Eight

"K9 out!"

Geo released Bosch from his tether and the dog streaked off into the darkness.

"Copy that," the reply crackled in his ear. "Decoy ready."

Trotting after Bosch, Geo muttered into the comms, "Steak dinner says he pancakes your ass."

"In your dreams. Get ready to pay up, bitch."

He and the decoy, a white guy named Laz, traded a few more insults before they went silent to let the dog work. The wind buffeted Geo from all sides, and he peered through his NVGs as Bosch, nose to the ground, chased the elusive scent eddies being tossed around like leaves in a river. He winced. Bosch would have to be on his A-game to even locate the decoy, much less get the drop on him.

For his part, it took all Geo's concentration to dodge the manzanita bushes that seemed to be everywhere.

"Prickly motherfuckers," he muttered, freeing himself from yet another thorn snagging his uniform sleeve. Ahead, Bosch zig-zagged across the rocky terrain, changing course multiple times until at last he sat down, ears up, and stared off into the distance.

Ha, ha, Laz. You're toast.

After hissing the "attack" command, Geo followed the dog as he bounded up the side of a small hill. He scanned the area ahead, his NVGs giving him a sight advantage Bosch didn't have, and…there! Laz was crouching next to a small rocky outcropping, an otherworldly green silhouette in a glowing alien landscape.

"I see him," Laz murmured in Geo's ear. "And I'm gonna dodge him, no problem."

Geo bit back a curse. If Laz could see Bosch heading for him, he'd be able to sidestep his attack. That meant no free steak dinner tonight.

Suddenly Bosch veered from his straight-line trajectory, darted around some scrub brush, and disappeared. Shouting, Laz leapt to his feet, whirling around just in time to catch Bosch's sixty-five-pound body square in the chest.

"Holy shiiiittt!"

He slammed down on his back in a mighty explosion of dust. Geo ran up to see Bosch clamp hard onto Laz's bite sleeve and shake him like a rag doll.

Barely able to contain his laughter, Geo gave him the "out" command, and Bosch immediately dropped Laz's arm. Once he was safely tethered, Geo tossed him a Kong, and Bosch set about happily gnawing on it while Laz sprawled out drunkenly.

"What the fuck was that?" he slurred.

Geo grinned. "A goddamn hair missile, that's what."

Laz groaned and sat up to lean against a nearby boulder. "I saw him comin', clear as day. *Still* managed to pancake my fuckin' ass." He shook his head in grudging admiration. "That's some dog."

"He's the best." Geo crouched down and patted Bosch's neck and sides.

As Laz caught his breath, Geo dug Bosch's water bowl from his pack and gave him a drink. Then they trudged toward the road where a helo would soon pick them up. In fact, Geo could already hear the faint echo of rotor blades off in the distance, the sound of the 160th Special Operations Aviation Regiment conducting their own exercises by flying through mountains and canyons that closely resembled Afghan terrain.

"Those guys are badass," Laz commented, his head tilted back toward the dark sky. "I've seen 'em get so close to a cliff face that I swear sparks were shooting from the rotors, but the pilot acted like, 'No big.' Cool as a damn cucumber."

"They love to make us shit our pants," Geo agreed. "Pucker factor is real high with those guys."

"You ever ridden with them on a Little Bird?"

Geo shivered as remembered thrill flowed through him. He'd never felt so alive in his life than when perched on the skids of the two-man helos everyone called Little Birds. Used for urban assaults, they were highly maneuverable, and it was like riding a rollercoaster into battle. "Hell, yeah."

That led to the two of them comparing war stories, and at one point Laz punched Geo hard on the upper arm. "Man, sounds like you've done it all." His voice was full of admiration. "You ever been shot?"

"No."

"How'd you go ten years in this job without getting

shot?" Laz held up his hands to forestall Geo's reply, saying, "And don't give me no bullshit about how you're just that good."

Chuckling, Geo shrugged. "Lucky, I guess."

With a shake of his head, Laz said, "You know that luck's bound to run out sooner or later. Watch your back, my friend."

The clatter of rotor blades suddenly grew louder, indicating their ride was here. Once on board, Geo sat tethered with his legs dangling out the open door, his hand twined firmly in Bosch's harness. On the floor behind him, some PJs shouted back and forth to each other as they treated a realistic training mannequin with an amputated leg. The helo dipped and rolled, simulating evasive maneuvers, while the PJs fought to keep their balance and their hands steady.

Twisting around, Geo watched them start IVs and an airway with unbelievable skill.

"You guys are good," he called to the nearest one, a tall, lanky Latino dude who'd sat back on his heels and was wiping the back of his gloved hand over his forehead.

"Fuckin' lost him, though," the PJ said, indicating the mannequin's flat-line computer readout. "Femoral artery. Never stood a chance."

Geo winced. "Sorry."

"Yeah, me, too."

"What was the scenario?"

"Stepped on an IED. What else?" The PJ gestured toward Bosch. "Too bad their imaginary 'patrol' didn't have a K9." After holding his knuckles out for a bump, he turned back to his teammates.

Sucking in a deep breath, Geo let the familiar smell of dust and exhaust settle in his lungs, his body swaying with the motion of the helo. Bosch sat placidly next to him, his dog-sized goggles and muzzle on. Yeah, the two of them had definitely saved a lot of lives these past couple of years.

Geo closed his eyes. It was a good feeling, knowing they'd made a difference. Because of them, hundreds of families had gotten their loved ones home intact. All the IEDs they'd found, the ambush nests they'd broken up, the structures they'd identified that were rigged to blow with just a touch of the door, meant a few more men and women safe for another day.

Behind him, the PJs sprawled disconsolately about, their dead "patient" between them. With a nicked femoral artery, the odds had been against him from the start, no matter the top-notch trauma care he'd received.

Geo had seen guys bleed out on dusty roads thousands of miles from home, their shattered bodies struggling to hang on. He'd held their hands, and in some cases comforted their dogs. One long, terrible night, he'd sat with a dying K9 while her handler was rushed into surgery with wounds so extensive no one expected him to survive. He had, and when he'd finally woken up, the first words he managed to mumble were, "Where's my dog?"

When would *his* luck run out? Maybe it never would. Maybe it'd continue, as Geo grew older and slower, as young guys with shiny new Tridents flooded the ranks, eager to get in the fight. Geo flinched. That'd be a lingering death all its own, for fuck's sake, being the guy who stuck around past his prime in an environment where thirty-five was considered old.

He stared unseeing at the ground flashing below his boots.

Passing the torch to the next generation of SEALs would be something he'd have to do eventually. Maybe he should think about doing it on his own terms. What that would look like, he had no fucking idea, but for the first time, he let the reality seep in—that someday, this all would end.

Then what?

By the time the helicopter landed at the naval air station, Geo was bone-tired. Wearily, he got Bosch settled in his kennel for the night, then trudged out to the parking lot, where one of the PJs was being picked up by his family.

"Daddy!" A little girl wearing a cowboy outfit hurled herself into her burly father's arms, and he picked her up and tossed her high over his head before catching her and swinging her around. Propping her on his hip, he bent to kiss his wife, then the baby she was holding.

Geo watched them. What would it be like, to have a tiny human dependent on you for everything? To know that you were responsible for their most basic of needs, for just keeping them *alive*, during those first few months? Then as they grew, to have the responsibility for raising them to be people of integrity, well-rounded individuals with a healthy outlook who treated everyone around them with respect?

He shook his head. Dang. Commando shit had nothing on parenting. No wonder Lani was scared. He would be, too. Still, as the PJ buckled his little family safely into their SUV, Geo couldn't help but think, "Lucky guy. You don't have to go home alone tonight."

As he was about to turn away, he caught a glimpse of Matt ambling across the parking lot toward a beat-up old truck. "Hey!" he called impulsively, waving his arm to get Matt's attention. "Dude!"

Changing course, Matt jogged over. "What's up?" he asked as they bumped knuckles in greeting.

"Eh, just wondered if you wanted to grab a drink? If you don't have anywhere else to be, that is."

Glancing at his watch, Matt said, "Well, I'm picking Shane up at the airfield in a few hours, but sure, we could grab something."

"Danny's?"

"Meet you there."

Twenty minutes later they were both seated at the bar at Danny's, a SEAL hangout and Coronado staple. Business was slow on this Tuesday night, although there were several older men, lean and leathery, grouped together near the end of the counter.

Retired team guys.

Geo ordered a beer, raising an eyebrow when Matt stuck with club soda with lime.

"I actually don't drink," he explained with a wry grin. "It's a long story."

"Well, if you feel like sharing, I'm all ears."

Geo listened as Matt told him about being a bored kid in a small North Dakota town, and how his recreational drinking had gotten out of control, coming within a hair's breadth of derailing his dreams of becoming a SEAL. He credited his uncle, a former SEAL himself, with helping him get his head out of his ass and into BUD/S.

"I had no idea you were part of a SEAL dynasty," Geo exclaimed. "Master Chief MacMillan is your uncle?"

"Yeah." Matt took a pretzel from the basket in front of them and broke it into tiny pieces. "So I had big fuckin' shoes to fill."

"No shit." Geo couldn't even imagine. Rick MacMillan was a legend in the teams, a SEAL sniper who'd been part of the special operations joint task force sent to Mogadishu, Somalia.

With that sort of background, the pressure on Matt to succeed must have been intense, almost suffocating, yet here he was. Raising his glass in a silent toast, Geo said, "Now you'll get to carve out your own path, have your own stories to tell. It's a different world than when he was in."

"For sure."

They fell silent, both staring up at the walls and ceiling of the bar, which over the years had turned into a memorial for the West Coast SEALs lost to the wars in the Middle East.

For some reason, an unsettled, unmoored feeling started swirling in Geo's gut. He drained his beer quickly, then ordered another. Instead of blunting the edges of his agitation, the alcohol only increased it.

Matt eyed him. "You okay, man?"

"Yeah, I'm fine," Geo muttered. His gaze skittered over to one particular section of the wall that was dedicated to the loss of Cobra Three-Five. Throat tight,

Geo scanned the twenty-four bearded faces, gone six years now.

And the community was *still* dealing with the fallout.

"Did you know some of them?" Matt's hushed voice broke into his reverie.

Geo took a long, slow gulp of his beer. "Yeah, I did." He pointed to a photo near the top of the pyramid. "Talked to him, in fact, right before they got on that helo."

Matt squinted to read the name. "Greg Petronis."

"Helluva dude. We called him 'Mooch' because he was *always* out of Copenhagen, but shit, he'd give you the shirt off his back if you asked." Geo shook his head. "He carried a copy of this little book by Marcus Aurelius. Quoted from it constantly and drove us all fuckin' nuts."

"'Death smiles at us all. All a man can do is smile back,'" Matt said softly. "*Meditations*."

"Yep, that's the one." Shoving his empty bottle away, Geo grated, "I know those guys weren't smiling at death when that punk shot them down. They all had their middle fingers up high and were screaming 'Fuck you!'"

Matt nodded somberly, still gazing at the wall. "MPC Callie? There was a dog team on that Chinook?"

"Yeah." Geo swallowed hard. "You know how they were found? Dog in the guy's arms, like he'd just had enough time to wrap himself around her as they were going down."

As always, picturing that handler's tragic desperation stole Geo's breath. It was something he himself wrestled with when he was alone in the dark with his thoughts, the fact that Bosch hadn't asked to be there. He hadn't volunteered to go to war, hadn't signed a contract offering his life to the Navy. He had no choice in the matter, didn't have the ability to reason that the odor he was being praised for finding was capable of blowing him to smithereens, or that the man he was so enthusiastically tracking might shoot him.

As the human, it was up to Geo to protect him, and that's what the handler in that doomed helicopter, in those last terrifying moments of his life, had been frantically trying to do.

Protect his dog.

He opened his eyes to meet Matt's.

"Were you there, Geo? I heard there was a SEAL unit sent out as the quick-reaction force and first responders."

"I wasn't, but a buddy of mine was. Cade's the one who found the—found the dog."

"Damn." Matt winced. "You wonder how those guys handled that, seeing what they must've seen, so many dead friends."

"Some of them didn't handle it," Geo snapped. "Some of them—"

One of them spiraled downward into his own personal hell and took a bunch of us with him.

He glanced up at the chronological line of pictures, which ended with some dude who'd been killed about two years ago. Nothing since then.

The low-grade anger bubbling inside him suddenly burst into flame. "Hey!" he called to the bartender, a tattooed young white woman with short spiky hair and a nose ring. "There's a picture missing." He stabbed his finger toward the memorial wall. "A guy who died last year."

"Really?" The bartender pursed her lips in confusion. "I'll ask the manager. Usually he has the pictures up within a few days of hearing about someone's passing."

She tore a piece of paper off her pad and rooted around for a pen. "What was his name?"

"Cade Barlow."

The retired guys at the other end of the bar snapped their heads around, and Geo immediately tensed. "Got that? Cade Barlow," he said loudly, clearly, staring them down. "B-A-R-L-O-W."

"Don't even bother, Luce," one of the men said, his tone dripping with disgust. "That wall's for *heroes*."

In an instant, Geo was on his feet and in the dude's face. "Excuse me? What was that?"

The guy didn't back down. "You heard me. That wall's for heroes who gave their lives in service to their country, not weaklings who decide to check themselves out."

His whole body shaking with rage, Geo growled, "You have no idea what he'd been through, asshole. He—"

"We've all been through it," the guy broke in. "Every single one of us has demons we wrestle with, but you know what? We don't shame our community by taking the coward's way out."

"He was *not* a coward," Geo shouted. "You don't know the first thing about him!"

"Well, the fact he ate his own bullet tells me everything I need to know, now, doesn't it?"

"You don't know *shit*." Geo planted his hands on the guy's chest and shoved.

The dude staggered back a few steps but quickly righted himself. Geo could feel Matt's warmth at his shoulder as the other man's friends leapt to flank him.

Pointing at Geo, the man growled, "You'd better watch who you're fucking with, son."

"Fuck *you*! Cade was my teammate…"

"And I'm sorry for your loss. But a SEAL who gave up, who *quit*, doesn't deserve—not while I have breath left in my body—to have his picture on this wall."

A huge lump rose in Geo's throat, almost choking him. When he didn't say anything, the guy went on, "Those men—" he pointed "—died fighting. They died honorably, bravely, SEALs to the end." He paused, lips twisted in a sneer. "Can you say the same about *him*?"

The disgust on his face, on all his friends' faces, plus the open-mouthed shock on Luce's, convinced Geo it was futile to continue the argument. Still, unwilling to back down, he took a step closer to the man, until their noses were only inches apart.

"It shouldn't be how he died, it should be how he *lived*," Geo hissed. "Cade Barlow gave eighteen years in service to his country. His bravery under fire was unquestioned, the lives he saved too numerous to count. For those reasons, he fuckin' *deserves* to be on that wall with his brothers."

The man shook his head. "Tell that to their families, son. Convince them that someone who *chose* to die should hang next to these men who fought death all the way to their very last breath. Tell them, or get the *fuck* outta my face."

They stared at each other, bodies rigid, Geo's anger mirrored back at him in the other guy's expression. Matt's hand coming to rest on his shoulder broke the spell. "Let's go, George. There's no point to this."

The older guy flicked his gaze to Matt, a renewed sneer twisting his lips. "Hey, I've heard about you. The spitting image of your uncle, aren't you? I had the pleasure of serving with him early in my career." He smirked. "Oh, the master chief must be *so* proud."

Derisive snickers came from the guy's friends at the sarcastic inflection to his words. Matt's voice remained calm, unruffled, as he said, "He is, and I'm sure he'd *love* to discuss it with you. Go ahead and call him."

The guy snorted. "Nah, cupcake. I wouldn't bother him with something as ridiculous as you." He lifted his chin toward the door. "Now prance on outta here, would ya? This bar's for *real* men."

Geo's muscles coiled, his fingers balling into a fist. "What the fuck," he started to say, but Matt tugged on his sleeve.

"It's not worth it. Let's go."

The group's mocking laughter followed them through the door. When they reached the sidewalk, Matt took a deep breath, his cheeks puffing out as he exhaled. "You okay?"

"Yeah." Geo stared at him. "You?"

"I'm fine."

By silent agreement, they turned and started ambling along Orange Avenue, hands stuffed in their pockets.

Geo couldn't help stealing looks at Matt, unsure what to say, until Matt glanced at him.

"Yes, I'm gay," he said quietly. "And out."

"Dude…"

"My task unit is fully supportive," Matt went on, "although the El-Tee says I can't serve in the same platoon as my boyfriend anymore." He chuckled. "One of us has got to go."

Geo stumbled over his own feet, saved in the nick of time by Matt's strong grip on his biceps. "Your boyfriend is in your platoon?" he croaked. "Jesus Christ."

"Well, we didn't plan it that way," Matt said, laughing. "We met in BUD/S, got assigned to different platoons, and then somehow Shane ended up in mine."

"*Shane?*" Now Geo stopped short, his eyes widening. "The wounded guy you kept driving for?"

Matt's smile faded. "Yeah. Lieutenant Bradley says he never wants us put in that position again. Shane and I know how to keep things professional at work, but one of us dying in front of the other, well, that'd be hard to come back from."

"No shit." Geo stood frozen, still gaping at him. For Matt to have kept on driving while the man he loved was bleeding to death a few feet away…

At last Geo held his knuckles out for a bump. "Goddamn, son. Respect."

Matt's eyes held a tinge of relief even as he grinned. "Thanks."

They resumed walking, feet scuffing along the pavement. After a moment, Matt said, "My uncle went to Cade's funeral. There, uh, weren't a lot of people there, I guess."

Including Geo. He hadn't been able to bring himself to go, the anger and guilt flooding him too strong. Besides, how could he face Renae?

"He was a good man, Matt. The best. I—" Geo couldn't go on, and luckily, Matt didn't push, just gripped his shoulder and, with a gentle tug, turned Geo toward his truck.

"C'mon. Let's get you home."

About to protest that he could drive himself, a sudden wooziness swept over him, a product of both too much beer and emotion. Still, he rasped, "Nah, I can get an Uber…"

"No way. We're swim buddies, right?"

Geo couldn't help but smile at that. The swim buddy ethos had been drilled into them from day one at BUD/S, sometimes painfully, and it wasn't anything a SEAL ever took lightly.

"Right," he whispered. "Thanks, brother."

It was a short drive to the barracks, and when Matt pulled up to the curb, he said, "I'll give you a ride back to get your bike first thing in the morning, if you want."

"Oh, God, no. I'll get an Uber for that." Geo got out of the truck and leaned his forearms on top of the window frame to look inside. "Sleep late with your man."

At those words, Matt's cheeks took on an attractive flush, his eyes sparkling. "Well, I definitely won't argue with you about that. I haven't seen him in a month."

Geo winked. "Enjoy. Talk to you later." He stood back, swaying just the slightest bit on his feet, as Matt put the truck into gear and drove away with a jaunty wave. He watched until the taillights disappeared around the corner. Wow. Shane was a lucky guy.

Wearily, he made his way up the walk toward his room, envying their upcoming reunion, the fact that Matt would soon be sleeping in the arms of someone who loved him. What was it like for them as a couple, being fully out in the teams? Even a few short years ago, it wouldn't have been possible, DADT or no. They wouldn't have been accepted; the reaction of the older team guys in the bar was proof of that.

Now, at least, the younger men moving into leadership positions were bringing with them their increasingly progressive views, slowly but surely replacing the old guard. The fact that the military as a whole was a largely conservative organization meant there was still a long way to go, but for the most part, he was finding the shift in attitudes encouraging.

Too bad it didn't extend to mental health.

He flopped fully clothed onto the bed, his thoughts churning as he replayed the altercation at the bar.

"We've all been through it. Every single one of us has demons we wrestle with."

It was true. He'd seen some gruesome shit during his career, heartbreaking stuff that sometimes flashed in his mind's eye with the clarity of a CGI movie: Fighters blown inside out by U.S. planes' powerful bombs, their body fat still sizzling from the white phosphorus. Women and children used as human shields or caught in the crossfire. Dead friends.

So many dead friends.

But grieving was a luxury no one could afford. They all learned pretty quickly to stuff it away, to move on. There were things Geo'd seen, and done, that he'd locked away so tightly, if he had his way they'd never again see the light of day.

"I don't want to compartmentalize so much that I stop caring," Matt had said.

"Well, you're gonna have to," Geo whispered to the empty room. "You'll have to."

Because theirs wasn't a sports team, where a player had the luxury of riding out a slump, of being able to take the time to get some extra help from the coaches and get back on track. Here, if someone couldn't keep up or got emotional and lost their edge, they were gone.

Even in the SEAL teams—*especially* in the SEAL teams—no one was irreplaceable. In their world, asking for help meant being seen as weak, cowardly, a breakdown of the mental toughness SEALs were legendary for. It meant possibly losing the confidence of teammates, of brothers, the very way of life they'd all fought so hard to be a part of.

And that was a risk almost no one was willing to take.

With an unhappy sigh, Geo struggled back to his feet and grabbed his phone, which he hadn't checked all day. As the various notifications popped up, one in particular caught his eye. A text from Lani.

Catching his breath in anticipation, he opened it up.

Hey! Tonight I saw one of the prettiest sunsets I've ever seen in my life, so have a pic of the beach, and also a "beetch" who's very glad to have met you. Not gonna lie, I've been pretty lonely, and talking to you is a real bright spot in my life these days. Now I'm off to make myself a delicious dinner, and nope, I won't exercise after. So there.

When he clicked on the first attachment, Geo's breath caught.

The Pacific Ocean shimmered in the fading sunlight, the blue-gray waves a white froth as they crashed down onto the shore. The brilliant purple-and-pink sky scudded with clouds, and he could just *smell* the breeze that'd carry the faint scent of brine to his nose.

"Ah, thank you, Lani," he whispered. "I really needed that."

He opened the other picture. Soft brown eyes gazed out at him, the waning San Diego sun highlighting a smattering of freckles that danced across a pert nose and along softly rounded cheeks. Lani was smiling, the light sheen of gloss on her lips emphasizing their shapely fullness.

Thick black hair shone, teased into a halo about her head by the sea breeze. A few strands clung to her lips, and Geo reached out a finger as if to brush them away. Instead of lush, pliable skin, the impersonal coldness of his phone screen greeted his touch, and he settled for tracing the shape of her mouth once, twice, a quiver starting low in his belly that made his heart thud painfully in his ears.

Dropping his hand, he ran greedy eyes along bare shoulders, the hint of cleavage swelling over the scooped neckline of her tank top. A small heart-shaped pendant drew his attention to the hollow of her throat, and the thought of pressing his lips to that enticing hollow swelled his cock to a painful hardness. He gulped, suddenly disgusted with himself. She was his pregnant *friend*, not a potential fuck buddy.

He had plenty of *those* in his life, more than he'd ever need.

Friends, though, were in short supply, especially ones outside the community who understood the demands of his job, who wouldn't expect more of him than he could reasonably give. Someone who enjoyed his friendship almost as much as he did hers.

Who knew what it was like to lose someone in an instant, in a way almost too painful to bear.

Geo sucked in a ragged breath, forcing back the toxic brew of anger, of guilt, of *shame*, that'd been his constant companion since the night Cade Barlow—his mentor, his friend—had lined up his personal effects on a shelf above his rack, stuck a Post-it note on his computer with his password written on it, then put a Sig Sauer nine-millimeter pistol into his mouth and pulled the trigger.

"What was that? Did one of you assholes have an accidental discharge?"

The crunch of booted feet, the shouting, as everyone in the platoon rushed through the hooch, looking for the source of the unmistakable sound.

Geo had flung open the door to Cade's room. "Dude, did you hear that?"

The smell of cordite had almost knocked him down. Before the roaring in his ears took over, a steady *drip-drip-drip* had registered, the sight of a wall splattered with…

His heart galloping, Geo fought the memories as Lani gazed steadily back at him, the gold flecks in her eyes giving them a warmth, a depth, that seemed to flow through the screen straight into his soul. He didn't look away from her, but clung to her, until the anguish crested, receded, then mercifully flowed away, leaving him limp and drained.

Clearing his throat, he clicked Reply with a shaking finger and typed, Thanks for the pics, pretty girl, and enjoy your dinner. See you soon.

Chapter Nine

"I'm coming!"

Lani could hear the irritation in her own voice, but she didn't care. Whoever was knocking so insistently on her door was about to get a piece of her mind.

"I don't need any—" she snapped as she jerked open the door, only to stop short. Instead of the salesperson she'd been expecting, a woman stood on the stoop, a woman who was girl-next-door beautiful, with fair skin and silky brown hair gleaming with blond highlights. Her workout leggings and layered tank tops emphasized a taut, athletic body, and oversized sunglasses perched on the top of her head.

Lani's stomach dropped to her toes, and her heart started to pound in abject fear.

"Hi," the woman said. "I'm—"

"I know who you are, Devon," Lani snapped. "Did something happen to Rhys?"

"What?" Her eyes widening, Devon took a step forward. "Oh, shit, no. Rhys is fine. I just talked to him. He's perfectly fine, I promise."

Her knees going weak in relief, Lani slumped against the doorjamb. "Thank God."

Because she couldn't take another loss.

"I'm so sorry." Devon's voice throbbed with remorse, her eyes shining with it. "I should've realized that's where your mind would go first."

"Yeah." Still trembling from residual fright, Lani blew out a shaky breath. "What're you doing here?"

"Well, other than scaring the shit out of you, I, uh, wanted to invite you to lunch." Devon gave her a tentative smile. "My treat."

Lani blinked. "Huh?"

"Lunch." Devon's smile wavered a bit. "I thought maybe we could have lunch today, get to know each other."

Her shock made Lani's tone sharper than she intended. "Why would we do that?"

Hearing it, Devon bit her lip. "Well, it's, uh—"

"It's what? Did Rhys put you up to this?" Raking one hand through her hair, Lani growled, "I swear to Christ, I'm gonna kick that man's ass. I'm *fine*. It's not his job to worry about me anymore."

"He still will, though."

The rueful tone gave Lani pause. "Well, Rhys and I are through. He only texts me once in a while to ask how I'm doing. We don't talk, or see each other. You don't have anything to worry about."

"I know that." Heaving a sigh, Devon said, "Okay, listen, here's the thing. You said it's not his job to worry about you, but he still will."

"Well, if that's true, he can stop."

"I don't think he can. And I don't want him to."

Lani rolled her eyes. "Yeah, right."

"I don't," Devon said confidently. "A part of him still

loves you, and his love for you, what you went through together, makes up a lot of who he is. He can't just turn that off, and maybe it sounds crazy, but no, I don't want him to. I don't want him to lose that piece of himself."

"Okay, I get it." Lani crossed her arms over her chest with a cynical chuckle. "What's that old saying? 'Keep your friends close but your enemies closer'? Is that what we're doing here?"

"See, that's exactly what I mean," Devon exclaimed. "Where is it written that two women automatically have to be enemies because of a man? Where's the rule that says we can't be friends? Ex or no, I'd still like to be your friend."

"Why? For Rhys's sake?"

"And mine. And yours. Women should empower each other, not be in competition to tear each other down. Sometimes we're all we've got, right?" A spasm of pain crossed Devon's face before she smoothed it out. "I'd really like to get to know you. We don't have to be rivals."

Studying her, Lani thought she seemed sincere, and maybe her motives were pure. Besides, she knew Rhys, and he wouldn't fall in love with a jealous, vindictive bitch, no way, not when he himself was kindness personified. And Devon had done some sort of advocacy work with women in Afghanistan, hadn't she?

God, the two of them were so perfect for each other. Both caretakers and healers, with all their shit together...

Totally unlike her, the one everyone thought still needed rescuing. That old crippling sense of inadequacy swept over Lani once more, and she heard herself blurt, "No, thanks. I'm fine. I have an appointment today anyway."

Devon's encouraging smile died. "Fair enough. I don't think I could've bungled this any more if I tried." She proffered a folded-up piece of paper. "Will you take my number? If you need anything at all, if you change your mind, please call me. I didn't mean to upset you. I'm sorry."

Numbly, Lani took the paper from her hand, her stomach churning. Devon turned and jogged lightly down the stairs toward a red compact parked at the curb, and once inside, she dropped her forehead to the steering wheel for several long moments before starting the engine and driving away.

Lani watched her taillights disappear off into the distance, then looked at the note crumpled between her fingers.

"Lady, I'm never going to call you," she muttered under her breath, but something made her stuff the paper in her pocket instead of tearing it into a thousand pieces like she wanted to. Back inside her apartment, she flopped into her chair at the table with a groan. She pulled her journal to her and flipped to a new page, where she scrawled the date across the top, then wrote:

Well, I met Devon today, and ugh, I was a total bitch to her. A part of me feels like I should apologize, but a bigger part of me doesn't give a shit. She actually thought we could be friends. That's impossible, isn't it?

* * *

"Isn't it?" she said aloud to the empty room. "It'd be weird, right?"

"Why? It's not like you want Rhys back," a little voice inside her head whispered. "Be honest. You were a bitch to her partly because you were shocked and surprised, and partly because she showed up looking all thin and cute."

God, was she really that petty?

Not wanting to think too closely about the answer to that, Lani picked up her pen again.

There's nothing wrong with not wanting to be friends with an ex's new girlfriend. It's not petty. Maybe it's just self-preservation.

With a sigh, she closed her journal and tossed her pen down. She grabbed her purse and keys, then headed for her car. As she drove, she thought about how earnest Devon seemed, how her face had crumpled when Lani kicked her out.

Had she really cared that much? Or was she just going to call Rhys and tell him, oh well, she'd tried?

Hot, tired and crabby, she thrust Devon from her mind and concentrated on finding a parking spot at the busy medical complex. She made her way into her OB's office, where she signed in and wedged herself into a chair next to a couple who were whispering and giggling together.

"She's moving so much today. Feel it?" The woman grabbed the man's hand and placed it low on her bulging belly.

He gasped. "I feel it!" Bending over, he put his lips near his fingers and crooned, "Hi, baby girl. Mommy and Daddy are so ready to meet you."

The woman stroked his hair, her eyes glowing with tenderness, and Lani glanced away, her own eyes stinging. The loneliness burning its way through her was a physical ache, this oh-so-painful reminder that the world largely moved by twos.

She looked around the busy waiting room, hoping, praying, to see someone else sitting alone, but she was the only one. What would she do when her time came? A picture formed, of a solitary Uber ride to the hospital in the dead of night. She'd be dropped at the curb, alone, in labor. Who would comfort her, and ease her fears, and celebrate with her when her baby was finally placed in her arms? Who would drive her *home*, for fuck's sake?

The memory of Devon's hopeful smile swam before her eyes, and suddenly, Lani couldn't help but put herself in her shoes. It had to have been hard, admitting to Lani that Rhys still cared for her. How much courage had it taken for her to show up at Lani's door and make herself vulnerable like that, not sure of her reception? What would she have done if Lani'd actually accepted her invitation?

"Well, I think we're about to find out."

Determination stiffening her spine, Lani fished the phone number from her pocket, and before she could change her mind, she texted, I'm sorry. Lunch sounds good. When?

An almost immediate reply popped up. Yay! How

about Friday, my house? That way we can sit and talk as long as we want, no pressure.

Lani hesitated. Was she really gonna do this?

Devon's not the enemy. We're not in competition. She's the woman Rhys loves, and since a part of me will always love him, too, maybe it's a good idea for her to have a place in my life.

Her thumbs flying, she replied, I'll be there.

Devon texted her the address along with a string of smiling emojis, and Lani couldn't help but snort a little at her enthusiasm.

Just then the giggling couple was called back, and the man leapt to his feet and assisted the woman to hers with such tender solicitousness that tears sprang to Lani's eyes anew. Before the self-pity could dig its claws any deeper, her phone chimed again.

She glanced at it impatiently, her heart giving a giant leap when she saw what it was, a picture of Bosch in full combat gear, along with an accompanying text. Ready to meet me? I'm free tonight if you are.

A grin spread over her face. I'd love to!

Great. My dad'll pick you up at six?

Snickering at the realization she was having a "conversation" with a dog, she typed, Perfect.

Anticipation buoyed her through her appointment and all the way home, where she took a long, hot shower and then spent an inordinate amount of time on her hair and makeup.

"No, I *won't* feel stupid about it," she lectured herself in the mirror. "I have a date tonight with a great guy, and I deserve to look and feel my best."

Besides, how many more dates was she likely to

have? At thirteen weeks, she could be starting to show soon, and she couldn't imagine that men would be lining up to get involved with her. After she had the baby, the last thing *she'd* have time for was a man.

"So, basically, I'm gonna enjoy it while I can," she said, pointing her mascara wand at her reflection. "No promises, no strings, just two people enjoying each other's company. Nothing more, nothing less."

Still, when the quiet knock on the door sounded precisely at six, her breath caught in a way it hadn't in years.

"Jesus, he's a SEAL," she lectured herself. "You're *not* going to fall for a SEAL. It's not gonna happen. So *what* if he cleans the kitchen without being asked? Or offers pity-free hugs and a shoulder to cry on without expecting anything in return? Lots of non-SEALs would do that, right? Tons of them. Men like that grow on trees."

Rolling her eyes at her own absurdity, Lani paused and fluffed her hair out one last time before reaching for the security chain.

"Seriously, now. Geo's amazing, but he's not for you. Go out, have fun, but try not to lose sight of that, okay?"

Taking a deep breath, she swung the door open, only for her mouth to go dry as an Arizona desert. Damn. Geo wore a faded Green Day T-shirt and soft jeans that molded themselves to slim hips and muscular thighs. His broad shoulders seemed to take up the entire doorway, the hands shoved in his pockets pulling his waistband down just enough to give her a peek of taut belly.

God, she could so lick him like an ice cream cone right now.

"Hey," he said, smiling, raising an eyebrow when she continued to stand there and gape.

Her cheeks heated. "Hey," she croaked, hoping he hadn't noticed how red they must be. "Ready to go?"

"Yep, if you are." Standing to the side, he waited until she'd closed and locked her door before ushering her on ahead of him down the stairs. At the bottom, he put his hand lightly on the small of her back and steered her toward a sleek, gunmetal-gray Toyota Tundra.

The touch, impersonal as it was, still managed to turn her knees to mush. Once seated inside the truck, Lani pressed her thighs together, doing her best not to squirm as he swung up into the driver's seat, his corded forearms making her mouth water. In fact, he looked so tasty it was a wonder she hadn't grown fangs.

Sucking in a deep, calming breath, she asked, "So… what's next for you and Bosch?"

He completed the left turn out of her parking lot before answering, "We leave tomorrow for a few weeks at Fort Benning, and then on to Langley for a, um, workshop."

A pang went through her. So this was the last night he'd be in town for a while. She kept her voice light. "Oooh, a workshop. Sounds exciting."

"Just another day at the office." They chuckled together. "How about you?"

"Eh. Work. Therapy." *Lunch with my ex's new love.* "More work. More therapy. You get the picture. Lather, rinse, repeat. *Super* interesting," she finished drily.

"When's your support group?"

She blinked, amazed that he'd remembered. "It's the, uh, last Saturday of the month, actually. Why?"

He shrugged. "Thought you might want an account-ability call. I can imagine it's not something you're looking forward to."

Her throat tightened at his perception. "That'd be amazing, Geo. And yeah, I'm pretty much dreading it."

The understatement of the year. The thought of sitting in a room full of total strangers and sharing her deepest, most private pain with them made her stomach tie itself into knots.

"There's strength in numbers," Maura had said. "In finding a community of people who've been through exactly what you have, who understand it, and are surviving it."

Aware of Geo's gaze, Lani made a concerted effort to relax. She was *not* going to ruin their night together.

After navigating through the sentry gate, Geo turned down a side street and parked in front of what she assumed was the kennel. Like every other building on every other military base in the country, it was an unassuming dun-colored block, the only identifying feature the large number on the corner of it.

"How many dogs are here?"

"Right now? I'm not sure. Three or four, maybe." He unlocked the front door and led her inside. "The kennel master's room is right there." He pointed. "And he has a couple of assistants who live here, too. There's always someone on-site who checks the dogs, feeds them, exercises them, does some light training. I try to work with Bosch every day, too."

When they reached Geo's assigned kennel area, Lani couldn't help but tense and move a tiny bit closer to him. He stopped short, then turned to look at her.

"Are you afraid of dogs?" he asked gently.

She shook her head, her voice a tiny bit tremulous as she said, "I'm not usually, but all of a sudden I'm thinking about what you told me, about him chasing the decoy up a fence and jumping out a window to pile-drive that guy. Maybe this isn't such a good idea."

Geo didn't answer, just snagged a folding chair that was leaning up against the wall and set it up well away from Bosch's cage. "Why don't we sit for a minute?"

After she'd lowered herself onto the chair, Geo crouched at her feet, his face solemn. "I would *never* bring you around Bosch if I thought he was in any way a danger to you. Never."

"I know."

She must not have sounded all that convinced, because he rested his hand on her knee and waited until she met his eyes. "On our last deployment, right before coming home, we were out clearing this compound, looking for bad guys. We found some."

Lani darted her gaze over his shoulder to where Bosch lay quietly.

"There was a firefight, and the drone pilot saw some people running away—just heat signatures in the dark, leaving the compound. We knew from earlier surveillance that there were a ton of irrigation ditches out in this field they were headed for, some palm groves."

She gulped. "Lots of places to hide."

"Yeah. Because of the threat of ambush, it was too dangerous to just blindly charge out there after them, so I sent Bosch first to try and track them down."

As he spoke, Geo moved his body around so they were both facing Bosch's cage. The dog was on his mat, ears up, his head cocked slightly to the side, for all the world looking like he was enthralled with the story, too.

Geo squeezed her knee. "Try to picture this if you can. It was pitch dark, the middle of the night. Our guys at the compound were fully engaged with the enemy there, our combat controller was trying to coordinate some air strikes, and we had squirters hiding somewhere in ambush territory."

His voice grew tight with remembered excitement.

"Fuck, we were totally amped, adrenaline pumping, ready to neutralize the threat. Suddenly Bosch veered off, and I could tell by the way he was running that he was locked on a target. We followed him, weapons up…"

When he paused, Lani reached out and dug her fingers into his shoulder. "Oh, my God, don't leave me hanging. What happened?"

"He stopped," Geo said simply. "Planted his feet at the edge of this ditch and stopped short, wouldn't engage. The whole point of using K9s is to give ourselves the element of surprise, a split-second advantage with someone aiming an AK-47 at us."

"Because they don't expect a dog to be coming at them?"

"Maybe they're expecting it, I don't know, but they never see or hear him coming. All of a sudden he's there, teeth clamped on your gun arm. When he full-on bites, those teeth slice through skin, and muscle, all the way to the bone."

He lifted his forearm to display his own scar.

"You're flailing, trying to get him off you, but his

grip is too tight. Everything is ripping, blood is flying, you're screaming…"

"And you're too busy to get a shot off," Lani said breathlessly.

"Some guys try. They try to shoot the dog, or reach for a grenade, or clack off a vest. Those guys don't live very long." His eyes looked straight into hers. "Not because *he* kills them, but because I do."

She nodded. That was his job, after all.

"Some give up, and then I call Bosch off. Those guys are put in flex-cuffs and taken back to base. That particular night, he stopped, went into what we call a bark-and-hold. Usually that's not something we want. We want him to go in, no hesitation, put the hurt on the bad guy."

"So why didn't he?"

"Because the people in the ditch weren't bad guys. They were women and children."

She gasped. "Oh, no!"

"In that instant, when he was in full attack mode, with four SEALs behind him ready to shoot to kill, he stopped." Geo paused. "He saved their lives. He recognized in a split-second that they weren't threats, and he stopped."

"How does he know?"

"Because he's trained. Exhaustively. He can run through a crowded bazaar and ignore everyone except the person he's chasing. If he corners a guy and the guy surrenders, he doesn't bite him. He's not some loose cannon I send out there to bring the pain to whichever random person he can run to ground."

"I know. But what if I do something wrong?" she whispered. "Something he doesn't like?"

"Well, let me tell you the two rules I have when it comes to interacting with Bosch." Pushing to his feet, Geo unlocked the cage and opened it. "Wait for me to introduce you, and don't try to kiss him."

With an incredulous laugh, Lani said, "Don't worry about that, Jesus." She put her hand to her mouth. "Did someone—"

"Yep, this overly enthusiastic Marine who was missing his Lab back home or something. Dropped to his knees and put his arms around Bosch, tried to kiss his nose."

"Oh, God. Did he get bitten?"

"Nice little rip in his tear duct. Hey, the guy was stupid," he went on when she groaned in sympathy. "You never put your face near a strange dog's mouth, no matter if it's a chihuahua wearing a fuzzy pink coat or a Malinois in a war zone."

Lani sat rigidly in her chair as Geo gave Bosch a command, and almost delicately the dog got up and crossed the floor to stand in front of her. He sniffed her knees, then down to her sandaled toes, before sitting with an eager, expectant look.

"Pet him if you want to," Geo said softly. "He loves a good ear scratch."

After a long moment's hesitation, she reached out tentative fingers and rubbed the top of his head. When Bosch didn't react, she fondled his ears lightly, then more firmly, at last scratching behind them and even down his neck. "Hey, Bosch. Nice to finally meet you."

Geo knelt next to them. "This beautiful lady is my

friend," he informed him, and Bosch thumped his tail as if in reply, which made her giggle.

"You're so handsome. Thanks for helping to keep the guys safe," she said with another hearty scratch to Bosch's neck. "You're such a good boy."

Lani could've sworn she saw the dog smile.

Geo had her feed Bosch treats from the palm of her hand, and taught her a few Dutch commands, like "lie down" and "sit." By the end of their little get-to-know-you session, she'd completely relaxed.

"I think I'd built him up in my mind to be some sort of lion," she admitted, "and while I wouldn't exactly call him a teddy bear, he's not as scary as I was picturing."

"There're some guys in the platoon who won't go near him if they can help it, and that's fine. Like I tell them, he's not there to be a mascot or a pet. He doesn't have to be loved, but he needs to be respected for what he's trained to do."

She watched as Geo led Bosch to his cage and ushered him inside, the affection in his body language, his voice, making her chest ache with something she couldn't define. Despite Bosch's toughness, not to mention *Geo's* toughness, it was obvious how much they loved each other.

The ache deepened into longing and, clearing her throat, Lani glanced down at her knees. Was she really envious of a dog? No way.

As Geo flipped the lights off and pulled the kennel door shut, he asked, "You want to go for a walk?"

"Mmm. I do if you do."

"Yeah." He thought for a moment. "Why don't we

head over to the beach by the Navy Lodge? It's just about a mile from here."

"Perfect." She grinned up at him, her nose wrinkling. "Close to bathrooms. I'll probably have to pee ten times while we're there."

He eyed her. "The joys of pregnancy, huh?"

"I wouldn't say *joy* is the word for it, but…" She sighed. "I'm sure all of this is nature's way of making sure I don't dread what's to come."

The parking lot at the beach seemed surprisingly full, although the beach itself looked deserted. Luckily, Geo found a spot close to the path leading down to the water. Once they'd reached the sand, the reason for all the cars became clear.

"I think there's a wedding over there." He pointed to a small reception hall and gazebo about a hundred yards away from where they were standing. The amplified voice of the DJ echoed over to them, along with the throbbing beat of some dance music. "You want to go somewhere else?"

"Nah. We won't hear them down by the water."

It seemed like the most natural thing in the world for her to take his arm while they strolled. She hugged his muscular biceps, enjoying the warmth and closeness. When they reached the reception hall, they stood just outside the pool of light, watching while the wedding couple danced together on the gazebo. The bride was radiant in a light pink cocktail dress, her groom in khaki pants, the sleeves of his matching pink button-up shirt rolled to his elbows.

"Aww, they look so beautiful and happy together,

don't they?" Lani whispered. "Best wishes to them both."

Loud laughter drew their attention to a knot of young men leaning against a nearby railing, bottles of beer in hand, their boisterousness and camaraderie instantly recognizable. Geo nodded at them. "Team guys."

She grimaced, her pleasure at the sight of the happy couple draining away. The bride had not only married her husband, she'd married the whole community and the demands it brought with it. It wouldn't be an easy or glamorous life, not by a long shot.

"Well, good *luck* to them both, then," she said. "They're gonna need it."

Geo quirked his lips at her. "Been there, done that, got the T-shirt, huh?"

"Hell, yeah, I got the T-shirt." Tugging on his arm, she steered them past the wedding and on down the beach. "How about you? What sort of relationship skeletons do you have in *your* closet?" She'd said it lightly, teasingly, and was surprised to feel his biceps tense.

He didn't say anything for a few beats, then, "I lived with someone for about a year once. His name was Jake."

It took a moment for his meaning to sink in. Careful to keep both her face and voice neutral, Lani said, "*His* name?"

"I'm bi. So yeah, 'closet' is a pretty good word for it."

Risking a glance up at him, she could see how rigid his jaw was, his lips compressed into a tight line. How much trust had it taken for him to reveal that? A pang shot through her. More than she'd ever know.

Instinctively, she hugged him tighter. "Thanks for

telling me that," she said softly. "What happened with you and Jake?"

He took a deep breath, the stiffness in his body slowly, incrementally, draining away. "He got tired of pretending to be my roommate. It was during DADT, so he couldn't ever be anything else."

Lani didn't reply, because what was there to say? She leaned her cheek on his shoulder as he went on, "I loved him, but not enough to fight for him, you know? When he walked out, I…let him."

"I'm sorry," she whispered.

After a lengthy pause, he shrugged. "Me, too. It was a long time ago, though."

"No one since?"

"No one serious. I really don't let myself do serious anymore."

"Yeah." She grunted. "I'm with you on that, even if my one foray into a no-strings hookup didn't end with, uh, no strings."

Geo cast her a sympathetic glance. "A baby is one hell of a string, isn't it?"

"I know! Jesus Christ, can't I do *anything* right?"

She'd meant the words to sound flippant, but they came out throbbing with pain, and hot embarrassment immediately burned its way through her. Before she could babble on, he reached over and covered her fingers with his.

With an internal sob, Lani clutched on to him, grabbing hold of the silent comfort he offered. "Wow, I'm sorry," she forced out. "You're sitting ringside to a real shitshow, aren't you?"

"What?" He chuckled softly. "And here I was thinking how brave you are. Silly me."

She just shook her head.

"Look." Geo slipped his arm around her waist and turned her to face the ocean. "See those guys?" He pointed, and under the weak moonlight glowing on the water, she could just make out some black rubber boats with shadowy figures inside, rowing away. "Those are BUD/S students. It's mid Hell Week."

Unbelievably, a laugh bubbled up in her chest. "Are you saying my life is like Hell Week?"

He threw her a reproving look. "I'm saying that by this point in the Week, those guys are so punchy from lack of sleep, they're hallucinating all sorts of crazy shit. Their skin is so chafed that the saltwater feels like acid, but you know what? They keep going."

She stared at the tight group of boats.

"Those dudes out there are the most determined sons of bitches on the planet right now. They've made it this far, and no way are they gonna fuckin' quit. Not when they're already halfway there. They're exhausted, in pain, scared of what's next, but they're gonna keep going." He gave her a squeeze. "Just like you. You're brave as fuck, Lani."

Before she could protest, he went on, "You are. You told me what you were going to do, therapy and whatnot, and by God, you're doing it." He grinned. "*That's* what I have a ringside seat to, and I gotta tell you, I'm sorta diggin' it."

She couldn't help but huff out a laugh, even as she dug her elbow into his side. "You're weird. I don't feel all that brave or anything, but whatever."

Geo didn't reply, but he left his arm where it was, and after a moment she let hers creep around his waist in return. Nestling against him, Lani soaked in his solid warmth, a shiver going through her at the sight of the little boats being buffeted by the cold, dark water.

"Did you hallucinate when you were going through it?" she asked curiously.

"Oh, fuck, yeah. I was convinced there was an evil clown following us. I kept shouting, 'Better not come any closer, motherfucker!'"

She giggled.

"Another dude saw snakes crawling in and out of the boat, and this one guy swore he saw his mom's face in the sky. I'd never met his mom, but when I looked at the sky, I saw her, too." He shook his head. "Surreal."

Her "geez" was hushed and heartfelt, and Geo said, "Sometimes, more times than I want to admit, the only thing that kept me going was the thought of Cade losing that bet. If it wasn't for him, I probably would've f-failed—"

A sudden tremor went through him. Immediately he shook off her arm and turned his back, shoulders rising and falling as he sucked in a few ragged breaths. Lani stood frozen, aching to comfort him but unsure what he needed, or more importantly, what he'd accept. So she just waited, tummy in knots, until he finally faced her again, his eyes dry, jaw set.

"Ready to go?"

When she nodded, he strode off across the sand toward the parking lot, tension in every line of his body. She followed more slowly, a sneaking suspicion growing inside her, a worry that Geo wasn't letting himself grieve for his friend.

Don't make the same mistake I made, she pleaded with him silently. Don't stuff it down and think it's just going to go away.

By the time they reached his truck, he appeared composed. "Sorry about that," he said, his tone discouraging any sympathy, any questions.

They rode in silence to her apartment, and as they turned into the parking lot, she ventured, "Geo, if you ever need to talk about it—"

"I'm good," he interrupted. "That memory just caught me off guard, that's all."

"An ambush moment."

"What?" He stopped in the middle of shoving his door open, his voice tight.

"That's what my therapist calls those, the memories that sneak up on you like that. Ambush moments."

"Hmmph." Slamming his door, Geo trotted around to hand her from the truck, his touch gentle, but his eyes bleak, distant. They didn't speak all the way up the stairs, and when she'd slid her key in the lock, she glanced up at him.

"Would you like to come in?"

He blinked, and for a moment she thought he was about to say yes. Then he shook his head. "I can't."

Disappointment shot through her, but she refused to let it show. "Okay. Well, thanks for taking me to meet Bosch. He's amazing."

A ghost of a smile touched his lips. "He is. And you're welcome. I love showing him off."

As he turned to go, she blurted, "If you ever want to talk, I'm here."

Geo's throat worked. Then he gave a terse nod, jogged down the steps, and was gone. Inside her apartment, Lani collapsed onto the couch, her thoughts in a jumble. Finally she struggled to her feet and into the kitchen to make tea. As she did, she caught sight of her journal. Pulling it to her, she picked up her pen.

It really is sad, she wrote, *that a man can trust me enough to reveal one of the most intimate aspects of who he is, yet at the same time can't bring himself to cry in front of me.*

Her heart aching, she stared at her silent phone.

Boys do *cry, Geo. Even SEALs.*

Chapter Ten

"Fuck, fuck, fuck!"

Pounding the steering wheel with the heel of his hand, Geo inched forward, the red brake lights glowing over the horizon as far as the eye could see.

Goddammit, what he wouldn't give for his bike right now. Adrenaline and speed, *that's* what he needed, two things guaranteed to clear the mind and quiet unwanted emotions. Instead, he was trapped inside the cab of his truck with nowhere to go, no escape from the inexplicable anger boiling through him, along with crushing sadness, and *guilt*.

So much fucking guilt.

When his phone rang, he stabbed the Bluetooth button. "What?"

"Guess who's in town?" The velvety smooth voice washed over him, and Geo smiled in spite of himself.

"Hey, Tariq."

A pause. "You okay? What's up?"

"Nothing." Geo blew out a breath. "Just a lot of things on my mind."

Tariq gave a low chuckle. "Well, you know I'd be

happy to, er, *suck* all your problems away. Just say the word."

Geo waited, but there wasn't a shred of temptation, not one. He couldn't help but wonder why, even as he said, "I have to be on a plane in the morning, T, so the only thing I'm taking to bed tonight is a bottle of vodka."

"Shit, baby, I'm down with that. Where d'ya want to meet?"

Sighing in resignation, Geo named a bar east of the city that wasn't known to be a military hangout. "Twenty minutes?"

"See you there."

Thankfully, the traffic eased up after the transition onto the I-8 freeway, and so did a bit of Geo's tension. As he relaxed, the inevitable regret started to creep in.

What was the deal with him? One minute he'd been talking to Lani, the next swamped by a tidal wave of grief so strong he'd almost started howling. An ambush moment, she'd called it, and like any ambush, he'd immediately fought back against it. He'd won, but it was a narrow victory, and he'd managed to wound Lani during the battle.

He gripped the steering wheel, his knuckles whitening. She had her own war to fight. She didn't need to be dragged into his.

After turning into the parking lot of the neighborhood bar, Geo locked his truck and strode inside. It was the type of place where people simply went to talk, and drink. No music blared in the background, there was no dance floor, just the bar counter and some tables scattered throughout, along with a pool table and dartboard.

He spotted Tariq even as the other man waved him over. Stuffing his hands in his pockets, he ambled in his direction, smirking at the sight of the vodka shots lined up on the table in front of one of the empty chairs.

He dropped into the seat and downed three of the shots in quick succession, welcoming the burn. "Ah, thanks, I needed that."

"I could tell." Heavy-lidded topaz eyes traveled slowly over Geo's face. "I've missed you, *habibi*."

At the sound of the Arabic word, more memories rose to the surface—of raw need, brown skin slick with sweat, begging whispers in a velvety mixture of languages breathed in his ear…

Geo downed another shot. Tariq lifted an eyebrow, although he didn't say anything, just poured him a beer chaser from the frosty pitcher in front of him. They studied each other over the rims of their glasses.

Lean and wiry, with black hair and those unforgettable eyes, Tariq Aimen—although Geo was sure that wasn't his real name—worked for one of the alphabet agencies in their counterterrorism unit. He spoke English, Arabic and Spanish with flawless accents, and was able to morph in and out of various personas like a snake shedding its skin. They'd met in Afghanistan on a long-ago op, and added benefits to their friendship during a long, drunken night in Germany.

"So what're you doing in San Diego?" Geo asked, leaning back in his chair and kicking his legs out.

Tariq mirrored his pose, his long fingers cradling his own beer glass. "Eh, following up on a case I was working way back in my narcotics days." He shrugged. "Overseas, I'm mujahid. In the States, I'm just a cop."

Geo drank steadily as they caught up, and he was drifting in a most pleasant haze when he felt Tariq's foot nudge his, then slide discreetly up to stroke his calf. Their eyes met.

"It's been a long time," Tariq murmured. "Spend the night with me. I'll make sure you get on your plane."

The pleasant haze sparked into a flame of desire, which almost immediately fizzled out. Geo cleared his throat. "Don't think I'd be good company tonight, T."

Disappointment flitted across Tariq's face even as Geo wondered at himself. Not only was Tariq a satisfying lover, he was a good friend, and Geo enjoyed spending time with him. Besides, booze and sex had *always* been his favorite training trip send-offs. What the hell was the matter with him?

Tariq's foot fell away. "Maybe next time."

In the sudden awkwardness, Geo mumbled, "I'll get another pitcher," and stood to weave his way toward the bar. As he did, a beefy white guy bumped into him.

"Excuse me," they both muttered, and when Geo glanced at his face, saw that he was wearing a black ball cap, nothing special, except for the words stitched across it: SEAL Team M4.

White-hot anger instantly shot through him, the intensity of it making him shake. The guy continued on to sit at the bar, an attractive blonde woman soon joining him.

Geo ordered the beer and picked his way back toward his table. "Did you see that douchebag's hat?" he demanded, plunking the pitcher down with a slosh.

"Yeah. Team M4. Gotta love those *Call of Duty* wannabes, man."

"Love them?" Geo's voice rose. "That's some stolen valor shit, T." He poured himself a glass of beer and drained half of it in one gulp.

"Eh, he's harmless. Let him have his fantasy."

Geo wanted to let it go, but found his gaze darting back to the man and his date again and again. They were sitting close together, the woman squeezing his biceps admiringly as if measuring the muscle.

"Fucker's misrepresenting himself to get in her pants," he grated, then shoved his chair back and stalked toward the couple.

"Geo, wait—"

Before Tariq could stop him, Geo was tapping the guy on the shoulder. "You're a SEAL, huh?"

The guy puffed up his chest. "Sure am." Smirking, he turned on his stool and propped his elbow against the bar top.

"Dude, that's pretty cool," Geo gushed. "You been in the shit?"

Taking a swig of his beer, the man said, "Oh, fuck yeah, I have. Afghanistan, Iraq. Top secret missions." He glanced around, then said under his breath, "My kill count's in the thousands. Way more than Chris Kyle's."

The anger in Geo's blood exploded into full-blown boil. "Really."

Suddenly, Tariq was there, gripping his arm. "Easy, bud. He's just some dumbass trying to boost his self-esteem."

"I actually know some team guys myself," Geo went on as if Tariq hadn't spoken. "Which BUD/S class were you?"

The man's gaze flickered a tiny bit, but he tried to

bluff it out. "Well, you know, the Class of 2002. Went in right after 9/11."

"Class of 2002, huh?" Geo said loudly. "I thought BUD/S classes had *three*-digit numbers. Learn something new every day!"

By then the guy had caught on that Geo might be the real thing. He paled, stammering, "Hey, look, dude. I was just joking."

Geo kicked the bottom of his barstool. "You lying sack of shit."

"That's enough." Tightening his hold on Geo's arm, Tariq tried to ease him away. "You humiliated this asshole in front of his date." He nodded his head toward the woman staring at them, wide-eyed. "He's learned his lesson, I think."

Jerking his arm free, Geo growled, "This piece of trash is impersonating a brotherhood he doesn't have any right to even *think* about, much less pretend to be." He grabbed the guy by the front of his T-shirt, yanked him to his feet and shook him hard. "You think it's funny to brag about kill counts? You think it's cool to pretend to be something you're not, compare yourself to Chris Kyle? How about other SEALs who died? You gonna bring up their names, too, you fucking loser?"

Geo was shouting now, and the guy put his hands up. "C'mon, man," he babbled. "I was just trying to impress a lady. Didn't mean nothin' by it, no disrespect, I swear."

"Fuck you and your *no disrespect*. How about we step outside?" Geo swung the man around and shoved him toward the door, only to find his path blocked by one of the bartenders wielding a baseball bat.

"I'm about to call the cops, buddy. Let him go."

Tariq grabbed his arm again. "George, knock it the fuck off," he whispered urgently. "I can't be picked up by the cops, you know that."

The words bounced off Geo's rage like water on Teflon. He let out a bitter laugh when the poser scuttled around behind the bartender. "Fucking coward," he sneered. "A real SEAL would stand and fight."

"Okay, no one's gonna fight," the bartender grunted. "And you need to leave. Now." He planted his legs wide, brandishing the bat, his face glistening with nervous sweat.

"What? You're kicking *me* out?" Geo snarled through clenched teeth. "*He's* the asshole!"

"I'm *asking* you to leave before there's any more trouble." When Geo took a step toward him, the bartender raised the bat to his shoulder.

"Goddammit, George!" Digging his fingers hard into his biceps, Tariq dragged him across the bar and through the door. "Sorry!" he called back over his shoulder. "We're leaving."

Once outside in the parking lot, Tariq shoved him away. "You came *this* close to getting us both arrested," he snapped. "What the actual fuck? If anyone runs my prints, man, my cover's blown to hell."

Geo wanted to care, but the rage coursing through him hadn't abated. When he caught sight of the wannabe SEAL hovering in the doorway to the bar, gloating, he charged toward him. "What're you looking at, dickstain?"

As he drew closer, several of the bar patrons aimed their phones at him and started recording. Tariq saw them at the same time. "Fuck, I'm out," he hissed, and melted away into the darkness, leaving Geo alone.

Spreading his arms wide, he faced the crowd. "If anyone wants some of this," he yelled, "come and get it!"

Despite the fact that Geo was intoxicated and outnumbered, when some dude—*his* balls firmly in a bottle—took a swing at him, the fight was on. Grunts and shouts, the smack of fists on flesh, along with the high-pitched screams from the onlookers, all coalesced into a maelstrom of sound and exhilaration that buffeted Geo like the winds of a hurricane.

In the moment, his only goal was survival. He didn't have to think about Lani, or Tariq, and how he'd disappointed them. He didn't have to think about *anything* that hurt, especially Cade and that stupid bet, the bet that'd ended up carrying Geo through BUD/S and into a career most men could only dream of.

Most of all, he didn't have to think about the fact that while he owed Cade everything, when Cade needed *him* in return, Geo'd been nowhere to be found.

Crack!

The lucky punch caught him directly in the jaw, and as he crashed to the ground, as his vision filled with flashing blue and red lights, then dimmed, he thought, *"How much longer can I go on like this?"*

Then everything went black.

"Let's go, Monteverdi."

The metal door whirred as Geo pushed himself up from the hard plastic bench. He waited for the detention officer to cuff his hands in front of him, then shuffled next to him down the hallway where they were buzzed through yet more sets of metal doors. At last the uniformed man unlocked the handcuffs and pointed toward a counter. "Go get your personal property."

As he processed out, he could see his troop's command master chief, Alex Cairel, pacing in the waiting room on the other side of the bulletproof glass. The officer handed Geo a manila envelope containing his wallet, phone and keys.

"You're free to go."

One more metal door, and then Geo was facing Alex, a tall Filipino man with colorful tattoo sleeves on his arms and a thunderous look on his face. "What the fuck, dude?"

Geo knew better than to say anything as they made their way outside to Alex's SUV.

Alex railed on. "You're the last guy I'd expect to get arrested in a fucking bar fight. Jesus *Christ*."

The drive was made back to the bar in a miserable silence. Alex pulled up next to Geo's truck, but before Geo could get out, he ordered, "Wait."

Geo froze with his door halfway open.

"I know you went through a lot with your last platoon," Alex said quietly. "I'm wondering if you're dealing with it."

Swallowing hard, Geo croaked, "Yeah, I'm—"

"Because I don't think you are," Alex interrupted. "When you first came on board, I talked with your former CMC. He told me you refused to see the Navy psychologist they sent over after Barlow's death."

His gut churning, Geo let out a bitter snort. "That guy was a fuckin' joke, Master Chief. He wasn't there to help us, he was there to satisfy his own morbid curiosity about what happened."

Painful memories flooded him, of how the psychologist's questions in their group session had focused on what everyone saw and heard, and what they thought Cade was feeling the moment he pulled the trigger.

"Who cares? The dude's dead!" Geo had wanted to shout. "*We're* the ones who need help now!" But he didn't shout it. Instead, he'd clamped his lips shut and stared at the toes of his boots. Afterward, when the guy tried to set up one-on-one appointments with the platoon, Geo had refused to go.

He glanced over at Alex in time to see his face soften.

"Look, I get it. Guys like us aren't programmed to ask for help. I'm not saying it's easy, or that I'd be first in line myself. But I want you to know that the leadership of this task unit is as committed to your mental health as we are to the physical side. We're here for you, George, so come to us."

Yeah, right. Sure. And have the guys think he was weak, or that he considered himself worse off than anyone else. They *all* had shit to deal with. He wasn't special.

"Thanks, Master Chief," Geo managed. He paused. "Am I, uh, still getting on the plane?"

Alex nodded as he clapped him on the shoulder. "You'd *better* be on that fuckin' plane. See you in a few hours."

After he'd driven off, Geo leaned against the bed of his truck, hands stuffed in his pockets. He shivered in the cool night air, jaw throbbing, his head aching from the effects of too much alcohol and too little sleep. God, what a fucking mess.

Tilting his head back, he stared at the predawn sky. His life choices really sucked ass. If he'd accepted Lani's invitation, none of this would be happening. Instead, he was hung over, beat up and lurking in a deserted parking lot at four in the morning.

At least the bar had declined to press charges, since there hadn't been any damage done and he'd been the only one injured. He reached up to probe the bruise on his jaw, wincing in both pain and shame.

Tonight he'd acted like the worst kind of thug, accosting and intimidating someone who clearly wasn't a threat. A douche and a liar, for sure, but not a threat. In that moment, with his anger raging out of control, he'd thought it okay to set Tariq's safety aside in order to "expose" an asshole and "save" a woman who hadn't asked to be saved.

All because he'd been looking for a fight. Any fight. *I'm sorry, Tariq. I'm sorry, Lani.*

On a tidal wave of remorse, Geo texted them both. He stuck his phone in his pocket not expecting any reply, and when it buzzed loudly, it startled him so much he jumped. Heart pounding, he pulled it back out and stared at the screen.

Believe me, I've my share of ambush moments. No apology necessary.

Geo pinched the bridge of his nose, Lani's gentle understanding making his tired eyes burn. Then he sucked in a deep breath and typed, I don't know how to deal with them. How the fuck do you deal with them?

A pause. By letting them happen. There's no cure, no way to avoid them, so instead of seeing them as something to run from, I'm learning how to just let them happen.

"Goddammit," Geo ground out, suddenly wishing he hadn't started this. He didn't *want* to let them happen, he wanted them to leave him alone, to stop making him angry, to stop *hurting*.

Before he could figure out a way to put a breezy end to the conversation, his phone buzzed again. Since Tyler's death, even the smell of hot chocolate makes me cry. The other day I was getting a tea at Starbucks when the girl in front of me ordered some. I immediately teared up, and then it hit me. What if my child wants it someday? Am I going to cry every time? Refuse to make it? Fall apart? So I made myself stay in line, made myself smell it. Made myself remember.

A giant fist squeezed his chest.

Tyler fixed it so carefully that day, just the way I liked it. That whole last hour of his life, even as he planned to end it, he took care of me. He made sure I felt loved, and with that hot chocolate, he was also saying goodbye.

A ragged sob escaped from his lips, a single tear tracking its way down his cheek. "Dammit, asshole," he berated himself, dashing the back of his hand over his face. "You will *not* do this."

Choosing to see hot chocolate as love instead of the precursor to horror is helping me and honoring my brother. Does that make sense?

Geo wanted to reply, but his fingers were shaking so badly he couldn't type. He was about to put his phone away when it buzzed one last time. I know it's not easy. I know I'm at a different point in my grief journey than you are, but if you want to talk, I'm here, okay? Always.

Lani followed up the text with a heart emoji, and a sudden warmth cut through Geo's numbness. Thank you.

He slipped his phone in his pocket and swung up into the truck, then dropped his forehead to the steering wheel. Fuck. Once again, he'd managed to spew all over this amazing woman he was coming to admire more and more each day.

With a long exhale, he sat up to turn on the engine. He did have to admit he felt better, though, stronger, less brittle, as if a valve had been opened to release some of the pressure building inside him. What the fight hadn't managed to do, a simple understanding conversation had.

You shouldn't dump on her, though. You should find a professional.

Geo's jaw tightened as all of his tension came roaring back. Right. No matter what Alex said about support, anyone in the teams who openly sought mental health services would immediately be taken out of the deployment rotation. He'd be sidelined and forced to watch his brothers go to war without him.

Hard-earned trust would be lost. He'd have to prove

himself again, prove that he wasn't gonna crack under the strain. They'd all be watching him, waiting for him to fuck up, scrutinizing every move he made, because if he made a wrong one, people could die. In a high-risk, high-consequence environment like special operations, any sign of weakness was taken seriously and dealt with accordingly.

Geo firmed his lips. He wouldn't let his teammates down. He wouldn't let *himself* down. No way. It all ended here.

Time to get a motherfucking grip once and for all.

Chapter Eleven

Beep, beep, beep!

Lani dragged her eyes open and stared at the bed-side clock. Ugh. Much too early. Slapping the snooze button, she pulled her pillow over her head. Getting up at ten in the morning after working the closing shift at the bar was nothing but pure torture.

"My bed, too comfortable," she grumbled. "Me, too tired. Verdict? Just stay home."

Flopping out her hand, she located the phone tangled up in the covers and pulled it to her. She peered blear-ily at it for a few seconds before scrolling in search of Maura's number, thinking she'd just text her with some excuse.

The effort proved too much in the moment, and clos-ing her eyes again, she laid her phone on her chest. "In a minute," she mumbled. "I'll do it in a minute."

Drifting in a most pleasant haze, she yelped as the buzz of a new notification startled her awake again. "Huh?" she gasped. "What?" She fumbled for the phone and forced herself to focus on the message.

The name on it said Geo.

Completely awake in an instant, Lani pushed to sitting and plumped her pillows up behind her, heart thudding painfully. Geo was contacting her? In the weeks since their impromptu text therapy session, she hadn't heard one word from him. She'd agonized over it, considered calling him, but something deep down told her not to push it.

Why the text now? She took a deep breath. Well, there was only one way to find out.

"Oh, my God!"

It was a picture of Bosch, a soaking wet and sudsy Bosch. He gazed directly into the camera, the accompanying text reading, Bath day for me, meeting day for you. If I can do it...

She clapped her hand over her mouth, a delighted giggle welling up in her throat. The dog's expression was one of a long-suffering stoicism, his dark eyes stony, frothy white suds piled high between his ears like a unicorn horn.

The incongruity of Bosch's toughness with the playful suds had her full-on laughing, and before she knew it, she was swinging her legs over the side of the bed and heading for the shower.

She found herself grinning through the whole of her morning routine. Geo hadn't forgotten. He'd promised her an accountability call, and he'd delivered, in a way that still managed to respect the boundaries he'd needed to set. With one silly picture, he'd made her laugh, and most importantly of all…she was up and out of bed.

An hour later, juggling a plate of raw veggies with the shishito pepper dip she'd made the day before, Lani slipped behind the wheel of her car. She set the plate on the passenger seat and snapped a pic of it, texting it to "Bosch" with the words, On my way to the meeting with goodies!

A few seconds later, a string of paw print emojis popped up, followed by one of a fist. The canine version of a knuckle bump? Well, she'd take it.

Her good mood lasted all through the drive to Coronado, only to evaporate as she parked and lingered in her car, tempted to turn around and take her ass right back home. Getting out of the car took a monumental effort, and the walk to the door seemed to take forever, every step leaden, like slogging through quicksand. As she reached for the pull handle, the door swung open to admit her.

"Hello, my dear." Maura's face held a reassuring smile. "Welcome."

Clutching the hors d'oeuvres in front of her, Lani burst out, "But I don't want to be here."

She'd tried a grief group not long after Tyler's funeral, and all it'd managed to do was re-traumatize her all over again. A light touch on her arm cut through the roaring in her ears.

"This will be a much different experience than the one you told me about," Maura said, her tone soft. "And I'm so glad you're giving us a chance. Please, come in and join us."

The room was bright and airy, with floor-to-ceiling glass panels that could be opened to let in the breeze and the roar of the ocean. A small group of people milled around a long table set up against one wall. Various crockpots emitted mouthwatering smells, and the delicious-looking selection of appetizers and desserts made Lani's empty tummy rumble despite herself.

Shyly, she approached the table and put her plate down next to where a white woman fussed with some crackers and a cheese ball.

"It turned out so lumpy," she complained, then caught sight of Lani's pepper dip. "Ooh, that looks scrumptious! Is it spicy?"

"Maybe a tad. Not like jalapeños, though." Already a little more at ease, Lani took the plastic wrap off the plate and arranged the cauliflower, carrots, snap peas and broccoli into a colorful, eye-catching pinwheel around the bowl of dip.

"All right, everybody." Maura raised her voice to be heard over the laughter and conversation. "Let me get this introduction out of the way, and then we can all dig in to our delicious food while we chat."

Lani stiffened as Maura stepped over to her and took her hand between both her own. "Friends, this is Lani, who's ten years out from the firearm suicide of her older brother, Tyler. After Tyler's death, she received no therapy, except for one generalized grief group session—" Maura paused "—that was held at a church with a clergy person facilitating. I think we all know how that turned out."

Soft exclamations went around the group as Lani was catapulted back in time to a room smelling of stale coffee and the sickly-sweet aroma of donuts.

"Suicide? That's a mortal sin!"

The young woman who'd been crying about losing her eighty-year-old grandmother to cancer glared at Lani in disgust, then moved her chair away.

"Suicide isn't catching, bitch," Lani snapped, her hands balling into fists. "Fuck off."

The woman flinched, and the minister broke in. "Tyler's soul is lost to God's mercy through his sinful act, but we can still pray for your salvation." He stretched out his hand as if to put it on Lani's head, and with a sob, she pushed it away and shouted, "Assholes! My brother is not in hell!"

She clattered up the stairs into the frigid night air, every gasping breath stabbing her lungs like a thousand knives.

Lani opened tear-filled eyes to see sorrow, as well as empathy, on every single face looking back at her. The words welled up and spilled out. "I stood outside that church and screamed, 'Fuck you, God' until the preacher came out and told me to go home before he called the police."

The woman with the cheese ball nodded. "I flipped God off at my son's viewing when someone came up and said his suicide must be part of God's plan. I said, 'Well, his plan sucks,' and stuck both middle fingers up at the ceiling."

Lani tried to hold in a laugh, but it came out through her nose as a loud snort. "Oh, shit. I'm sorry," she gasped.

Maura chuckled. "No need to be sorry. In our group, you can say, think and feel any way you want. Sometimes we laugh, sometimes we cry. We get angry, too, a *lot*, and above all, nobody judges anyone else for anything."

"During my daughter's wedding rehearsal," a different woman said, "I got so angry at my husband for killing himself and missing out on walking our girl down the aisle that I kicked over the guest book stand.

A couple of people tried to intervene, and my son-in-law told them to leave me alone."

Lani blinked back tears. "Well, I'm going to have a baby, and sometimes I feel so *cheated* over not having Tyler here, so *angry* at him. It doesn't feel right to be angry at him, but how could he leave me? Why wasn't I enough?"

"Ah, Lani. These are questions we've *all* wrestled with in regards to our loved ones' suicides," Maura said softly. "But the truth is, we're in a club that nobody wants to be in, and we're going to get through it together."

After that, everyone headed for the potluck table, and balancing their plates on their laps, they sat around in a circle, the smell and sound of the ocean backdrop soothing.

"This is beautiful," Lani ventured. "I was afraid it'd be another church basement."

Maura smiled. "I had a client once who lived in a condo in this building. He arranged for us to use this room at no cost, because what suicide survivor wants to meet in a church basement, or a conference room in a hospital? That implies there was something wrong with our loved one, or with us, when instead we're simply friends, sharing food, drink and conversation." She took a sip of her iced tea. "So, my dears, how has your story changed since we last met?"

The discussion flowed easily, and just like Maura promised, there was plenty of laughter to go along with the tears.

"As your homework assignment until we meet

again," Maura said at last, "I'd like you to think about the word *acceptance* and what it means to you."

"What does it mean to *you*?" This came from a man whose twenty-year-old daughter jumped off the Coronado Bay Bridge the morning after they'd had a bitter argument.

"Well, for me it means making peace with the unknown and accepting that I'll never know the *why* of Vincent's suicide. Ending his life was a decision Vincent made, and even if I don't agree with it, I must respect it the same way I respected the decisions he made while he was alive."

When the man's face crumpled, Maura went on gently, "But acceptance is going to look very different for you, Bruce. Maybe it's forgiving yourself for the words you said to Christie the night before she died. Maybe it's forgiving *her* for—"

"For not giving me a chance to fix it?" Bruce's voice was ragged. "For dying without letting me say, 'I'm sorry'?"

Someone handed him a tissue as Maura nodded. "Yes. Maybe that's what acceptance will mean to you, that you forgive yourself for not realizing mental illness might've been the reason for Christie's erratic behavior and drug use. That by confronting her about it that night, you were only doing what you thought was right at the time."

As Bruce sobbed, Maura glanced around the room. "For others of you, acceptance might simply be conceding that even though your loved one's life ended, yours goes on. There's no right or wrong answer here, but I can tell you firsthand, there *is* a measure of peace that comes along with identifying it."

A little while later, as Lani slipped her empty plate and dip bowl into a plastic bag to take home, Maura approached her. "How are you feeling?"

"Drained," she admitted. "But a little more grounded, I think. It does help to know I'm not alone, and I'm grateful that at least my last memories of Tyler are good ones. We didn't argue, or say awful things to each other, things that I have to try and live with now."

"Yes. I think we could all look around and very easily say to one another, 'I'm so glad I'm not *you*.'" Maura smiled. "But out of that realization grows the gift of empathy, of compassion, too. Gifts we can then use to help others, especially other suicide survivors."

She walked Lani to the door.

"As always, my dear, be a little extra good to yourself today."

Instead of heading to her car, Lani walked along the narrow path to the beach. She slipped off her sandals, relishing the cool sand between her toes.

The roar of the ocean wrapped itself around her, the thundering power behind it making her feel insignificant, yet so profoundly glad to be alive. She took deep breaths of the salty air.

"You know what I'm finally realizing, Ty? That I can miss you, and still be grateful for the path my life has taken." She closed her eyes briefly. "It's so weird to think that I'm standing here, in this moment, in this place, only because you're not."

Rhys. The military. Her baby. All of these ripple effects.

"In so many ways I love my life, too. I got to be with Rhys, and watch him grow up and become the wonderful, caring man he is now. Would he be that man today if it wasn't for you? I'm not sure."

With a sigh, she dropped to sitting in the sand and leaned back on her hands to watch the frothing waves.

"Part of the complexity of suicide grief," Maura had said, "is the realization that good things, that *blessings*, can also come from it. As hard as that is, doing our best to embrace those blessings helps honor our loved one's memory."

Lani closed her eyes and tilted her head toward the cobalt sky.

"Maybe this is what acceptance looks like to me, Ty. Learning to accept the hidden gifts your death has given me and using them to make me a better person, a better mom. Maybe it means being grateful for the path my life has taken, no matter how much I wish it still had you in it."

One lone tear slid down her cheek. "I miss you, and I'll always love you. But I think, just maybe, there's a chance your baby sister grew up a bit more today."

Pushing to her feet, she dusted off the seat of her capris and ambled toward her car, another tiny piece of the wall around her heart chipping off and falling away. Instead of scaring her this time, though, she welcomed it.

Of course there'd always be pain, and sometimes it'd be sharper than others, but maybe now it wouldn't define her. Maybe now she wouldn't be so afraid to let a little happiness in, a little peace.

Before she started the engine, she checked her phone,

and her tummy gave a flutter at the sight of another text from Geo.

"Oh, I'm sorry. From 'Bosch.'" She giggled and opened the pic. In it, Bosch had his head cocked to one side as if he was listening to something important. It said, Guess what? I jumped out of an airplane three times in a row! How was your day?

She smiled, and replied, It was a good day, Bosch. It was a really, really good day.

Later that evening, Lani rang the doorbell, her nervousness hitting fever pitch.

Inside the house, a laughing voice called, "I'll get it, Shane," and then the door swung open.

For the space of a few heartbeats, she and Devon appraised each other.

Lani tugged up the strap of her knit floral sundress, aware of how it clung to her sixteen-week baby bump and hips. In contrast, Devon wore a white V-necked T-shirt and some faded denim shorts, both of which emphasized her golden tan and lithe athleticism.

Her brown hair fell in silky waves about her shoulders, her eyes holding nothing but friendliness. "Hey. I'm so glad you could make it."

Lani gave a tremulous smile. "I'm sorry I had to cancel lunch before. It was just—"

Too much. It was just...too much.

Devon moved back to let her step inside. "No explanation needed," she said softly. "I'm happy you're here now."

Despite the nondescript appearance of the small house from the curb, the interior was warm and in-

viting, and looked recently renovated. "This is nice,"
Lani said tentatively. "So, uh, Rhys doesn't live here?"

"Nah. He still has his same apartment, so I pretty
much split my time between both places. Let me introduce you to one of my roommates."

Roommates? Lani's curiosity intensified as Devon
led the way to the kitchen, where a tall blond man stood
at the island chopping a cucumber. "Lani, this is Shane
Hovland. Shane, this is Lani, um…"

"Abuel." Lani came to her rescue. "Hey, Shane. Nice
to meet you." Her voice trailed off as a sense of déjà vu
crept over her, and Shane's stunning blue eyes widened
in recognition at exactly the same time.

"Hey, I know you," they exclaimed in unison.

Out of the corner of her eye, Lani could see Devon's
mouth drop open. "You two know each other?" she demanded. "What? How?"

"My engagement party. Shane's the dude who—"

"—fought with the cops." Shane's voice was rueful.
"That's what I'm always gonna be known as, I guess…
'The Dude Who Fought with Cops.'"

They snickered together as Devon huffed a disgruntled sigh. "That's right. Man, I think everyone in the
world was there that night but me. I missed all the fun."

"Fun, no," Shane said drily, fingering his eyebrow,
which had been split open by an off-duty cop's lucky
punch. "Memorable, definitely."

"I thought the guy you came with was gonna tear the
place apart when you got hit," Lani commented. "He,
um, wasn't happy."

With a chuckle, Shane went back to his chopping.
"Matt won't admit it, but he's pretty protective of me."

He glanced at her. "If you didn't already know, he's my boyfriend."

Before Lani could react, Devon elbowed him with a loud, "Ahem. *What* is he?"

Shane blushed. "My fiancé," he mumbled. "As of this past weekend."

"You're engaged? Whoa, congratulations! And no, I didn't know, but looking back, I should have. He couldn't take his eyes off you."

And shit, who could blame him? Despite a livid scar on his forehead that skirted the edge of his hairline, Shane Hovland had to be one of the most beautiful men she'd ever seen. His cheekbones could cut glass, his lips shapely and full, and those dimples...

"He took me totally by surprise when he proposed, because he's been telling me he doesn't feel the need to get married, you know, since it's such 'heteronormative bullshit,'" Shane said, complete with air quotes. "Typical Matt."

"What changed his mind?" Lani accepted the glass of iced tea that Devon handed her with a grateful smile.

"The fact I might be getting off active duty." Shane pointed to the scar. "Need the bennies."

With a grunt Devon reached out and whacked him on the arm. "And because he's so in love with you he can't see straight. The benefits just gave him an excuse."

Shane shot them both a killer grin. "Hey, whatever gets him to the altar, I'm all for it."

"He's making a big show of grumbling about it, but I bet he bawls like a baby when he actually says his vows." Devon glanced at Lani, a wicked light in her eye. "Five bucks says he cries."

Lani flashed back to that night at the bar. She smirked, doubting that dude would cry even if his feet were held to a blazing fire. "Ten says he doesn't."

"Ha. Done."

They bumped knuckles and then Devon gave the "sucker" cough into her fist, all to Shane's enormous amusement.

Lani glanced at his scar. "Do you mind if I ask what happened?"

She listened in horror as he told her about an RPG exploding over the gun turret he was in.

"I don't remember anything about that day at all," he said. "Woke up at Landstuhl with my head bandaged and everyone telling me how lucky I am. The piece of metal that sliced across my forehead could've taken my eyes out, or lodged in my brain. Instead it just cracked my skull and peeled me open like an orange." He grinned. "Thank God for good plastic surgeons."

After dumping the diced cucumbers into an enormous bowl of salad, Shane led the way to the back patio, where there was a small table set for two. With a flourish, he put the bowl down next to what looked like a soup tureen.

"Chicken and dumplings, and salad. Enjoy, ladies, I'm off to the gym."

He disappeared back inside the house, and Lani couldn't help but watch him go. "Wow."

She snapped her gaze guiltily to Devon, whose eyes twinkled at her. "I know, right? He's gorgeous, and also one of the nicest people you'll ever meet." She sighed. "I love him to death, which is why I'm staying with him right now. He's still recovering, and Matt doesn't want him to be alone."

"What's Matt like?" Lani asked.

"Focused, intense. A SEAL down to his soul. He and Shane complement each other beautifully." Devon laughed. "You'll see it when we're all together some-day."

At Devon's invitation, Lani dished herself up a bowl of the piping hot chicken and dumplings. She waited while Devon did the same, then blurted, "How did you and Rhys meet?" She hadn't meant the question to come out quite so abruptly, but the open friendliness in Devon's eyes didn't waver.

"Actually," she said, "I met him in Afghanistan about five years ago, during my very first op as a member of the Cultural Support Team." Her lips curved. "He was so kind to me that night, helped show me the ropes. When the mission was over, he went back to his original squadron, and I—" She shrugged, a haunted look flickering over her face. "Anyway, one day, I walked into my new platoon here in Coronado, and there he was. We just—"

Fell in love.

A pang went through Lani, but it was manageable. She nodded. "What's next for you both?"

When Devon put her spoon down, her hand trembled a bit, and that slight hint of vulnerability loosened some of the knots in Lani's chest. She was nervous, too.

"Well…" Taking a deep breath, Devon leaned forward and propped her elbows on the table. "I've already separated from the Army, so I'll be starting on my Master's in Social Work in a few weeks. My goal is to work with veteran survivors of trauma, with an emphasis on sexual assault."

"And Rhys?"

Devon's eyes widened just as a pair of big, warm hands settled on Lani's shoulders from behind. With a squeak, she tilted her head back and gazed right up into Rhys's smiling face. "Oh, my God," she exclaimed. "What're you doing here?"

Devon seemed just as surprised as she was. "Thought you'd be halfway to Florida by now, babe."

"Nah, departure got pushed back to tomorrow." Rhys squeezed Lani's shoulders once. "Thought I'd come say hi." He sounded a little tentative, as if unsure of his welcome, and Lani reached up to pat his hand.

"Well, I'm glad you did. Why don't you join us?"

The expression of relief that spread over his face made her heart ache, and as he snagged a chair from the stack next to the wall, she thought, "Devon was right. He needs to see for himself that I'm okay."

After all, he'd gone down into that basement to protect her. The instinct to watch over her was deeply rooted, and anchored in place by their shared trauma. Devon had intuited that need and worked out a way to satisfy it—by offering her friendship to Lani, no matter the risks that entailed for her own personal happiness.

Oh, how she loves you, Peanut Butter. Way more selflessly than I ever could.

She waited until Rhys was settled next to Devon, his arm slung casually along the back of her chair, before asking, "Okay. What's next for you?"

"Eighteen more months in the Air Force," he said. "Then PA school, hopefully followed by a job in emergency medicine." He grinned at Devon. "A house with a white picket fence, two-point-five dogs."

"Uh-uh. One dog."

"Aww, honey, we can't have an only dog. It wouldn't be fair to him or her."

As they bickered amicably, Lani's hand fell to her tummy. That was another facet of hers and Rhys's incompatibility, the fact he'd never wanted kids. Afraid to lose him, she hadn't wanted to examine her own feelings about that too closely.

He really is where he needs to be, isn't he? And so am I.

Everything was delicious, and as the meal went on, she relaxed even more. Devon and Rhys's easy affection spread to include her, and by the time the three of them had cleared the table and cleaned the kitchen, Lani felt like she'd known Devon forever.

She excused herself to use the restroom, returning just in time to see Rhys pull Devon into his arms. "Thank you for this. You have no idea…"

Devon reached up to cup his stubbly cheek. "Love you," she whispered. "Mean it."

The kiss they shared was achingly gentle, and Lani backed slowly out of the doorway to give them some privacy. Her eyes fell on a black-and-white picture of Matt and Shane on the beach. They were sitting side by side, Shane's arm draped over Matt's shoulders, their fingers entwined.

She smiled. The four of them were so close, bound together by experiences she'd never had and never would. She was a true outsider, a mere ex-girlfriend, not to mention a painful reminder of the past. Yet Devon's simple gesture—as well as Rhys's gratitude for it and Shane's kindness toward her—told her their friendship circle would expand to admit her, a generosity of spirit she'd be an absolute fool to reject.

Yeah, it'd suck being a fifth wheel. Seeing Rhys's happiness with someone else no doubt would cause the occasional twinge, but what a small price to pay for the chance to be a part of it all.

Lani squared her shoulders. Time to grow up a little more and accept this olive branch for the gift it was.

She slipped back into the kitchen, where Devon and Rhys were swaying together and giggling over some private joke.

"Okay, lovebirds," Lani said, amused. "Think I'm gonna take off. Been a long-ass day."

"I'll walk you out." Rhys released Devon with a kiss to the tip of her nose, then waited while Lani gathered up her things.

Devon approached her, worrying her lower lip between her teeth. "Thanks for coming," she said huskily. "I really enjoyed it."

With a reassuring smile, Lani said, "Me, too." She hesitated. "Maybe we could do it again sometime?"

Their eyes met and held, understanding arcing between them. There'd be no rivalry, no pettiness. They could both love Rhys in their own way, and maybe—someday—they'd grow to love each other, too.

"I'd like that," Devon said softly. She reached out her hand. Lani took it, and after a tight squeeze, they let go.

Outside, the cool evening air caressed Lani's flushed cheeks. She and Rhys ambled silently down the walk toward her car, parked a little ways down the street. At last he said, "Thanks for giving her a chance."

"I like her. I enjoyed myself tonight."

Rhys's voice was a little rueful. "You're being a thousand times more mature than I'd be if the situations were reversed. It's—"

When he broke off, she touched his shoulder. "I'm not about to cut my nose off to spite my face, and believe it or not, it makes me happy to see *you* happy."

"Ah, Lee-Lee." He opened his arms and she went into them, choking back a tiny sob. She clung to him as he hugged her tight. "I don't think I'd be truly happy unless you're a part of my life. I hope *you* believe that."

"I do. And same."

With a brush of his lips over the top of her head, Rhys let her go. He waited until she was safely in the car, engine started, before he lifted his hand in a final wave and turned to jog eagerly back toward the house.

All the way home, she let the memories flood her, both the good and the bad, as she closed the Lani-and-Rhys chapter of her life once and for all. Whatever memories they made from here would include Devon, and Lani's child, fresh new pages of a book yet to be written. Instead of scaring her, the thought sent anticipation tingling through her.

I think maybe, just maybe, I got this.

Once inside her apartment, she tossed her keys into the basket by the door and hung up her purse. As she did, her phone buzzed, and pulse kicking into a sudden gallop, she fished it out. The picture that greeted her made her laugh out loud.

In it, Bosch sprawled on his back, paws in the air, sound asleep.

Still giggling, she texted, Someone's tired, huh?

Someone's very tired. TWO someones, actually.

I bet. She paused, then said, Thanks for this morning. It means a lot that you remembered.

You're welcome.

And thank Bosch for me, too.

I will.

With a wicked grin, she typed, Don't tell him, but I just enlarged the pic and kissed his nose.

What?? Now I'm jealous of him! But I won't tell.

Lani's tummy gave a flutter, even as she rolled her eyes. I'd be happy to kiss your nose, too, if it's that important to you, geez.

After a delay of several seconds that felt like hours, the phone buzzed, and quivering, she opened the selfie. In it, Geo looked tired, and stubbly, his hair overly long, but his incredible eyes glowed with warmth. He pointed not to his nose, but to his slightly parted lips. The text read, Suggested kiss target.

Her own lips started to tingle. Kissing her finger, she pressed it lightly to the screen, then typed, Done.

Mmm, that was nice. A pause. Call me?

Her breath caught. She wanted to, but the emotions of the day had left her raw, her vulnerability dangerously close to the surface. In her current state, it'd be *so* easy to take Geo's light flirting as more than he intended it to be, and the last thing she wanted to do was risk their as-yet delicate friendship, a friendship she sensed they both needed right now.

Talking to him would be a big mistake.

She was just about to hit Reply and make up some excuse when the phone vibrated again.

You know what? I'm sorry. You've had a long day. Another time?

His perception warmed her, even as she sighed in a combination of relief and disappointment. Yes, please.

You got it, beautiful. Until next time.

A couple of heart emojis followed that, and groaning, Lani pressed the phone to her chest.

Fate, you're such a fucking bitch. I hate you. Why does he have to be a SEAL?

Chapter Twelve

"She likes you better than me."

Bosch cracked an eye open at Geo's disgruntled tone, then went right back to sleep.

"No comment? Thanks," Geo grumbled. "Lazy dog." On impulse he aimed his phone and snapped another pic of him, anticipating maybe texting it to Lani at some point with the caption, "Exhausted from pile-driving SEALs all day. How about you?"

That led to thoughts of her tackling some dude from behind in order to wrest his beef jerky from his hand, and the visual made him cackle all over again.

He flopped to his back on the bed, and idly scrolled through his photo album to the one of her on the beach. Oh, yeah, those gold-flecked eyes, that sexy half-smile. He traced his finger over her lips, aching with something he couldn't define.

He sighed. The sharpness of his disappointment over not getting to talk to her surprised him a bit, even as he sensed that what she needed after a difficult day was a little decompression and quiet time.

And maybe a pity-free hug, if I was around.

Sitting up again, he glared at Bosch asleep in his

cage. "But I'm not around, am I?" he said aloud. "And *you're* getting free nose kisses. I had to ask for mine."

Just then the lock on the barracks door whirred, startling him, and he glanced up as Matt pushed it open.

"Talking to yourself again?" Matt asked with a grin. "You do that a lot."

"Shut the fuck up," Geo growled, though the words were without heat. In the past couple of weeks, through rooming and working with Matt, he'd come to like him a lot. As a no-nonsense SEAL with a strong work ethic, he'd endeared himself to the entire platoon, so much so that Alex had offered him a permanent slot with them.

"You thought any more about that job offer?" Geo asked him now. "Love to see you come aboard."

"Yeah, I've thought about it." Tossing his sweaty T-shirt aside, Matt skinned off his running shorts and wrapped a towel loosely around his hips. Then he dropped to sitting on the bed next to Geo. "The thing is…"

"What?"

Matt drew in a breath. "I screened positive for Green Team."

"Development Group?" Geo blinked. "Holy shit, dude! That's great!" Of course Matt would accept the chance to join the elite SEAL Team Six, the highly mobile unit which specialized in time-sensitive missions. "Sucks to be us, but congrats!"

"I'm also getting married." Although Matt's voice sounded rueful, his face glowed with happiness. "Proposed last weekend, got down on one fuckin' knee and everything."

"Wow. Congrats again." Geo eyed him, trying to picture serious, sometimes taciturn Matt ardently asking someone to marry him. Damn. Lucky Shane. "So…?"

"So now I have a decision to make. Stay with a West Coast team, or uproot us both."

Geo winced. DEVGRU was based out of Dam Neck, Virginia, so accepting the slot definitely meant moving. "What about Shane's job?"

"That's the thing." Matt leaned forward and rested his elbows on his knees, hands clasped loosely between them. "His injuries mean going before a medical board, and if they keep him on operational status, he'll be staying on the West Coast."

"Why? Why can't he transfer to an East Coast team?"

"He could, but…" Matt sounded stressed, and frustrated. "He owns a house in Imperial Beach. His sister and brother-in-law are in El Cajon, as well as his niece and nephew. I'd be asking him to give everything up in order to follow *my* dreams, but I also don't want to start my marriage off with a long-ass separation."

"Well, as someone single, footloose and fancy-free, I got nothin' in the way of advice." Geo clapped Matt on the shoulder and squeezed. "Kinda regret proposing now, huh?"

"I should, for his sake." Grinning, Matt stood, his towel slipping perilously low. "But no, no regrets. Shane's the best thing that could ever or will ever happen to me, and I can't wait to marry him." He pointed at Geo. "Just don't tell him that, okay? I have an image to maintain. Mushy Matt is reserved for special occasions only."

"Ha. Noted."

After Matt had disappeared into the bathroom to shower, Geo stared unseeing at the dingy carpet. Screening for DEVGRU had never appealed to him— why, he couldn't say. Maybe it was the thought of living his life tied to a government cellphone on a one-hour leash. No matter what he was doing, if a DEVGRU guy was called, he had one hour to get his ass on a plane. Missions spun up, and more than half the time, they spun right back down, creating a push-pull that tended to wreak havoc on personal lives.

Nope, Geo didn't envy Matt the difficult life decisions coming up, not one bit. He sighed and hooked his nearby duffel bag with his foot, intending to drag it over and dig out some clean clothes. As he did, Matt's phone, tossed negligently on the bed next to Geo's hip, lit up.

Hey sexy. Where's that dick pic u promised?

The screen faded, then went off again.

Need it now.

Geo was reaching for the phone when it lit up one last time. J/k miss u baby. Be safe. Love u.

Choking back a laugh, he tossed the phone facedown onto Matt's bed, something that felt very much like envy coursing through him. He immediately shook it off. No way. He didn't envy Matt. Uh-uh. Matt should envy *him*, because *he* didn't have to answer to anyone, consult anyone, over the decisions he made, plus he had a contacts list *full* of people who'd request dick pics from him.

An unwilling pang shot through Geo. The "love u" part, though?

Not so much.

"Jesus, save some beer for the rest of us."

Geo paused in the act of refilling his glass. "What?"

"We all pitched in for that pony keg, and you've already had half of it." The guy met Geo's stare challengingly. "When did you become such a lush?"

"Ever since I started working with you, Lennox." A chorus of "ooohs" broke out from the other guys as Geo deliberately filled his glass to the brim. "Fuck off."

The man bristled and drew himself up to his full height, which Geo had to admit was impressive. "It's not 'Lennox' to you anymore, Monteverdi, it's 'sir.'"

Geo rolled his eyes. "Okay. Fuck off...*sir*." He finished pulling his beer, and just for shits and giggles let a goodly amount spill on the floor of the bar before he shut off the tap. Aiming a mocking salute at Lennox, he strolled away, only to be intercepted by Alex.

"Hey, George," Alex said, lips twitching a bit. "You shouldn't bait the good ensign like that."

"Why? He's a prick."

"Agreed." Alex's lips twitched even more. "But he's already put a letter of reprimand in your service record over that arrest. Another one might hurt your chances at making Chief."

That gave Geo pause. Moving from E-6 to E-7 in the Navy was a huge accomplishment, one that only ten percent of servicemembers achieved. He'd been eligible for Chief the last two promotion cycles, been passed over, and was pinning his hopes on this go-round.

"Chief's board is in four months," Alex went on, "so you gotta keep your nose clean at least till then, okay?"

He clapped Geo on the shoulder and headed over to join the boisterous group next to the pool table.

Sipping his beer, Geo leaned against the bar top, brooding. Making Chief meant a small bump in pay and a *huge* jump in status. It meant a deeper layer of brotherhood, one that could never be broken. It meant more responsibility, more respect—a respect that was far-reaching, even into the officer ranks. "Ask the Chief" was a well-known maxim, and one that any smart officer would adhere to.

Geo grimaced, his gaze tracking Lennox from across the room. Present company excepted, of course.

"What's your beef with that guy?" Matt appeared at his elbow, his fresh club soda fizzing and popping. "Who is he?"

Swallowing a gulp of beer, Geo grunted, "Lennox Parnell is everything that's wrong with the system." As Matt's brow furrowed, Geo clarified, "He's a mustang."

A mustang was a former enlisted guy who'd applied and been commissioned as an officer. The good ones took that experience and used it to make themselves better leaders. The bad ones...

"Pretty hung up on who calls him 'sir,'" Matt observed, and Geo tapped his own nose as if to say "bingo."

"Exactly. I knew him two platoons ago when he was a fuck-up E-5. How they gave him a commission..." Shaking his head in disgust, Geo drained his beer. "I wouldn't follow that guy to the shitter, much less to war. Good ol' No-Mag."

Matt choked on his sip of club soda. "Was that his nickname?"

"Yep. He was part of my fire squad during a long night of house-clearing with some Marines. When it was over, it turned out he'd accidentally ejected his magazine while breaching the first house." Remembered anger tightened Geo's fingers around his glass. "He didn't even notice, one of our interpreters did—when he found it on the ground."

"Jesus." Matt's gaze shot to Lennox. "The whole time he only had a single bullet in the chamber?"

"Yeah. The worst part? He didn't own it, but tried to blame everyone from the gun manufacturer on down to the terp." Geo grit his teeth. "I don't care if he puts on Admiral someday, he'll always be fuckin' No-Mag to me."

"Unfortunately he's also our AOIC," Matt said drily. "Not much we can do about that."

The thought made Geo shudder. As assistant officer-in-charge, Lennox would be responsible for planning some of the missions they'd conduct while on deployment.

"Just watch your back, brother," he cautioned. "Dude's gonna get someone killed someday through sheer arrogance and incompetence."

"Noted. And thanks." After bumping knuckles, Matt wandered off, while Geo continued to glare at Lennox.

Fuck, he hated that guy. Lennox knew it, too, which was why he delighted in forcing Geo to call him "sir" at every opportunity. One of these days, that asshole was gonna push him too far, and then all bets were off.

Bring it.

By midnight, the keg was empty and the rowdy pool game had finally burned itself out. Inebriated team guys sprawled around several tables pushed together, talking shop, talking trash, until someone raised his glass and slurred, "Hey! Did you know it's five fuckin' years today since Loomis bought it? Miss you, man."

"Shit, five years? 'til Valhalla, brother."

"Rest easy, Loomy."

After the initial mutters died down, someone else made a different memorial toast, and soon they were going down the line, everyone taking turns. It made Geo's gut churn, how many names there were.

"To Jon Robinson," Lennox called out. "Helluva SEAL, helluva friend."

Next to Geo, Matt stiffened, his knuckles whitening around his glass. A muscle ticked in his jaw, nostrils flaring.

Geo stared at him. Jesus. What was the story there?

Matt's stony face didn't invite any questions, so Geo glanced away, his chest hollowing out as he realized it was almost his turn to toast.

Myriad names and faces flashed before his mind's eye—guys taken too soon. They'd been men he'd looked up to, men he'd loved, men he'd gladly trade places with if he could. They were heroes, every single one of them, and Geo would miss them for the rest of his life.

But none as much as Cade.

Geo's mouth dried up, his pulse throbbing behind his eyes, all the alcohol he'd drunk sloshing its way through his veins. Why *shouldn't* he toast Cade? Cade was as deserving as anyone, his exploits legendary in the special operations medics community. Geo had seen him run through a hail of gunfire to reach the wounded, cover shattered bodies with his own as the enemy closed in…

That's what he should be remembered for, goddammit! Nothing else, and damn if Geo wasn't going to try to keep his memory alive.

"Who you got, Georgie?"

His heart thundering, Geo glanced around the group, then raised his half-empty beer glass. "To Cade Barlow—"

Before he could even get the words out, Lennox thumped his glass on the table and crossed his arms over his chest. Geo rocketed up and out of his seat. "What's the matter, *sir*? My toast not good enough for you?"

Lennox shrugged. "I don't toast cowards."

"No, only rapists." Matt's grunt barely registered over the roaring in Geo's ears.

He leaned across the table and got right in Lennox's face. "Whatever your personal feelings about his death," he hissed, "I'm toasting a friend, and what I'd appreciate is a little goddamn respect while I do so."

"Friend?" Lennox smirked, a malicious light in his eyes. "Some friend, huh, Monteverdi? That's not what I heard. I heard you egged him on—"

With a howl of rage and pain, Geo swung at him… and missed. In the next instant he was flat on his back, breath knocked out of him by Lennox's vicious tackle. Years of resentment, and contempt, burst into flame, with Geo's guilt acting like gasoline thrown on a campfire. His second punch didn't miss, slamming into Lennox's jaw with a satisfying crunch.

Lennox roared and returned the favor, and Geo's head bounced off the floor so hard he saw stars. Before he could regroup, strong hands pulled him to his feet, arms like steel bands around his shoulders.

"Let me go," he shouted at Matt and Alex, his struggles futile against their iron grip. Across from him, other guys had Lennox similarly wrapped up, and amidst the demands from the bartenders to "Get 'em outta here, *now*," they were both muscled outside.

In the parking lot, Geo broke free, but his head still rang from the blow and the beer, and he staggered. Lennox yanked against his bonds, the guys holding him fast, spittle spraying from his mouth as he bellowed, "I'll have your Trident for this! I'll fuckin' take your Trident and shove it up your *ass*!"

Still shouting, he was dragged away.

Dimly, Geo felt Matt's arm slide around his waist. He sagged against him, nausea and emotion clogging his chest, the toxic brew suddenly surging into his throat in a sickening wave that had him jerking away.

Dropping to his knees, then all fours, Geo vomited in heave after wrenching heave. Matt knelt next to him, his hand between his shoulder blades, firm and warm.

"Stop it," Geo choked. "Go away."

"No."

"God—*dammit*—"

"Swim buddies, remember?" Matt whispered. "Not going anywhere."

With his stomach finally emptied, he collapsed on his side, away from the mess. After waiting a moment to let him catch his breath, Matt coaxed him to standing and helped him to a nearby bench.

The platoon's medic jogged over and crouched at his feet. "You hit your noggin pretty hard, Geo. I'm worried you might have a concussion."

Gut still churning, Geo submitted to a quick exam, his head drooping as the medic gave Matt instructions on what to look for during what remained of the night. "Keep a close eye on him, and call me if he vomits again."

"Roger that."

After the medic had gotten up, Alex took his place. "You know Parnell's gonna call for a Trident review board," he said without preamble.

"I know." Geo pinched the bridge of his nose and swallowed hard. "What are the chances he'll get my bird pulled?"

After all, he'd swung first. He'd let his anger get the best of him, and now Lennox could end his career. With Geo's Trident yanked from him, he'd be sent out into the fleet, his life as a SEAL over.

Oh, my God. What have I done?

"We'll figure something out," Alex said softly. "I'm gonna sleep on it, so let's meet with the El-Tee in the morning, okay?"

At Geo's miserable nod, Alex squeezed his knee and stood. Matt turned to Geo. "C'mon, bud. Let's get you home."

Home? Geo's eyes stung. Yeah, right. Another transient barracks in yet another city—white walls, industrial-grade linoleum, bleach-scented sheets, lumpy pillows. Some home.

They were silent as they trudged down the sidewalk, Matt not touching him but sticking close in case he stumbled. Once in the room, he sat on the closed toilet lid while Geo showered.

"I'm fine, Matt," he croaked at one point. "Really."

Matt shook his head stubbornly. "Swim buddies," was all he said.

"You gonna crawl in bed with me, too?" Geo kept up the grousing as he pulled on some boxer briefs and yanked back the covers. He curled up on his side, his back to Matt.

Matt didn't say anything, just filled a glass with water and put it on the nightstand, his hand coming to rest briefly on Geo's shoulder. The comforting touch brought more tears rushing to his eyes. He choked them back, his head throbbing, and listened to the quiet rustle as Matt undressed and slipped into his own bed.

"I'm here if you need me," Matt said quietly, then switched off the lamp, plunging the room into darkness, except for the soft glow of his phone. He wouldn't sleep, Geo knew—he'd stay awake in order to check on him periodically, a swim buddy to the core.

"I'm sorry," he mouthed into his pillow. *I'm sorry, Matt. I'm sorry, Cade. Oh, God, I'm so fucking sorry.*

To his horror, an audible sob broke from his chest. He stiffened, but Matt didn't rush to his side or demand to know what was wrong.

"Do you want to talk about it?" he asked, and when Geo croaked a "No," he murmured, "Okay. I'm here if you do."

"Thanks, bud," Geo managed, burying his face in

his pillow. How could he ever talk about the night Cade died, what he'd seen? What he'd done?

Or not done.

Suppressing another sob, Geo twisted his fists in the pillow, trying not to gasp under the weight of the grief and remorse crushing him. He'd had a chance. For one brief moment in time, he'd had a chance to stop the course of events that'd led to Cade eating that bullet.

But he hadn't.

And living with that was proving to be the hardest thing he'd ever done.

Chapter Thirteen

"We've given this a lot of thought, George."

Still weak and shaky, his head pounding like a bitch, Geo stood at attention in front of Alex and the officer-in-charge, a newly minted lieutenant not long out of the Naval Academy. Like all Academy grads, the lieutenant carried himself with the sort of polish that made Geo think of a politician.

A lot of the enlisted guys distrusted him for that, but Geo saw a thoughtful, deliberate man underneath the Academy veneer. In his opinion, the dude would make an outstanding leader someday, so Geo'd done his best to ease the lieutenant's transition into the platoon.

Would that act of support and loyalty pay off now? He couldn't tell by the expression in the lieutenant's eyes, which rested on Geo's face with their now-familiar coolness. "Ensign Parnell is already pushing for a Trident review board," he said quietly. "This incident—striking an officer—along with your arrest of a few weeks ago, makes me think it's warranted."

Geo kept quiet.

"Your drinking has increased exponentially. Several of your teammates have remarked on it," the lieutenant went on. He paused. "A few have raised concerns about operating with you."

The words hit Geo like a hammer blow, and he had to fight not to stagger. If his teammates were losing trust in him, wouldn't operate with him, then he was finished.

"Sir—" he choked, but couldn't go on.

The lieutenant nodded toward Alex. "Master Chief?"

After a long moment, Alex said, "Geo, if you agree to it, I think we've come up with a work-around to the disciplinary action."

"Anything," Geo burst out. "I'll do anything—"

"We're sending you home," Alex cut in. "As of today."

"What?" A fresh wave of horror weakened Geo's knees even more. "You want me to leave the platoon?"

"Temporarily."

"What do you mean, temporarily?" With all his might, Geo tried not to sound belligerent, especially since right now Alex was his only ally. "How long?"

Alex seemed to brace himself. "At least ninety days."

"*What?* Master Chief—"

Holding up a placating hand, Alex waved him toward an empty chair. "Have a seat and hear me out."

The last thing Geo wanted to do was sit, but he gritted his teeth and did it anyway. Alex propped his butt against the table next to him, arms crossed over his chest. "Ninety days. And during that time, you'll seek mental health services."

Geo dug his fingernails into his thighs. "I'll do what now?"

"You'll see someone for your post-traumatic stress."

The lieutenant took over, his gaze implacable. "Witnessing the suicide of a battle buddy isn't something you're equipped to deal with on your own. Period."

"I didn't witness it—"

"You were steps away when it happened. You heard it. You were first on the scene. Don't quibble with the semantics, Petty Officer."

Images that were burned into Geo's brain fought to materialize. In a surge of desperation, he beat them back.

"Don't do this," he said hoarsely. "I'll do better. I won't drink as much. I'll work harder—"

"Work harder at what?" Alex interrupted. "Forgetting? The last thing you need to do is stuff this down anymore, Geo. We think it's time you deal with it once and for all."

"By sending me *away*?" Now Geo didn't bother to modulate his tone. If he was going down, he wasn't gonna go down easy.

"Yes." The lieutenant's voice was equally firm. "If you were bleeding out on the side of the road, we'd do everything in our power to get you help. A mental injury is no different, and I'm not about to sit here and watch you suffer when I can do something about it."

"You're not helping me, you're—"

Consigning my career to the Dumpster. These guys will never, ever trust me again.

He clenched his fists, the starburst of pain shooting up his arm startling him. Geo stared at his swollen knuckles while the lump on the back of his head gave a sudden throb as if to say, "Remember me? You're a screwup no matter which way you look at it."

Blowing out a shaky breath, he forced himself to straighten. "So what you're saying is that I have a choice: Trident review board, or going home to see a shrink." When the lieutenant nodded, he made a bitter sound. "Basically, I'm fucked."

"Well, if you look at it that way, I guess you are."

Before Geo could respond, Alex held up a piece of paper. "This is Ensign Parnell's statement. What it contains is enough to send you to captain's mast at best, a Trident review board at worst. If we forward this up the chain of command, yeah, you're fucked. Even if you beat it, the fact it's in your permanent record means you'll never make Chief."

Geo flinched. Upward or out. If he didn't make Chief this time, his days were numbered anyway.

"If you agree to go home and seek mental health services, this statement goes in the shredder, never to see the light of day." Alex crouched in front of him. "We've cleared this with the task unit CO," he said softly. "He bought off on it with zero hesitation."

When Geo didn't reply, he went on, "Don't you get it? We're worried about you, and we care. The drinking, the discipline problems, the aggression, that's not you, and we would be remiss—as your leadership and as your friends—if we didn't say something, *do* something." He paused. "Isn't that what you tell yourself when you think about Barlow? 'Why didn't I fucking *do* something?'"

The truth of that stabbed Geo like a knife to the throat. Tears sprang to his eyes, and for once he didn't try to hide them. Seeing them, Alex reached out and gripped his shoulder. "That's a burden you shouldn't have to carry alone, brother. Not anymore." He squeezed. "Take some time, figure some stuff out, and come back when you're ready. There'll always be a place for you here."

Geo bowed his head.

The piece of paper crinkled as the lieutenant took it from Alex and slipped it into a manila file folder. "This will stay in my safe for ninety days. It's up to you what happens to it."

Dismissed, Geo stood. Alex walked him out into the hallway, where they turned to face each other.

"I just want it noted that I think this is bullshit, Master Chief," Geo managed.

"It's noted."

"I assume there's someone in Coronado I'm supposed to check in with periodically?"

Alex rattled off the name of a friend of his, and with a start, Geo recognized him as the OIC of Matt's original platoon, Lieutenant Bradley.

"They're coming off block leave in the next few weeks and starting workups, so go ahead and hook up with them for the close-to-home stuff." Alex forced a grin. "Show 'em what a badass K9 team can do, okay?"

When Geo just stared straight ahead, the smile faded from Alex's lips. "Rotator flight to San Diego leaves at 1300. Be sure you're on it."

"Aye, Master Chief," Geo said stiffly, and without another word, he turned on his heel and strode away. Once in his room, he slumped on the edge of the bed, waves of anger and despair washing through him.

How the hell had it come to this? When had he become so weak, so lacking in self-discipline, that he was letting jerks like Parnell affect him to the point he was being sent home in disgrace, his very future in jeopardy?

Geo clutched his hair. And why couldn't Cade stay in his goddamn mental box where he belonged?

"Fuck you, Cade," he gasped. "You kill yourself and now it's *my* life being ruined?"

The anger intensified until Geo was shaking with it.

"You're gone. Checked out. Outta here. And the ones who loved you the most are left holding the bag. Fuck you!"

The pressure inside him built. Fighting the urge to scream, or punch the wall, he finally picked up a heavy boot and flung it across the room with all his strength.

Crash!

It hit the doorframe, inches away from where Matt now stood staring at him, frozen like a deer in headlights.

As quickly as it appeared, the anger leached away, leaving Geo limp and drained. He sank to the edge of the bed and buried his face in his hands. After a moment, the mattress dipped. "I'd ask if you were okay," Matt said softly, "but I think I know the answer to that." He lifted his chin toward the black mark on the doorframe.

"Yeah. Sorry."

"It's all right." Matt hesitated. "What did Master Chief say?" He listened quietly while Geo told him everything, about being sent home, about being ordered to see a therapist.

"Obviously you're pissed about it," he said when Geo finished. "I mean, Exhibit A: the boot."

"I'm pissed at myself, mostly." Geo heaved a sigh and fell backwards on the bed. "I'm disappointed and angry in *myself*."

"For what, being human?"

Geo shook his head. "For being weak. For not setting the example."

A brief silence, and then Matt said, "Five years ago I made a promise to myself, a promise that I would never touch a drop of alcohol again. I've kept it, too, through hazing, peer pressure, even those times when I'm just fuckin' stressed and a beer sounds like heaven."

When he didn't go on, Geo rolled to face him. "And?"

"Now it's all I can think about. Like, if I drink enough beer, maybe I'll be able to forget the sound of Shane's blood splashing everywhere while I kept on driving."

Geo flinched.

"Maybe I won't think about those hours when I didn't know if he was dead or alive. Maybe it'll erase the knowledge that *I'm* the one who triggered the goddamn ambush in the first place."

His own misery forgotten at the anguish in Matt's voice, Geo sat up and gripped his shoulder. "It won't. Take it from me. It won't erase any of that."

"I know. That doesn't stop me from wanting it, though." Sucking in a ragged breath, Matt went on, "So what I need right now is an alternative to taking that drink, something that doesn't have anything to do with 'rah-rah SEALs,' 'rah-rah mental toughness,' 'rah-rah compartmentalize everything and suck it up.' I can get that anywhere in this community."

He turned to Geo.

"I need honesty. I need someone to tell me it's okay to struggle with this shit. That it's okay to maybe need help." Matt paused. "Like it or not, you *are* being an example, even if it's not the kind you thought you'd be, or the kind you *want* to be. For what it's worth, I do think it's the kind I need."

"Well, if what you need is to watch me spiral right on down toward rock bottom, enjoy."

Matt nudged him with his elbow. "I also get to watch our leadership recognize that and do everything in its power to make sure that doesn't happen. Maybe after all this, other guys who are hurting won't be too ashamed to ask for help when their time comes."

With a pat to Geo's arm, Matt slipped out the door, and long after he'd gone, Geo sat slumped on the bed, his thoughts in a tangle.

It was true. The SEAL narrative was firmly focused on mental toughness, their status as "elite" and "special." No one talked about the darkness, the brokenness. They didn't talk about the destroyed marriages, the isolation, the disconnect, or how it felt to stuff charred bits of beloved teammates into body bags and a week later come home to a world whose idea of a bad day was that their car wouldn't start.

He'd bought into that narrative, too. He'd ignored his own concerns about Cade, and convinced himself that he just needed time, because someone so capable, so larger-than-life, so *tough*, couldn't possibly be in such a deep well of agony that death would seem like the only way out.

Geo squeezed his eyes shut, the echo of that single, lonely gunshot ringing in his ears.

"Maybe after watching you..."

No. He didn't want to be anybody's trailblazer or poster boy. He wanted to stay with his unit where he belonged.

Until what, the next time you fuck up? If you can't control your anger, eventually someone's gonna get hurt. Eventually something's gonna happen that you won't be able to come back from.

He still had a chance to come back from this. As much as it sucked, if he jumped through enough hoops like a good trained SEAL, that statement from Parnell would get shit-canned and Geo could get right back where he belonged.

At last he dragged himself up from the bed and started to pack. It didn't take long, and soon he was strapped into a cavernous C-17, Bosch's travel kennel locked down at his feet.

As the ramp slid closed and the engines spooled up with a whine, Geo put everything he was leaving out of his mind and turned his focus toward what he needed to accomplish—getting back to his unit.

The problem was, he had no idea where to begin. Who should he call? A Navy psychologist? Memories of past mental health briefs welled up, and Geo shuddered. They'd been a joke, something they all had to sit through, yet even the presenters had looked bored, their message clear: "You don't really need this. You're SEALs, right?"

Geo firmed his lips. No way. Whoever he saw would have to be someone outside the Navy, yet ideally someone who also had a basic understanding of military culture. He let out a grunt. Yeah, good luck with that. He had *no* fucking idea where to start.

Right then his phone buzzed in his pocket. Geo dragged it out, a pleased warmth washing through him as he read Lani's text. Hey, Bosch and Geo, what're you up to? Hope you're out there living your best life. The message was followed by a few paw print emojis and a heart.

Geo stared at the screen. Holy fuck, was he an idiot. Maybe *he* didn't have a clue where to start, but he certainly knew someone who did. He snapped a quick photo of Bosch in his crate, and thumbs flying, replied, Heading somewhere top secret. Shhh.

Lani answered with a string of zipped-lips emojis, which made him chuckle.

You get it, don't you? You understand things about me I don't even understand myself.

A sudden aching need to see her, to be with her, swept over him. When I get to where I'm going, can we talk?

There was no hesitation. Anytime.

Geo's tension slowly leached away, and he slumped in relief. Okay. He had someone in his corner, someone he liked, someone he'd already grown to trust. Lani could help him.

He just had to be honest with her first.

"Thanks, girls!"

Lani stepped out of the SUV before turning back to wave at the driver and the two other women inside. "I had a great time."

"Love ya, sweetheart."

"Catch you later!"

"We'll do lunch soon."

After the car roared off, she ambled up the sidewalk toward her apartment, smiling to herself. Her tummy was full, her heart even more full, the happiness a low hum that made her swing her purse back and forth playfully and lent a skip to her step.

What a fantastic night.

Still grinning, she caught sight of a lone figure perched on the stairs leading up to her door, and she paused. The man sat just outside the pool of light cast by one of the lamp posts that lined the walkway, his elbows propped on his widespread knees, head down.

Unsure what to do, Lani continued to hesitate. Her apartment complex had roving security, so maybe she should call the number and request an escort before she went any further. She'd just fished her phone out to make the call when the man lifted his head.

She gasped. "Geo!"

She hurried toward him, slowing once again when she caught a clearer glimpse of his face. His eyes looked bleak, lines of misery bracketing his mouth. Stress tightened his shoulders, his fingers clenched together so tightly the knuckles were white.

Holy shit. What was going on?

Her heart pounding, Lani leaned against the railing next to him. "Hey," she said softly. "How're you?"

Geo shrugged. "I've, uh, been better."

His voice sounded scratchy, hoarser than usual, and the way he was sitting, muscles bunched as if ready to flee, warned her to keep it light. "Well, I just happened to have made a cheesecake this morning that'll knock your socks off. Wanna come inside and have some?"

A shadow of a smile touched his mouth. "Sure. If you feel like sharing."

"Oh, I won't let you hog it, buster, believe me." Holding out her hand, Lani said, "C'mon."

She pulled him to his feet and, entwining their fingers firmly together, led him up the stairs. Once inside the apartment, he headed for the bathroom while she flipped the lights on and started some soft music playing.

She was busy slicing the cheesecake when Geo reappeared, the neckline of his T-shirt damp as if he'd splashed water on his face. Gesturing toward the fridge, she said, "Help yourself to a beer if you want."

"No. No beer."

He sounded so adamant that she paused. "Okay. Coffee?"

After a long, slow exhale, he nodded. "Yeah, that sounds good. Thanks. I'll make it."

She pointed out where everything was, then left him to it, her mind racing. What was going on? From what she understood, he was supposed to be headed to Langley right about now for his CIA "workshop." Why was he home, so visibly upset?

And why had he come to her?

Her instincts still screaming to keep it casual, Lani said, "Lemme tell you about *my* day."

Busy scooping out the coffee, he didn't answer, but she saw the stiffness in his shoulders ease a bit.

"Remember the night we met?"

Geo threw her a wry glance. "As if I could forget." He pantomimed someone puking.

"Not that part," she grumbled, secretly delighted in the glimmer of humor. "I meant the part where I told you that I'd lost all my friends, the team wives."

He turned to face her, coffee abandoned for the moment. "Yeah, I remember. Did something happen?"

"Hell, yeah, something happened." She leaned in close, and lowering her voice dramatically, hissed, "I... stopped feeling sorry for myself."

"Yeah?"

"Oh, yeah. So get this: the other night I was bored and lonely, my self-pity game *super* strong. 'Boo-hoo, poor me. I don't have any friends anymore. They don't call me. Why don't they call me?' blah, blah, blah." She paused. "You know what I realized?"

He raised an eyebrow. "That the phone works both ways?"

"Yes!" She punched him on the arm in her enthusiasm. "If they won't call me, maybe I should try calling them, right? So I screwed up my courage and called this one girl, asked if she wanted to go to dinner sometime. Not only did she say yes, she brought a bunch of our other friends with her!"

"Oh, wow, that's great."

"We *totally* cleared the air. I mean, their husbands still have to work with Rhys, so they felt caught in the middle. No one knew what to say to me, or how to act, so they told me it seemed easier just to drift away." She shrugged. "I get it. It was pretty much the same when Tyler died. Hardly anyone stuck around."

At those words, the spasm of pain that crossed Geo's

face made her reach out to touch his shoulder, but before she could say anything, he spun away and snatched up the coffee carafe. "Gotta finish this," he muttered. "'Scuse me."

Lani moved aside so he could fill the carafe with water, then turned back to her own task.

Geez. Getting this dude to open up was like pulling teeth.

She sensed he needed to, though—that he *wanted* to. She also knew damn good and well what these guys were like. Vulnerability had no place in their world. They'd die before admitting any sort of weakness, their ability to push past their limits honed to an art form.

With all that in mind, she resolved to be patient.

When the cheesecake was plated, sliced strawberries scattered over the top, she carried it all into the living room and switched on the TV. After a moment he joined her, mug of steaming coffee in hand, and they ate their cheesecake accompanied by the laugh track to an episode of *Friends*.

Geo still didn't speak, although he seemed to enjoy the dessert. Lani took their empty plates to the sink and, returning to the living room, propped her feet firmly on the coffee table. "Go on. Get comfortable," she ordered. "Feet on the furniture, unbutton your pants, rip a giant belch, whatever."

He rolled his eyes, but he pried off his sneakers and crossed his socked feet next to hers. Delighted with her small victory, she nudged his toes. He nudged her back, setting off a mini foot war, which ended with Geo's big toe caressing her instep in surrender.

At the touch, she shivered, nipples tightening, goose

bumps springing up everywhere. She glanced at Geo to see if he noticed, but he just sighed and sank back into the couch, coffee mug resting on his stomach. As the *Friends* episode ended and the next one started, his eyes drifted shut, his breathing going long and slow.

Lani rescued the mug just in time, a lump rising into her throat.

I wish you could talk to me, she said to him silently. I wish you could let yourself trust me. Whatever it is, I'm here.

Even as she watched, he startled himself awake with a snore, so she took a chance. Grabbing up a small throw pillow, she put it on her thigh and urged him to lie down.

Blearily he did, head on the pillow, one leg crooked against the back of the couch, the other one stretched out, foot on the floor. She stroked his hair, which was soft and springy. She was combing her fingers through it, sifting it gently, when suddenly he murmured, "No wonder Bosch likes this so much."

"Whoops." She gave a self-conscious giggle, hand stilling. "I guess I *am* sort of petting you, aren't I?"

"Yeah. But don't stop," he said hoarsely, his voice a tiny bit ragged. "Please."

"I won't." Her eyes stinging, she ran her thumb lightly over his forehead, fingers delving back into his hair. "I won't. Shhh. Go back to sleep."

It's okay to trust me, Geo. It's okay to let me in.

When his body finally went limp and he let out another soft snore, she couldn't help but smile.

She'd take it.

Chapter Fourteen

Something tickled Geo's nose.

He waved it away, only for it to reappear on his forehead. A damn fly. God, he hated the barracks.

Yawning, he cracked open his eyes, but instead of drab white walls and industrial furnishings, the soft light coming in through the windows revealed pictures scattered everywhere, a floor lamp with a funky shade…

"Oh, shit!" Awareness returned in an instant, and he jackknifed to sitting, the blanket covering him dropping to the floor.

Lani's apartment. Jesus, he fell asleep on her!

With a loud groan, he flopped back down on the couch. Fucking hell, he was such a tool. Not only had he shown up uninvited, he'd probably scared her the way he'd been lurking in the dark like that. Then after she'd graciously asked him in, he'd eaten her food, refused to talk—the whole reason he'd come here in the first place—and finally passed out cold with his head in her lap.

What the fuck? True exhaustion, or just avoidance?

He didn't want to think too closely about the answer to that.

Finally unable to ignore the demands of his bladder anymore, Geo got to his feet and tiptoed down the hall to the apartment's one and only bathroom. When he'd finished, he paused in front of Lani's door, which was slightly ajar.

Holding his breath, Geo peeked in, catching a glimpse of long, tangled hair and one bare shoulder, the rest of her covered up by a thick gray comforter. He backed away, careful not to make any noise, and retreated to the kitchen.

The sight of their cheesecake plates in the sink brought a lump to his throat, along with the memory of gentle fingers in his hair, soothing murmurs, and a sense of peace and safety that'd enabled him to fall so deeply asleep he hadn't even felt her disentangle herself from him.

He couldn't remember the last time that'd happened, if ever.

Sighing, he filled the sink with soapy water and washed the plates and silverware. When he was done, he stood uncertainly in the middle of the kitchen, the soft ticking of the appliances the only noise.

What else could he do? She'd probably be getting up soon, and it'd be nice if—after everything she'd done for him—she could wake up to *something*.

He discarded the idea of running out to buy breakfast. Lani would appreciate the effort more than the result, homemade over store-bought every time. Geo gazed at the fridge, imagining it covered with childish creations someday—finger paintings, crayon drawings, even stick figures.

Each one would get a pleased exclamation, and a hug and kiss, before finding its place of honor amidst all the others...

He squared his shoulders. Okay, he'd cook for her. It wouldn't be amazing, but he'd try. Searching her tiny pantry, he came up with a box of pancake mix. Ah, perfect. Pancakes were idiot-proof, weren't they?

"Well, almost," he thought ruefully a few minutes later as the one he was trying to flip broke apart. "Not as easy as it looks."

"Good morning." Lani's husky voice behind him made him jump and whirl around, spatula in hand. "What's going on?"

Oh, my. In a spaghetti-strap tank and cotton pajama pants, she looked sleep-warmed and cuddly, and the sudden, overwhelming desire to take her in his arms had him spinning back toward the stove.

"Um, you know, breakfast," he grunted. "Although I'm not doing so great a job." He lifted his chin toward a nearby plate and its pathetic stack of uneven, broken pancakes, wincing when she crossed the room to look at them.

"Mmm. They don't have to look pretty to taste good, do they? I can't wait."

Despite a sneaking suspicion that she was only being polite, warmth flooded him at her approval. As he finished with the last few pancakes, she sliced some bananas and made a pot of coffee, both of them working in a companionable silence.

When they were finally seated across from each

other, Lani lifted her glass of orange juice and tapped it against Geo's mug. "Cheers."

"Cheers," he mumbled, holding his breath as she forked up her first bite. She chewed thoughtfully for a moment, then pronounced them delicious, her tone grave but her eyes twinkling.

"Thank you, Geo. What's the occasion?"

He knew she meant more than the breakfast—she meant his sudden appearance, then the way he'd clammed up and fallen asleep on her lap. Still, her demeanor was relaxed, and there was no demand to her words. That strange sense of peace and safety wrapped itself around him again.

"My platoon sent me home."

That surprised her, he could tell, but her gaze remained steady on his. "Because?"

He carefully laid his fork down and clasped his fingers together in his lap, his heart starting to pound.

I'm going to say this, and afterward, nothing will ever be the same.

"Because one year ago, my teammate killed himself. And it's all my fault."

Lani could feel the blood drain from her cheeks.

"I'm sorry I didn't tell you before," Geo went on shakily, "but I couldn't—" He squeezed his eyes shut, anguish in every line of his body, as she struggled to process what she'd just heard.

One year ago? Was he talking about Cade? Cade the bet-maker, motivator, hero and mentor?

In the next instant, she was up and out of her chair. She dropped to her knees next to him. "Breathe, Geo," she murmured, taking one of his ice-cold hands in hers. "Take a deep breath."

He did, and it sounded so much like a sob that he flinched and tried to pull away. Lani hung on to him, moving her thumb in soothing circles over his wrist. "First of all, I need you to know something, something I wish even one person had told me back when Tyler died."

His throat worked as he swallowed, his eyes still closed.

"You're not alone, okay? No matter how much you think you are, you're not. If nothing else, I want you to trust me on that." Steeling herself, she went on, "And secondly, despite what your brain is telling you, Cade's death is *not* your fault."

Immediately he ripped his hand from hers. "You weren't there. You don't know—"

"It's not your fault," she said, making her voice as firm as she could. "The responsibility rests with Cade and Cade alone."

"You weren't *there*," he repeated through clenched teeth, then surged to his feet. Afraid he was about to bolt, she stood, too, and planted herself in front of him.

"Why did your platoon send you home?"

When he shook his head, she tamped down her frustration at his stubborn reticence.

"Why did your platoon send you home, Geo?"

"Because I'm a fuck-up," he burst out. "I've been drinking a lot. Been in two bar fights the past few weeks…"

Shock roared through her, but she forced herself to sound calm. "What did your command say?"

"They ordered me to talk to a shrink. Gave me zero say in the matter, zero choice. If I don't, it's all over for me." He grimaced, jaw tight. "The problem is, I don't have a clue where to start, and I'm scared to fucking *death* I'm flushing my entire career down the toilet right now."

Despite her roiling emotions, his reluctant admission brought a flash of relief. Now they were getting somewhere. She had to keep him talking.

"Well, my support group is amazing—"

Before she could get the words all the way out, he was already shaking his head. "No groups. That kind of stuff isn't for me."

She wanted to argue, tell him that her group wasn't whatever he was picturing, but she forced herself to be patient. "How long are you in town for?"

He let out a bitter snort. "Until further notice, or until I get my shit together, whichever comes first."

"So what can I do?"

He stared at her, and then with a helpless gesture, slumped back against the counter. "I don't know, Lani. I just don't know."

The weary defeat in his voice made her heart ache. "Well, nothing has to be decided right now, does it?" she said gently. "Let's finish our breakfast, or would you maybe want to take a shower? We can talk later."

He glanced over at her, his relief at the proffered escape palpable. "A shower sounds good. Can I?"

"Of course."

She laid out some towels for him while he jogged down to his truck to fetch his duffel. Once he was safely in the bathroom with the water running, she unplugged her phone from the charger and called Maura.

She told her the whole story before saying tearfully, "I have no idea what I'm doing."

"Sounds like you're doing a beautiful job." Maura's smooth, reassuring voice wrapped around Lani like a weighted blanket. "What he needs right now is an empathetic friend, and that's exactly what you are."

"I just feel so clueless—"

"Nonsense," Maura broke in. "Whether you realize it or not, you've been modeling healthy grief work for him. That's why he came to you."

Lani told her what he'd said about the drinking and the fights.

"Well, his grief has to go somewhere, doesn't it? Anger is an easy outlet." Maura made a frustrated sound. "I'm willing to bet Geo's story is the same one I've heard over and over from servicemembers I've counseled. After a suicide, units are often dismantled, which takes away from any source of support they might find in each other. Commands don't allow surviving teammates to hold their own memorial service, sending the message that the death was shameful, something not worthy of being acknowledged and mourned."

She paused.

"I think Geo's drawn to you because you've been where he is. You're also in a unique position to understand his world, and what he needs is someone to give him permission to grieve, to let him know it's okay to fall apart."

Lani grunted. "I'm the queen of falling apart, aren't I? He's definitely in the right place."

"And you've also realized that falling apart doesn't make you weak, and that letting your grief evolve doesn't diminish your love for Tyler in any way." Maura paused again, a bit longer this time. "But, my dear, you're not obligated to put yourself through any of this. Give him my number—"

"Oh, I will," Lani broke in, "but I want to do what I can from here, too. I want to pay it forward, what I've learned. It's my way of honoring Tyler."

Lani promised to call if she needed her, and after they hung up, she stood for a long time, Maura's words echoing in her ears.

"You're in a unique position to understand his world."

Painful memories surged—of Rhys and his post-deployment nightmares, of those times he'd tried to turn to her for comfort but she was incapable of or unwilling to give it.

He went into that basement for me, and all I managed to do in return was let him down. Nothing will ever change the regret I feel about that.

She squared her shoulders. No. She wouldn't repeat her past mistakes. It was too late for her to be there for Rhys, but she could be here for Geo. She could take *every one* of the painful lessons she'd learned over the past ten years and pass them on to the man now walking in her shoes.

A man she was growing to care for more each day. Through blurred eyes, she gazed at the cold, misshapen pancakes—Geo's sweet attempt at meeting her needs even in the midst of his own distress.

She swallowed the lump in her throat. Why? Why

did she have to find him now, when anything between them would be impossible? The best thing—the *smart* thing—would be to give him Maura's number and let her refer him to other people who could help. No one, least of all Geo, would blame her for that.

As if he was reading her mind, his husky voice sounded behind her. "Lani? Do you want me to leave?"

She smoothed out her expression and turned to face him, her heart skipping a beat. He wore a clean, though rumpled, T-shirt and cargo shorts, his feet bare, hair damp. Despite his obvious attempt at stoicism, his eyes also shone with a vulnerability that tugged at her.

She couldn't abandon him now. No way.

So she summoned up her most incredulous tone. "Leave? When it's time for pancake-flipping lessons? Come here, you." Lani extended her hand to him, a quiver going through her when he took it without hesitation. "No, I don't want you to go. In fact, I'd like you to stay here with me as long as you're in town."

His eyes widened. "What?"

"Don't go to the barracks. Stay here with me." Suddenly, she'd never been so sure of anything in her life. "We can cook together, watch TV, talk when and if you want to…" She shrugged. "Maybe you'll even convince me to exercise a little. No promises, though."

Indecision had been flitting across his face, but at those last words, the mischievous look he shot her weakened her knees and stole every last bit of her breath.

"Oh, you gotta know them's fightin' words," he drawled. "No SEAL can resist a challenge like that."

"Um, hate to break it to you, but you're no match for my aversion to exercise," she fired back. "SEAL or no."

"Well, then, challenge most definitely accepted." He still held her hand, and he gave it a gentle squeeze. "You sure?"

"Totally sure." *My head is, at least. My heart? Not so much.*

They stared at each other for another few beats, and then Geo nodded. "So what's this about pancake-flipping lessons? I thought you said they didn't have to look pretty to taste good."

The tinge of indignation in his voice made her giggle. "Well, why not have both? Watch this."

He leaned against the counter nearby as she whipped up some fresh batter and reheated the griddle. In no time she had a thick stack of fluffy, perfect pancakes. "Voila."

"Hmph. You make it look easy," he grumbled as he took his seat at the table. "At least I tried."

He sounded so disgruntled that Lani wrapped her arms around his shoulders from behind in a hug. "Geo, those pancakes were the nicest thing anyone's done for me in forever. They were delicious and I loved them, okay? Every bite." She gave him a squeeze. "Thank you."

"You're welcome." Smirking, he turned his head and pointed to his nose with a questioning sound.

She bit back an answering smile. "Somehow I don't think Bosch would approve."

"Silly dog doesn't know what he's missing."

Another giggle escaped her. "Well, he doesn't get to change his mind. No nose kisses for him, he's too scary."

"He *is* pretty scary when it comes to nose kisses."

Geo paused. "I'm not scary, though, and I love nose kisses. All kisses, really."

A little shiver went through her. "Mmm, you *did* give me an alternate target once."

He shrugged. "That one's my favorite, to be honest." Despite the nonchalant tone, his pulse throbbed visibly in the hollow of his throat, and her own heart started to thud.

"I guess if that's your favorite…"

The sound of his hoarse chuckle echoed in her ears even as their lips met and clung together for several breathless seconds.

"*Definitely* my favorite," he whispered, the words little puffs of air against her cheek.

"Mine, too." She kissed him again, lingeringly, her arms tightening around his shoulders at the hot slickness of his tongue, which danced briefly along hers. When it ended, Geo took her hand and eased her around into his lap.

He linked his arms loosely around her waist as she nestled against his chest with a sigh. For several long minutes they held each other without speaking, his face buried in her throat while she stroked his hair.

Finally he croaked, "I'm sorry."

"For what?" She knew he didn't mean the kiss. "Geo, one year ago a bomb went off in your life. It's okay to need help with that."

At those words, a giant shudder passed through him.

"I get it. I've been there. I'm *still* there, in a lot of ways. It's not anything I'm ever going to 'get over.'"

His ragged breathing stilled, as if he was holding it, waiting.

"But I'm also not going to let his death define me anymore. Tyler's life and suicide were his, not mine." She paused, then said gently, "Just like your responsibility as a teammate and friend was *to* Cade—to always treat him with respect, honor and loyalty—but you were not responsible *for* him, okay? You weren't responsible for his thoughts, his actions, his happiness…"

Geo gazed up at her, his eyes liquid with a pain he had no idea what to do with. "How did you—" He broke off, his throat working as he swallowed hard, and she pressed their foreheads together.

"I started talking about it. I started sharing it with other people who'd walked in my shoes, and I didn't hold back. Realizing I'm not alone is when I took that first step toward healing—*true* healing."

He nodded, his lips tight.

Lani kissed his temple, then climbed off his lap. "Easier said than done, I know."

She watched him get to his feet and move to the sink, where he began to wash the plates, his movements sharp, purposeful, shoulders bunched.

"We were good at compartmentalizing grief before we were even adults," she thought, *"and the SEALs taught you how to become a master at it, didn't they? But all of a sudden those boxes won't stay closed."*

Sensing he was once again on the verge of bolting, Lani picked up a dish towel and started to dry, feverishly racking her brain for something to say that'd lighten the mood. A dollop of suds landed on the back of her hand, and without thinking, she flicked them at him. "Take that."

He huffed. "Oh, yeah?" Scooping up a handful of

bubbles, he plopped them on her head, where they immediately slid down her cheek, onto her chest and right into her cleavage.

His eyes widened in consternation, but before he could say anything, she patted herself dry with the neckline of her tank top. "I didn't know this was a wet T-shirt contest." With that, she dunked her hand in the sink full of water and plastered her open palm right in the middle of Geo's chest. "Now we're even."

He looked down at the soggy palm print, then back up at her. Laughing, she danced backward as he stalked toward her, until her butt was up against the counter. Geo caged her in with his arms, his body close but not quite touching hers. She gazed up at him with a smirk, a lock of wet hair annoyingly stuck to her cheek. Before she could brush it away, he reached up with gentle fingertips and did it for her.

"Beautiful girl," he murmured, his thumb lingering on her cheekbone. "I love your laugh."

"I love how you *make* me laugh." Biting her lip, Lani toyed with the hem of his T-shirt. "Are you going to stay with me?"

After a brief hesitation, he nodded, and she let out a long, slow breath. "Good. And just so you know, forcing you to talk isn't part of the deal. If you *want* to, though, I'm here."

"I want to." He tucked the hair behind her ear, his mouth looking a bit less pinched. "I know I *need* to. It's just—I have no idea where to start."

The memory of that first time walking into Maura's office washed over her, along with all of its accompanying anxiety. She forced it back, hoping it didn't show on her face. He needed her to be empathetic, cool and capable right now, not an emotional basket case.

"I know it's not easy," she said again, proud of how calm she sounded. "In fact, it'll be one of the hardest things you've ever done, not gonna lie."

He studied her for a moment, his expression smoothing out, that hint of vulnerability still in his eyes. "I appreciate your honesty. It, uh—" He swallowed. "It does help to know I'm not alone."

"You're not alone," she said fervently. "And we'll get through this together, okay?"

"Okay." Pulling her to him, Geo hugged her tight. "The sooner I can stop disrupting your life and get back to my platoon, the better, right?"

Her heart gave a painful throb. "Right."

"I think I'm gonna go pack some stuff, check on Bosch. You need me to pick anything up while I'm out?"

With sheer force of will, she managed to sound breezy. "Nah, I'm good." Pulling away from him, she rummaged in her junk drawer and extracted her spare key, which she pressed into his hand. "Make yourself at home. I'll be around most of the day." She paused. "I do have my support group tomorrow…"

"Okay." With a noncommittal sound, he stuck the key in his pocket. "See you later."

After he'd gone, Lani ran for the bathroom and her shower, where she stood under the spray and let the hot tears flow unchecked. "Fuck, what am I doing?"

Despite her best efforts, all of her old insecurities reared their ugly heads. They started hissing that she wasn't strong enough, or smart enough—that not only had she failed Tyler, she'd failed Rhys, and soon it would be Geo…

"I think you're doing a beautiful job." The memory of Maura's words echoed in her ears, drowning out the strident voices. *"What he needs right now is an empathetic friend."*

Lani leaned back against the wet tile and scrubbed her hands over her face.

"Remember, he doesn't need you to fix him," she reminded herself. "What he needs is someone to listen, and to understand. You can do that."

Feeling a bit more calm, and proud of how quickly she'd turned it around this time, she got out of the shower and dried herself off with brisk motions. She *would* do it. She'd use her pain to help Geo navigate his, and hopefully in the process find a way to give meaning to her own journey.

Wiping off the mirror, she stared at her foggy reflection.

"You'll also protect your heart at all costs, you hear me?" she said fiercely. "You know damn good and well that the minute he can, Geo's gonna walk out that door for good."

He would leave. And he wouldn't look back.

Because that's what SEALs do. Don't you ever forget it.

Chapter Fifteen

"Geo! Hey!"

Geo spun around, a jolt of surprise and pleasure going through him at the sight of Matt's welcoming smile. "What? You're here, too? Why aren't you at Langley?"

They bumped knuckles as Matt said, grinning, "Some of the CIA instructors got re-tasked at the last minute, so Master Chief gave us the option of coming home for a few days if we wanted." He turned to the blond man at his side. "This is the K9 guy I was telling you about, babe, the one whose dog almost took a chunk out of my ass?"

"Oh, yeah. That was funny." The man shot Geo a devastating grin. "I'm Shane, by the way. Matt's fiancé."

Dazzled almost speechless by Shane's movie-star good looks, Geo mumbled a greeting as they gripped hands in a tight shake.

Holy. *Shit*. No wonder Matt wanted to come home. Geo'd be on the first plane, too. Damn.

"Trust me, this dog is so badass," Matt was saying

enthusiastically. "Are you busy right now, Geo? Can we take Shane to meet him?"

"*He* might not be busy, but *I* have that brief in ten minutes," Shane reminded him. "Some other time."

They started walking again as Geo fell into step beside them.

"Shane's been offered a billet as a BUD/S instructor until his medical board meets," Matt said. "Second Phase." He grunted. "Talk about a destroyer of dreams."

Geo shuddered. It was true. So many guys survived Hell Week only to fall victim to Second Phase's pool competency, arguably the most challenging training evolution in all of BUD/S. He'd squeaked through it himself by the skin of his teeth, the specter of Cade losing that bet hanging over his head like a sword waiting to fall...

He must've made some kind of noise, because Shane glanced at him curiously. Geo cleared his throat. "Right. Second Phase is *not* a fun memory."

"It ranks up there as being some of the worst weeks of my life," Matt agreed. "This clown aced it, though."

"What can I say? I'm comfortable in the water." Shane rubbed his hands together theatrically before saying, "In all seriousness, I'm eager to get a glimpse of BUD/S from the inside out, and now the guy I'm replacing can get back to operational status a few months sooner. It's basically a win-win."

Geo and Matt parted ways with Shane at the entrance to the Naval Special Warfare Center, then ambled along the sidewalk in the direction of the kennel.

"So how are you doing?"

At Matt's soft query, Geo shrugged. "Okay, I guess.

I've been talking to a friend who's a suicide survivor herself."

"Yeah? You think it'll help?"

He thought about Lani's quiet empathy, her understanding, even in the face of her shock at the true nature of Cade's death. "I think it will, given some time. I'm gonna be staying with her at her place."

"Really? That's great." Matt looked like he was debating with himself, then said, "I'd, uh, been planning to talk to Shane about you staying with *us* for a while. Didn't want you to be alone," he added. "Those barracks are depressing as fuck even in the best of times."

Geo blinked, warmth sprouting in his chest, but before he could say anything, Matt went on, "Swim buddies, you know? Least we could do."

"Thanks, Matt." Geo elbowed him in the side. "You're a great swim buddy."

An embarrassed but pleased look flitted over Matt's face, and suddenly, Geo found himself offering to bring Bosch by their team room to meet anyone else who was interested.

"It's my opinion that every troop should have a multi-purpose K9." He grinned. "Lemme pitch it to your lieutenant."

"Ha. Done." Matt dug his phone out of his pocket, thumbs flying. "Just texted the El-Tee. I'll let you know."

After he'd trotted off to run his errands while he waited for Shane, Geo headed for the kennel, where he leashed Bosch up and took him for a punishing run. Forty minutes later, dripping with sweat, endorphins coursing through his blood, he crouched to give him a drink. "Exercise is the only therapy I need, right, boy?" he panted. "Fuck that psychologist shit."

Or the support group. The thought of walking into a room full of wild-eyed, tearstained strangers made him queasy. He didn't want to hear their stories, or relive their pain, or feel like a bug under a microscope. Besides, SEALs weren't supposed to need their hands held, weren't supposed to be perceived as failures who couldn't figure their shit out on their own. That went against everything he'd learned, everything he stood for, and the last thing he wanted to do was expose his weaknesses.

Tamping down a flicker of discomfort, he said to Bosch, "You know I don't mean Lani, right? It's different for her. She was a *kid*."

Bosch didn't have an opinion to offer, just gazed at him with his dark, impassive eyes.

"It's fucking different, okay?"

After getting back to the kennel, Geo dug out his phone and found a text from Matt.

Meet us at the O-course!

He slipped Bosch's muzzle on, grabbed a small duffel of equipment, then headed over to the SEAL obstacle course, a sadistic collection of apparatus that had sent many a BUD/S candidate stumbling to ring the infamous bell.

Once there, Matt introduced him to Lieutenant Bradley. "Okay, convince me," he said, grinning. "And if you can fit in a workout for us somewhere in there, all the better."

His blood racing with anticipation, Geo faced the semi-circle of men waiting expectantly. A few of their expressions held smirks, a few trepidation, and a couple more excitement.

At his feet, Bosch sat quietly, his ears pricked.

"Okay, here's how it's gonna go," Geo said. "I'll pick him up and hand him to you. You hold him for a minute, then hand him back to me. Do *not* hand him off without giving him back to me first. Got it?"

A few murmured "Checks" went around the circle, and then Geo bent his knees and picked up Bosch, one arm under his chest and the other under his hindquarters. He approached the first man in line, a short, muscular Black guy.

"This is Bosch. What's your name?"

"Aaron." With a confident grin, Aaron took Bosch from him, held him for a minute, then passed him back to Geo.

"What's the purpose of the name shit?" a blond white man next to Aaron asked almost belligerently. He was one of the apprehensive ones.

"Introducing yourself is only polite. Plus, this is all to indicate to Bosch that I trust you, so he should, too. Your name?"

"Mullet."

"Okay. Nicknames work, too. This is Bosch."

Mullet took Bosch gingerly, screwed his nose up in distaste and immediately pivoted to hand him off to Matt, who raised his hands and backed away.

"Whoa. Way to follow directions there, asshole."

"Take him. Take him." He thrust Bosch at Matt, who had no choice but to take him or else Bosch would fall to the ground.

A few grunts and mutters of "Weak" went around

the circle. Mullet wiped his hand over his forehead and glared at them.

"I had a bad experience with a dog as a kid, okay? Fuck all y'all."

Geo took Bosch from an apologetic Matt, shooting him an "It's okay" look.

"The point here isn't to force you to like dogs," he said evenly. "The point is to establish a trust reference. Out in the field, in the confusion and heat of the moment, now Bosch won't go after you." He couldn't help but add, "In theory, anyway."

More razzing as Mullet visibly paled. "Don't need no fuckin' K9 in our unit," he muttered. "Fuck that dog."

Geo approached the next man in line, a tall, freckled redhead.

"Hey, Bosch," the guy said with a smile as he reached for him. "I'm Rhys."

This time *Geo* almost dropped him. This was Rhys? Lani's Rhys?

No, not hers. Her ex.

Geo studied Rhys covertly. Gah, the dude was gorgeous, with that red hair and those striking green eyes. A wholly unaccustomed, idiotic spurt of jealousy slithered through him. Stiffly, he reached for Bosch. "Okay, you're done."

Rhys raised a questioning eyebrow, then shrugged, handing Bosch back without comment.

At last, the introductions over, Geo bent to dig a bite sleeve out of his duffel and slip it on his forearm. "I'll play decoy, if you want to do the honors." He took off Bosch's muzzle and handed his leash to Matt. After giving him some quick instructions, Geo trotted a little ways off and took up an offensive stance. He nodded to Matt, who hissed, *"Reveiren!"* and unclipped his leash.

Bosch streaked toward Geo, a black-and-tan blur of motion, and then he leapt, body fully extended, to clamp hard onto Geo's protected forearm. They fought, Geo doing his best to dislodge Bosch's grip on him, but the pressure exerted by a canine in full bite was impossible to loosen.

Shouts from the guys echoed in Geo's ears as he stumbled around in the sand, sixty-five pounds of fur and muscle firmly attached and not going anywhere. At last Geo raised his free hand in surrender. Immediately, Matt trotted up and gave Bosch the "release" command, then tossed him a Kong.

"Okay, pretty cool," Mullet called begrudgingly. "But no way can that thing run the O-course with us."

"Wanna bet?"

Instantly one- and five-dollar bills started flying. A grinning Shane took charge of the money. "I'm restricted from the course at the moment, so I'll be the bookie."

Geo took off the bite sleeve and slipped into a chest harness. "I'll need a swim buddy," he started to say, glancing at Matt, but Rhys raised his hand.

"I'm in."

Geo couldn't help but stiffen as Rhys strolled toward him with a loose-limbed, lazy grace that sparked the jealousy right back to life, a little stronger this time. He and Lani must've made a beautiful couple…

"Okay," he grunted when Rhys reached his side. "There'll be times you have to lift and attach Bosch to me—"

"I've worked with K9 teams before," Rhys broke in. "I'm an 18-Delta medic, too, so I have vet training. You and Bosch are in good hands."

If he'd been *anyone* other than Lani's ex, Geo probably would've indulged in a brief fantasy of the gorgeous Rhys's hands literally being on him, but under the circumstances, he could hardly keep a snarl from twisting his lips.

Jesus, where the fuck is this coming from? I don't have any claims on her!

Sucking in a deep breath, Geo pushed Lani back into her designated mental box.

"Okay, Bosch. Let's show this fucking Mullet asshole what's what."

"Amen," Rhys muttered, and then they were off.

Bosch ran easily next to them as they navigated the different apparatus. He crawled when they crawled, and jumped over the lower obstacles with ease. When it was time for Geo to climb, he waited as Rhys lifted the dog up and hooked him to Geo's chest harness.

Bosch hung calmly as Geo climbed up a metal ladder, then attached a cam to the thirty-foot rope and slid back down. The whole time Rhys stayed next to him, and as the course went on, they slowly meshed into one smoothly operating unit.

When they crossed the finish line, Geo couldn't help but reach out for a knuckle bump. "Good work, swim buddy."

"Thanks." Rhys's face was attractively flushed and glistening with sweat. "I wish Devon—my girlfriend—could've been here. She would love this."

Devon? Why did that name sound familiar?

"She's a badass in her own right," Rhys went on. "This would be right up her alley."

Ah, Devon! The CST Matt mentioned. She was Rhys's girlfriend?

In an instant, the stupid jealousy melted away, and Geo shot him a more genuine smile. "Hey, if you wanted to bring her out sometime, we can do this all over again."

A bemused expression crossed Rhys's face in response to Geo's change in attitude, but all he said was, "Awesome."

As the guys sprawled about with water and Gatorade to take a break, Bradley approached Geo. "Impressive demo," he said admiringly. "I can't even imagine how many hours of training that's taken you."

"Bosch and I have been together for years."

Bradley asked about their previous deployments, his interest gratifyingly sincere. They were deep into talking shop when Mullet suddenly interrupted, "You were in Kalach? Oruzgan Province? Isn't that the outpost where the dude offed himself?"

Geo stiffened as Mullet went on, "I heard that guy was one *crazy* mofo. Unraveling in plain sight, and no one did jack shit about it."

"That's an unfair judgment." Rhys's voice was mild, but his eyes were like chips of ice. "Suicide deaths are very complex. His teammates weren't responsible…"

"Bullshit." Mullet rolled to the side and spat in the sand. "Someone's fuckin' crazy enough to kill themselves, those dudes shoulda seen it." He shrugged. "Guess they figured they were all better off just lettin' him do it."

A bolt of white-hot anger shot through Geo. "Why don't you shut the fuck up?" he growled. "You weren't there."

"Were you?" Mullet sat up, a prurient curiosity in his gaze. When he read the answer on Geo's face, he smirked. "Ah. Was the tough love part your idea? Solved your problem, didn't it?"

A red haze descended over Geo's eyes, and he lunged, but Rhys was ready for him, his arms wrapping tightly around Geo's shoulders. "Don't give this asshole the satisfaction," he said urgently. "Your teammate wouldn't want this."

Across the way, Mullet had surged to his feet and was beckoning to him, his lips twisted in a mocking grin. "Got a lesson you wanna teach me, dog boy?" he taunted. "Don't worry. I promise not to kill myself after."

With a howl of rage and pain, Geo fought against his bonds, dimly aware of Shane dragging Mullet out of reach, both fists twisted in the back of his shirt. "Get out of here, you colossal prick," he snarled, shoving Mullet into the arms of his buddies, who hustled him away, their faces red with embarrassment.

The remaining guys stared at the ground, at the sky, anywhere but at Geo, discomfort written all over them. Fighting back sudden tears, and with a strength born of desperation, he wrenched away from Rhys, snatched up Bosch's leash and strode off in the opposite direction.

Rhys and Matt appeared to walk next to him, silent while he wrestled for control. At the kennels, they leaned against the wall as he brushed Bosch's fur clean of sand and fed him some kibble, their quiet, supportive presence along with the routine of caring for his dog bleeding away Geo's tension and leaving a leaden sadness behind.

Back outside in the parking lot, he waved toward his bike. "That's me. I'm gonna take off."

"Geo…" Rhys moved around in front of him. "I don't think you should ride right now. Please, let me drop you somewhere."

Geo met his eyes, the empathy in them sparking fresh tears. "I'm okay," he said thickly. "But thanks, though."

"You don't seem okay." Rhys's voice was soft. "And believe me, I know something about what you're going through."

Of course he did. He'd been the one to find Tyler, like Geo'd been the one to find Cade…

He shook his head, and Rhys rested a hand on his shoulder. "Let me at least put you in touch with a friend of mine, okay? She's a suicide survivor and has recently started counseling. Her name is—"

"Oh, I'm already talking to someone," Geo broke in hastily before Rhys could go any further. "I'm going to see her now."

Rhys still looked troubled. "I don't think you should ride," he said with quiet insistence. "I'll be happy to take you over to your friend's."

At the thought, an almost-hysterical laugh bubbled up in Geo's throat. How would Rhys react upon being directed to Lani's apartment? Was he a possessive ex? A protective one? Geo didn't think he wanted to find out. Not now, not when things were so new and tentative with Lani, when the last thing he'd ever want to do was upset her.

So Geo dredged up a smile. "I swear I'll be fine, and if I do end up smearing myself over the I-5, I absolve you of all responsibility, okay?"

Rhys flinched. "Not funny, man." With a resigned sigh, he stepped aside, and Geo nodded.

"I appreciate the concern, I really do." He grunted. "And if you ever wanted to give Mullet a swift kick in the ass—"

"Oh, I look for those opportunities on a daily basis," Rhys assured him. "I fuckin' hate that guy."

Straddling his bike, Geo yanked his helmet on and fired it up. He peeled out, Rhys and Matt watching helplessly as he roared away. Geo weaved in and out of traffic, speeding, taking reckless chances, welcome waves of adrenaline spurring him on.

He clenched his teeth so hard they throbbed. Would it really matter if one of the cars got lucky and took him out?

Downshifting, Geo leaned into the next curve, whipping past cars as if they were standing still. Faster, and faster, he accelerated again, anger toward Mullet, Cade, himself, blurring his vision and tightening his chest.

Who cares if I crash? Who'll miss me? Who gives a shit?

Right then, his phone rang. Punching the Bluetooth, he croaked, "Yeah?"

"Hey, it's me." Lani's soft voice cut through the chaos in his head. "I was about to run to the grocery store. Is there anything in particular you *don't* like?"

In an instant, he snapped back to reality. What the

fuck was he doing, taking chances like this? Slowing to a more manageable speed, Geo took the next exit off the freeway.

"Geo?" Now she sounded anxious. "You there? Is everything all right?"

No. Nothing was okay.

"Yeah," he grunted. "It's fine."

"You don't sound fine. Do you need me to come get you?"

"No." Geo exhaled, long and slow. "In fact, I'm here." His heart gave a giant leap as he roared into the parking lot and saw her running down the stairs to meet him. He killed the engine and pulled off his helmet as she hurried over, her gaze searching his face.

Doing his best to smooth out his expression, Geo called, "I'm fine."

God, he was such an asshole for upsetting her, after everything she'd been through.

He'd just opened his mouth to say he'd changed his mind about staying with her, that it'd probably be best if he went back to his room, when she reached his side and took his hand.

"I'm so glad you're home," she said with a squeeze.

And suddenly, there was nowhere he'd rather be.

"I, uh, met Rhys today."

Geo held his breath when Lani glanced at him before carefully setting down the cantaloupe she was inspecting. "Really? Where?"

He told her about the impromptu demonstration at the O-course, and Rhys's volunteering to be his swim buddy. "He seems like a good dude."

"He's the best." She smiled. "And I'm sure he enjoyed working with Bosch. Rhys has always loved dogs."

There wasn't any longing in her voice or on her face, just a fondness, a touch of nostalgia that flitted by and was gone.

Relaxing slightly, and wondering why her residual feelings for Rhys should even matter, Geo asked, "You guys never had one?"

She started pushing the shopping cart again. "Nah. Those first few years, we moved around so much, and I worked so many nights. It didn't seem fair to get a dog."

"Why bartending?" he asked curiously, suddenly wanting to know everything about her. What had been her hopes, and dreams, all the things that'd become secondary the moment Rhys entered the special operations pipeline?

"It was practical." She shrugged, confirming his suspicions. "Every time I got a job, and got settled, it was time to move again. I eventually realized I needed something that I could get quickly, and could get anywhere, so I took a bartending course."

"Do you like it?"

"I do. It's not something I want to do long-term, though, so I'm thinking about other options."

"Such as?"

"Not sure yet. I'm figuring things out one day at a time." With a grin, she bumped him with her hip. "Prioritize and assess, right?"

"Right." He bumped her back. "Now all I gotta do is get you exercising, and then you're practically a SEAL, like it or not."

She rolled her eyes. "Ha ha. Not gonna happen."

They bantered and bickered as they wandered the brightly lit aisles of the grocery store.

"You sure learn a lot about someone from their food choices," she commented at one point, glaring at the frozen dinners Geo'd piled up on one side of the cart.

"What?" He propped his hands on his hips. "I don't know how to cook, and I certainly don't expect *you* to do it all."

"Well, I'm happy to teach you. It's not hard to learn how to make simple, healthy, filling meals."

"How'd you learn?" Geo took over pushing the cart, and almost absently, Lani threaded her arm through his.

"My dad, mostly, although my mom liked to cook, too. I loved those Saturdays, when we'd go to the farmers' market, and then come home loaded down with produce, meats and cheeses. Sometimes he'd let Tyler and me have a tiny splash of French wine while we all worked together."

"Tyler was there?" Geo spoke softly as to not break the spell of her memories.

"Oh, yeah. His specialty was nilagang baka, a Filipino beef stew he learned from my Lola. So good." She inhaled deeply, as if still smelling it. "We'd play music really loud, and talk about anything and everything—politics, spirituality, sex. My dad used to say that preparing and eating a meal together is one of the oldest, most simple rituals we have. Those Saturdays definitely brought us closer as a family."

And yet Tyler's suicide had *still* come as a complete shock, even to the ones who knew him best.

For the first time, Geo caught a glimpse of the mag-

nitude of that shock, and how, like an earthquake, it'd
shaken Lani's life off its secure foundation and sent her
plummeting into a well of pain, neediness and confusion.

Geo glanced at her, unable to keep from marveling
at how far she'd come in the few months he'd known
her. The brittle, emotional woman of that first night in
the bar had been replaced by one of quiet strength and
calm understanding, a woman who could show up for
a friend in crisis and know exactly what he needed.
A woman who—in being there for that friend—was
forced to confront her own pain, her own trauma, again,
but wasn't letting it control her anymore.

A true survivor.

His eyes started to burn. *I don't want to just endure
this, because I don't know how long I'll be able to. I
want to survive it, too.*

"If I go to your group," he said roughly, "I won't
talk, okay? I'll just listen."

He heard her tiny intake of breath.

"You don't have to say anything you don't want to,
Geo." Her voice was hushed. "And yes, sometimes just
listening is the best therapy."

She gazed up at him with those beautiful gold-
flecked eyes, and almost helplessly Geo bent his head
to brush his lips against hers. They caught, and lingered, the plush heat of her mouth sending a delicious
shiver down his spine.

His need was reflected back at him in her slightly
flushed cheeks and the pulse beating visibly in the hollow of her throat. "I've never made out in a grocery
store before," she whispered. "It's, uh, sorta hot."

Sliding his hands onto her hips, he backed her up against the dairy case. "Yeah? Does the skim milk turn you on, baby?" he leered, loving how she dissolved into laughter.

She glanced around. "It's all this…*heavy cream*," she hissed. "I can't control myself."

It was hard to kiss a woman who kept snickering, but Geo managed a few decent ones, decent enough that when a dry "Excuse me" from behind broke them apart, he had to keep his back turned for a moment until his body calmed down.

"Oh, I'm so sorry!" Lani exclaimed to whomever had spoken. "We were just goofing off."

"Y'all are so darn cute, I really hate to interrupt, but I need to grab this and get home."

The female voice was familiar. So familiar, in fact, that Geo's blood instantly turned to ice.

It can't be her. Oh, God, please don't let it be her.

"Geo? You okay?" Lani's innocent question caused the woman to suck in a sharp breath.

"Geo? Oh, my God. George? Is that you?"

Steeling himself, his heart beating so hard he felt sick, Geo turned around. The woman clapped a hand to her mouth.

"It *is* you," she breathed. "Geo…"

He was surprised by the strength of her hug, the genuine pleasure she seemed to find in seeing him.

You should hate me. Why don't you hate me?

While he stood there mutely, wrestling with his agonized thoughts, the woman turned to Lani and held out her hand. "I'm Renae Barlow," she said. "Geo's an old friend. It's so lovely to meet you."

Lani smiled and introduced herself, but her eyes asked Geo the one question he dreaded answering: *Barlow?*

The wave of pain coursing through him almost knocked him down.

Renae Barlow. Cade's wife.

Chapter Sixteen

"I didn't know what to say to her."

Lani wanted to shout her relief at Geo's muttered words. He'd been silent all through paying for their groceries, the drive home and lugging them upstairs. Resisting the urge to press him to talk, she'd clamped her tongue firmly between her teeth and waited him out.

Now she was careful to keep her voice neutral. "You haven't seen her in a while?"

"Not since Dover." He stopped in the middle of unloading one of the bags, his knuckles clenched white around a can of stewed tomatoes. "I'm the one who escorted him home."

"Oh, Geo. That must have been so incredibly difficult," she said quietly. "I'm sorry."

Having to escort the body of his friend all the way from Afghanistan to Dover Air Force Base in Delaware would've been a solitary, emotional task in and of itself. Then to be confronted with Cade's horror-stricken and grieving wife...

"I'm going for a run." Abruptly handing her the can of tomatoes, Geo disappeared in the direction of the bathroom, and Lani stared after him, wrestling with indecision.

She knew the run would calm and exhaust him. By the time he got back, he'd be locked down tight as a drum again. Frustration burned its way through her. He'd finally cracked open the door, so now all she needed to do was find a way in.

But how?

A sudden lightbulb went off in her head, and she shoved the rest of the perishables into the fridge before dashing to the bedroom to exchange her sandals for sneakers.

When Geo emerged, dressed in his running gear, she was waiting for him, bottle of water in hand.

He stared at her. "What's this?"

"Going with you. A run sounds good."

Eyeing her floral sundress, hoodie and tiny cross-body purse, he said skeptically, "You're going running like that? The woman who hates exercise?"

She winked. "First time for everything, right? Actually, I'll walk and carry the water."

To her satisfaction, he didn't argue, just went into his warm-up stretches on the porch while she locked the door.

"There's a cute little business district to the north of here," she said. "I walk over that way sometimes when I can't sleep. Nice quiet streets, no traffic. That's where I'll be, okay?" As she passed him on the stairs, she reached out and squeezed his arm. "Have a nice run."

She set out at a brisk pace, and when he finally caught up, he muttered, "You lied to me. I think you're a secret exerciser."

"Ha, no." She crinkled her nose at him. "I like to walk, and my job means I'm always on my feet and moving, so—"

He nodded before jogging off into the distance. Lani crossed her fingers and prayed, her breath escaping in a muffled groan of relief when he soon circled back around and fell into step beside her.

He didn't say anything, but he also didn't seem ready to bolt, so she took a chance. "Tell me about escorting him home."

After a few beats of silence, Geo let out a grunt. "What's there to tell? Bosch and I rode all the way from Bagram with him in a C-17." His tone was carefully noncommittal, but Lani detected a thread of *something* else there…

Before she could probe any more, he went on, "There was this one fucking airman, though, who couldn't even look at me. When he brought me the transfer paperwork, he practically shoved it in my face and ran back down the ramp."

Geo's jaw rippled, and suddenly, as if a lid had been lifted on a violently boiling kettle, the words spewed out. "I wanted to grab that little pissant and shake him. I wanted to scream that that metal box didn't contain just *anyone*, it contained a man who'd loved his country and his family. It contained a decorated SEAL who'd saved countless lives. A husband, a father, a *friend*, not just—"

When he broke off, she finished softly, "You wanted him to know that Cade was more than the way he died."

"Yes." That one word burst out of him. "He was, Lani. He was so much more than that."

"Then tell me. Tell me about him."

Taking his arm, she listened as Geo told her about a guy who guzzled Rip Its and red licorice like they were going out of style, who could quote the movie *Tombstone* from the opening credits to the very last line, and who'd once—accidentally, famously—taken a huge swig of someone else's dip spit when reaching for what he thought was a bottle of water.

She gagged. "Ewww, gross."

Barking out a laugh, Geo said, "Damn, that was funny as hell. We were all like, 'Noooo! Don't spit it back out in here!'"

"Ugh." She shuddered. "Poor Cade."

"Some of the guys tried calling him Spittoon." Geo shook his head, still chuckling. "He never protested it, just refused to answer to it."

He fell silent, and desperate to keep the momentum going, Lani threaded their fingers together and dragged him toward a nearby convenience store.

"Ooh, that gives me an idea. C'mon."

Inside the store, she picked out a couple of energy drinks and some Twizzlers, paid for them quickly, and headed for home. Once there, Geo stood by, clearly mystified, as she dug through her Blu-Ray collection, at last emerging triumphant holding a copy of *Tombstone*.

"I hereby declare this the First Annual Cade Barlow Memorial Movie Night," she announced, pointing at the couch. "Have a seat."

He did, staring in bemusement as she popped the tab on one of the drinks and set it at the end of the coffee table. She handed Geo the other can before opening the bag of Twizzlers and dividing them up three ways.

As the opening credits of the movie rolled, she could see him glancing at the solitary can and licorice, over to her, and back to the TV screen. Her heart thudding, praying once again she was doing the right thing, she said, "Put your feet up and relax. Let's watch his favorite movie with him."

After a long, silent moment, Geo at last raised his can toward the other one in a toast, took a swig, then put it down carefully. Turning to Lani, he wrapped her up in his arms.

"Thank you," he whispered into her hair. "I love this."

"Mmm." She nestled against his chest, her whole body going limp in relief. "Every year on my birthday, Tyler would take me to a movie and buy me some Milk Duds and a Dr. Pepper. He'd have Raisinets." She shuddered. "Yuck. I *hate* Raisinets, but now on my birthday I go to a movie and buy them anyway. It makes me feel close to him again."

Sighing, he settled back into the couch, still holding her. "This is perfect—Rip Its, Twizzlers and *Tombstone*. I can almost picture him slouched over there, quoting his favorite lines."

"What about Renae? Were you close to her, too?"

Geo stiffened, but he didn't let her go. "Their door was always open, if any of us needed a couch to crash on, or someone to talk to. She never made us feel unwelcome, as if we were intruding, although a lot of times we were. *Most* times." He swallowed hard, his voice roughening. "I abandoned her, Lani. I couldn't even go to his funeral."

Lani's heart ached, but she didn't say anything, just rubbed her palm in soothing circles over his chest.

"I never called her or went to see her. It's been a whole fucking year, and I..."

When he trailed off, she sat up and looked at him. "What about now? It's not too late."

He blinked. "What?"

"In a lot of ways, the second year is the hardest, simply because you're past all those 'firsts'—first birthday, first anniversary, first holidays. There are no more milestones, and now you've just gotta slog through life. She'll need friends more than ever. It's not too late."

"But—but what do I—"

"Just show up, maybe take care of something she hasn't had the time or ability to. Trim the hedges, clean out the gutters, take a load of stuff to the dump." Lani patted his chest. "You don't have to say anything profound, or think you're going to 'fix' what she's going through, because you can't. Just be there, Geo. Just show up. It's not too late."

Shaking his head, he mumbled, "You make it sound so simple..."

"Sometimes the simplest things mean the most." She paused. "You're worried that she's angry at you for not going to the funeral."

When he nodded, she said, "To be honest, she probably didn't even notice, as focused as she was on getting herself and her kids through it. But if you *really* want to show up and make a difference, now is a great time. It's not too late, I promise you."

Geo's arms tightened around her as he mulled that

over. "Is this the kind of stuff you talk about in your group?"

Lani's tummy flipped over, but she managed to keep her voice even. "Sometimes, sure. We talk about anything and everything. Guilt, fault, anger, all of it."

He squeezed his eyes shut.

"Whatever you're feeling," she said quietly, "I guarantee someone in that group has felt that way, too. It's a safe space. A *welcoming* space. And it's freed me in a way I never thought possible."

He didn't reply, so—the seed having been planted— she grabbed up a Twizzler and took a huge bite. "God, I haven't had one of these in forever." Then she grimaced. "Bleah. Now I remember why."

"Says the girl who likes Milk Duds."

"What?" Lani glared at him in pretend outrage. "What's wrong with Milk Duds?"

"Oh, I don't know. They rip your fillings out?"

She opened her mouth to counter, then snapped it shut.

"Uh-huh," Geo said. "I'm right, aren't I?"

"Hmph. It was a loose tooth, okay? Not a filling." She narrowed her eyes. "What's *your* favorite candy?"

He shrugged. "All of them. Well, except for Milk Duds. Obviously."

"Good. More for me." After elbowing him lightly in the ribs, she leaned forward to pick up her water from the coffee table. As she did, she lifted her hair away from her neck, sighing in relief at the cool air on her sweaty skin.

God, I don't know how you do this day in and day out, Maura. You're a fucking rock star.

"Hey, what's this?" Geo asked. "You have a tattoo here?" Gentle fingertips brushed over her nape. "What is it? I mean, I can see it's a cardinal, but…"

His calloused thumb traced the small tattoo, over and over. The slight rasp tightened her nipples, made her shiver. Goose bumps springing up everywhere, Lani swallowed her gulp of water. "I got it, what," she said huskily, "maybe three years ago now?"

Suddenly restless, needing to move, she pushed to her feet and headed for the kitchen. After a moment, Geo followed, propping his hips against the counter as she started to put away the neglected groceries. "You don't have to talk about it if you don't want to." His voice was hushed. "I'm sorry."

She snapped her head around to look at him. "Oh, Geo, don't be sorry. It's not a bad memory, at all. It's just—"

"An ambush moment?"

Her chest tightened. "It used to be." Putting down the box of pasta she was holding, Lani crossed to him and mirrored his pose. "Tyler was a huge St. Louis Cardinals fan. Like, huge. During baseball season it was all he could talk about. For a long time after his death, I couldn't handle seeing or hearing anything about them, which sucked, because I loved them, too."

She tilted her head back to stare at the ceiling.

"One night, some dude came into the bar. Kind of like you, he was toasting a friend who'd passed away, and I remember asking him about this really elaborate tattoo on his forearm. It was a Stormtrooper helmet, and he said he'd gotten it because his friend loved *Star Wars*. So that got me thinking."

"A cardinal for Tyler."

"Yes. Because he loved the Cardinals, and because whenever I picture him now, it's always as a bird flying free, at peace." She shrugged. "It seemed fitting."

"But why here?" Geo touched the nape of his own neck. "You can't even see it. Why…?"

"I don't *have* to see it to know it's there." She smiled. "Kind of like Tyler being at peace. It's not something I can see, but I need to believe it exists, for my own sake."

Geo went still. "I've struggled with that, too. Is Cade at peace now? Is that how it works?"

Lani's heart ached at the thread of anguish running through his words. "A suicide-attempt survivor came to talk to our group a few weeks ago. He told us that when he finally made his plan, it was the first time in a long time he'd felt relief, that knowing there would soon be an end to his pain was a strange sort of peace all on its own." She swallowed hard. "So yes, I believe that's how it works."

Geo closed his eyes, and with a pat to his shoulder, she went back to the groceries. As she stood on tiptoe to put the box of pasta high on the shelf, she heard his footsteps behind her.

"You have no idea how much you've helped me tonight. Thank you."

"I'm glad."

"You're amazing," he went on softly. "Wise, compassionate, patient…" A pause. "Not to mention so beautiful it hurts."

She let out a hoarse chuckle, a pleasurable tingle going through her. "Well, as to the first part, I have a great therapist. The second? All a matter of opinion."

"Hmm. It's definitely my opinion that you're beautiful." Geo rested his hands lightly on her hips. "And sweet. Oh, and sexy. Should I go on?"

The tingle turned into a blaze of heat that pooled low in her belly. "Umm, sexy?" she quavered. "Nah."

"Mm-hmm." Leaning down, he brushed his lips over her bare shoulder. "Sexy. As. Hell."

Lani's knees turned to jelly as he placed tiny, open-mouthed kisses along her shoulder and up into the curve of her neck. Helplessly, she tilted her head to the side, and Geo let out a low growl, biting down lightly on the tendon there, his tongue soothing the tiny sting. His breath was ragged in her ear, the hard ridge pressing into her hip unmistakable.

Her heartbeat immediately kicked into overdrive, her blood racing hot through her veins. It'd been *so long* since she'd made love to a man she cared about, and one who cared about her in return. The overwhelming desire to be held by him, to feel him against her—*inside* her—swept over her in a dizzying wave.

All she'd have to do was turn around and take him in her arms.

"Lani?" he whispered hoarsely in her ear. "Do you want me to stop?"

Did she? She'd be going into this with no illusions, no stars in her eyes. Geo wasn't right for her, and he'd made it crystal clear that getting back to his unit was his only goal.

As for her, she could handle her burgeoning feelings. She'd *have* to, because life with a SEAL wasn't in the cards for her and never would be. But he was here now, and he wanted her, and Lord knew she wanted *him* with every fiber of her being.

So Lani drew in a deep breath…

And turned.

Chapter Seventeen

"I don't want you to stop."

Geo went boneless as she ran her palms up over his chest to wrap her arms around his neck. She lifted her face and, heart thumping, body aching, he brushed their lips together lightly, once, twice.

"Mmm," she breathed. "More."

Her kiss this time was lusher, deeper, a melding of mouths that stole every last bit of his breath. He poured all of his longing into it, his need, and he fought to keep his hands gentle despite wanting to crush her close and never let her go.

When she pulled away, he grunted a protest, but Lani just threaded their fingers together to lead him down the hall to her bedroom, where she turned and moved languidly back into his arms.

He rested his hands on her hips as she gazed up at him, her eyes soft, her face dappled by the moonlight streaming in through the blinds on the window.

"So beautiful," he murmured. "I wish…"

That I could freeze this moment in time.

Her voice a mere thread of sound, Lani whispered, "Kiss me."

He did, his senses awash in the heat of her lips and tongue, the yielding softness of her body against his. Linking her arms tightly around his neck, she pressed closer, and they danced their way toward the soft, inviting bed.

Right as they reached it, though, she eased away and pushed Geo to sitting on the edge of it. He spread his knees, and she moved to stand between them, his mouth drying up completely when she reached for the buttons on her dress and teasingly flicked them open, one by one.

"You're killing me," he gasped, twisting his fingers in the comforter, his hungry gaze fastened to each tantalizing bit of skin as it was revealed. When the dress was open to her waist, she shrugged it off her shoulders and it fell away to pool softly around her feet, leaving her in a pink bra and bright purple panties.

"Sorry," she said, watching his face. "My sexy matching sets don't fit anymore."

He almost couldn't speak from the desire surging through him. Putting his hands on her hips, he pulled her closer and buried his face between her breasts. "Sweetheart, if you were any sexier," he croaked, "I might spontaneously combust."

She ran her hand down the back of his head to rest it on his nape. "How come you always know the right thing to say?"

"Not speaking anything but the truth." He brushed his mouth against her. "Mmm. You feel so good, you smell so good. I'm so hard…"

Huffing out a laugh, Lani pushed him back on the

bed and sprawled out next to him. He leaned over to kiss her softly.

"Is there anything you don't like?" he asked. "In bed, I mean."

Grabbing the back of his T-shirt, she wrestled it up and over his head, then pulled him on top of her. "Guys wearing too many clothes while in it." She draped her arms around his shoulders. "Other than that, um, my feet are super ticklish."

"So don't suck your toes?" He took her giggle into his mouth, his own lips curving. "Noted."

A warm, comforting silence fell as she stroked his back, her knees hugging his ribs. He breathed in the scent of her skin, wishing he could bottle it and take it with him, and he closed his eyes, purging his mind of everything except the need to give her pleasure.

To make love to her.

He ran his palm along one silken thigh as he kissed his way up her throat to her lips. Lani was waiting for him, her mouth welcoming his, her tongue a slick heat that curled his toes and wrenched a moan from deep in his chest.

He broke the kiss and climbed off the bed to strip off his shorts—well, tried to—his arousal making him clumsy.

At last he kicked them away and spread his arms wide. "What do you think? Should I take a second job as a stripper?"

Her eyes danced. "I think you might need to work on the presentation a bit."

"Yeah?" Geo did a little shimmy, feeling silly,

and free, amazed at the level of comfort he'd already reached with her.

"Oh, yeah, shake that booty." Leaning back on her elbows, she braced one heel on the edge of the mattress and waved her knee idly back and forth. "More. Do your best *Magic Mike* impression." She lifted an eyebrow. "Did you see that movie?"

"At least three times." Geo shrugged. "Channing Tatum is fucking hot." He watched her carefully to gauge her reaction to the reminder of his sexuality, but all she did was give a thoughtful nod.

"He is. Although I like Matt Bomer more."

"Hmm." Geo pretended to consider it. "I guess I wouldn't kick him out of bed either."

"Well, you're sexier than both of them put together. Damn." Her eyes fell to his cock, and her eyes widened. She scooted to the edge of the mattress, and when he drew close enough, wrapped her arms around his hips. Then she tilted her head back to gaze up at him. "Can I—?"

Tenderness made his hand shake as he smoothed her hair away from her flushed face. "I'm all yours," he whispered.

She bit her lip, then leaned in to place a shy kiss on the slick, aching tip of him. Geo widened his stance, his abs tight with the effort of holding back. "Oh, yeah," he encouraged her, then clenched his teeth as she took him deeper, her mouth a tight, moist heat that gripped him, her rhythmic tugging rapidly eroding his control.

At last she sat back and licked her swollen lips. "Tastes so good."

He forced himself to remain still as she ran exploratory hands up his sides and along his chest, stringing little open-mouthed kisses between his hipbones. When she tweaked his nipples, he gasped. "Driving me crazy, darlin'."

"You're so beautiful." She sounded a little tremulous, her breathing as unsteady as his. Her gold-flecked eyes glowed with desire, and awe, and unbelievably, his cheeks heated in a blush.

Seeing it, she chuckled low in her throat. "Yep, you are." She stood and wrapped her arms around his neck. "And I'm dying for you to touch me."

He smoothed his palms along her back and down to her silk-clad buttocks, which he plumped and squeezed, unable to keep from groaning as she arched against him, his cock trapped between their bellies.

"Don't stop," she breathed, her fingers digging into his shoulders. When he hesitated, her gaze flew to his, then sharpened. "What's wrong?"

"I—I don't—" he stammered, then swallowed hard. "I don't want to hurt you."

Lani's mouth curved. Reaching back behind herself, she unfastened her bra and let it slip down her arms, then took his hand and placed it gently on her breast. "You won't. Touch me."

She was heavy and warm, her nipple digging into his palm. He shaped her with tentative fingers, thumb circling, which made her gasp. Yanking his hand away, Geo flushed again when she pressed her lips together to hold back a smile.

"I promise, you won't hurt me." She slid her arms back around his neck and moved sinuously against him. "I *need* you. Please."

She gave a gigantic tug, and they fell onto the bed together, her breathless giggle as they bounced and settled in a tangle of limbs easing Geo's anxiety a bit. He kissed her softly, then buried his face between her breasts, the feel of her fingertips stroking his nape raising delicious goose bumps all over his body. Nibbling along one lush curve, he flicked his tongue against the taut, pebbled bud.

"Mmm," she hummed, her hand tightening on his neck, holding him to her. "Feels so good."

Encouraged, Geo drew her nipple deep into his mouth and sucked hard, her husky moans of enjoyment brushing along his skin and making him shiver. When he finally released her with a pop, her hips were moving restlessly, her heart hammering beneath his cheek. He rose up above her, groaning as she lifted and spread her knees.

Anticipation burning like fire through his veins, he nuzzled his nose against the swell of her belly, the scent of her driving him wild.

"I want to taste you," he murmured, brushing his lips along the waistband of her panties. "Please."

Her "yes" was so husky as to be almost inaudible as she helped him make quick work of the scrap of purple fabric. Geo ran his hands down her inner thighs, pressing them wide.

Her intimate flesh was as juicy as a ripe peach, silky and wet. His nostrils flared, mouth watering, his cock so hard it hurt. He kissed the inside of one knee, then drifted his lips down, attuned to her every breath, every sigh, all the little noises she made deep in her throat.

Propping himself up on his elbows, he searched her

face, a blaze of satisfaction going through him at the sight of her with her eyes squeezed shut, teeth sunk in her lower lip. Even as he watched, she gave a sharp tug on his hair, a "get on with it" motion that made him suppress a smile.

He thought about teasing her, thought about edging her pleasure, but her growing need was evident in the moisture beaded on her curls, the hard, swollen nipples, and the way her pulse throbbed in the hollow of her throat.

"Gorgeous," he breathed, then bent his head and dragged the flat of his tongue along her clit. The salty-sweet taste of her exploded in his mouth, and he growled, even as she cried out, "Geo!"

He licked her, sucked on her, his shoulders holding her legs wide as he slipped one, then two fingers inside her. She was hot, and slick, and he trembled as he thrust into her, over and over. Lani writhed on the bed, her fists twisted in the covers, back arching.

"Come for me, love," Geo whispered, his fingers plunging deep once more. She froze, her high, thin cry music to his ears. The feel of her spasming around him, the gush of moisture, the swelling of her clit between his lips, had Geo riding the knife's edge of control.

When the orgasm eased its grip on her, she sank back into the bed, her face flushed, eyes drowsy. "Holy shit."

He couldn't help but grin. "Good?"

Flicking him on the nose, she grunted, "You know it was." Then she stroked his cheek, thumb drifting over his lower lip. "Condoms in the side table." She watched as he retrieved one and shakily rolled it on, then pushed him to his back. His fingers digging into her thighs, Geo let out a groan when she sank down onto him.

"Lani, Jesus!" Her body clasped him tight, and he found himself gritting his teeth, fighting to hold back.

She circled her hips, eyes falling shut, her lips parting. Tamping down his own need for release, he slowed his breathing, hands drifting up and down her silky thighs. As she moved, he gave her short, hard thrusts, her little whimpers of pleasure tightening his chest all over again.

"Geo…" Lani planted her hands on either side of his shoulders, her hair falling in a scented curtain around them and cocooning them in their own little world. Everything else faded away, until there was only the feel of her lush curves, her lips on his. "You feel so good inside me. You're so deep… I need…"

At her gasping plea, he braced his feet on the bed and lifted his hips fully into her downward strokes, hilting himself, over and over. "Take what you need, sweetheart," he encouraged, his hands cradling her breasts, the hard curve of her belly pressing against him.

When her breathing roughened even more, and her whimpers became breathless cries, he licked his thumb and pressed it to her clit, circling it, flicking it, then rubbing it hard, until she threw her head back and came with a long, low moan.

Digging her nails hard into his chest, Lani rode out the pleasure, and the sweet pain, the thought of her marks on his skin, kicked him over the edge. He arched clear off the bed with the force of it, his jaw clenched to keep from shouting something he had no right to shout:

Mine!

* * *

"Did you always want to be a SEAL?"

Lani's voice was drowsy, her head heavy on his chest.

"Nah." He sifted her hair through his fingers, his other hand drifting up and down her back. "I'd never even heard of them until one of my buddies decided he wanted to enlist in the Navy. For shits and giggles I went with him to the recruiter, and on the wall was this rah-rah poster of buff dudes doing what looked like some really awesome shit. I couldn't stop staring at it."

"Ah. The recruiter smelled blood in the water."

He shook his head in disgust. "He really did, and I fell for it hook, line and sinker. These days guys who pass the initial assessment go to a separate bootcamp that feeds directly into the SEAL pipeline, but back then, you went to regular bootcamp and applied for Naval Special Warfare. Took me two years to get in."

"So you did your time on a big old gray ship." Lani splayed her palm over his abs. "And the recruiter met his quota."

"Exactly. I made my share of dumb-kid mistakes along the way, too, which didn't help."

"But yet here you are."

"Here I am."

She propped herself on her elbow to gaze down at him, hair tangled, eyes heavy-lidded. The sheet slipped down to pool at her waist, leaving her full breasts gloriously bare. Reveling in the freedom to touch her at last, Geo cupped one gently, his thumb caressing the lush curve.

"So what's it like?" she whispered. "Over there?"

"Afghanistan?"

When she nodded, he let his hand drop away and fall to the bed. "Certain parts of it are absolutely majestic, with some of the most beautiful scenery I've ever seen."

"What are the people like?"

"Stoic. Weary. Hard-working. Proud. Most of them have never known peace in their lifetimes."

Before he knew it, Geo was telling her about the remote villages high in the mountains of eastern Afghanistan, some of them completely cut off from the rest of the country during the winter months.

"And all we did was bring the war to their doorstep," he said quietly. "Sometimes when I think about it, I—"

He fell silent, aware of her hand rubbing in soothing circles over his chest and stomach. Fuck, how could he explain his complicated feelings about what he'd seen and done? He wanted to, though. He wanted to tell her everything.

Forcing a smile, he reached up to tuck a lock of her hair behind her ear. "Why are you so easy to talk to?"

"Well, I'm a bartender. Listening is part of the job description."

"Uh-uh. I don't think it's the job. I think it's all you." *And I'm* this *close to falling for you.* His throat closed. *But I know you don't want me.*

How could he blame her? He himself had seen the fallout from the marriages, the relationships, that'd broken apart under the strain of so many long absences. Of course she wouldn't want to bring her child into that.

He suppressed a wistful sigh. Her child. A part of her, a tiny human who'd hopefully inherit her beautiful eyes, her loving heart, her intelligence and wisdom…

"What're you thinking about?" Her voice was soft.

Shoving his ridiculous feelings down deep, Geo summoned up a more genuine smile. "About what an incredible mama you're going to be."

Her eyes crinkled. "I actually felt the baby move the other day. It was this tiny popping and fluttering sensation, almost like gas bubbles."

"Wow."

"I may have cried a little, you know? It hit me like a ton of bricks—this is *real*."

"Were they happy tears?"

"Mostly." Her palm came to rest between his pecs. "I'm still scared to do this alone, but I'm in a *much* better place than I was the night I met you."

Geo listened as she told him about meeting Rhys's plane after his deployment. "We'd been broken up for about six months by then. I'd just found out I was pregnant, which sent me into a total panic. Instead of a Welcome Home sign, I made one that said Let's Try Again and totally put him on the spot in front of his entire platoon." She let out a groan, dropping her forehead to his chest. "And in front of the woman he's actually in love with."

"Ouch." Aching for her, Geo asked, "How did he handle it?"

"With grace and forgiveness, far more than I deserved. When I realized my desperate stunt wasn't going to work, I tried to play it off as I'm a jealous bitch who can't stand seeing him happy with someone else."

"I'm sure he didn't believe that, not if he knows you at all."

She lifted her head to gaze down at him. "He didn't.

That's the moment I realized that if I told him about the baby right then, the idiot would try to sacrifice his newfound happiness for me. I couldn't let him do that, not again. I convinced him to go away, climbed into the shower, bawled my eyes out, and then went to work." She smiled ruefully. "Where I met you. That's the unfortunate aftermath you walked into that night."

"Mmm." Geo pulled her close and kissed her cheek. "All I noticed was how tough you were when you sent that creep packing. I, uh, was a little afraid of you, to be honest."

She gave him a swat. "Oh, stop. You were not."

"Just a little." He grinned up at her to show he was joking, and her face softened. She ran her fingertip along his jaw to trace it lightly over his lips.

"One of the first things I noticed about *you* is this gorgeous smile. It lit up the room."

His heart turned over. "Really?" he croaked, then smirked. "Not my hot Navy SEAL bod?"

She rolled her eyes. "This is San Diego. I can go to the beach and see a million hot bods."

He couldn't help but snicker. "True."

"That night I was sick, and hurting, and your kindness toward a complete stranger, your *smile*, is what stood out to me the most. What I needed the most." Bending her head, she kissed him gently, the tip of her tongue tracing his lower lip. "I'm so glad I met you."

Geo wrapped his arms around her as she settled in to taste him leisurely, her little murmurs of pleasure arrowing straight to his cock. He shifted restlessly on the bed, gasping when she broke the kiss only to mouth her way down the length of his neck.

With a wicked smile, she licked each of his nipples in turn, the sensitive buds drawing up into tight points. "Okay, I have to admit," she murmured, the light flicks of her tongue making him grit his teeth, "your body *is* pretty hot."

"Ha, I knew it." He put one arm up behind his head and flexed, making his six-pack pop.

"Oh, yeah." Rolling on top of him, she kissed her way down his chest to his belly, where she nuzzled her nose into his navel. "So damn hot."

Geo wallowed in a haze of enjoyment, his fist twisting in the pillow, as she mouthed along his abs, at last twitching the sheet away from his hips. His cock, the broad purple head glistening with renewed arousal, bobbed up between them.

Lani licked her lips. "Mmm, nice." Wrapping her fingers around him, she gave him a few long, slow strokes, thumb circling the crown. "*Very* nice."

Lifting a trembling hand, he cupped her flushed cheek. "Sweetheart, whatever you want," he gasped. "I'm all yours."

She turned her head and kissed his palm, her voice whisper soft. "Then make love to me."

Falling to her back, she pulled him over on top of her. His heart thudding painfully in his ears, Geo settled between her widespread legs. It was her turn to gasp as he dragged the base of his shaft against her clit, her slickness easing the way.

"So beautiful," he murmured, shaping her breasts in his hands, plumping them gently. He bent to kiss her, his tongue rubbing along hers, hot and wet. She dug her nails into his shoulders, tiny moans welling up in her throat.

Eager to taste her, Geo worked his way down her body with nibbles and soft licks. At the gentle curve of her belly, he paused for the briefest of moments, then brushed his lips against it, too. He glanced up at her to see her watching him, her eyes warm. She combed her fingers lightly through his hair.

"No six-pack here. Sorry."

He chuckled. "Nope, just one sexy mama."

"Ha. Will you say that when I'm big as a house?"

As soon as the words left her mouth, he could see her wince and bite her lip. To hide his own reaction, he bent his head to kiss her tummy again, whispering, "You'll always be gorgeous to me, no matter what."

Even big as a house. Even if I won't be here to see it.

Her fingers drifted along his jaw, the breath she blew out a little shaky. "I need you. Please, Geo."

Oh, God, he needed her, too. So much he ached with it, an ache that went far beyond the physical. It was a need to *belong* to her, an unfamiliar longing that welled up from deep inside him and flooded him with a combination of joy and pain.

"I'm here, darlin'," he murmured, kissing her gently. "I'm all yours."

Fumbling in the side table for a condom, Geo rolled it on, then notched himself at her entrance and started a slow rock, a raspy groan breaking from him when she pulled her knees back to let him inside. Inch by inch he filled her, his lips never leaving hers.

His first strokes into her were careful, unhurried, almost languid. Lani moved with him, lifting her hips to meet him, one hand on his nape, the other riding the motion of his flexing back.

Squeezing his eyes shut, he let the sensations wash over him, determined to commit them to memory. He nuzzled her neck, groaning when she raked her nails lightly across his shoulders, her silky thighs hugging his ribs.

"Geo," she breathed. "You feel so fucking good."

He wanted it to last forever, but all too soon his body took over, clamoring for release. Sliding his hands under her to change the angle, he buried himself to the hilt and pulsed his hips, rubbing against her clit. With a shuddering cry, she arched her back, knees falling wide. Alternating short, hard pumps of his cock with long, deep strokes, he growled low in his throat when at last she spasmed around him, her body milking his.

Helpless against it, he threw his head back and let go with a low moan, pleasure sweeping over him in wave after shivery wave. When it was over, she drew him down against her and wrapped him up tightly, so close he could feel the pounding of her heart.

Geo kissed her shoulder, her neck, and finally her lips, his tongue caressing hers as their breathing slowed. He slid from the bed to take care of the condom and practically ran back to where she held the covers up for him, giggling at his exaggerated shivers and squealing when he tucked his cold feet next to hers.

With a sigh, she spooned back against him and was soon asleep, while he lay and listened to her breathe, relishing the closeness. His hand crept down to cradle her belly, and in the haze between waking and sleeping, a sudden fantasy sprang to life—the fantasy that they both were his. His to cherish, to protect, to come home to…

To love.

I guess I don't have to worry about falling for you anymore, sweetheart.

The truth settled in his chest with an unexpected warmth that brought a huge lump to his throat.

Because it was too late. He already had.

Chapter Eighteen

Lani had never felt so decadent in her life.

Her body throbbed, her nipples so deliciously sore they tingled, and if she moved just right, she could still feel the echoes of Geo deep inside her. Squirming in her chair, she watched him fork up huge bites of lasagna.

"What do you think?" she asked anxiously. "Good?"

He swallowed, put his fork down and wiped his mouth with a napkin. "I think lasagna for breakfast is the best idea anyone's ever had."

She rolled her eyes. "It *is* underrated as a breakfast food, but how does it *taste*?"

Pronouncing it delicious, Geo carried his empty plate to the sink. As he washed it, he glanced over at her. "This is what you're taking to your group?"

"Yep. You've just been my lasagna guinea pig."

Unable to resist him in all his shirtless glory, she wrapped her arms around his waist from behind and kissed his bare shoulder. "We're eating at noon, and the meeting itself will start at 12:30."

She could feel him tense, but he didn't try to pull away. At last he blew out a breath. "Where is it?"

"Coronado." Reluctantly letting him go, she pulled

out her phone and texted him the address. Then she propped her hips against the counter. "No pressure," she said quietly. "I'm gonna go early and help set up. If you make it, great. If not, that's okay, too."

His shoulders slumped in relief as her meaning sunk in, that she was leaving it up to him. No begging, no pleading, no riding together, nothing that could smack of coercion at all.

Leaning over, Geo gave her a short, hard kiss, then headed toward the bedroom, reappearing several minutes later pulling a T-shirt over his head. "Gonna go run a few errands," he said noncommittally.

After the door had closed behind him, she sank into a chair at the kitchen table and buried her face in her hands.

Please, God. Please let me be doing the right thing.

A furtive twist of guilt went through her, one that she quickly banished. Yeah, sleeping with him might not have been the *wisest* course of action, but goddamn, what a night. Three times they'd made love, three glorious times that'd left her limp with satisfaction, the last one right as the sunrise started peeking through the blinds.

She shivered at the memory of his sleepy kisses, lazy hands and languid thrusts from behind, her top knee hooked over his forearm. They'd showered together before heading into the kitchen for their unconventional breakfast, Geo declaring himself famished.

"No wonder," she'd teased him. "Good sex is hard work!"

He'd pulled her into his lap and kissed her thoroughly in agreement before letting her go.

Sighing, her lips still tingling, she pushed to her feet and padded into the bedroom to strip the sheets and tidy up, only to stop short in the doorway with a gasp. "Oh, my God!"

He'd already stripped the bed and remade it with crisp, perfect corners. Their scattered clothes had been picked up and stuffed in the hamper, the bathroom sink wiped down, wet towels hung neatly back up.

Lani clasped her hands to her chest and spun around in a circle before sinking to sit on the edge of the bed. "You're a keeper for sure," she said aloud to the empty room. "Husband material, boyfriend material…"

A pang shot though her. He might be a keeper, all right, but *she* couldn't keep him. So what if he was a dishes whiz, a good listener and a generous and considerate lover? So what if she'd woken in the night to find him splaying his palm low on her belly, as if hoping to feel the baby move?

The pang morphed into an ache so sharp that tears sprang to her eyes. No, she couldn't keep him. Not as long as he was a SEAL.

How many of her friends over the years had given birth alone, their husbands gone—out of touch, out of reach? How many of them had had to deal with missed birthdays, forgotten anniversaries, serious injuries, illnesses?

So many things left for them to handle alone, married as they were to men who were gone far more than they were ever home.

Lani squeezed her eyes shut.

An afternoon on Tabitha's porch while the kids were all in school. The laughter flowing along with

*the wine, excited plans bandied about for the guys'
homecoming in only two weeks. Suzette had a pregnancy to announce to a husband she hadn't seen in almost six months.*

"Harry's gonna shit *when he sees me," she said,
cackling. "We've only been trying for two goddamn
years, and then with one last goodbye fuck, boom...
knocked up! I can't wait to surprise him!"*

*Hoots and jokes from the women about all the home-
coming babies about to be conceived, and then Suzette
pushed to her feet. "Y'all, I bought the cutest maternity
lingerie the other day. Lemme show you!"*

*Caressing her baby bump, she hurried to her house
across the street.*

*A little envious of her happiness, visions of her own
childless future with Rhys swirling before her, Lani
hadn't even noticed the government car that'd turned
the corner until someone gasped.*

*Frozen in horror, they watched it creep along be-
fore pulling over to the curb and stopping—in front of
Suzette's house.*

*Anguished shouts of "No!" interspersed with the
tinkle of wineglasses crashing to the ground...*

For the rest of her life, Lani would never forget the
sight of Tabitha's long blond hair streaming out behind her as she ran barefoot across the street, desperate to get to her friend before the Navy chaplain did.
Before Suzette's world crashed down around her ears.
Before she learned that Harry would never meet his
long-awaited son...

"I can't do it," she gasped, the painful memories

splintering her heart into pieces all over again. "I can't live my life like that. I *can't.*"

She'd had enough of goodbyes.

Geo killed the engine and gazed up at the small house.

"In a lot of ways, the second year is harder than the first. She'll need friends now more than ever."

Lani's words echoing in his ears, he pulled off his helmet and tucked it under his arm. Then, his heart thundering, the lasagna he'd eaten a lump in his stomach, Geo made his way slowly up the walk toward Renae's front door.

At the sight of the chairs on the porch, his eyes burned. How many beers had he shared here with Cade over the years, their feet propped on the railing as they talked about work, love and life?

He'd been the only one in the command who knew the truth about Jake.

"I'm here for you one hundred percent, brother, whatever you decide to do."

In the end, of course, he'd chosen his career over his relationship, and after Jake had moved out, Cade's unwavering support was what got him through those first emotional weeks.

"Couldn't have done it without you," he whispered to the empty porch. "Best swim buddy ever."

Before he could change his mind, Geo put his helmet down on a chair and then knocked softly. If Renae didn't answer in thirty seconds, he would—

The door swung open almost immediately. "Hey, Geo." Renae smiled up at him, her face thinner than he remembered, the sharpness of her cheekbones highlighting the deep ocean blue of her eyes. "I heard you pull up."

And then waited to see if he had the guts to go through with it.

Shame twisting him into knots, Geo stammered for a reply, then choked off when Renae simply opened her arms and gathered him close. He clutched onto her, her presence a sudden, tangible connection to Cade—one he hadn't known he so desperately needed.

"I'm sorry," he whispered.

She stroked the back of his head like she was comforting a child. "For what?"

"For not being here. For not—"

Once again he couldn't go on, and Renae pulled away, then reached up to cup his face in her hands. "Well, you're here now. Come on. Let's have some coffee and talk."

Discomfort still roiled through him, but Geo nodded and followed her inside. The living room was much the same, except for the big wooden Trident that Cade'd had commissioned. He'd been so proud of it, and hung it in a place of honor over the couch.

Now it was gone, replaced by a photograph of a stunning beach sunset.

A lot of other SEAL memorabilia that Geo remembered being scattered throughout the house was gone, too.

He bit his lip. Well, why wouldn't it be? Who'd want those reminders?

"I had my brother come pack it away," Renae said, answering his unspoken question. "I'll go through it all someday when my girls are ready."

Swallowing hard, Geo croaked, "How are the girls?" He accepted the cup of coffee Renae handed him as they took their seats at the table.

She sighed. "Ava is—well, she's Ava. Wears her heart on her sleeve, gets it all out. Ari? She's my stoic one, the quiet one. Spends all her time reading or playing soccer."

Geo nodded, his heart aching for Cade's nine- and ten-year-old daughters.

"I think the permanence of it's been a little hard for them to understand, because he'd always been gone a lot." She shook her head. "Hell, even *I* think that sometimes: 'Cade's not dead, he's just on deployment.'"

Geo had no idea what to say, and just in time he remembered Lani's words.

"She doesn't need you to 'fix' anything about what she's going through. Just be there. Just show up."

So he reached across the table and covered her hand with his. "I miss him, too. And I'm really fucking sorry it's taken me so long to get here."

Renae's eyes met his. "You're the only one from his platoon who's come to visit," she said, with just the faintest trace of bitterness. "It's like my husband went from hero to zero in the blink of an eye."

He couldn't deny that's what a large part of the community thought, and he didn't want to insult her intelligence by trying to. Squeezing her hand, he said, "Well, he'll always be a hero to me."

Her eyelashes grew spiky. "Thanks, Geo. Even getting to talk about him is nice. People avoid the subject like it's the plague."

Once again Lani came to his rescue.

"Just so you know, asking about him, about the person he was, is always the right thing to say."

He quirked his lips. "Well, before I knocked, I was standing out on the porch remembering all the times I invaded your home, drank your beer."

With a chuckle, she let go of him and picked up her coffee. "God, he loved you, George. He used to say you were the little brother he never had."

"Really?" Warmth flooded him, banishing the discomfort, and suddenly Geo was glad he'd come. "Then no wonder he busted my balls so much, Jesus."

"He was beyond proud of you. I mean that."

"Well, it's because of him that I'm even here." Ignoring the tears pricking at the backs of his eyes, he wrinkled his nose at her. "Did he ever tell you about the time he accidentally drank some other dude's dip spit?"

She gasped. "No! He didn't!"

Before long they were laughing, trading stories about a man they'd both loved. Renae raked her hair back with one hand and grinned. "This is great. You're telling me stuff about the side of him I never got to see. You seriously pulled a knife on that bouncer?"

Geo groaned. "I did, convinced I was a badass impressing my teammates. Afterward, when Cade made me cut my brand-new Trident patch off my uniform…"

"Yikes." She winced. "It was a lesson you never forgot, huh?"

"Never. He said, 'This symbol doesn't make you a hero, your actions do. There are plenty of heroic guys who don't wear Tridents and plenty of pieces of shit who do. Which one do you want to be?'"

She picked at the donut she'd dug out from a box of

them on the counter. "He loved mentoring new SEALs. Whenever he had those bouts of depression, I'd remind him of that. 'Those kids are counting on you.'"

Geo froze with his own bite halfway to his mouth. "Depression?"

Renae's gaze met his. "He'd suffered from anxiety and depression since he was in high school."

In growing shock, Geo listened to her tell him about Cade surviving a car crash in which his two best friends died.

"He was sixteen, and he never got professional help," she said. "Instead, his parents told him to pray about it." Her jaw clenched. "Then when he was twenty-two, his BUD/S swim buddy was killed in a training accident right before their first deployment. No time to grieve, just suck it up and go to war. Then…"

"Then Cobra Three-Five," Geo whispered.

"Yes." She nodded. "The husband I knew died on that helicopter with his friends. After he came home, his depression got worse—longer, more pervasive. I begged him to get help, but…"

"He wouldn't?"

"He was a SEAL," she said quietly. "To him, it wasn't a legitimate mental illness, it was a character flaw. A weakness. He was always apologizing to me for not being stronger and 'more of a man.'"

The horror washed through Geo in wave after wave. "I wish I'd known," he said shakily.

"The night he died," Renae went on, "he called me on the sat phone. I asked him again about getting help. He said he would, that he needed to, that things were going to be different from now on."

She shook her head. "He sounded good when he said that, more like himself. I—I believed him. Never dreamed that as soon as he hung up the phone, he would—" Her voice broke.

In an instant, Geo flashed back to what Lani had said about the suicide-attempt survivor who'd visited their group. Turning his palm up and entwining Renae's fingers with his, he told her about it, about Cade's possible relief at having made his plan, his pain eased for maybe the first time in years.

A single tear streaked down her cheek. "How I hope and pray that's the case." She squeezed his hand. "When did you get so wise?"

He squeezed back. "Well, I have this friend..."

After he'd told her about Lani, she smiled. "Bring her over for dinner sometime. I'd love to get to know her better."

He said he would, then got up to rinse his coffee mug out. As he did, he gazed out into the backyard, at the seed pods, brown leaves and other debris that covered the ground. Renae snorted when she saw what he was looking at. "That stupid-ass tree."

"Cade hated it," they said in unison, then laughed. Geo slid his arm around her shoulder and kissed the top of her head.

"I'll come take care of it," he promised. "Soon."

She leaned against him. "I'd appreciate that more than you know."

They held on to each other for several long minutes, and then she determinedly pulled away. "Now shoo. I have hair and nail appointments this afternoon." Putting her hand on his back, she began walking him to the door. "I'm going out with some girlfriends tonight for a bachelorette party. Hers is the third wedding this year and they *refuse* to let me back out this time."

"Good."

"Yep. I'm going to go, and I'm gonna take joy in my friend. If I need to cry, I'll cry, and then I'll get right back to dancing." She stood on tiptoe and kissed his cheek. "I'm *so* glad you stopped by."

After she'd closed the door behind him, Geo sat on his bike at the curb for a while, staring at the house, not quite willing to leave her yet.

"You were right, Lani," he whispered.

Renae hadn't needed him to "fix" anything. What she'd needed was for someone who also loved Cade to show up, to listen, to not be afraid to talk about him. He'd needed that, too, more than he realized.

Firing up his bike, he gazed at the unkempt yard.

He could also honor his friend by being there for the family Geo knew had meant everything to him. His joy and pride in his daughters was front and center in almost everything Cade did, from carrying their picture in his helmet to taking along the tiny stuffed bear that Ari had given him for "luck" on every single mission.

His jaw set with a new determination, Geo activated his Bluetooth and made a call.

"A SEAL brother's wife needs help," he said without preamble when Matt picked up. "You free tomorrow?"

After Geo explained the situation with the tree, Matt promised to be there with all the manpower and lawn tools he could muster.

"Be sure people know this is Cade Barlow's family," Geo grunted. "'Cause if anyone shows up and has a problem with that—"

"Got it," Matt assured him. "There won't be any problems."

As they hung up, a fragile sense of peace wrapped around him.

It was a small thing, trimming a tree, cleaning a yard. But it was a start, and he couldn't deny that taking direct action against his anger and grief was giving him back a much-needed sense of control.

Thank you, Lani.

Would he have ever had the courage to visit Renae if it hadn't been for her?

His throat tightened. Of course he wouldn't have. He'd have continued to avoid her, drowning as he was in the toxic brew of his guilt and shame. In her own gentle and inexorable way, Lani'd thrown him a lifeline, the same one she'd been thrown by the others who'd gone before her.

Geo glanced at his watch and took a deep breath. He could make it. He could keep this momentum going. After all, he was one of the guardians of Cade's memory, and his mentor—his *friend*—deserved no less.

Kicking his bike into gear, he eased away from the curb and headed toward Coronado.

Chapter Nineteen

"I don't think he's coming."

Lani glanced at the door, then at Maura, who smiled at her reassuringly. "It's okay if he doesn't."

"What?" Agitation and worry sharpened Lani's voice. "Geo needs this."

"Well, not everyone is a candidate for group therapy," was Maura's surprising answer. As Lani gaped at her, she went on, "People tend to grieve how they live. How is Geo in life? Is he open with his feelings and emotions, or is he reserved, stoic, self-reliant?"

"He's a SEAL," Lani snapped. "What do you think?" Then she winced. "I'm sorry. I'm just worried about him."

"Of course you are." Maura touched her shoulder. "But sharing in a group isn't everyone's style. It might not be Geo's, and that's okay."

Frustration made Lani's voice sharp once again. "But it's not enough just to talk to *me*, is it?"

"For some people, the relationship is more important than the expertise," Maura said gently. "He obviously trusts you, and I have a feeling that trust isn't easily given. He also knows you've been where he is, that you'll listen to him with empathy and compassion, and without judgment. Don't underestimate the power of any of that."

With a final pat to her shoulder, Maura moved off to greet some other new arrivals. Lani stalked out through the open door to the large patio and sucked in huge gulps of the sea air, her stomach churning.

Being a part of this group had helped turn her life around. Before it, she'd been isolated, convinced she was alone. Learning to understand herself, and her grief, had enabled her to loosen her grip on the past and embrace her new life without the self-doubt that used to dog her every step.

She wanted that for Geo. With every bit of her heart and soul, she wanted that for him, too.

"Hey."

The husky drawl behind her made her whirl around, the sight of Geo's tentative smile flooding her with relief. "Oh! Hey, you."

"Guess I'm in the right place after all," he said. "Wasn't sure for a second. Wow." He gazed over her shoulder at the stunning ocean view. "I totally didn't expect this."

"I think everyone expects the dingy church basement." Lani studied his face, and although his cheeks looked a little pale, the warmth in his eyes was genuine. "How was your morning?"

"Good. Spent some time with Renae."

She listened as he told her about his visit. "Going over there is something I never would've wanted—or had the courage—to do on my own. Thank you. It helped both of us, I think."

He seemed to stand a little taller, as if some of the weight on his shoulders had finally been lifted.

"Oh, I'm so glad."

After a quick glance around, Geo bent his head for a kiss, which lingered just long enough to turn her knees to jelly. "So what do we do now?"

Still quivering, she took his arm and led him back into the bright, airy room. "Now we eat."

The laughter and conversation flowed as the fifteen members of the group helped themselves to the delicious spread of food. Geo loaded his plate sparingly and barely touched what he did take, his discomfort apparent in the set of his jaw and compressed lips.

Maura was right, Lani thought anxiously, watching him. *He's not going to open up here in front of all these strangers.*

As the lunch went on, though, several people approached him to introduce themselves, like this was any old social gathering. Their friendliness, along with the beautiful setting and casual vibe, eventually seemed to put him more at ease.

"This is, uh, different," he muttered at one point, slinging his arm over the back of her chair and leaning close. "Not what I was expecting at all."

"Which was what? A bunch of wild-eyed people clutching tear-stained Kleenex?"

"Umm…"

She chuckled. "Sometimes it's like that, if someone is having a particularly bad day. What's wonderful is how we all help each other. Whatever someone might be struggling with, it's likely that someone else has already experienced that, and maybe found a way through it. We're here to support each other, which is all we can do."

Blowing out a breath, he sat back again, leaving his arm where it was, his thumb idly stroking the ball of her shoulder.

After the meal wound down and everyone settled in with their desserts, Maura said, "For those who haven't had a chance to meet him yet, this is Geo."

Some murmured greetings, which Geo acknowledged with a lift of his hand.

"Geo's loss is fairly recent, within the last year, so we all know he's still trying to find his footing in a lot of ways." Maura turned to him. "Feel free to just listen and absorb today, okay?"

Lani could see a bit more of his tension ease, and he nodded, his hand heavy and warm as he relaxed it against her upper arm. She reached over and squeezed his knee, leaving her palm splayed over his muscular thigh.

"So, my friends," Maura was saying, "how has your story changed since we last met?"

A few people shared their victories, and ongoing struggles, before Bruce said abruptly, "I keep going over what you said about acceptance, and I don't think there's any way to *accept* that I drove my daughter off that bridge almost as surely as if I'd pushed her myself."

As Bruce spoke, Lani couldn't help but remember Maura's earlier words about grieving styles. If Geo's style was to hold it close to him, Bruce's was to talk about it. He described his daughter Christie's struggle with addiction, her unwillingness to go to rehab, the untold chances he'd given her to seek help before finally drawing the line in the sand and telling her that she had to move out.

"She begged me for just two more weeks," Bruce sobbed. "Just two more weeks. But I'd already given her months, and I'd had enough. Tough love, right?"

Despite the fact everyone in the group had heard this story countless times before, nobody acted impatient, or bored, their attention fixed unwaveringly on Bruce as he struggled to live with something Lani wasn't sure she herself could bear.

Once again, she breathed a silent prayer of thanks that her last memories of Tyler were good ones. Geo sat frozen next to her, the muscles of his thigh bunched tightly under her hand.

"The next morning she drove onto the bridge, parked her car and jumped off." Bruce sucked in a breath. "I killed her!"

The people on either side of him reached out to grip his shoulders in support.

"No, Bruce," Maura said. "She killed herself."

"Because of me! If I hadn't kicked her out, she'd still be alive!"

Lani's heart ached as Maura took him through it once again, reiterating the fact that he hadn't been responsible for Christie's actions. "You were only doing what you thought was right at the time. If you'd known Christie was going to kill herself, you would have acted differently, but you're not omniscient. You can't blame yourself for something you didn't know would happen."

His face pale, Bruce whispered, "I've never told anyone this before, but—" He seemed to steel himself, then blurted, "A few minutes before the cameras on the bridge said she jumped, sh-she called me."

Around the circle, eyes widened, and even Lani had to fight an involuntary gasp.

Maura remained unruffled, her voice calm. "And you didn't answer."

"No, I didn't! I didn't want to talk to her."

"Because you were angry."

"Yes. I wanted to teach her a lesson!"

Next to Lani, a giant shudder went through Geo's body, and his fingers dug almost painfully into her arm.

"I wanted to show her that Dad wasn't going to be at her beck and call anymore," Bruce said raggedly. "I declined the call, and a few minutes later, she jumped. How the fuck am I ever gonna *accept* that or live with the guilt of knowing I killed her?"

The people next to Bruce continued to hold on to him as Maura got up from her seat and pulled her chair over to sit in front of him knee-to-knee.

"Let's try something," she said softly. "Let's try replacing the word *guilt* with the word *regret*, okay? When you think of Christie, instead of 'I killed her,' try saying, 'I regret that I chose that particular time to draw my line in the sand.' Or, 'I regret my anger in that moment.'"

Bruce mopped his face.

"Something else to add to that," Maura said, "is to make what I like to call 'living amends' to your loved one, which is taking the action with others that you wish you'd taken with *them* in that moment. For example, Bruce, you might say: 'My living amends to Christie is that I will always answer my phone, especially after an argument.'"

Bruce was already shaking his head. "That's too simple—"

"But sometimes the simplest things are the most obvious," Maura broke in gently. "Not answering the phone didn't cause Christie's suicide—her mental illness did. The fact you had a complicated relationship with her, and the fact that your last interaction was acrimonious, doesn't negate the fact that Christie was ill and she lost her battle with that illness."

She reached out and took Bruce's hands in hers. "I'm not saying it's easy, or that it ever goes completely away. Some days I struggle with regret so crippling I can barely breathe. Vincent was my *son*. As his mother, how could I not know he was in so much pain?"

Bruce squeezed his eyes shut.

"My work here is part of my own living amends to my son. Finding meaning in his death has helped me move forward, and I want to help others find their way forward, too." Maura released him and sat back. "You regret the things you said to her. You regret not answering the phone that morning. But you're not 'guilty' of anything except being human."

Letting her gaze drift around the room, she said, "My friends, thank you for being here, for witnessing Bruce's grief. Thank you for letting him witness your own. Sharing our pain, and having it reflected back at us, reminds us that we're not alone."

Next to Lani, Geo grunted, his hand slipping off her shoulder. Then he got up, yanked open the sliding glass door, and walked away.

* * *

"Should I go to him?"

Indecision roiled in her gut as Lani gazed out over the sand toward Geo's distant figure. He sat facing the ocean, unmoving, his arms linked loosely around his upraised knees.

Next to her, Maura said, "I don't know him as you do, my dear. What are your instincts telling you?"

"That if he really wanted to leave, he would've taken his bike and gone."

"But instead, he's sitting on the beach in plain sight." Maura's voice was soft.

Raking her hair back from her forehead, Lani bit her lip. "If I go to him, I wouldn't know what to say."

"Well, to start with, just sit with him. Whatever he's trying to work out, he'll let you know if he wants to talk about it or not. If he does, then listen. That's all."

With a reassuring pat to her shoulder, Maura went back inside to join the rest of the group.

After another long hesitation, Lani finally made her way down the stairs and headed out across the sand. She could tell the moment he heard her scuffing toward him, because he turned his head slightly, shoulders bunching up.

She fought the impulse to turn and scurry away. What if he didn't want her here? How dare she intrude?

Before she could retreat, Geo swiveled around to face her. "Hey," he said, then reached out his hand.

Relief making her knees weak, she grasped it and lowered herself to sit at his side. For a while, neither of them spoke. She could see him watching her out of the corner of her eye, so she kept her expression smooth, serene.

"Are you mad at me?" he finally asked.

She shook her head. "No."

"I'm sorry I left like that."

"It's okay."

"It's just—" He combed his fingers through the sand, sifting it, his throat working "—that Bruce guy, you know? His story hit a little too close to home for me."

She waited, and when he didn't go on, asked gently, "Why did it hit close to home?"

"Because—" Tilting his head back toward the sky, Geo sucked in a few deep breaths. "Because, like him, I missed my chance to stop it. Stop Cade."

"So tell me."

He cleared his throat. "It's not an easy story to hear—"

"I know. Tell me anyway."

Lani kept up the comforting touch as he described Cade pulling a gun on Bosch after threatening an unarmed prisoner. "That was him unraveling in plain sight, and everyone had an excuse: 'Cade's burned out.' 'He's been through a lot.' 'He just needs time.'"

When he paused, she said, "I think most people have preconceived notions about those who die by suicide. We don't picture them as high-achievers, popular or larger-than-life." *Like a Navy SEAL.* "Instead, we picture someone who cries all the time and is clearly depressed."

Geo gave a jerky nod. "He *had* been through a lot. But the guys were getting sick of his unpredictability, and I was still pissed about how he'd pointed his gun at my dog, his own *teammate*. So when—" He broke off, his body coiling, tensing.

Before he could push to his feet, Lani slid her arm around his waist to anchor him. "No. Don't run away from this anymore, because it's eating you alive. Talk to me, please."

A giant shudder went through him, and he clenched his fists, the knuckles white. Just when she was sure he wouldn't answer, he ground out, "In our team room, we had a message board with all of our names on it. One night, after a clusterfuck of a mission, I was headed to bed when I saw that someone had—" He swallowed hard. "Someone had written 'We don't fucking want you here' next to Cade's name."

"Ah." She closed her eyes briefly. "Did you write it?"

"No!" The word burst out of him with a vehemence that left no doubt he was telling the truth. "But I—" His head drooped. "I also didn't erase it. I left it. To teach him a lesson. To let him know that his actions were affecting unit cohesion."

Her thumb rubbed his nape in soothing circles. "Which they were."

"Yes, but—"

"Had you seen that kind of thing before? A message on the board like that?"

"Shit, yes. Dozens of times."

"So it wasn't anything out of the ordinary. When you saw them before, would you ever erase them?"

"No, because they didn't happen unless the dude deserved it."

"Did Cade?"

Geo didn't answer.

"From what you're saying, it sounds like he was becoming a danger, not only to unit cohesion, but to people's lives. *Bosch's* life."

When he still didn't answer, she took another tack. "What would happen when the other guys would get those messages intended for them?"

"They'd either get their act together or be forced out of the unit."

"Did they kill themselves?"

He blinked, his jaw bunching. "No."

"Did any of them?"

"No one did. They fixed their shit or got out."

"Okay. So I think we can conclude that messages on a white board don't make people kill themselves."

"But—"

"If you'd known Cade's state of mind in that moment, you *would* have erased it." She squeezed the back of his neck. "If the guy who wrote it knew, he wouldn't have written it. But you *didn't* know, and the things that were done, the things that were said, were things that'd been done and said dozens of times before. Right?"

Geo stared straight ahead.

"You didn't do anything differently that night than what you'd always done. Someone thought Cade needed a wake-up call and wrote that on the board. You agreed, and you didn't erase it." Lani paused. "That message didn't kill him. He killed *himself*."

A tiny sob broke from Geo's lips, quickly suppressed.

"You regret that it was the last straw for him—"

The next sob was harsher, deeper, and she wrapped her arms around his shoulders.

"—but you didn't know. You. Didn't. Know. And it's not your fault."

She held on to him while he shuddered against her, although he managed to hold back the tears.

All around, beachgoers went about their daily lives, while the two people huddled in the sand right in front of them were fighting to put theirs back together.

"You're not alone, Geo," she whispered in his ear. "I'm here with you."

And I don't know how I'm ever going to let you go.

Chapter Twenty

Lani followed him home, the cherry-red of his motor-cycle taillight glowing bright in the gathering darkness.

Inside her apartment, she turned into Geo's arms, her palms sliding up his chest to link around his neck. "Why don't we get in the shower and have a good cry?"

He smiled, his hands settling on her hips as he started inching her down the hall. "How about we get in the shower and skip the crying part?"

"But that's the beauty of it." She stood on tiptoe to brush her mouth against his. "Whether you choose to cry or not, no one will ever know, will they? It's between you and the shower."

Geo didn't answer, just reached behind his neck to unclasp her arms and ease them to her sides. "Turn around," he said softly. When she did, he gathered her hair in his hand and draped it over her shoulder before leaning down to place an open-mouthed kiss on her exposed nape.

"Mmm," he breathed. "There's a distinct possibility that you're overdressed for this shower. It's a, er, way more casual event."

"Ha. Did I misread the invitation?"

"I think you did." Trailing his tongue along the side of her neck, he murmured, "Luckily, I'm here to help."

"Yes. Lucky, lucky me." She'd meant the words to sound teasing, but instead they came out fervent, with an emotional undertone that flushed her entire body hot.

"Baby…" Mouthing her earlobe, Geo eased the zipper of her dress down, inch by inch, until it sagged to the waist. With an expert flick of his fingers, the fastening of her bra popped open, making her gasp.

"Wow. You're pretty good at this wardrobe director stuff," she quavered. "I'll be the best, uh, *un*dressed woman at the party."

"Everyone will want to know what you're *not* wearing," he agreed modestly. "It's true."

Chuckling, he moved around in front of her and tipped her chin up to gaze down into her eyes. "So beautiful," he whispered before brushing the softest of kisses over her lips. Holding on to her hand, he helped her step out of the dress and bra now pooled around her ankles. Then he knelt in front of her and hooked his fingers in the sides of her delicate lace panties.

As he eased them down her legs, Lani stroked his hair, her hand shaking with so much tenderness she felt choked with it. Geo glanced up at her, then leaned forward to nuzzle the swell of her belly, his arms wrapping around her hips.

"Oh, how I wish…" Lani mouthed the words as he drifted his lips slowly, almost worshipfully, up her body until he was standing again, his breathing slightly ragged.

"Is it time to go to the party?" she croaked. "'Cause I'm ready."

"Yeah? Me, too." Geo yanked his T-shirt over his head and shucked his jeans. Her eyes dropped helplessly to his cock, which bobbed in between them, the swollen tip already slick with excitement.

"Oh, my." She gave him a few strokes, which made him hiss. "Lovin' this party favor."

He pulled her close, letting out a sigh as her breasts flattened against his chest. "I'm thinking—" Geo bent to kiss her "—that we skip the party—"

"What?" Her eyes widened. "No!"

"—to go to a better one." Swinging her up in his arms, he carried her to the bed.

"Ohh." She cupped his cheek and drifted her thumb over his lips. "I do like the way you think."

Bracing one knee on the mattress, he laid her gently in the middle of it, then eased over top of her, his kiss warm and coaxing. He licked, nipped, and tasted, as if savoring her, his hands gently arousing, until Lani arched up against him with a breathless moan. "Please."

"Mmm." He trailed his open mouth between her breasts and nuzzled his nose against the curves. "Please what, darlin'?"

She writhed when he sucked each nipple in turn, teeth gently scraping the pebbled flesh. As she lifted and spread her knees, he let out a soft hiss. "Tell me what you need, sweetheart."

She was already beyond words, so Lani yanked on his hair and showed him. The first touch of his lips on her clit had her crying out, hips moving restlessly. Geo didn't tease her, didn't make her wait, just opened her wide, the hot swirls of his tongue driving her out of her mind.

Yet all too soon it wasn't enough. "Please," she gasped. "Need you inside me."

He thrust one finger deep, then two. "Fuck, baby, you're so wet," he growled, the tip of his tongue rasping across her clit. The hoarse note of satisfaction and possessiveness in his voice sent Lani careening over the edge, her orgasm sweeping through her in a sweet rush.

He took her through it, easing her back to earth with soft licks and gentle sucks, at last brushing a kiss along the inside of one inner thigh before leaning over to the bedside table for a condom.

Her blood still surging through her veins, she stopped him with a trembling hand on his shoulder. "I had a full testing panel at my OB's when I found out I was pregnant. Everything's negative."

Geo froze for the briefest of seconds, then straightened and sat back on his heels. "Negative at my last physical three months ago."

Her eyes dropped to his cock. Even as she watched, he wrapped his fingers around it and gave it a few rough strokes. She licked her lips and relaxed fully back into the mattress. "Then no condom."

A flush staining his cheekbones, Geo came down over top of her, his palms flat on the bed next to her shoulders. Slowly, deliberately, he circled his hips, dragging himself against her from base to tip. "This what you want?"

The hard, thick column sliding over her hypersensitive flesh made her gasp. "Geo!"

"Is it?"

Reaching up behind herself, Lani grabbed onto her pillow and wound her legs around his waist. "Yes, it's what I want," she panted. "Please. I need you inside me."

Flush deepening, teeth bared, Geo notched the broad head against her entrance and started a slow, insistent rock. "Oh, *God*," he ground out. "Fuck, you feel so good."

His head tipped back almost helplessly, eyes sliding closed. Planting his knees wide on the bed, he started to move, his thrusts starting out slow, but getting longer and harder as his need grew.

Lani wrapped her arms around his neck and held on to him with all her strength, reveling in his pleasure, his low moans. She arched up into him, the hair on his chest teasing her swollen nipples, his cock driving deep, stretching her wide.

As her second orgasm built, she squeezed her own eyes shut, not wanting it to end, but he cupped her chin in his hand and kissed her with such tenderness that she was lost. She spiraled into bliss as he stiffened, his body throbbing inside hers, the words he breathed into her mouth sounding very much like, "I love you."

Love won't be enough, Geo. It's not going to be enough.

She clutched onto him and buried her face in his neck.

But God help me, I love you, too.

"Will you go somewhere with me tomorrow?"

Anywhere. Lani turned onto her side to face him. "Where?"

Haltingly, Geo told her about a plan to get together with some team guys and work on Renae's yard. "I guess that can be part of my—what did Maura call it?—living amends to Cade. Being there for his family."

"Yes." Reaching up, she stroked his cheek. "Of course I'll come."

"I want to surround her with the community, show her that—" he took a deep breath "—that she's not been completely abandoned."

Her heart aching, she thought again about her friend Suzette, and how hard it'd be for her to see Cade's death in the same light as Harry's.

"I'm happy to go." Pulling his head down, she kissed him softly. "Thank you for asking me."

A relieved sigh escaped him, and he pressed their foreheads together. "You are, hands down, the most incredible person I've ever met. I wish..."

When his jaw tightened, she smoothed her thumb along it, tears pricking the backs of her eyes. "I wish, too," she managed.

With twin sighs, they settled down, her back to his front, his knees tucked up behind hers. Before long, he was asleep, his soft snores rumbling comfortingly in her ear. Lani lay awake, staring into the darkness, thoughts in a tangle.

Could they make this work? *How* could they make this work?

Geo twitched, his hand splaying low over her belly. As if in response, the baby moved, the sensation sharper than she'd ever felt it. She gasped, on the verge of waking Geo to tell him about it when she caught herself.

It's not his child.

Does it matter? she argued silently. *He's invested, both in me and this pregnancy.*

Sure. It's easy to be invested when the baby is an abstract, not a living, breathing reminder of another man.

Geo's not like that, she scolded her inner voice. *He's not the type of person who'd hold anything against an innocent child.*

But he'd be gone so much. Would they ever get to bond? You don't want your child to have a part-time father.

A father whose first priority—first *love*—would always be his job, his teammates. And besides, when had he said anything about wanting more? Could she really see him as a dad?

Try as she might, Lani couldn't picture it. She and Geo would always want different things, and when it was time to move on, they'd both move on.

Eyes stinging, she stroked the back of his hand, whispering, "But damn, you do throw one hell of a party."

Chapter Twenty-One

I wonder if anyone will show.

Geo gripped the steering wheel, his stomach in knots.

Next to him, Lani sat quietly, a container of cookies on her lap. In the backseat was a large cooler holding the variety of sandwiches she'd insisted on getting up early to make.

"They'll bring the beer, so *someone's* gotta bring the food," she'd said jokingly.

He was just afraid no one would show up to eat it.

As he wound his way deeper into the pleasant Chula Vista neighborhood, his anxiety grew. He wanted this for Renae, wanted to show her that there were those in the community still there for her.

He glanced at Lani, the uncomfortable truth making him squirm. *He* wouldn't even be here now if it hadn't been for her gentle encouragement. If it'd been left up to him, he would've kept his head buried in the sand, would've kept on running.

And missed out on so much.

Reaching over, he took her hand and threaded their

fingers together. No matter what happened between them, she'd touched his life in ways he'd never forget.

One last gradual curve, and Renae's house came into view. Geo gasped, his hand tightening on Lani's. Lining the curb on each side of the street were several large pickups and more than a couple of motorcycles.

Team guys milled on the sidewalk dressed in jeans and T-shirts, some in loud-patterned board shorts and tank tops, all of them boisterous and—he rolled his eyes—holding cases of beer.

"Told you!" Lani crowed with a triumphant smirk. "I think it's going to be all right."

As soon as they got out of the car, Matt jogged up, and he and Geo bumped knuckles before flowing into a back-slapping hug. "You really came through, man," Geo said fervently. "Thank you."

Matt grinned. "You're welcome." He turned to Lani, eyes widening. "Well, hey there, bartender lady. Remember me?"

"Well, of course I do," she exclaimed. "And congrats on your engagement! Shane's a lucky guy."

"Nah, I'm the lucky one."

Faces animated, hands waving, they were talking about some bar fight Shane had been in when Rhys snuck up behind Lani, finger to his lips. She talked on, oblivious, until Rhys reached out and flicked her on the earlobe.

"Ouch!" She whirled around. "Rhys, you asshole. You know I hate that!"

Cackling, Rhys feinted and dodged the playful punches she threw. "Too slow," he taunted after each one. "Missed me. Weak."

It was a game they'd obviously played many times before.

The warmth in Geo's chest splintered into painful shards of jealousy. He gritted his teeth, not quite sure what to do with it all, just as a pretty brunette walked up to them.

"Now, children," she said drily, and grinning, Rhys wrapped his arm around her waist and hauled her close.

"Well, hello, gorgeous," he murmured. "Where have you been all my life?"

Geo immediately tensed, berating himself for putting Lani in the position of having to see Rhys's new girlfriend. Racking his brain, he was feverishly looking for a way to extricate her from the situation when Lani held her knuckles out to Devon.

He could only gape in shock as Devon returned the fist bump.

"Help me with the food?" Lani asked, and before he knew it, the two of them were headed for the car, chattering, laughing.

His mouth hanging open, he stared in bemusement, dimly aware of a big white dude with a shaved head walking up to elbow Rhys.

"That's some next-level shit right there, man," he rumbled, "your ex and your current squeeze gettin' all chummy like that. Can't imagine the stories those two tell each other about you." He gave a dramatic shudder. "Poor bastard."

Rhys laughed. "More like *lucky* bastard, Grizz."

Grizz barked out an incredulous laugh. "If any of my exes dared show their faces around my wife, she'd—" Like the thought was too horrible to contemplate, he shook his head, popped open a beer and gulped down half the can.

After he'd wandered away, Rhys crossed his arms over his chest and turned to Geo. "I didn't realize you knew Lani."

Fighting the urge to fidget under his steady gaze, Geo grunted, "We're friends. Have been for a few months now."

They both caught sight of Matt struggling to unload a tall ladder from a nearby pickup and jogged over to help him. As they set it up against the side of the house, Geo said quietly, "I'm lucky to have met her when I did. She's, uh, helped me a lot in dealing with Cade's death. I don't know where I'd be without her right now."

Rhys's face softened. "Yeah, she's a good person."

"The best."

"She deserves to be happy." Rhys's eyes bored into his. "I'd hate to see her hurt."

"I'd never hurt her."

I love her.

But Geo didn't say that, and after a moment, Rhys smiled. "Of course she can take care of herself, but Devon would have my head if I didn't at least *attempt* to warn you, so there, consider yourself warned."

They both chuckled, and with that, Rhys headed to join the group unloading a small cherry-picker from the back of someone's trailer. Soon the air was filled with the sound of leaf blowers and the whine of a chainsaw. A few of the guys had brought their older kids and put them to work raking and bagging debris.

His heart full, Geo was heading for the ladder to climb up to the roof when Renae called his name. They hugged each other tightly. "God, you don't know how much I've missed this."

He pulled back to grin down at her. "What, a bunch of assholes invading your home? We used to do that a lot, didn't we?"

"And I loved every minute of it." She blinked a few times, her eyelashes spiky with unshed tears. "So did Cade. This all feels like—well, it feels like old times. In the best possible way."

After a kiss to his cheek, she went to greet some new arrivals.

Gripping the sides of the ladder, Geo was about to continue his climb when some movement in his peripheral vision caught his eye. Over at the far end of the yard, near the fence, Cade's oldest daughter, Ari, was kicking a faded soccer ball into a small net.

He hesitated, one foot still on the rung, wanting to approach her but not sure of his welcome. After all, it'd been so long since he'd seen her...

On the verge of chickening out, he saw Ari glance over her shoulder at him, then quickly look away when she noticed him watching her.

Okay. He had to go through with it now. His heart pounding, he stuffed his hands in his pockets and started wandering her direction. What the fuck did he say to a ten-year-old who'd just lost her father?

His "Hey, kiddo" came out as nothing but a hoarse croak, so he cleared it and tried again.

"Hey." Ari glanced over at him, her blue eyes— so much like Cade's—holding a wary bitterness that punched Geo right in the gut. "Haven't seen *you* in forever." She snorted. "Uncle Geo."

He was on the verge of playing it off as if he'd just been busy, when a long-forgotten memory popped into his head—his dad's visitation, and the hushed, pitying voices whispering stupid euphemisms for death.

He's dead, okay? He's not "asleep" or "in a better place." He's just fucking dead!

What his eleven-year-old self wouldn't have given for some simple goddamn honesty. If nothing else, he could offer that to Ari now.

Praying for wisdom, he said, "I know. I've been really sad because your dad died."

Ari froze, then kicked the ball hard into the net.

"I'm sorry. I still should've come to see you." He waited, agonized, but she didn't reply, her kicks getting harder and more vicious.

Once again, Lani's words popped into his head. *"Asking about him, about the person he* was, *is always the right thing to say."*

Geo dropped to sit cross-legged on the ground, well out of her line of fire, and watched her for a minute before saying, "I remember once, when you made this awesome game-winning goal, your mom emailed your dad a video of it."

Ari abruptly put her foot on the ball to stop it, her head cocked in his direction, although she didn't look at him.

"He showed it to everyone on our base, you know?" he went on. "Whoever walked by got to see it."

Silence, and then, "Did *you* see it?"

Chuckling, he said, "At least five times, no lie. Maybe more."

Ari shrugged, her toe worrying the ball back and

forth. "Did he—" She took a deep breath. "What did he say about it?"

What did he say about me?

Her unspoken question lodged in Geo's throat like a shard of glass. "How proud he was of you. That he knew how hard you'd been practicing to get better. That he—" Despite his best efforts, his voice broke. "That he wished he could've been there to see it."

Ari's lips tightened, but for the first time, her eyes met his directly. The pain in them almost stopped his heart. "Then why—?"

"I don't know," he said with quiet honesty. "I wish I did."

After a moment, she turned away and resumed her kicking. Instinctively, he stayed put, even as his stomach twisted itself into knots of inadequacy. At last she grunted, "No one wants to talk about him with me. Most people just say stupid shit."

She flicked another glance at him, as if gauging his reaction to the profanity, but Geo nodded. "I know. I remember getting pissed off about that, too, when my dad died." He gave her a tentative smile. "Tell you what. Whenever you want to talk about your dad, just call me, okay? Anytime. I'll make sure your mom has my number."

For one heart-stopping moment, Ari started to smile back, but then it faded, her eyes going blank again. "Sure. Except you'll be on deployment," she said flatly. "You'll be gone all the time, too."

The truth of it was like a soccer ball to the face. "Not for a while," he managed. "I'm gonna be home for a little while, you know? We could—would you like to talk now?"

"Nah." With her foot, she expertly flipped the ball up into her arms and, without another word, walked away.

Geo struggled to his feet and trudged back toward the ladder, the knots in his stomach tightening.

He *wouldn't* be here. What the fuck was he thinking? He couldn't be what she needed. He couldn't be what *anyone* needed.

"Geo?" Lani's soft voice cut through the roaring in his ears, and before he knew it, she was in his arms. He clutched her tightly, her comforting warmth, the feel of her for some reason keeping him together, from splintering apart.

Pulling her into the shadows next to the house, he threaded his fingers through her hair and tilted her head back to kiss her, softly, gently.

"Mmm." Linking her arms around his neck, she relaxed against him. "This is nice." With one last nip to his lower lip, she whispered, "You okay?"

He buried his face in her hair, breathing in the scent of her shampoo, her subtle perfume. "No," he croaked. He told her about his conversation with Ari as she stroked his nape and listened quietly.

"I'm not a trained therapist," he fretted. "What was I thinking?"

"Hmm. That you were someone who loved her dad, too. Maybe what she needed in that moment wasn't necessarily a therapist, but a friend."

"Uncle Geo." He let out a ragged sigh. "That's what they called me, the girls. And all I've done is let them down."

He appreciated when Lani didn't rush in with a bunch of empty reassurances that he probably wouldn't believe anyway. All she said was, "Well, you're here now."

For a while anyway. Not long enough.

He could see the truth of it on her face reflected back at him, but she only cupped his cheek and gave him one more soft kiss. "You're here now," she repeated, then took his hand and led him back around the house. After letting go with a gentle squeeze, she headed toward the group on the porch, the skirt of her dress swishing around her thighs.

With a lovesick sigh, Geo turned to climb the ladder and get to work cleaning out the rain gutters. Wrist deep in wet leaves and other trash, he was startled several minutes later when a frosty can of Coke landed on the roof not far from him. A tousled blond head popped up at the top of the ladder.

"Thought you might be thirsty," Ari said.

"Um…" He craned his neck and desperately sought out Renae, who was watching them. She nodded imperceptibly at him from her seat on the porch.

"You want it or not?" Ari's voice now held a note of belligerence, so he hastily stripped off his work gloves and extended her a helping hand.

"Of course I want it," he said, hovering until she was safely seated on the sloping roof, her knees drawn up, arms wrapped around them.

He pried open the top of the can and got a spray of Coke in the face for his trouble, not even caring about the cold stickiness when he heard her give the faintest of giggles.

"No, really, thanks," he said drily, taking a huge swallow as her shoulders shook with silent laughter.

When the Coke was gone, Geo crumpled up the can, tossed it to the ground below, and waited.

"Did you cry when my dad died?"

Her abrupt question startled him, and for a long moment he was at a loss for words.

Be honest. Just be honest. It's what you *wanted back then, remember?*

"No," he said softly. "I didn't. Did you?"

She rested her forehead on her knees. "No."

"Why, sweetie?"

Ari shrugged. "Dunno. How come *you* didn't?"

Pursing his lips, he leaned back on his hands. "I think it's because I was afraid if I started, I'd never stop. I really miss your dad a lot."

"Yeah, me, too." Her voice quavered a bit as she toyed with one frayed shoelace. "My mom and sister cry all the time, too, so I thought maybe—"

His heart ached. "You thought maybe *you* should try to be strong?"

"Mm-hmm. My dad used to tell me that when he left. 'Be strong for Mom and Ava. I'm counting on you, Love Bug.'"

A sudden bolt of anger toward Cade made Geo clench his fists. How dare he put that burden on her shoulders and then check himself out?

You bastard. You left such a fucking mess behind, you know that?

Ari was looking at him anxiously, so he strove for calm. "It's not a kid's job to be strong," he said evenly. "It's a kid's job to be sad if you want, to cry if you want, to scream into your pillow if you want, and know your mom's gonna come hug you, take care of you."

She didn't reply, her lips still tight, and suddenly, Geo couldn't help but chuckle. "You look so much like your dad right now, you don't even know."

Her eyes flew to his. "Really?"

"Yep. And you're stubborn like him, smart like him. He also played soccer like a *badass*." Before he knew it, Geo was telling her about a game that'd sprung up on their outpost one night, SEALs against the Army. "Your dad was goalie, and he made all these awesome saves." He pantomimed diving and twisting as best he could in a seated position.

"Did he win?"

"Yep. The Army guys had to give him a box of homemade cookies this one dude's wife had sent him. That was the bet."

Bet.

A pang went through him, but it was softer, muted, more nostalgia than sorrow. The realization loosened the knots in his chest a little.

"You remind me a lot of him, in all the best ways," he finished softly. "And, kiddo, he was so proud of you. So proud."

Ari's shoulders slumped and she sighed, like a balloon letting out all its air. He waited, until at last she looked over at him. "Will you come watch me play sometime?"

A huge lump in his throat, Geo reached out and tugged on her ponytail. "I'll be there with bells on."

After he'd helped her down the ladder, he leaned against the side of the house and watched her tuck her soccer ball under her arm and head for the porch. On the way, a couple of younger kids ran up and, with excited gestures and animated faces, asked if she wanted to play.

Ari shrugged. "Sure."

Soon there was a small group of them kicking the ball about. She proved to be a patient and knowledgeable coach, and finally he turned away to climb to the roof once again, a cautious satisfaction swirling through him.

Of course she still had a lifetime of grief work ahead of her, but Geo would always remember that first pressure-valve release of emotion that came from simply talking about it with someone who understood, who cared.

And if what he'd gone through as a child would help her...

Helplessly, his eyes sought out Lani, who was sitting in the sun laughing with Devon and Renae. She'd learned to take the things that hurt the most and use them to light the way for others walking in her shoes. What an amazing tribute to Tyler.

He moved his gaze to Ari, who gave him a tiny smile when she saw him looking.

And you've helped me give some much-needed relief to a devastated little girl.

"How am I going to leave you, Lani?" he whispered.

How the fuck was he ever gonna leave?

"Hey, can I say something real quick?"

Someone turned the music down and all eyes settled

on Renae, who'd stood and was nervously twisting her fingers together.

Geo slung his arm along the back of Lani's chair and kicked his legs out in front of him before doing a quick scan of the assembled group on the deck. Night had fallen, and full of beer and steak—courtesy of some of the SEALs' wives who'd showed up—everyone was mellow, chill and enjoying each other's company.

Most of the kids were in the living room watching a movie, but since their talk on the roof, Ari had stuck close to Geo's side. She'd been peppering him with questions about Bosch when Renae tapped her steak knife on a nearby beer bottle.

"I just wanted to thank you all for coming," she said. "Of course the yard looks absolutely beautiful, but more than that, it's been so nice to feel a part of things again." She hesitated. "Did any of you know Cade?"

A few hands went up, and to Geo's surprise, Rhys said, "I remember him from a few years ago when his platoon rotated through our outpost." He grinned. "We were bored, and frustrated from planning missions only for the head shed not to approve them."

The SEALs grunted their understanding—they'd all been there. Most people pictured spec ops units as mavericks who got to do whatever they wanted, when in reality, missions were carefully planned based on gathered intelligence and then sent up the chain of command for approval.

Most were denied, and even the approved ones tended to spin up and then spin right back down.

"So anyway, Cade heard us bitching and organized a baseball game, but not just any baseball game." Rhys paused. "An *opposite-hand* baseball game. Whatever your dominant hand was, you could only pitch, throw, bat, whatever, with the other one. That was some of the funniest shit I've ever seen, oh, my God. He really saved our sanity."

Several other guys chimed in with stories about running into Cade over the years, and almost all were about when he'd used humor to boost morale, to motivate or to encourage.

The ever-present lump rose into Geo's throat. Like that stupid bet. That stupid, wonderful bet.

Miss you, Cade-Man.

At the end of the impromptu memorial service, Renae wiped a few tears from her cheeks. "I loved hearing this. Thank you for letting me see my husband through your eyes."

Glasses were raised all around.

"To Cade!"

"'Til Valhalla, brother."

"Long live the brotherhood."

The toasts finished, someone turned the music back up and the SEALs settled in to party. Renae approached Geo and gave him a long, fervent hug. "I can't tell you how much today has meant to me and the girls. You've helped us feel normal again, and I'll never, ever forget it."

He hugged her back, then said tentatively, "Ari invited me to watch one of her games. Is that—"

"Of course it's fine with me, but Geo, it's not your job to play dad, you know. If you don't want to—"

"I want to." Taking a deep breath, he went on, "I lost my own father at about her age. Yeah, it's different, but in some ways it's the same. I know what it's like to be a grieving little kid."

Standing on tiptoe, she pressed a kiss to his cheek. "You'll be a blessing to her, then, George. And to me. Thank you."

After she'd headed inside to check on the kids, Lani walked up and took his arm. "You okay?"

He told her about his conversation with Ari on the roof. "I keep taking your advice to talk about the person Cade *was*. Hands down, it's the best advice I've ever gotten."

She smiled, a warmth in her gold-flecked eyes that sent an answering quiver through him. "Every life has meaning, no matter how it ended. Focusing on that makes all the difference."

He couldn't help but tilt her chin up to give her a gentle kiss. "*You've* made all the difference."

Her face softened. "Geo, I—"

Whatever she was about to say was lost when Devon called out, "Hey, Lani, get over here! We have baby shower questions!"

With an apologetic wrinkle of her nose, she squeezed his arm and headed over to the lively group of women. Not far away from them, Rhys leaned against the railing talking to Matt and Shane, who were standing arm in arm, Shane's hand resting possessively on Matt's hip.

Something Rhys said made them burst into laughter, and Shane pulled Matt closer and kissed the top of his head.

"That's some fuckin' next-level shit."

Turning, Geo saw Grizz sprawled out with a beer

in hand, staring at Matt and Shane. He grunted. "Apparently *everything* is to you, man. What is it now?"

"That." Grizz lifted his chin toward the two men, in the next instant letting out a yelp when his wife leaned over and swatted him on the arm.

"Are you serious? Two guys in love and showing affection? That's surreal to you?"

"What?" An expression of sincere confusion flitted across Grizz's face. "No! What I mean is, look at him! Knytych's *smiling.* Baby, he never smiles, not like that."

Geo had to agree. "It's true."

Indeed, Matt's happiness radiated from him, the kind of happiness that came from having found his place in the world, and from knowing that he was loved.

"They're some of my favorite dudes, you know," Grizz went on indignantly. "I'd *never* hate on them."

His wife wrapped her arms around his neck and pulled him into a repentant hug. "I misunderstood. I'm sorry."

"You should be," he groused, even as he hugged her back. "They're my *friends*, babe."

Geo left them nuzzling, and wandered closer to the group just as Rhys crouched behind both Lani's and Devon's chairs and whispered something that made them both look at Matt.

"You can *sing*?" he heard Lani say. "Really?"

"Like an angel," Devon assured her as Matt rolled his eyes.

"Arts and theater, not much else to do at a North Dakota high school," he said jokingly. "I wanted to stay *warm.*"

"Except he's really, really good," Devon said. "*I'm*

the one who looked like a chump singing karaoke with him."

"Lani can sing." Rhys squeezed her shoulder, laughing when she turned to swat at him. "Get her drunk enough and she'll serenade you."

Hoots from around the group as she raised her voice to be heard over them. "Whoa, whoa! It'll be a *long* time before I'm ever that drunk again." She pointed to her baby bump. "So don't hold your breath, people. I don't sing sober."

"And *I* only sing when I'm trying to convince certain clowns I don't care about the date he's flaunting in my face," Matt chimed in, yanking away from Shane in mock disgust. "I never asked, who was that guy anyway?"

"Nobody, my love," Shane said as he wrapped his arms around Matt's waist and pulled him back against him. "Absolutely nobody."

Wistfulness and a feeling of disconnect drove Geo off the deck and out into the shadows of the backyard. After all, he didn't really belong here. His time in this platoon was only temporary, and it'd be over soon enough.

Then what?

Then he'd focus on his career. He'd make Chief, and move into leadership, where he'd be able to mentor young SEALs. Yeah, it'd certainly be rewarding, to help usher the next generation of young men—and maybe soon young women—into the ranks.

But what about when it was over? When he hit his twenty, twenty-five, maybe thirty-year mark? Eventually he'd have to retire, and what would he have to show for it? A rank on his sleeve, maybe a few medals, a trail of broken relationships scattered in his wake?

He gazed up at the now-neatly trimmed tree in the moonlight, a sudden wave of loneliness, of sadness, crashing over him and nearly driving him to his knees.

What if I'm alone?

As he bent double, struggling for air, footsteps rushed through the grass and then an arm wrapped around his waist, anchoring him. "I'm here. I'm here, Geo."

At Lani's whispered words, the last of the walls he'd built around his heart started to crumble into dust.

"God, I just miss him so much," he gasped. "I'm so fucking angry at him, and I love him, and I *hate* him."

"I know," she crooned, holding him tight. "I know."

"You had it all, Cade. A *family*," he whispered brokenly. "You belonged. You were *loved*."

And suddenly, for the first time, Geo caught a glimpse of how deep, how pervasive, how *black* the hole of Cade's pain must have been. It'd overshadowed everything, and stolen his hope for tomorrow. It'd rendered him unreachable, having grown too big, too vast, for him to climb out of.

Or for anyone to simply stick their hand down and rescue him from it.

The first sob that broke from his chest came out muffled, like a hiccup. The second was a ragged, gasping explosion that had Lani pulling him closer.

Clutching onto her, he sank down into the grass. She never let go, and under the shadow of Cade's tree, safe in Lani's arms, Geo wept.

Chapter Twenty-Two

"Will you go somewhere with me?"

Geo's voice was quiet, hoarse.

Brushing her lips over his forehead, Lani whispered, "Anywhere."

They stumbled to their feet and lurched toward the car arm in arm. Once there, she slipped behind the wheel, Geo slumping in the passenger seat, head back, eyes closed. She couldn't help but glance at him frequently as she drove, wondering if he was donning his armor again even as she watched.

He didn't speak except to mumble directions, and at last they pulled up in front of an unassuming tattoo studio named Scars & Ink. A short, barrel-chested white man met them right inside.

As he and Geo clasped hands and then embraced, she heard Geo croak, "It's time, Spike."

"I got you, brother," Spike murmured back. "I got you."

He took them to a room at the rear of the shop, and as he got set up, Geo turned to her. "Spike's a former team guy. We did one tour in Afghanistan together, the one where Cade—"

When he couldn't go on, Spike came over and squeezed his shoulder. "C'mon, buddy, let's do this."

They didn't discuss tattoo designs, and Geo didn't look at any of the flash on the walls or page through a book. Instead, Spike asked one simple question: "Where d'ya want it?"

After Geo indicated his right biceps, Spike configured the chair and tray accordingly. Geo stripped his T-shirt over his head and sat down, his elbow crooked on a padded armrest. He held his other hand out for Lani, who perched on a stool next to him, their entwined fingers resting on her thigh.

For a long time the only sound in the room was the buzzing of the tattoo machine. Geo stared straight ahead, unmoving, although his thumb drifted in almost unconscious circles on her inner wrist.

I'm here, baby, she whispered to him silently. *I'm here.*

At last Spike sat back and snapped his gloves off before running a rag over his sweaty forehead. "Outline's done. Wanna see?" He handed Geo a small mirror, then got up and left the room, leaving them alone.

Geo's hand was trembling, so she reached over and gently took the mirror from him. "You ready?"

"Yes." His voice still scratchy from crying, he rasped, "Will you look at it first?"

A huge lump rose into her throat. "Of course," she managed. Pressing a kiss to his bare shoulder, she stood and moved around to his other side, where she immediately caught her breath. "Oh, my."

The stark black outline of a frog skeleton wrapped itself around his muscular biceps. Eerie, yet beautiful, each individual bone was rendered so lifelike that she couldn't help but shiver.

"A bone frog. It's amazing," she whispered, then held up the mirror for Geo to see. He stared wordlessly for several seconds before nodding.

"It's good," he said to Spike, who was now hovering quietly in the doorway. "Real good."

Lani laid the mirror down carefully and returned to her seat as Spike donned fresh gloves and resumed his work. She traced her eyes over him, letting them linger on the many tattoos decorating his own arms.

One of them, a shiny red apple with a snake wrapped around it, caught her attention. She peered closer. Was the snake's tongue comprised of someone's initials...?

"M.S.," Spike said. "Mike 'Snake Eyes' Slidell, one badass Marine."

"Ah, I get it." She sat back. "'Eat the apple, fuck the Corps.'"

Spike smirked in appreciation at her knowledge of Marine culture. "Yeah. Ol' Snake Eyes saved my life on a joint op in Fallujah, and the day after that stepped on an IED. Here one minute, gone the next." He shook his head. "Ain't war a bitch."

"Ain't it, though."

"Lots of good people died, but Mike's death is the one that hurts the most." His voice was matter-of-fact, but Lani could still hear the thread of pain running through it. "On the days that I'm struggling, I look at this." He lifted his chin at the tattoo. "It reminds me that I'm a living, breathing memorial to Mike, and it's up to me to honor his memory. It helps me put that drink down, you know?"

They stared at each other for a few brief moments, and then Spike turned back to his work. "You get it, lady, don't you?"

"Yeah, she gets it, man," Geo broke in, sounding a little stronger now. "She fuckin' gets it."

The tattoo machine buzzed on as the tension in Geo's shoulders gradually eased, although every now and then a stray tear trickled down his cheek. He made no move to wipe them away, or to hide them, still staring straight ahead, his thumb caressing Lani's wrist.

In the end, Spike wouldn't take any payment. "Anything for a team guy," he said quietly before pulling him into another tight hug. "You know I got you, brother."

She drove them home, and once inside her apartment, they stood facing each other in the darkened living room. At last Geo reached out to run the backs of his fingers down her cheek, his swollen, red-rimmed eyes meeting hers. "Lani, I…"

When the words seemed to fail him, she moved closer. "Let's go to bed."

Letting out a hoarse groan, he swung her up in his arms. He carried her to the bedroom and set her gently on her feet, then stood quietly as she eased his T-shirt up and over his head.

"I'm sorry," he whispered when she undid his jeans. "I'm all dirty and sweaty…"

"Shh." She ran her palms over his chest and shoulders. "Do you have any idea how beautiful you are to me?"

His lips started to tremble.

"So beautiful," she breathed, brushing her fingertips

oh, so gently over the stark white gauze on his biceps. "Inside and out."

He made a choked sound. "Will you—will you just—"

Without a word, she drew him down to the bed and pulled him into her arms, his body starting to shake as the storm swept over him once again.

She held him tight through it all, her fingers combing through his hair, her own tears dripping from her chin. When at last he fell asleep, his head heavy on her shoulder, she whispered, "I love you."

Tonight, it didn't matter that he was a SEAL and she a mom-to-be. Tonight, all that mattered was that she loved him, and because he loved her, too, he was finally letting her in, finally letting her witness his vulnerability and pain.

It was a gift of trust she'd cherish to the end of her days.

We'll be back in town next Friday.

Geo barely had time to register the first text from Alex when the next one popped up.

Got a great report from your therapist! A thumbs-up emoji, and then, Looking forward to having you back with us, G.

Several weeks ago, those words from his master chief would've had him dancing in the streets. Now, they sat like a lump in the pit of his stomach.

He crammed his bite suit into its bag, then headed for the locker room shower to scrub off the sweat that crusted him from head to toe. It'd been a long, exhilarating afternoon playing decoy with the San Diego County Sheriff Department's K9 unit. He'd gotten to hide in buildings, in cars, conceal himself in bushes, even once behind an air-conditioning vent. It was such a rush each time the dog found and dragged him out, although that meant ending the day covered in scratches and bruises.

Yep, he'd gotten a lot of teeth hugs from some badass hair missiles.

As he soaped up, Geo canted his arm to gaze at his tattoo, now mostly healed, the scabbing having finally flaked off, the oozing dried up. It calmed him to look at it, especially during those difficult, emotional sessions with Maura.

"Why did you get that tattoo?" she'd asked.

Geo had stared at her and fought not to fidget on the couch. "Well, it's tradition. Most SEALs get a bone frog to memorialize fallen brothers."

"I know. But why did *you* get it?"

Unable to sit still anymore, Geo surged to his feet and paced around her office. "I wanted one, okay?"

"Why?"

He gritted his teeth, resisting the urge to shout that he just did, so fucking move on already. Instead, he'd let the memories of that night flow through him—Cade's family, his tree, crying in Lani's arms...

He'd taken a deep breath. "Because I'm trying to forgive myself, and I don't ever want to forget. That's the deal. If I'm going to carry this with me, it's gonna be out in the open, visible. No more hiding."

"Yes. Forgiveness is a process, a lifelong process.

Sometimes you'll feel like you're starting from square one all over again."

It was true. He'd already experienced that a lot, when anger at Cade would well up out of nowhere, along with his own self-loathing that was like acid burning him from the inside out. Some days it felt like all he was doing was forgiving, and it took every bit of his strength.

Geo had said as much to Maura, finishing with, "I'm processing it so much better, though. I'm not drinking, no fights."

"Well, that's certainly progress. I hope you're giving yourself credit for that, even on those difficult days."

"I am." He'd looked down at his hands, then back at her. "I know Lani's disappointed about the grief group. I just—"

Maura smiled. "Not everyone is wired to share in a group setting, Geo. I know she understands."

He knew she did. By her own admission, her disappointment had been fleeting.

"It was *my* fantasy about us sharing together in the group," she'd said when he haltingly told her he wouldn't be going back. "A fantasy that I've been trying to impose on you. This is your journey, not mine."

Thoughts of Lani made Geo rush through the rest of his shower. They were meeting at Ari's game tonight, the last one of a hard-fought season. She would be making cupcakes for the team, and he'd volunteered to stop off and grab some pizzas.

As he jogged to his truck and tossed his duffel in the bed, he couldn't help but snort. Here he was, looking forward to spending his evening eating cupcakes with a bunch of ten-year-olds. Not that long ago, if anyone had suggested he'd enjoy that, he would've laughed and promptly dumped a beer on their head.

What had changed?

The sudden buzzing of his phone made him smile, and he swung up into the truck before opening Lani's text.

Cupcakes done. Whaddya think?

Instead of the cupcake itself, the attached pic was a selfie. In it, she had chocolate frosting all over the tip of her nose and lips, obviously from sampling her handiwork.

A pleasant tingle went through him. Mmm. I think I have a sudden hankering to lick the spoon. And by spoon, I mean you.

She sent back a string of laughing emojis, saying, Good thing I saved us a bowl of frosting to, uh, eat later.

The tingle turned into a blaze of arousal, and Geo reached between his legs to palm himself soothingly. "Jesus. Down, boy."

To Lani he said, You're killing me, beautiful. Can't wait.

As he drove, his happiness couldn't help but dim a bit. At some point he'd have to tell her about Alex's text, which would burst the idyllic little bubble they'd been living in these past two months, the one in which he came home every night and woke up next to her every morning.

He didn't want it to end.

Geo clenched his fingers on the steering wheel as he reminded himself that they'd turned a corner, too. That night at Scars & Ink, he'd felt it—something had shifted between them, something good.

Sighing, he turned into the parking lot of the pizza restaurant with a resolve to make sure they talked about it tonight, after the soccer game. He wanted a future with her, and he was more than ready to make some big changes to get it.

The stack of pizza boxes made the cab of his truck smell so good, Geo couldn't resist sneaking a slice on the way to the soccer field. When he arrived, most of the team was already there, milling around, and a cheer went up when they saw him.

"Pizza! Pizza!" they chanted, swarming the boxes when he put them down on a nearby picnic table.

He gave Renae a hug and a kiss on the cheek, then looked around for Ari. She was a short distance away from the rest of the group, seated on the grass, doing some desultory stretches. Stuffing his hands in the pockets of his jeans, he wandered in her direction.

"Hey, kiddo," he said softly as he approached.

She glanced up at him and shrugged. "Hey."

He dropped to sitting next to her and leaned back on his palms, his legs crossed at the ankle. "How's it going?"

"Good."

These pre-game talks had become their own private ritual. Mostly Ari wanted to hear about her father, and it delighted Geo to dredge up all the funny and inspiring Cade stories he hadn't thought of in years.

How could I forget for one moment how amazing you were, bud? Because you were, and I miss you.

He waited for her to ask, but tonight Ari was quiet for a long time. Geo didn't push, just sat next to her, letting her take the conversational lead. At last she drew her knees up and wrapped her arms around them. "Do you ever think it's your fault?"

His breath froze in his chest. "Think what's my fault, honey?"

"That your dad died."

Geo paused. "*My* dad?" he asked carefully, wondering if he'd heard right.

"Yeah. Do you ever think it's your fault he died?"

What?

"Some of Ari's questions to you might be her way of expressing her *own* feelings," Maura had said when he'd asked for her guidance early on. "Just listen, and use honesty and your best judgment when answering them. That's all you can do."

Tamping down his nausea at the thought of Ari blaming herself, Geo swallowed hard. "He'd been sick—"

Suddenly, a memory roared to life, the memory of a disappointed eleven-year-old boy and an impulsive, selfish prayer.

Just be honest.

"Well, a couple of months before he died, a friend's dog had puppies, so I asked my mom if I could have one."

He remembered how he'd been building up his courage for weeks, bolstered by the thought of having a warm, furry little creature to love, something that'd become a bright spot of hope and anticipation in those last days of his dad's slow, inexorable decline.

"What did she say?"

At her hushed question, he drew his knees up and mirrored her pose. "She said no. Right away. Wouldn't listen to my plan to take care of it, nothing. Just a big fat no. Period. The end."

"Ugh. Were you mad?"

"I was furious. I thought it was so *unfair.*"

Looking back as an adult, Geo could recognize her decision as one of an exhausted caregiver who only saw a puppy underfoot as yet another burden, but in his childish selfishness and grief...

"I shouted that I hated her, and then I stormed outside and kicked some stuff over, like my bike and the garbage can. After that I ran to the park down the street and sat on the swings for a long time, thinking about my dad being sick, and I—"

He squeezed his eyes shut and blew out a long, slow breath.

God, help me.

"I prayed that he would just die already."

"Oh, shit." Ari clapped her hand over her mouth. "And he did?"

"He did, several weeks later." Turning to face her directly, he waited until she met his eyes. "But because he was sick, Ari, not because I prayed that. Okay? That was me being mad, and for some reason praying that made me feel better, but I was a little *kid.* I didn't have the power to make him die."

Her lips trembled the tiniest bit before she broke their gaze and looked down at her knees.

Steeling himself, Geo asked, "Why, sweetie? Why did you want to know that?"

She shrugged. "Dunno."

Despite her attempt at nonchalance, he could see her knuckles turn white as she clenched them together.

His instincts screaming at him not to let this go, he nudged her foot gently with his own. "You don't know? C'mon, it's me. We've had a lot of good talks, haven't we? I won't get mad, no matter what you tell me."

Ari's shoulders hunched in on themselves, and for a moment Geo thought she was about to bolt when suddenly she blurted, "I took Daddy's lucky bear."

His mind immediately flashed to the tiny tie-dyed bear Cade always kept in the front pocket of his ruck. Had he mentioned not having it on that last deployment? For the life of him, Geo couldn't remember.

Carefully keeping his face and voice neutral, he said, "You took it out of his bag?"

"Yeah, I wanted to sleep with it before he left." Ari dragged her head up to look at him, her eyes stark. "But I forgot to put it back. He went on deployment and he didn't have his lucky bear…"

Lips trembling, she buried her face once again in her knees. His heart aching, Geo rested his hand lightly on her shoulder. "So you've been thinking that might be why he died?"

When she didn't respond, he gave her a squeeze. "Honey, your daddy died because his brain got sick, just like *my* dad's *body* got sick. Nothing we did made them die. Nothing."

Another moment of absolute stillness, and then she shrugged his hand off and jumped to standing. "Gonna go warm up with the team." Without another word, she jogged off.

Geo stayed where he was, his gut roiling with sorrow for the burden she'd picked up and carried all this time. Hadn't he himself carried that exact same burden for years, until the wisdom that came from maturity and life experience finally convinced him otherwise?

He swallowed hard. But how much damage had that done in the meantime, damage to his psyche that in a lot of ways he was still dealing with today?

Guilt, responsibility, blame, anger...

Surging to his feet, Geo sought out Renae and told her what happened. Her cheeks paling, she clutched his arm.

"That explains so much," she breathed. "I'll let her therapist know. We've been searching for a way to break through to her, to understand her, and this might be it." Her voice broke. "Oh, Jesus, help me help my baby."

When she couldn't go on, he pulled her into his arms and hugged her tightly.

"I'm so glad you're here," she whispered over and over. "So glad you're here."

The game was in full swing when Lani finally arrived, breezy and beautiful in a colorful maternity top and leggings. Geo's pulse throbbed at the sight of her, the desire to whisk her away and make love to her almost overwhelming him.

Their eyes met, and she put the cupcakes down before sauntering over to him, her lips quirked in a sexy half-smile. "Hey, you."

"Hey, gorgeous." Geo reached out and drew her to

him. With a contented sigh, she tucked herself into his side, her arms linked around his waist.

The game was a close one. Ari played with a ferocity that Geo recognized as an attempt to exhaust her body as well as quiet her mind. His gaze met Renae's more than once in shared concern.

She saw it, too.

A sudden burst of cheering caught his attention, and he left Lani at the snack table to move closer to the field, where Ari drove toward the goal with seconds left, her feet a blur as she worked the ball. A quick pass to a teammate, a dart into scoring position, and then...

"She made it! She scored!" Renae pumped her fist wildly in the air. "She scored the winning goal!"

"Way to go, Ari!" Geo put his fingers in his mouth and let out a piercing whistle. "Yeah!"

He and Renae jumped up and down in their excitement, and Ari turned in their direction, her lips stretched in the widest grin he'd seen yet. Renae caught her breath and threaded her arm through his in sheer happiness. "You see that? She's *smiling*!"

Suddenly, Ari charged toward them, her smile morphing into an expression of red-faced fury. Geo barely had time to brace himself before she slammed into him, fists flying.

"I hate you!" she screamed. "I don't want you here!"

He staggered back, horror turning his blood to ice. "Ari, what—" he choked.

Tears streamed down her cheeks, her face a mask of anguish. "I don't want you here! I want my daddy!"

Sinking to his knees, he pulled her close, ignoring

the blows that continued to rain down on his chest and shoulders.

"I want my daddy! I want my daddy! I want my daddy!" Her howls at last trailed off into sobbing as she sagged against him. Falling back on his butt, Geo hauled her into his lap and wrapped her up tight.

"I know, baby," he whispered, rocking her, his own tears flowing unchecked. "I know you want your daddy. I'm so sorry he's not here."

Renae knelt beside them as the rest of the team parents linked arms to form a protective circle around them, a barrier against the phones suddenly pointed in their direction by seemingly every bystander in the vicinity.

Her hand shaking, Renae stroked Ari's sweaty hair. "That's it," she crooned. "Let it out, my love. Let it out. You're safe."

Geo attempted to let her take his place, but Ari clung to him, her fingers digging into the back of his neck. He subsided, holding on to her, in that moment a willing stand-in for the dad she so desperately missed.

Lani stood at the edge of the group, her hand over her mouth, her eyes full of empathy and pain. Geo lost sight of her when Renae pressed her tear-stained cheek to his. "Whatever fate brought you here to us now, I'll be endlessly grateful for it. She's grieving, thank God. Because of you, she's finally letting herself grieve, and now I can get her the help she needs."

By the time he assisted her in getting Ari home and settled, it was late, approaching ten o'clock. He drove to Lani's apartment in his pizza-smelling truck, his body numb, drained. All he wanted to do was fall into bed with her and hold her close all night long.

"It won't matter if we wait to talk in the morning," he told himself. "I have a week left. Plenty of time."

He trudged up the walk and slipped the key in the lock. The tiny entryway was dark, although judging by the slight glow emanating from the kitchen, the light over the stove was on. Heading to turn it off, he about jumped out of his skin at the sight of Lani sitting at the kitchen table, her fingers knotted tightly in her lap.

A jolt of unexpected fear made him croak, "Babe? What's wrong?"

Her eyes darted back toward the door. He turned to look, and what he saw there made his body go leaden with a weary sadness.

"Oh." He cleared his throat. "Can I ask why?"

"Because I can't do this." Her voice was brittle, like glass, the way it'd been when they first met. "This isn't the life I want."

What life? A life of loving each other? A life of respect, and happiness? Of family?

He wanted to argue, to plead his case. Whirling away, he scrubbed his hand over his jaw, searching desperately for the words that would convince her to try.

As he did, his eyes fell on the picture of Lani and Tyler. It struck him anew, how Tyler's seemingly-happy smile masked so much internal pain, a pain so severe it'd wrenched him away from everyone who'd loved him—

He glanced back at Lani's bowed head in sudden understanding. Her beloved brother had died. Rhys had fallen in love with someone else. The baby's father abandoned her by not returning her messages. Geo's job would take him away for months, a job there was always a possibility he'd never come home from.

She'd already dealt with so much loss, uncertainty and—Geo squeezed his eyes shut—far too many good-byes.

On shaky legs, he made his way over to her and rested his hand lightly on her nape. With a muffled sob, she lifted her face to look at him, her eyes dark with misery yet her mouth firm with resolve. They stared at each other even as a strange sense of peace swept over him.

If what you need right now is for me to leave you on your *terms, then sweetheart, that's what I'll do.*

Because he loved her. And because in asking him to go, she trusted him to know what she needed, and to understand it.

Tears stinging his eyes, Geo took that trust and tucked it away deep inside, even as he cupped her cheeks in his hands and kissed her oh, so gently.

Then he strode to the door, grabbed up his neatly packed bags, and left.

Chapter Twenty-Three

She missed him with an unrelenting ache.

It was always there—at work, at home, everything in between.

One morning there came a knock on the door, and Lani swung it open to see Devon standing there holding a bag of fresh bagels.

"Food and friends," she said with a tentative smile, "the best cure for a broken heart."

"Ha." Lani stepped back to let her in. "If there's a cure, I'll take it."

They unpacked the bag and made coffee in a companionable silence. When at last they were seated at the table, steaming mugs in hand, Devon said, "If you want to talk about it, I'm listening."

Lani toyed with a piece of blueberry bagel. Her appetite was nonexistent, like it'd been the whole three weeks Geo'd been gone, but for the baby's sake she forced herself to take a bite. "I guess the gossip finally reached you, huh?"

Devon gazed at her over the rim of her coffee cup. "Well, when Geo went back to his original platoon and you went radio silent, it didn't take much of a detective to figure it out. C'mon, honey, talk to me."

"What's there to talk about?" Lani shrugged. "We were friends with benefits and the benefits ended."

"Bullshit." Devon's eyes were steady on hers. "If you don't want to talk about it—especially with me—I'll respect that. But at least be honest with yourself about what you two were to each other."

At those words, Lani's attempted belligerence drained out of her, leaving that ever-present ache behind. "I love him," she said quietly. "And I sent him away."

"Oh, honey. Why?"

"Fear."

Devon's face softened, and she reached out her hand to cover Lani's. "Of what? What are you afraid of?" Her voice was exquisitely gentle. "Talk. To. Me."

The memories crashed over her, of Geo on the ground with Ari in his lap, rocking her, crying with her. The protective tenderness on his face, in his voice, as he'd comforted her...

One tear leaked out, then another.

"Because that night," she whispered, "for the first time, I could picture him as a father. An amazing, loving, *wonderful* father, and he'd take such good care of us—when he was around, that is."

Suzette. The son Harry would never meet. A government car. Tabitha's long, blond hair...

She wiped her cheeks. "I can't be with a SEAL. I can't do this again, risk losing someone I love, that my child loves."

As she clutched Devon's hand, those years with Rhys

swirled before her eyes—the sum total of his absences far outweighing the togetherness; the neediness she couldn't hide, couldn't overcome; the vulnerability that made her feel like a bug, speared by a pin and writhing in failure…

Devon's eyes shone with sympathy and understanding. "No one can blame you for that," she said quietly. "Least of all Geo. What did he say when you talked to him about it?"

That brought Lani up short.

"He, uh, didn't really say anything," she admitted. "I'd made my decision, so it was time to rip the Band-Aid off, you know?"

"Oh." Devon was quiet for a moment. "Well, obviously you have to do what's best for you. Always."

She left not long after, with hugs and reassurances that Lani's village was just a phone call away. When she'd gone, Lani puttered around the silent kitchen, Devon's question echoing in her ears.

"What did Geo say?"

Her heart gave a painful thud at the memory of his stricken face, then his silent departure. What *could* he have said? She'd packed his bags and had them waiting by the damn door, for fuck's sake! Short of planting her foot firmly on his ass and shoving him out, she couldn't have made her wishes more clear: Leave *now*.

Besides, what would she have done if he'd insisted on talking? Listened calmly, rationally?

No way. The walls around her heart had sprung back up, thicker and higher than ever, infusing her with a clawing desperation to leave *him* before he left *her*. If he'd pushed it, she would've gotten angry, defensive, possibly said things she didn't mean...

Things like, "I don't love you."

The ache in her chest disintegrated into splinters of pain, and Lani dropped her forehead to her folded arms, the sudden truth sweeping over her. Geo had let her push him away, had gone without a fight, because he'd realized—in that moment—it's what she'd needed him to do.

With that, the last wisps of the mental fog that'd been her constant companion for the last three weeks finally cleared. Springing to her feet, she ran to the hallway closet, where she reached up on the shelf and pulled down Geo's Metallica T-shirt, neatly folded.

Clutching it against her, she headed to her bedroom. After Geo had gone, she'd cleaned her apartment like a crime scene. All his favorite condiments? In the trash. A half-finished grocery list written in his distinctive scrawl? Thrown out. After that, when she'd dumped her basket of clean laundry on the bed, there, at the bottom of the tangled pile, she'd found Geo's T-shirt.

The sight of the faded material had broken the dam of her tears. She'd wept for hours, remembering the last time he'd worn it—the morning he'd surprised her in bed with a beautiful stack of pancakes he'd gotten up early to perfect. He'd fed them to her, interspersing each bite with a sticky, syrupy-flavored kiss, until at last she'd wrestled him out of his clothes and made love to him with a fervency that'd left hickeys on her neck and scratch marks on his back.

Eyes stinging at the memory, Lani traced her fingers over the cracked, faded letters, finally letting the enormity of what she'd done sweep over her.

Geo loved her. Without a shadow of a doubt, he loved her, and not only that, he understood her. But when the time came for her to understand *him*, be there for *him*, all she'd managed to do was regress back to the old Lani, the one who reacted by curling up into a spiky, self-protective ball.

"It's like you haven't learned a thing," she berated herself. "Not a goddamn thing."

Maybe it wasn't too late.

Her fingers trembling, she snatched up her phone and texted Renae: Do you know when Geo's platoon is back in town?

A few minutes later, a reply: Day after tomorrow, I think?

Lani's heartbeat kicked into a gallop. Okay. She had time. She had time to make this right, to at least let Geo have a say before she unilaterally decided their future.

I'm coming. Don't write me off just yet.

The C-17 touched down with a thump and whine of the engines.

"We're home, buddy," Geo said wearily to Bosch, who stood up in his crate before performing a perfect downward dog.

"Oh, my God, kill me now," Lennox groaned as he limped toward the open ramp at the rear of the plane. "Everything hurts."

Geo glared at him for a moment, then shrugged. For once he agreed with the prick—everything hurt. He fought not to groan himself, but the hours of sitting in a cramped webbed seat got the best of him.

"Damn those Greenie Beanies," he muttered, bending stiffly to unlatch the door to Bosch's crate and snap a leash onto his harness. "Those are some tough-ass motherfuckers."

And he was getting too old for this shit.

The hazy Coronado sky was a beautiful sight. At the base of the ramp, the ragged platoon gathered around Alex. "Well, we got our butts kicked, fellas," he rasped. "Those dudes hiked us into the ground. Fuckin' embarrassing."

"Not embarrassing, more like humiliating," someone else grumbled.

It was true. The Army Special Forces, or Green Berets, were known for their brutal ruck marches, their ability to hike for days with heavy combat loads. When an SF friend of Alex's had challenged him to bring his platoon and join them deep in the forests of West Virginia, the SEALs had been enthusiastic, and confident they'd at least be able to keep up.

Instead, most of them had struggled even to finish.

By the second day of the four-day ruck, Geo's heels were so blistered he'd had to cut out the backs of his boots to ease the agony. SEALs were popping ibuprofen like candy, their self-confidence growing dimmer by the day. At the end of the march, egos in tatters, they'd had to admit defeat.

"Let's see you fast-rope onto a moving ship in high seas now, asshole," Alex had growled to his friend, a Latino guy who'd barely seemed to have broken a sweat the entire march.

By the time everyone had showered, had their wounds patched up and taken a long nap, all was forgiven.

Now, safely back in Coronado, Alex dismissed them for a forty-eight-hour liberty. "Rest up," he said. "Next week we're headed for Langley and the CIA workshop that got rescheduled before. After that, well, you'll see."

He grinned wolfishly to a chorus of answering hoots, but instead of excitement, all Geo felt was weariness.

More of the same. It was all just more of the same.

And he'd lost Lani over it.

The FNGs would offload Bosch's crate and most of the gear, so Geo caught a ride to the kennel and gratefully handed him off to one of the staff, saying, "He could use a good bath and a brush. It's been a long week for this guy."

Instead of going on the ruck, Bosch had stayed behind to work with a couple of the new SF handlers in order to show them exactly what a well-trained K9 could do. The handlers had had nothing but the highest of praise for him.

After getting him settled, he ruffled Bosch's ears with a promise to come check on him in the morning, and then he headed for the team quarterdeck to downstage his personal gear and clean his weapon. He winced at the sight of his blood-stained and ruined boots.

"Fuck you, old man."

The next equipment cage over, Lennox flipped him off, and Geo desultorily raised his middle finger in return. As he'd expected, the team guys had treated him with a wary caution at first, but as the brutal exercise wore on, they'd thawed little by little, until by the end, everything was more or less back to normal.

Which was the reason Alex had arranged that particular training trip, he suspected.

Yeah, I owe you a big one, Master Chief.

Even he and Lennox had reached a sort of uneasy truce, which was a relief in and of itself. After all, they'd be deploying together by the end of the year.

Once his weapon was cleaned and secured in his locker, then and only then did Geo allow himself to turn on his phone. He held his breath as it booted up—which seemed to take for-fucking-ever—but once it did, not one of the notifications that scrolled past was the one he was looking for.

He closed his eyes. A little over three weeks now, and not a word.

How long should he wait? The more time went on, the more he started to doubt himself, to doubt that he'd done the right thing in walking away from Lani that night. He'd thought to give her a little space, a little time to think, and then wait for her to text him wanting to talk.

But she hadn't.

Geo blew out a ragged breath. Had he only imagined the feelings he'd sensed from her? He knew where she stood on his career, and if she'd sat him down and told him flat-out she couldn't do it, he would've respected that. Hated it, mourned it, but understood it.

Instead, he'd been left in some kind of hellish limbo, not sure if he was supposed to be trying to move on or not.

Standing and shouldering his backpack, he called

goodnight to the other guys and headed out, squinting into the late-afternoon sun. Damn. The week at Fort Bragg and then the week in West Virginia had kept him busy, but now an endlessly lonely forty-eight hours stretched out before him.

His phone buzzed with another notification, and Geo glanced at it before rolling his eyes. Well, apparently the next two days didn't *have* to be lonely: Been a long time since I've fucked your sweet ass. How 'bout it?

Ash had helpfully attached a pic of his erection, in case Geo missed the point.

With a laughing sigh, he texted back his regrets. Another time, hot stuff. I wouldn't be good company tonight.

An almost immediate reply. You know sex doesn't have to be on the table, G. Nick and I are always here if you just wanna talk.

He texted back a kissy-face emoji before putting his phone away, thinking that he'd go back to the barracks and grab a shower before seeing if he could take Ari for ice cream. Thank God that night at the game ended up being the breakthrough Renae had been waiting for.

"She's opening up to her therapist more and more," Renae said tearfully one night over FaceTime. "It's like a floodgate. She's held so much in, and she's been blaming herself the whole time. I had *no* idea. None."

With all his heart, Geo hoped their little family was finally on its way to healing.

As he rounded the corner toward where he'd parked his motorcycle, a slight movement to the left caught his eye. There, parked at the curb, was a little blue Nissan, one that looked a lot—his heart gave a twinge—like Lani's car.

Great. Now he was gonna see her everywhere.

"Hey, sailor."

The sound of a familiar husky voice had Geo snapping his gaze toward his bike, his breath catching in disbelief. Lani stood next to it, fingers twisted tightly together, a tentative smile on her lips. She wore a short denim skirt, some cute cowboy boots, and—his eyes widened—his fucking Metallica shirt!

"Hey, I've been looking for that," he grunted by way of greeting. His heart threatening to pound its way out of his chest, he dropped his backpack to the ground and stuffed his hands in his pockets.

When he didn't immediately approach her, her smile faded, and with an effort Geo kept his face stony—damn if he was gonna make this easy for her. "What're you doing here?"

"Waiting for you."

The soft answer shimmered between them like a fragile bubble, until it was popped by the sharpness of Geo's one word—"Why?"

She bit her lip. "Because I wanted to show you the sign I made."

It was only then that he noticed the piece of poster-board lying on the bike's seat, and even as he watched, she grabbed it and held it up.

There was no embellishment on it, nothing fancy, just the simple block letters: I'M SORRY.

Already shaking his head, he spun away, the pain and uncertainty he'd suppressed for the last three weeks crashing down on him with the force of a tidal wave. Gritting his teeth, he forced out, "Sorry for what?"

"For everything." Her voice was whisper soft.

He whirled back around to face her. "I want to hear you say it," he said fiercely. "What are you sorry for? Packing up my shit like you were getting rid of a transient sleeping on your porch? Throwing my ass out of your house like an unwanted pest?"

"Yes, to all of those things." Tears glistening in her eyes, Lani let the sign drop to the ground. "Especially for—" she swallowed "—for letting my fear get the best of me."

The simple honesty blunted the edges of his anguish a little. Of course he'd known her actions that night arose out of fear, but hearing her admit it—

He blew out a long, slow breath. "I would've talked about it with you, you know," he said more quietly. "We could've worked it out. I thought, silly me, that we were in this *together*."

"We *are* in this together."

"Are we?"

"I want to be." She took a step closer. "Despite the way I acted, I *want* to be in this with you. Whatever the future holds for us, I want us to decide it together."

With nothing more to lose, he said harshly, "I can tell you right now what the future holds. It holds four more years of *this*." He waved at the airfield behind him. "This isn't a job I can just quit, you know."

"I know."

"You need guarantees? I can't give 'em. You want to count on me? You won't always be able to. It'll be life with Rhys all over again, Lani, except this time you'll be doing it with a child."

She flinched, but said, "I know that, too."

"Yeah, I know you know." Exhaling, he tilted his head back to the sky, his eyes starting to sting. "And God, for some reason, I *still* thought maybe we had a chance. Stupid."

Lani's boots made clicking sounds on the asphalt as she approached him, stopping so close he could feel her warmth. "I want that chance with you, Geo."

He shrugged. "Funny way of showing it. Nothing says 'I want to try' like packing up your boyfriend's things and leaving them by the door."

"Not my finest hour, I admit." Her voice was soft. "But let's flip this around. You need guarantees? I can't give 'em either. You want to count on me? Well, I *hope* you know that you can." She paused. "Most of the time. Kinda goes back to that 'guarantee' thing."

Geo couldn't help but snort at that.

With a watery chuckle, she took his hands in hers, her own fingers ice-cold. "But if you want to be loved? You are. Completely. The no-guarantees-asked kind, the we're-in-this-together-even-when-one-of-us-screws-up kind."

When he shook his head, she reached up and cupped his cheek. "I love you. With everything that I have. And I know you love me."

A kernel of hope sprouted in Geo's chest even as he grunted, "Hmph."

"You know how I know? Because nothing says 'I understand you' like grabbing up the things your girl-friend packed and leaving without a fight." She crinkled her nose. "Well, when your girlfriend is Lani, that is. I can't speak to any other girlfriend you've had, or boyfriend, for that matter. All I know is Lani's not easy to understand, but somehow you understood what she needed that night. You must really love her."

He grunted again, the hope taking cautious root. Still, he didn't say anything, and she squeezed his hand again. "This morning I was lying in bed, wondering when I'd gotten so selfish. I've been acting like *my* needs are the only ones that matter. Worse, I've been superimposing my past with Rhys over the idea of a future with you."

Geo waited while she wrestled with her thoughts, his heart thumping painfully in his ears.

"Every time he left, I considered it an abandonment," she said. "I blamed him for loving his job more than me. He was a part of something that had its own language, its own traditions, a culture that, as much as I wanted to, I'd never completely understand."

He rubbed her fingers gently, and her lips trembled a bit as she went on, "But you're not Rhys. I'm not the same Lani I was back then, and it's so *fucking* unfair for me to compare my life with him to what it would be with you." A single tear slid down her cheek. "I love you. I'm *proud* of you, of the way you serve your country. The way you and Bosch keep people safe. And if you'll have me, I want to try and make this work."

Before he could say anything, she let go of him. "I'm gonna walk for a while. That way." She pointed to the beach. "Come find me and we'll talk some more. If you want."

Despite wanting to charge after her, Geo forced himself to wait until she'd disappeared. Anger and pain still coursed through him, along with uncertainty, because everything he'd said was true. She *couldn't* count on him to be there for her when she needed him. The birth of the baby? No promises. Anniversaries, illnesses, deaths in the family, on and on and on. For the next four years, he couldn't make her any fucking promises.

Except one...

Grabbing up his backpack, he headed in her direction. When he reached the sand, he toed his sneakers off, his lips quirking when he saw one cowboy boot, then the other a short distance away, as if she'd been leaving a trail of breadcrumbs for him to follow.

A wave of pure love weakened his knees. How much courage had it taken her to come to him like this, to recreate a scene that several months ago had led to heartache, and an ending? More than he'd ever know. Despite himself, the tiny kernel of hope grew.

Ambling closer, Geo caught sight of her standing at the water's edge, her arms crossed over her rounded middle. The gentle wind teased her hair, lifting it, then dropping it, her profile serene as she gazed out at the setting sun.

"Are you sure about this?" he called to her. "You've been there, done that, got the T-shirt, remember?"

She turned to face him. "Well, you know, that was a different T-shirt. I don't have this one yet."

"The fabric's pretty much the same, though. What's going to make this one different?"

She took a step toward him. "Because this time I'll ask for help if I need it instead of trying to take the weight of the world on my shoulders." Another step.

"I won't make you responsible for my happiness." Another step. "I'm going to continue my therapy, my grief group, so when stuff pops up that scares me, that makes me want to shut down—and it will—I'll have the tools to deal with it so I don't hurt you like that again."

Geo gazed over her shoulder at the ocean, aware of her eyes steady on his face.

"What about you?" she asked softly. "Are you sure you're ready for this package deal?"

He opened his mouth to tell her that he was, then snapped it shut. If there was anything she deserved, it was as honest an answer as she'd given him.

"I think I am. I *want* to be." Dropping his backpack to the sand, he said, "A husband and father isn't anything I ever saw myself as, for a lot of reasons."

She bit her lip. "Do you think you'll be able to love the baby? I mean, because it's—"

"Because it's not mine? Lani, it's a part of you, so loving the baby isn't the issue. It's just, the thought of me ever letting you down is—" Suddenly he was blinking back tears of his own.

"You will, sooner or later." Her voice was quiet. "Just like I'll eventually let *you* down, because neither of us is perfect."

She was close enough to touch now, so Geo reached out to stroke her cheek with his fingertips, whispering, "The only thing I can promise is that you'll get the best version of me I can possibly be."

"What more could I ask for?" Sliding her arms up around his neck, she drew his head down to kiss him gently. "I promise the same."

"Then I'm the luckiest man alive." Geo deepened

the kiss, their tongues dueling lightly before their lips separated with a lush *smack*. "I love you." He rested a hand on her tummy. "Both of you."

Smoothing her hands along his shoulders, she said, "You're going to be an amazing father."

Hearing it said out loud, he froze, and the panicked look that must have crossed his face made her giggle. "Well, not tomorrow, at least," she said drily. "You have a little time to really get used to the idea."

"How much—" He cleared his throat and tried again. "How much time?"

"Four months, give or take."

He breathed out a shaky sigh of relief, then panic surged again. "Oh, God. I don't know how to change a diaper, or fix a bottle, or soothe it when it cries." He dropped his arms from around her. "Um, are you sure about this?"

"Completely sure." Grabbing his hand, Lani started towing him back across the sand. "We'll learn together. You think I know how to do any of that?"

"You mean you *don't*?"

"Nope. We're on equal footing here, Daddy."

The jolt of fear lasted maybe another dozen steps before it drained away.

Daddy.

"I'm gonna be a daddy," he breathed, a dizzying mix of joy, wonder and trepidation swirling through him. He planted his feet. "Do you know if it's a boy or girl?"

"I'm supposed to find out next week." Swinging around to face him, she asked, "You think you'll be able to come to the appointment with me?"

Geo shook his head. "No." He watched her carefully.

"I'm leaving soon for Langley. After that, I'm not sure where we're going or when I'll be back."

"Aw, shit." Her eyes showed the merest flicker of disappointment before she smiled. "Well, there's our first dose of reality, I guess." She threaded her arm through his as they started walking again. "Okay, listen up. I'm gonna find out, but I swear I will *not* tell anyone until I tell you first, even if we have to do it over FaceTime."

"I'll move heaven and earth to be there if I possibly can."

The quiet fervor in his voice made her press her cheek to his shoulder. "I know you will," she said. "And if you can't, I'll be fine. We'll make it work."

"We'll make it work," he repeated softly.

They'd reached his bike by then, and Lani turned into his arms, her own twining around his neck. "Go pack your stuff and then come home?"

His heart so full he could barely speak, Geo kissed her gently. He danced her back toward her car, not wanting to let her go, and leaned in through the driver's window for more kisses as she started the engine.

"Bye." *Smack.* "Love you." *Smack.* "Hurry." *Smack.*

At last he forced himself to step away with a lovesick sigh, and after she'd driven off, he picked up the I'M SORRY sign that had blown against his front tire, tore it down the middle and stuffed it in a nearby trash can.

As he pulled on his helmet, his phone buzzed with a text. Hey, dude. Meet us for a beer?

Can't, he replied, then straddled his bike and fired it up, contentment and the promise of happiness stretching his lips into a grin.

'Cause I'm headed home.

Epilogue

Two years later

"Come on, bud. Let's go wake Mama."

Some scuffling and giggling at the doorway, and Lani buried her face in her pillow, hiding her smile. She feigned sleep as footsteps toddled toward the bed, little fists grabbing onto the mattress next to her.

"Mama, up."

With a loud pretend yawn, she rolled to her other side, away from Aidan, who said again, "Mama, up!"

Her shoulders shook with laughter when Geo scooped him from the floor and whispered, "I know what'll wake her up. Ready?" He plopped Aidan down next to her, and then with a shout did a giant belly-flop onto the bed.

Aidan shrieked as he was bounced several inches into the air. Lani grabbed him to pepper his face with kisses. "You surprised me!" she declared. "You woke me up!"

She hugged his warm little body close while he patted her cheeks and babbled at her, until a loud, ostentatious snore from Geo made her glance over to where he now sprawled on his back, arms thrown over his head.

"Uh-oh," she hissed. "Daddy's asleep."

"Dada up?"

"Right. Dada up."

She helped Aidan stand, and he turned around and sat down—hard—right on Geo's stomach.

"Oof!"

Cackling with glee, Aidan did it again, and again, each time Geo letting out a loud, mock-pained grunt. At last Aidan tired of the game, and Geo scooped him up in his arms, saying, "Go on and shower, love. You have a big day ahead, and I have everything under control."

She knew he did. Since Aidan'd been born, Geo had thrown himself whole-heartedly into family life, soaking it up like a thirsty sponge. Some careful planning, combined with being in the right place at the right time, had opened up an opportunity neither of them could've foreseen.

"I've been offered a billet with the LeapFrogs," he'd told her one night, his eyes bright with excitement.

Pulled exclusively from the spec ops community, the Navy's parachute demonstration team traveled to events all over the country.

"They want to add a K9 handler to the troop to raise awareness of what military working dogs can do."

He'd get to jump out of airplanes with Bosch, swoop in on a helicopter and fast-rope with him to the ground, and conduct mock searches and takedowns.

At first she'd been worried that he'd be bored, that he'd miss the close camaraderie of deployment or the thrill of combat, but to her surprise and delight, he didn't seem to miss either. He was still involved in the community he loved, he got to work with his favorite badass dog, and best of all, he was safely stateside, even if sometimes he was gone for a few weeks at a time.

Yeah, life was pretty damn good.

Oh, the joys of a leisurely soak under a hot spray! Lani took full advantage of it, running a deep conditioner through her hair and taking the time to shave her legs. She applied her makeup carefully, then put on a pair of dark jeans, a black tank and a sheer, emerald green blouse. Slipping her feet into some strappy sandals, she made her way next door to where Matt and Shane sprawled out on the patio, cups of coffee in hand. With a pleased exclamation, she bent to hug Matt and give him a kiss on the cheek.

"Welcome home. We missed you 'round here."

"Thanks. Good to be home." He squeezed Shane's ankle where it rested across his thigh.

Shane glanced up at her, his smile welcoming but his blue eyes shadowed with exhaustion. "Morning, beautiful." A huge yawn seemed to catch him off-guard, and he barely had time to cover it with his hand. "Sorry. Didn't get much sleep last night."

Lani waggled her eyebrows. "Ah, the joys of homecoming."

"I wish it was just that." Shane grunted. "Matt sprung a big decision on me."

"Oh?" Declining his offer of coffee, she sank down into a patio chair opposite them. "You finally decide about the DEVGRU slot?"

Shane huffed, and Matt shot him a warning look. "Don't start, clown."

Lani had been surprised to learn that a SEAL could delay reporting to Green Team, the training platoon for the elite SEAL Team Six. If a guy didn't feel ready, or if he wanted to go through another deployment cycle with his original team, he could choose to do that and not lose his spot.

Matt had been putting it off for over two years now.

She searched their faces. Matt himself appeared completely relaxed, but Shane's lips were tight. "Like I said last night, you don't have to make any grand gestures, okay? You're already stuck with me."

"Oh, my God. It's not a 'grand gesture,' so would you fucking stop calling it that?" Matt swatted Shane's leg. "And *I'll* say again, accepting the slot means us moving to Virginia. That means ripping you away from this house you've worked so hard on—"

"It's just a damn house—" Shane began, subsiding when Matt growled, "Let me finish, *please*."

"Humph."

Lani couldn't help but suppress a smile at the mutinous look that crossed Shane's face. God, these two could be stubborn, and passionate in both love and conflict. It'd made for some *very* interesting times during the year she'd been their neighbor.

"Your support system is here," Matt was saying. "Your pain doc. Your *school*."

She gave an internal wince. Finally accepting that he wouldn't be suitable for an operational command, Shane announced one night that he was seeking a medical discharge from the Navy and would enroll in the SDSU occupational therapy program, his ultimate goal to work with wounded warriors living with traumatic brain injuries.

"I can transfer schools. I'm willing to do whatever it takes—"

"To what? To make sure I'm living out *my* dream?" Matt waved his arm. "What about *your* dreams? *Your* happiness? *Your* well-being? You honestly think none of that matters to me?"

Shane's face softened. "Of course I think it matters."

"Then let me *show* you how much it matters. How much *you* matter. It's not a grand gesture, it's me saying that I don't need DEVGRU to feel complete, but I do need you."

Putting his coffee cup down, Matt slid into Shane's lap and draped his arms around his neck. "You're going to be my husband long after I'm done being a SEAL. At least, I hope you will."

"Oh, you know you're never getting rid of me." Shane lifted his face and they shared a lingering kiss, his fingertips drawing tiny circles on Matt's bare back.

Heaving a deep sigh, Matt finally moved from Shane's lap, picked up his coffee again and headed into the house. "Guess we'd better get going."

As soon as he'd gone, Shane leapt to his feet. "Okay. We're headed to the base to work out with the platoon and run the O-course, and then Rhys and Devon are meeting us at the courthouse at two to act as witnesses. Ceremony's supposed to be at three. You'll get everything set up here?"

"I've got it all under control," she assured him. "Geo's taken Aidan out for the day, and then he'll drop him at our babysitter's in time to be back for the big surprise."

"Good." Shane slid his arm around her shoulders. "I'm getting married today, oh, my God!" His voice sounded a little squeaky with nerves, and she gave him a squeeze.

"Yep, you are, and you need to get going. Don't worry about a thing here, just enjoy."

After he'd followed Matt into the house, she hurried back to her own house next door and called Grizz's wife. "They're leaving now," she hissed. "Operation Surprise Reception is a go."

Half an hour later, armed with her spare key, Lani let an excited group of team wives into Matt and Shane's house, and left them to decorate while she hurried home to cook. By the time the team guys started to show up with kegs of beer and the other assorted liquor needed for any good SEAL event, the counters were groaning with all of the grooms' favorite foods.

Geo burst in not long after. "Aidan's with the sitter," he said breathlessly. "She'll drop him off in the morning."

With nothing critical to come out of the oven, she wandered into the bathroom where he stood shaving at the sink, and wrapped her arms around his waist from behind.

"Love you," she whispered, kissing his shoulder.

His eyes met hers in the mirror. "I can't wait to have you all to myself tonight," he murmured, and heat sparked down low, making her squirm.

Splaying her palms over his ridged abs, she pressed closer, letting him feel the way her nipples jutted through the thin fabric of her blouse. "Can't wait to be yours tonight," she whispered back. When he groaned, she let go of him and sauntered away, his sigh of longing echoing in her ears.

Next door, it was a boisterous group both inside and outside the house. The gate was thrown open between the two yards in preparation, some music was turned on, and half-drunk, giggling team guys roamed the neighborhood doing Matt and Shane "recon."

At last one of them checked his phone and hollered, "One minute out!"

A couple of snickering dudes arrayed themselves on either side of the gate between the houses, each shaking what looked to be bottles of champagne. The music was lowered just in time for her to hear a deep voice on the other side of the fence say, "I thought you said Lani and Geo invited us for cake at *their* house…"

A murmured reply, and then Matt and Shane walked into the backyard from Lani's side. Matt's eyes widened. "What's this…?" Before he could finish getting the words out, a blast of champagne caught him right in the face.

"Congratulations!"

Loud cheers echoed in the waning light as champagne continued to drench both of them. Matt sputtered and coughed while Shane laughed, a steadying arm going around Matt's waist.

Using his hands as a megaphone, Grizz shouted, "Hey, fellas. Did you do it?"

"Yeah, did you do it? Did you do it?" Everyone else took up the chant, the volume escalating, until Shane raised his left hand to display a black ring encircling his finger.

"We did it!"

Immediately they were surrounded by their friends, who pounded their backs and grabbed them up in gigantic hugs, one laughing Black dude named Smudge refusing to let go as he walked around with Matt, whose feet dangled helplessly off the ground.

"Um, I'd like my husband back, please," Shane requested politely, the grin he was sporting threatening to split his face in two. With a grunt, Smudge dropped Matt like a bag of rocks, but then pulled him close one more time and scrubbed his knuckles over his hair.

"So happy for you, man," Lani could hear him say. "It's about time."

More champagne was opened and poured—with sparkling cider for anyone who didn't drink, including Matt—and the toasts commenced. Some were irreverent, some were bawdy and inappropriate, which left the whole group in stitches. Finally Shane raised his glass.

"Thanks, everyone, for being here tonight. I know this day has been a long time coming, but we did it. We finally did it!"

Laughter and cheers all around, and then Matt lifted his glass. "Y'all punked me," he said fiercely. "I thought I'd gotten my way with the city hall thing, and then I come home to find this shit." He paused. "Thank you."

Some scattered applause, some insults, before Matt shouted above the din. "I want to say something else, something I don't say nearly often enough." He put his glass down and turned to Shane. "I love you."

His eyes shining, Shane leaned down for a kiss, but

Matt wasn't done. "From the first moment I met you, clown, you got under my skin. You pissed me off. There were days I couldn't decide whether I wanted to kiss you, or punch you, or both."

"Oh, you definitely wanted to punch me." Shane slid his arm around Matt's waist. "Repeatedly."

"I tried *so fucking hard* not to want you," Matt went on. "I kept pushing you away, pushing you away, convinced there was no room for you in my life." Reaching out, he took Shane's left hand in his, and lifted it to his lips. "Thanks for not letting me," he whispered against his ring. "For not giving up on me. I'm so lucky—and so goddamn *happy*—to be yours."

With a choked exclamation, Shane cupped his chin with gentle fingers and kissed him. "I love you." Then he grinned. "Mushy Matt."

"Annnd of course you had to go and ruin it," Matt grunted in mock disgust, even as he twined his arms around Shane's neck. "Fuckin' clown."

After that, the music was turned back up to a deafening level, beer cups were filled to the brim, and the SEALs settled in to party.

Devon slipped over to Lani at one point and pressed a folded ten-dollar bill into her hand. "He didn't cry," she said, her tone dripping with disgust. "Cool as a damn cucumber."

Before she could saunter off, Lani grabbed her arm and hissed in her ear, "You're next, lady."

After a moment's hesitation, Devon towed her into the shadows next to the garage. "Well, we, uh, actually got married three months ago. In Vegas."

"What?"

"Don't be mad," Devon pleaded. "We were there, and we'd wandered into this cheesy little chapel. All of a sudden Rhys pulls a ring box from his backpack and says something like, 'I'm tired of carrying this around, waiting for the perfect moment. Here.'"

Lani gasped. "He didn't. Tell me he didn't say 'Here' and *shove* your engagement ring in your *face*." She looked wildly around for Rhys. "Where is he? I'm gonna give him a piece of my mind—"

"Simmer down, tiger." With a laugh, Devon pulled her into a hug. "It wasn't as bad as I'm making it sound, but Lani, it was just so *us*. Lots of laughter, a few snafus, and me marrying the love of my life. It was perfect."

Tears stinging her eyes, she firmly pushed aside *her* idea of what Rhys and Devon's perfect wedding should've been, and hugged her back. "We're sisters now," she whispered. "You know that, right?"

"Yeah." Pressing their foreheads together, Devon rasped, "Love you."

"Love you, too."

Not long after that, the raucousness of the party quieted down as the single guys left for more exciting pastures. Couples with young kids and babysitters at home started drifting away, too, and soon it was just the six of them left, sprawled out among the wreckage.

"Great party," Devon said drowsily, not even bothering to lift her head from where it was resting against Rhys's chest. Curled up on Geo's lap, Lani mumbled, "Thanks."

Shane sat on the floor of the patio, back against a support post, Matt between his legs, arms wrapped around Shane's upraised knees. Their heads were tilted close together as they whispered, every now and then sharing a lingering kiss.

Lani couldn't help but smile, and Geo brushed his lips over her temple. "What're you thinking about, sweetheart?"

She sighed. "About the first time I saw them, that night at the bar. Matt was so prickly, and Shane so arrogant, and yet they were so in love with each other they couldn't see straight. Who'd have thought I'd be sitting here with them on their wedding day? It just makes me so *happy*."

He leaned down and kissed away the tear that slid down her cheek. "It was your engagement party, too, wasn't it?"

She gasped. "Oh, my God, it was. I forgot for a second." In the process of casting Rhys a guilty look, she caught him with his hand sliding along Devon's silky thigh, where it slowly disappeared under her skirt.

Whoops.

Quickly looking away again, she snuggled down against Geo's broad chest. "It's scary to think how close I came to marrying the wrong man. What if *you'd* picked another bar to have a drink in that night? What if I hadn't gotten so sick at that exact moment?"

Then I wouldn't be here, a little bit tipsy on wine and a lot drunk on happiness, sitting on my husband's lap next to some of my most favorite people in the whole wide world.

Lani gazed up at the sky, Geo's arms around her, squeezing her tight.

Was it you, Ty, watching out for me?

She'd like to think that it was.

Thanks, big brother.

It might've been her imagination, or her tired brain, or the fact she'd finally let go of anger, of bitterness, and opened her heart, but she could've sworn she heard Tyler's voice whisper in her ear, *Love ya, lil sis*.

* * * * *

Author Bio

Melanie Hansen doesn't get nearly enough sleep. She loves all things coffee-related, including collecting mugs from every place she's visited. After spending eighteen years as a military spouse, Melanie definitely considers herself a moving expert. She has lived and worked all over the country, and hopes to bring these rich and varied life experiences to the love stories she gets up in the wee hours to write. In her off-time, you can find Melanie watching baseball, reading or spending time with her husband and two teenage sons.

Visit Melanie's website at melaniehansenbooks.com. Find her on Twitter, @MelJoyAZ. Find her on Facebook as Melanie Hansen: Facebook.com/profile.php?id= 100009084006829.

HARLEQUIN

Heartfelt or thrilling, passionate or uplifting—Harlequin is more than just happily-ever-after.

With twelve different series to choose from and new books available every month, you are sure to find stories that will move you, uplift you, inspire and delight you.

Love Harlequin romance?

DISCOVER.

Be the first to find out about promotions, news and exclusive content!

f Facebook.com/HarlequinBooks

Twitter.com/HarlequinBooks

 Instagram.com/HarlequinBooks

Pinterest.com/HarlequinBooks

You Tube YouTube.com/HarlequinBooks

ReaderService.com

EXPLORE.

Sign up for the Harlequin e-newsletter and download a free book from any series at **TryHarlequin.com**

CONNECT.

Join our Harlequin community to share your thoughts and connect with other romance readers!
Facebook.com/groups/HarlequinConnection

HSOCIAL2021